THE FIVE LOST DAYS

Published by Pearhouse Press, Inc., Pittsburgh, PA 15208
www.pearhousepress.com

First Printing: May 2010

Printed in the United States of America

Library of Congress Control Number: 2008934350

ISBN: 978-0-9802355-0-0

Cover and Book Design: Mike Murray
Illustrations: Lisa Kemper
Author Photo Credit: Andrew Holbrooke

. . . we make guilty of our disasters
the sun, the moon, and the stars; as if
we were villains on necessity; fools by
heavenly compulsion; knaves, thieves, and
treachers by spherical predominance; drunkards,
liars, and adulterers by an enforced obedience of
planetary influence; and all that we are evil in,
by a divine thrusting on: an admirable evasion
of whoremaster man, to lay his goatish
disposition to the charge of a star!

WILLIAM SHAKESPEARE, KING LEAR

WILLIAM PETRICK

THE FIVE LOST DAYS

PEARHOUSE
PRESS

For
Mary Ann Petrick and
Edward J. Petrick (1920-1998)

1

Sa'x jolom Chacmut: Rain forest plant used in treatment of madness and headaches; leaves are crushed in cold water, and the liquid is drunk and used to bathe the head

They drove along the Belize highway, a narrow, sun-beaten lane that wound through miles of savanna. The rainy season had just ended, but the lush grasses were already the color of straw. Scattered palmettos drooped listlessly, some of their crowns shriveled like dried tobacco leaves. Even the sky had lost its semitropical brilliance, the blue faded into the dull pewter of an overcast afternoon. It wasn't supposed to be this way. Burns had carefully planned his brief shoot for the shoulder season, when there would be few downpours to interrupt the filming and less of the oppressive, stultifying heat of the dry season.

"How much further to Cayo?" Burns asked as the van bounced over another dry pothole. Burns grabbed the shoulder strap and peered out the window. They were still the only car on the road.

"No to worry," Gilbert said. The driver grinned, his head bobbing to the reggae music. The same Bob Marley tape had been thumping from the front dash speakers since they had driven off the airport's dirt lot earlier that morning.

"What's that in hours, Gilbert?" Burns wanted to escape this maddening sea of parched grass and chalk it up to a bad dream.

"You smoke some ganja?" Gilbert offered, gesturing to the hand-rolled joint he kept handy just behind his ear.

Burns didn't get high even in normal circumstances. He rarely even drank alcohol, preferring the buzz of strong, sweet coffee.

"Your friends?" Gilbert asked, grinning again. Three crew members dozed shoulder to shoulder in the back seat like frat boys on a road trip. Burns had hired them for enough shoots over the years that he'd come to think of them as family. His cameraman's young son even called him "Uncle" Mike.

"We're all on the clock," Burns answered. "We can party when this is over."

Gilbert shrugged and motioned to the blowers that blasted cool air throughout the van. "We have air-condition. Relax."

Relax. Burns had been told this so many times that the word barely registered anymore. He picked up his bible, a three-ring binder stuffed with contact names, photocopied pages of books and articles, a shot list and a detailed production schedule for the week.

"I tell my wife we make a movie," Gilbert said. "She is very excited. I tell her maybe we stop at our home later. After."

"It's a documentary, not a movie," Burns said. "It's not make-believe."

He distrusted fiction and fantasy. Burns wanted facts and true stories. He sought people and places that really existed and were not merely the creation of someone's overactive imagination. The real world didn't need any embellishment.

Gilbert nodded agreeably, then described his house, which was set just off the highway with its own small milpa, which teemed with healthy stalks of maize and sugar cane.

"Your house is on this road?" Burns asked. He couldn't imagine anyone living or wanting to live in the middle of this emptiness.

"Si," Gilbert said. "Is very near."

Burns searched the grasslands.

Finally, pale green spikes of palmettos had begun to sprout in the distance like overgrown weeds. But there were no houses, still no sign of traffic on this road that had been grandly named the Western Highway.

"You have boy, girl?" Gilbert asked.

"Kids?" Burns said, surprised by the question. Even marriage was something he hadn't given much thought about. He was devoted to filmmaking. If he wasn't producing a documentary, he was watching one, studying images and techniques for something he might use.

Gilbert appeared puzzled, his wide, cueball eyes narrowing as he squinted through the dirty windshield. Suddenly, he screamed and slammed on the brakes. Burns grabbed the hanging strap and heard his crew tumble forward from the back seat, bouncing into each other and the seat backs.

Without an apology or explanation, Gilbert turned off the engine, cutting off his reggae music, then hopped out the door. The dank, humid air rushed in, sour-smelling, like a sewage drain in the city. Gilbert hurried around to the front of the van and stooped down by the front grill just out of sight.

"We blow a tire?" Vic Colt asked. It was the first time his cameraman or any of his crew had spoken for hours. Burns didn't answer, unsettled by the utter quiet that surrounded them. The empty lane continued far into the distance like the road to nowhere.

Moments later, Gilbert reappeared at the side of the van alongside Burns, wearing a big, scarecrow grin and holding a turtle the size of a hubcap.

"Beautiful, yes?"

"It's big," Burns managed to say, relieved they hadn't broken down after all.

Gilbert shuffled into the dry grass, his narrow shoulders stooped and his skinny legs bowed from the awkward size and weight of the turtle. He talked to the animal as he set it down, as if he were sooth-ing an old friend. Before he backed away, Gilbert bowed and wished the turtle a safe journey.

"I worry to run over him," Gilbert said, climbing back behind the steering wheel.

"He's not kidding," Vic said. He yawned and slid back into his seat.

Burns knew many of the Maya were devout animists, believing spirits dwelled in everything from a plant leaf to a jaguar. But he'd assumed the Creoles and islanders were more practical and less su-perstitious.

"No more stop," Gilbert announced as he powered the van back to highway speed.

"Good," Burns said. "We don't have much time as it is."

Five days on location, to be exact. Burns needed weeks, if not months, to get inside the subject, to get to know the people and their world. But this project was filmmaking-on-the-cheap. The budget was so low that Burns felt like he was part of a rapid deployment force. This was fast becoming the business model for all the networks and production companies. In the end, he had jumped at the chance, drawn to the prestige of a foreign story—so rare in television and even the big screen. Burns, like so many of his colleagues, was also hoping to hit "the one," the documentary that would make his name.

"I love to drive," Gilbert said, gazing ahead as if they were speed-ing through paradise. "Time all mine. That is what I will do when there is enough money. I go to the States and get a job driving a semi coast to coast."

"Well, the roads are better," Burns said. "But you'll have lots of company."

"That's what we do here," Gilbert said. "We get enough money, we leave. Go to New York or Los Angeles."

"You don't want to go to New York."

Burns was only too happy to have escaped the cold, hostile can-yons of Manhattan. It was less a home for him than a base from which to launch trips elsewhere.

"New York has jobs," Gilbert said. "And money. Many are rich."

Burns was reminded of his own tiresome struggle to pay the rent on his fifth-story walk-up. It wasn't the kind of life he had imagined for himself when he was younger. By now, he assumed he would have made it and not be living like a student.

"Not so many are rich," Burns said. "Not so many as you think."

"No. But more than Belize."

Burns had glimpsed the poverty as they drove past the outskirts of the city. There had been that tired group of skeleton-thin black men standing barefoot in puddles that glistened with turgid sewage. Behind them, under the palm trees, were candy-colored shacks perched uneasily on skinny stilts that looked out over mounds of scattered trash. But the image that stayed with him was the toddler playing in a cardboard box, a live toucan perched on the tattered edge like a stuffed toy. At the time, he decided that it was too National Geographic to stop and film. Burns wanted images that were unique and different, that would set his documentary apart.

In his view, filmmaking happened long before the camera was turned on. For this shoot, he had spent days working up a shot sheet, a long list of possible images and scenes they might film. He had scoured photo books, magazines and other films for inspiration. He knew what to expect. Except when it came to the old Mayan healer. There were pictures of bush doctors, village elders and shamans. But not a single curandero. He was believed to be the last surviving curandero in those mountains—what was once the heartland of the Mayan empire.

"You ever go to see a curandero when you're sick?" Burns asked.

"Brujos," Gilbert said without hesitation. Witches. "My wife's sister. She feeling very tired, not happy. Lonely. So she try anything. She go and pay him, and he tell her problem she have no lover."

"Like a psychiatrist," Burns said.

"Yes. But this brujo, he is very powerful. He keeps a blanc."

Gilbert explained that the old curandero was said to have put a spell on a white American woman who followed him everywhere. It was said they went into the forest together for hours at a time gathering dangerous plants and barks that the curandero used to put a spell on others. The blanc deferred to him like a servant, yet she was married and owned a huge estate near the Macal River that had electricity and clean water.

"The woman is a scientist, an ethnobotanist," Burns said.

"You know her?" Gilbert asked.

"Why do you think you're taking us all the way to Cayo?" Burns was about to explain the research partnership between the blanc woman and the curandero, but given Gilbert's distrust of the curandero and his traditional medicine, he decided it was best to leave the topic alone. Yet he was intrigued by Gilbert's opinion, if only because there were plenty of people in New York and Boston who also believed that the ethnobotanist might be under some kind of spell.

Burns was startled by what seemed to be a massive movement off to the west. At first, he thought it was a flock of birds rising out of the unending savanna. Instead, spinach green hills appeared on the horizon with the suddenness of an apparition. A dense, milky steam drifted languidly above the round, gentle peaks. He felt a quickening sensation, a kind of primal, anticipatory excitement.

"Cayo," Gilbert said.

Burns was about to give an order to stop so they could set up the video camera and get some beauty shots. But the rain started without warning. It dropped in heavy, thick sheets, pounding the roof of the van. Gilbert slowed the van and turned on his lights to try to see through the falling water.

"Rain," Gilbert said. "We have been without for long. Is good."

An hour later, they were churning through mud the color of peanut butter. Black men and women, their skin much lighter than Gilbert's, began appearing alongside the van, trudging through the rain. They walked without apparent concern, as if slogging through this weather were routine. Gilbert blew the van horn. Arms were raised in greeting without anyone's turning around.

"You know them?" Burns asked.

"Neighbors. They come to work in the big sugar cane milpa. As everyone does."

"But not you."

"Me?" Gilbert asked, not smiling. "No. Never."

"You drive."

"Yes," Gilbert grinned with the satisfaction of being understood. "Me drive all the time."

The heavy rains stopped abruptly when they finally reached the concrete bridge that led over the river into San Ignacio. The wet road gleamed under the van's headlights, the reflection offering a glimpse of the weathered, clapboard homes that were slung at the road's edge. They reminded Burns of the Mexican shacks in Baja, where he'd done a shoot a few years earlier. There, too, he'd been struck by the hapless poverty, a place far beyond development schemes.

Gilbert guided the van uphill toward a cluster of weak, flickering lights. The engine whined under the combined weight of the passengers and the television equipment, burning oil as it struggled up the steep slope. Gilbert pointed out the town's electrical generator as they crept by, apologizing in advance for its frequent breakdowns. Burns listened pensively, his attention riveted on the crest of the hill that was still fifty yards away.

"Is no trouble," Gilbert said.

The van was aimed at the starless night sky, inching along like a roller coaster on its final ascent, everyone acutely aware of each painstaking rotation of the tires. Burns peered ahead into the dark with a tense, forced stoicism. If the van lost traction on the wet road, he knew it would slide backwards, down the hill, careening into one of the distant shacks, maybe not even stopping until the black river. But he would not let himself think about this, would only listen to the whine of the engine as if it were a distant sound that demanded intense concentration.

When the front wheels slipped, Burns dug into the hanging strap, his eyes drawn to the ambient light that hovered at the crest of the hill. He sat on the lip of the seat, breathing faster, his head pounding.

Gilbert let out a small grunt of surprise. His face was taut and serious. The van was at a standstill, the engine shaking violently, threatening to stall. Gilbert gave it more gas and the wheels slid again, moving them sideways, the tires spinning uselessly. He stretched himself further over the steering wheel, muttering incoherently, and peered down at the road as if it were a living thing, threatening their progress.

"Lay off the gas," Burns warned. "You're going to lose control."

Gilbert ignored him, obstinately waiting for the road to cooperate. The crew was unnerved, their fear charging the close air. At once, all three men searched frantically for a door handle, groping over and across one another, desperate to be the first one to safety.

The wheels caught in the midst of the commotion. But the crew continued to scramble until the van began to creep forward once again, climbing toward the light. A squat, oversized bungalow appeared behind it, an American Express sign dangling from a rusted hook near the entrance. The van lurched over the crest of the hill, and the whining engine collapsed into the next gear as they leveled off, the wheels crunching over the gravel driveway of the hotel. Gilbert let the van drift up to the glass doors.

"Hotel San Ignacio," Gilbert informed them. "Three stars."

Burns stumbled out of the van, his crew following. The heavy, humid air drifted around them like a vapor, obscuring the outlines of the tin-roofed hotel, making the building seem to float in the gray mist. The air reeked of burnt oil.

Burns let his crew unload the huge anvil cases one at a time. The heavy silver boxes were packed with portable quartz lights and stands, rolls of light gels, screens and scrims, a battery-powered sound mixer, a selection of microphones from a boom to tiny, wireless lavalieres, a new composite tripod with a fluid head, one shrink-wrapped case of raw video stock, and a Beta-cam, complete with backup batteries and remote control.

Gilbert watched grimly as the cases piled up in the lobby, almost blocking the entrance. By the time the crew was finished, he stood so still and fearful that Burns worried for him. Maybe it was exhaustion.

"What's wrong?" Burns asked, wiping sweat from his forehead. The humidity clung to him like his damp clothes.

"Guns," Gilbert said, his voice low and soft. "It is like the army with all these equipment."

"What army?" Burns asked. There were fewer than six hundred soldiers in the entire Belize Defense Force, a token band of locals set up by Great Britain a few years earlier.

"Rebels," Gilbert said. "They cross the border to steal food, clothes, shoes, anything. Bandits. They shoot anyone."

"Guatemalans?"

Gilbert nodded soberly.

Even if there were wandering bands of soldiers, it hardly mattered. The landscape alone protected his assignment. The research camp and surrounding jungle where they were going was isolated and best reached by boat. Besides, Burns was certain no one was foolish enough to mess around with Americans.

"Well, Gilbert, the only thing inside those cases that can shoot anything is a camera. Nothing to fear."

Gilbert stared at the anvil cases, unconvinced.

"So we'll see you in the morning?" Burns asked. "You'll take us to the river landing?"

Burns was relieved to finally escape to solitude. He sprawled across the clean but musty bed, closing his eyes to the yellowed ceiling, the paint crumpled or peeling from the onslaught of humidity. There was no fan to stir the air, heavy with the ringing of insects that roamed outside in the darkness. The noise would not let him sleep. He tried covering his head, but that only made the thick, humid air more difficult to breathe. Burns finally relented and got out of bed. He tried taking a shower, but the warm water lasted only a few minutes before it abruptly turned cold and made him leap through the vinyl shower curtain.

Burns put on his jeans and unlocked the warped screen door that led to the small porch. The pale light of his bedside lamp leaked through, giving a faint definition to the plastic chair that rested against the cement wall. But beyond the porch, there was only a black wall of sound, the starless sky nearly indistinguishable from the land underneath. For a moment, Burns felt that he had truly reached one of the ends of the earth. The still, thick air reeked of decay like a hole filled with compost. A strange, hostile chatter seemed to grow louder as he stood peering out into the darkness, as if all those insects and birds and whatever else foraged through the night were somehow watching him, waiting. Burns yawned nervously and slipped back inside his room, latching the screen door behind him.

2

Ix-canan: Leaves of this shrub are boiled and applied
to sores, rashes, cuts and insect bites; the name,
in Mayan, means guardian of the forest

The late morning light shot through the dense canopy of trees,
tumbling down through rare gaps in the lower branches, thinning as it flowed to the forest floor far below. By the time the sunlight
fell on Kelly Montgomery, who was hiking on a narrow footpath, it
was a soft, white vapor, barely illuminating the plants that crowded
one another in the deep shadows of the tubroos trees. Kelly moved as
nimbly as a native Mayan in the dim light, her long, silent strides
barely leaving an imprint on the soft earth. But she struggled, as always, to identify each passing plant and tree. There were thousands
of species, maybe more. Despite her training, Kelly couldn't be sure.
Cayo contained one of the densest ecosystems in the world, and decades of research had identified only a fraction of what was believed
to exist.

Kelly treasured these morning research hikes, being alone in the vast emerald underworld, liking even the faint scent of decay that oozed from the mud and wet plants. There was a fluid, hypnotic stillness here, like being underwater. The weight of managing a research facility fell away. She could be herself in the forest, pursuing what she loved most, what had attracted her to Cayo from the beginning. C'ox Ca'ax, the Mayans called it. Into the mountains.

A burst of tropical rain rattled the leaves of the canopy high overhead. Kelly glanced up only to feel her right boot suddenly sink into the black mud. She knew what it could mean, but she ignored the danger because a flower growing off a strangler vine, dangling from a doomed tree, captivated her. The small, star-shaped petals were both butter yellow and snow white, blossoming on bamboo-like reddish stems. The doctrine of signatures—which dictated that the color of medicinal plants offered clues to its application—was difficult to decipher in this case. Bright yellow flowering plants often indicated use for liver and urinary tract problems. But white flowering plants were usually a sign of danger or toxicity. Red often had an indication for blood-related illness. This unusual understory plant combined all of them.

At first, she noticed surface similarities to the *Lindahermosa* flower, but those grew on thorny vines that could rip a person's skin off. This reddish vine was smooth and the petals were delicately spiked like *Dracaena*. It was an unusual combination, which suggested that the flower could be some new, uncharted plant that even Tato did not know. She hurried toward it, excited at the prospect of discovery. She remembered one of the first instructions the curandero had given about hunting for medicinal plants. "You will not find the plant," he had said with an uncharacteristically somber, serious expression. "The plant will find you."

But as she moved closer to examine the provocative flower, a gray, black-speckled smoke rose from the mud patch behind her, swirling even though there was no breeze. The odd, smoky cloud drifted toward her, and before she had even risen on her toes to examine the white flower, the cloud descended and the mosquitoes were biting her bare forearms.

Kelly was stunned by the sudden attack. The bugs whirred outside her ears, their stridency building quickly to a high-pitched whine. Squinting through the speckled smoke, she turned and ran down the path toward her research camp. Only a few mosquitoes bit into her neck and face. The rest, however, continued to prick her arms as she ran, some bursting into blood as Kelly slapped at them, desperate to stop the harsh stings. But there were too many to kill, too many swirling wildly as she charged out of the dank, morning shade. It wasn't until she reached the grass clearing and stumbled into the blaze of the hot, tropical sun that the biting finally stopped. Like Dracula, these monsters scattered in the face of sunlight.

Kelly bent over to catch her breath. She felt a nauseating chill run through her, and she was afraid for a moment that she was going to get sick. But as her breathing slowed, she became furious, not at the mosquitoes but at her own stupidity. For some unknown, indefensible reason, she had not coated herself in repellent as she had been urging everyone else to do ever since the WHO had issued the surprise warnings weeks ago about a possible new malarial strain in the hills of neighboring Guatemala. A father and his two sons in a small village—an otherwise lucky all-male household not conscripted by the Guatemalan army—had died from what researchers believed was a severe malaria spread by mosquitoes, impervious to any antiviral.

The WHO bulletin had reminded her of the curandero's belief that the rain forest was occupied by both healing spirits and evil spirits, each endlessly vying for supremacy. It had seemed like a simplistic folk tale until she considered the fact that viruses were as unseen to the human eye as spirits and the deadly H1 strains like HIV were traced to remote jungles—Uganda in the case of HIV. Now in medicinal research centers around the world, including her own here in little Cayo, ethnobotanists were combing the rain forests for a plant or a piece of bark that might hold an unseen cure to cancer, AIDS and whatever deadly viruses were yet to emerge. Good and Evil in their secular forms.

Kelly brushed a wisp of damp, tawny hair from her face and examined her thin, aging forearms. They were covered with red bumps. There were speckles of blood as though she'd been pricked by hundreds of sharp pins. She felt the need to scratch. It swept over her suddenly, inexorably. She fought the urge to tear into her arms with her fingers, to rip away the terrible itching. Tears welled in the corners of her eyes. But she knew that scratching would make the bites worse, could even end up scarring her arms. Instead of scratching, Kelly cursed loud enough to startle a spider monkey out of a nearby tree, and she hurried toward a prefab shack in the middle of the clearing. Inside was her lab, where she experimented with different herbal recipes to cure both common ailments like bites and rashes and the more serious illnesses like malaria. But she had no defense against a new virus. No one did.

As Kelly hurried to the shack, she heard Frank's voice calling to her from the hill. She waved without turning around, unwilling to stop. The itching consumed her attention. Nothing mattered but getting inside the lab and mixing the medicine. With each step, she could picture where each plant was stored—the red-tinted Ix-canan on the second shelf, the yellow flowers of the wild sage in a glass jar, the fresh kayabim wrapped in paper.

"Kel," Frank called again, "there's a telephone call for you."

"Take a message," Kelly yelled and ran inside the lab. Couldn't the fool see she was in a hurry, in pain, in danger of having contracted a disease? Was he blind?

Kelly grabbed a handful of Ix-canan leaves from the shelf and quickly crushed the red-veined leaves over her opposite arm. A faint, almost invisible oil dripped onto the swollen mosquito bites, cooling their feverish burn instantly. Kelly sighed. Ix-canan. The joy of Ix-canan. In Maya, the name of the plant translated as guardian of the forest. It was a sacred herb among the people in Cayo because it could treat a wide variety of ailments.

As Kelly took another handful of the plant leaves to use on her other arm, she heard Frank's pickup roar to life, the driver's door slam shut and the tired truck lurch into gear. She was annoyed that he had left without even checking to understand why she had been running. He was focused on his own agenda, and his self-absorption suddenly enraged her. He seemed to always be running off to another one of his endless meetings in the name of social justice and Mayan rights, oblivious to how it made her feel. No wonder their marriage was in the state it was in. You can't expect anything to grow if you don't cultivate it, give it regular, careful attention.

When the itching subsided, however, Kelly forgot her anger. She wondered about the telephone call. There were no telephones in San Antonio so it would have to be someone from San Ignacio or another working town. She guessed it was either one of her colleagues from Belize City or, possibly, another call from the TV crew who were expected later in the afternoon.

Kelly poured rainwater from an old ceramic jug into a pot and lit her propane stove. While she went to answer the telephone, the water would have time to boil and she could soak the wild sage and the tres puntas and the fiddlewood together to create a lotion to treat her mosquito bites further. She would also make a tea of the kayabin, a preventative for malaria, at least.

Kelly clambered up the hill to the house, a prefab rancher trucked and floated in all the way from Belize City. Inside, she felt a sudden chill run through her as she picked up the telephone receiver.

"Dr. Montgomery? Ma'am?"

A boyish but resonant voice laced with education and privilege. Every word carefully enunciated without a trace of regional accent. She'd grown up surrounded by voices like this, and hearing it made her think briefly and vaguely of Philadelphia and the world she had long left behind.

"We're boating our way up to you," the voice continued. It was the documentary producer from New York. Michael Burns. He sounded vibrant, excited, in a way he never did when they had first discussed the details of his shoot.

"Anything you might need from civilization before we climb in these canoes?"

Kelly wanted to remind him of the history of "civilization" in this part of the world. Before the Spanish conquistadors tore through the forest in search of gold, neither the Mayan nor any other Indians knew diseases. It took civilization to supply that.

But Kelly knew her history lesson would sound like ranting, and she didn't want to come across as a reactionary. She needed these TV journalists on her side. There was no question in her mind that a little publicity about her research would make it more difficult for the new regime at corporate to pull the plug despite the very real dangers of new viruses and other microbes. The new bean counters were impatient for results. Her operation had not contributed anything to the bottom line since it was created over a decade ago. They wanted a miracle cure, like the one found by an ethnobotanist team in the Fiji rain forest that had struck upon the Pacific yew tree and the ability of its bark to fight cervical cancer. Only two years on the market and it was already saving lives and making profits. The best thing Kelly had come up with was an anti-itch ointment that smelled like cat piss, a deficiency no industrial perfumer could figure out how to mask.

"We're pretty self-sufficient, here," Kelly answered, finally. "But a six-pack of Belikan might be nice. It's a favorite of my husband's. Have a safe trip."

As Kelly strolled down the hill to the medicinal lab, she began to feel like herself again. The itching had stopped, Frank was away and she would be left alone with her research. This time the subject of her experiments in medicine was her own arms, her own body. Kelly, not someone in an antiseptic laboratory, would be the guinea pig for the antimalarial tea and the new, scentless anti-itching bath she was concocting. This fact only made Kelly more enthusiastic about her work. There would be no guessing about the eventual findings. She would know immediately if they worked and under what circumstances. There would be no guessing about unknown variables. She would control the process from beginning to end.

The water was boiling by the time she reached the lab. She collected the plants and dropped their assorted leaves into the bubbling water. As each leaf slipped underneath, Kelly pressed her right hand against the flowering crosses embroidered on the neck and chest of her huipile blouse and chanted a benediction the curandero had taught her. Her enselmo. It was a simple call to the healing spirits of the Maya—the good spirits. Pedro Meza had been emphatic about the importance of praying when preparing any medicines. He believed the spirits activated the healing power of the plants. Kelly assumed chemical alkaloids and enzymes were equally responsible, but she chanted nonetheless. One could never be too sure.

THE FIVE LOST DAYS

3

Ca-cal-tun: Dried seeds of this herb are placed in eye overnight to rid phlegm and to discourage formation of cataracts

The dock was a small tree trunk hammered into the bank of the Macal. The wood canoes were tethered to it, bobbing like toys on the swollen river. The mocha-colored water churned silently by, as strong and thick as the cafe con leche Burns and his television crew had been served at the Hotel San Ignacio. A gaunt, dark-skinned Creole man stooped by the river's edge, adjusting the rope near one of the canoes.

"He called Mr. Green," Gilbert announced and turned off the van's ignition.

"That's the sack of bones that's going to take us six miles upriver?" Vic Colt glanced over his aviator sunglasses to make sure Burns had heard him. Like the rest of the crew, he was not happy with the planning that Burns had done for this shoot. First, they had endured a pounding, five-hour van ride on a dusty, potholed road through parched grasslands that smelled like urine. When they finally reached San Ignacio, they discovered their hotel was a dump at the edge of town without hot water and a hole in the floor for a toilet.

"The man takes elder hostel tourists further than we're going," Burns said. "Besides, it will be cooler on the river."

"This is ridiculous, Burns. You let Gilbert hire this grandpa?"

"Gilbert has been the best. He's gotten us around as good as anyone could in this part of Belize and he knows what we're trying to do. You can't ask for anything more."

Burns escaped from the hostile van into the sticky heat of midmorning. He steeled himself against the discomfort much as he had done during the night. He accepted it as just part of filming on location. What bothered him was the obvious fatigue of his crew. A producer was only as effective as his crew, a fact that had always made him take responsibility for the men and women who worked for him. For the duration of the shoot, at least, he considered them, if not friends, then family.

After Burns had descended the hill, he found their river pilot crouched over the bow of one of the dugout canoes, patiently tying a knot with his huge, bony hands. His long, narrow face was drawn with intense concentration.

"You must be our river captain," Burns said, offering his hand. Mr. Green's face suddenly brightened with a warm, gap-toothed smile that made Burns like him immediately. Cataracts clouded the old man's eyes, but his chestnut face was alert, the deep, prune-like wrinkles suggesting a long life under the harsh glare of the tropics. Burns reached over and grabbed the old man's hand.

"Mr. Green know every meter," Gilbert said, shuffling up behind them. "And he make the dory hisself from a giant tubroos tree."

"He's almost blind, Gilbert," Burns said. "I thought you said he was the best guide in Cayo."

Gilbert nodded, grinning with what was meant to be reassurance. Burns felt the swollen river and its swift, silent current as though it were underneath him. There was a faint gurgling sound where the water fell into rippling eddies, and it filled Burns with a sense of dread.

"How old is he?" Burns asked.

"Eighty-two. Mr. Green gran-son take other dory," Gilbert answered, pointing further down the riverbank, which was crowded with mahogany and tubroos trees and tall beds of light green bamboo stalks. The figure of the lanky teenager was barely discernible as he strolled under the lush shadows cast by the trees. Burns had to squint to see the boy, and it made him aware of the high contrast created by the brilliant tropical light and the dense, dark jungle. More bad news. It would present a problem for video, which could not record extreme contrasts with the sensitivity of film, especially when it came to photographing faces. The details of cheeks and forehead would be washed out while the eyes would be sunk behind harsh shadows.

"Gran-son is very good, too," Gilbert said with a show of concern. "No to worry."

An argument between Vic and the crew erupted behind them. They were carrying the heavy anvil trunks that protected the video gear and were arguing about whether to set them on the soft ground at the foot of the canoes or to pack them directly onto the barge that bobbed off shore. Vic wanted all the equipment checked and accounted for before it was set on the flimsy bamboo platform. He owned the Ikegami camera and most of the accessories and was as protective of his equipment as a new car owner.

"It's gonna sink in the mud, Victor," Elf complained. He was the shortest member of the crew, with a long nose and pointed chin, which had earned him the nickname. "You know how hard it's gonna be to get this stuff unstuck?"

"What are we going to do if batteries or a light or a lens gets left behind, Elf? You gonna swim back and get it?" Vic demanded.

"Why can't we check it on the barge, mister cinematographer?"

"Because we don't know if Kon-tiki here even floats," Vic said.

"It works," Burns interrupted. He wasn't sure the raft floated, but there was no other transportation option. The single dirt road that led to the camp turned impassable with a sudden downpour. He'd been warned it would be like trying to drive through wet cement.

"This is ridiculous," Vic said. "I'm not going to be treated like this. I've been in this business for fourteen years."

"I agree. It sucks. But we're here. So let's just do it."

"Why should I take the risk for a network that gives me this kind of treatment?"

"How's this any different than the Nantahala?" Burns asked. Years ago they had done a shoot together on Tennessee's Nantahala River about whitewater canoeists training for the Olympics. Vic had not only shot from the bow of a canoe but voluntarily climbed up a rugged cliff to get a towering shot that reminded everyone of the movie *Deliverance*.

"We had professionals in kevlar boats on the Nantahala," Vic said. "Not Pops and Junior on a floating log."

"The Nantahala had Class Four rapids," Burns said. "This is just a little river to the research camp."

"Look at the current, Burns. What do you think I am, an idiot? Anything goes under, including us, ain't never going to be seen again."

Burns closed his eyes to relieve the ache of squinting from the hazy, white sun. His pale, grey-blue eyes—usually cool and predatory—were defenseless against the tropical brilliance. He felt inside his empty pockets, realizing he had left his sunglasses back at the hotel, a simple oversight he knew would cost him even more in the coming days. A few years ago, this would never have happened. Maybe he was just losing his edge, Burns thought. He wasn't getting any younger, and most documentary producers his age were behind an executive desk, not out trudging in the field, hungry for experience.

"Vic, I don't want to argue. Let's get going. We don't have time for this. We've got five days to get this in the can, and the clock is ticking."

"All the more reason to pay Gilbert to take us in the van."

Of all the times for Vic to throw one of his fits, Burns thought.

There just wasn't time, no matter how good he was.

"You don't want to get in that canoe, Colt, you can pack yourself up and go home. Understand?" Burns said.

Elf and Big had been busy moving the television equipment alongside the canoes and the raft. Both stopped, waiting pensively for the confrontation to unfold.

"Go home," Vic said, dismissing the idea with a slight, mocking smile. "And you'll do what?"

Burns closed his eyes. Instead of relief, his pupils throbbed as if scratched by the sun. He pulled off his Yankee baseball hat, struggling to find patience. He'd dealt with Vic's arrogance before. But he didn't have it in him now. This wasn't just another gig. They had an opportunity to capture a story so rare and unusual that not a single film had ever been made about this curandero and his medicine. Not one. Vic's attitude was not going to stand in the way, even if it meant shooting the film himself.

"Gilbert. You can take Mr. Colt back to the hotel?"

Gilbert stood behind him, his bug eyes cast demurely to the ground at his feet.

"You're serious?" Vic said.

"I don't want you on the crew. I need people who are willing to follow orders. Now let's get going. It's hot out here."

Elf and Big immediately found something to lift. Burns instructed Gilbert to drive Vic back to the hotel and, in the morning, to transport his cameraman to the airport near Belize City for the daily flight to Miami. Gilbert nodded soberly, casting shy glances in the cameraman's direction as Burns spoke.

"What are you going to do without a camera and someone to operate it?" Vic asked. "Draw pictures?"

"I've got a free-lancer in Belize City. We'll be fine."

"A free-lancer. In Belize City. You expect me to believe that?"

"She's a phone call away."

"She? A she?" Vic said. "Give me a break. Hell, there's maybe two female shooters in all of NYC, let alone this backwater."

"Well, guess what? This is a different world down here," Burns said. He didn't know why he was creating such an outsized fabrication, but he couldn't help himself. He would not have the cameraman—even a longtime collaborator like Vic—question his authority. A producer gave orders, not requests.

"I don't see why you or I or anybody should take unnecessary risks. For what? For a story no one will ever see?"

"What do you mean, no one will ever see?" Burns asked, alarmed.

"C'mon Burns. It's a foreign story. No one watches foreign stories. You know that." In fact, that was a common complaint from executives. They viewed foreign stories as the broccoli of the doc world. Films about Africa or Asia or Latin America never delivered ratings or ticket sales. Usually, they lost money—lots of it.

"This is a science story and a cultural piece. This is something no one has ever seen before," Burns said.

"You keep saying that," Vic said.

"Don't you want to do something unique and important for a change?"

"What's that supposed to mean?" Vic asked.

Burns rolled his eyes. The vast majority of their documentaries had been about crime, police, murder or celebrities. They had filmed three docs about serial killers alone. The last big-budget doc was called "The Professor and the Call Girl."

"I'm not embarrassed by anything I've done. Maybe you are," Vic said.

"No?" Burns reminded him of a documentary they had done together about teen suicides, where they had chased distraught mothers to funeral homes and wakes in order to film an emotional moment. *How do you feel?* The question was asked over and over again, fishing for tears, for the stuff of tabloid television. Yet he and Vic had pretended to be above it all, filmmakers forced to be craven by ad-crazy executives. In fact, they had done the filming willingly and with enthusiasm.

"Well you have to make a living, right?" Vic said.

24

Burns felt the shift in attitude. It was like a balloon pricked with a pin, the pent-up air rushing out. He studied Vic, wondering what had come over him.

"If this were a job, I'd quit," Vic said with a short laugh of contrition.

"That's right, Vic. This isn't just a job. We're not just punching in."

"I don't need one of your pep talks, Burns. Let's just get on board Kon-Tiki and get the ride over with."

"You're a pain in the ass, Vic."

"By the way, what's the name of this she-shooter from Belize City you got in your pocket?"

"Wouldn't you like to know!" Burns smiled, relieved to have Vic back on track, at least for the time being.

Mr. Green stood in the back of the lead canoe, yanking the ripcord for the tiny outboard that hung on the stern. It sputtered with all the force of a model airplane. Burns clung to the plank seat with his long, skinny legs, hoping he hadn't misjudged Green. The old man turned the long, seamless log into the river, aimed the boat upstream, and the canoe slid forward, the toy motor pushing them effortlessly against the swift current. As they moved away from the dock, a warm, moist breeze kicked off the water and Burns felt a quickening burst of optimism.

The river snaked ahead, sliding past the bamboo thickets and the dense cluster of trees. Some of the uppermost branches stretched halfway across the river, like hands reaching for the other shore. Mr. Green muttered and, like a tour guide, pointed out an iguana resting motionless on one of the bare branches. The old lizard was drinking up the sun, oblivious to the putter of the little boats. Nearby, bats slept upside down, dangling from underneath the same branches. Burns checked to see that Vic was shooting close-ups. The cameraman was already standing up in the canoe, his Ikegami camera lens trained on the tree branch. What had all the protest on the riverbank been about? Burns wondered. Was it the new responsibility of his eight-month-old son? Cute kid, Burns remembered, but fatherhood changed priorities. Burns had seen it in other filmmakers, many of whom switched to management desk jobs not long after a family arrived on the scene. After all, this was an all-consuming business, a calling of sorts. There wasn't time for a normal life. Burns wouldn't have it any other way.

Burns noticed whirlpools that swirled silently near the banks, some bubbling at the center like water boiling in a cauldron. It reminded him of Saturday morning cartoons that had captivated him as a young boy, where the whirlpools swallow the heroes and take them to a subterranean world where they do battle with the forces of evil. Even with middle age within sight, Burns had not stopped dreaming of becoming a hero. He would ferret out wrongdoing, expose the attempted cover-ups. He would become famous as a beacon for truth, for keeping the public informed, the essential bedrock for the functioning of a democracy. But it was TV, and in TV you could have nobility and glamour. You could bring down a corrupt president and still get rich from the movie rights.

The rain was startling. It fell in silent, gentle sheets from a brilliant blue sky. A cool breeze whisked across the surface of the river, bubbling from the impact of the tiny droplets. They passed under the cold shade of outstretched branches, then back out into the warm sun. Abruptly, the rain vanished.

"Hey, check out the birds," Elf said. The tall, lean birds were a brilliant, downy white. With the pale green reeds behind them, they seemed etched into the landscape, as delicate as Chinese watercolors.

"White herons," Big said. "They're all over Florida."

"You're a regular birder," Elf said.

"I ain't no birder, Elf. I just know a white heron when I see a white heron, OK?"

The motors on their outboard canoes suddenly shut off.

"Hey what gives?" Elf snapped.

Burns studied Mr. Green with bony shoulders slumped over the engine, apparently checking a valve. Malsheet mahn, malsheet mahn, he grumbled in his thick patois. Finally, without any explanation, the old man stood up and pulled the engine's cord, bringing it sputtering back to life. As he steered back to the middle of the river, however, he remained standing. His grave expression worried Burns. He sensed the old man's calculation. It reminded him of a pilot silently gauging a difficult landing.

As they passed around the bend, the river exploded with the roar of white water. Burns stiffened, chilled by the cool, charged air whipping off the raging water. The swift change confused and disoriented him. He checked Green's long serious face—drawn and taut and somehow familiar—as their flimsy canoe puttered toward the roaring white water, head-on.

"Burns," Vic shouted, his eyes gleaming with fury. He turned from the bow, the precious Ikegami cradled in his lap, and his free hand clawing at the empty crawl space under their seats. "There are no life vests. No life vests! You hear me?"

Before Burns could react, a heavy wave slammed into the canoe and knocked them sideways. Burns clung to the sides of the canoe as it shimmied backwards, and he feared they were about to capsize. His breathing raced away from him. He knew there was little hope if they were thrown from the boat—not without life vests. The shore was close, but the river's powerful current would drown anyone who tried to swim it.

Burns prepared for the worst. But the canoe stopped its drift, and the bow swung back to face the white water again. A sheet of water leapt over the bow and drenched them. Vic cursed and curled himself even tighter around his camera, which he had swaddled in a towel. The canoe inched forward, the waves rumbling underneath. Somehow, the little boat advanced against the raging water. Burns felt buoyant.

"Vic. We need to be shooting this. Is the lens clean?"

Vic remained utterly still, then shook his head emphatically from side to side.

The old man stood straight, squinting through the wet spray. He steered the canoe off to one side, away from the biggest waves, keeping a steady course. He squeezed past the rocks, hugging the strip of calmer water near the bank.

The bow of the second canoe was being pummeled by the waves. The boy stood in front of the motor like his grandfather, studying the water. Elf sat grimly in the stern. He ducked as a sheet of water blasted over them. As the canoe turned toward them, a sense of dread gripped Burns long before anything else registered. It was a feeling he'd had only a few times before. The last was in college, a hot, sunny day like this, but there was something foreboding hovering over the atmosphere of the campus. He was fearful without knowing why. Only later did he learn about the freshman who had hung himself in his closet.

Big was gone. There was no mistake. It sent a sickening chill down into the small of Burns's back. Mr. Green stood up and shouted. He pointed to the mini-barge, floundering in the white water. The canoe and barge swung closer to the bank and gained momentum. The boy nodded to Mr. Green, who was still shouting. Burns willed himself to remain calm, to think clearly.

He had never lost anyone on a shoot, ever. Fourteen years and God knows how many remote locations—from the desert to Alaska to the murky slums of Haiti—not one of his people had even been harmed.

Burns avoided looking at Vic, whom he could feel watching him. He knew what his cameraman was thinking. People don't drown if they're driving in a van. And they don't drown if they have life jackets. But when Vic spoke, his voice was reassuring, not accusative.

"He couldn't have disappeared that fast," Vic said. "No chance."

The grandson guided the canoe over and around the waves nearly as expertly as the old man. Within moments, the second canoe was moving into the shallow, calm water near the shore.

"Hey guys!" The high voice came from the bank of the river. A broad-shouldered, blonde-haired Slavic kid dressed in long, baggy lacrosse shorts and an oversized "Good Morning America" T-shirt stood on the lush bank. Big. It was Big John. When he gave a small, mock salute, Burns laughed as much in relief as surprise. Big could not have seemed more out of place in the tropics if he'd been a mid-western farmer.

"The jungle kid made me get out, guys," Big told them. "Too heavy for the rapids."

"You got to stop popping the steroids, Big," Burns called. He loved these guys. They were fearless, and they would do whatever it took to get the shot.

"Take supplements. Never touched a steroid, Burnsie."

The old lizards sunned on the thick branches, uninterested in the video crew that slipped underneath them. The river was calm, the once-raging current now buried underneath a placid, gleaming sheet of mocha. The sputtering outboard engines pushed the boats steadily upstream, churning through the creamy water, leaving a smooth wake that fanned out behind their sharp bows. Unseen birds called from the densely wooded forest that lined both banks, sealing off the river like verdant cliffs.

Big John grabbed one side of the canoe for balance and crouched above his seat. He pulled a cellular telephone from the back pocket of his lacrosse shorts and flicked it open. He pushed the power button but no welcome to AT&T appeared on his LED screen. He kept turning it on and turning if off, waiting for the signal to kick in.

"Ain't going to do you any good," Elf called. "There's no towers, no relaying stations around here. We're in the boonies."

Big shook his phone, then held it above his head, desperately trying to extend the reach of his antenna.

"I told you, Big," Elf said.

"This is dual band, Elf," Big insisted.

High above the river, a buzzard scouted effortlessly on a thermal in the white, cloudless haze. Burns tried to relax in the humid silence. He loved being in the wilderness, away from all the noise and clutter and distraction. But his mind raced, untouched by the torpid still-ness.

He pictured Katz's bare white office. There were no pictures, plants or bookcases. A sleek, minimalist aesthetic. No clutter except for a trio of gilded Emmy statuettes on a black lacquer shelf. He was sitting across from Katz, who was dressed like a corporate lawyer in a sober blue suit and brick red tie. The executive producer was almost a decade younger, a fact that Burns tried hard to ignore.

"So are you available?" Katz asked.

"Five days," Burns said. "That's tight. We'd be like some platoon dropping into a hot zone, then getting pulled out before we knew what was going on."

Katz seemed to be reading a memo on the desk in front of him. A corporate intimidation tactic, Burns thought, like the way Katz positioned his desk in front of the window so whomever was being subjected to an interview had to squint to find Katz's eyes. It was a tactic popular with interrogators.

"What's that, Burns?"

"I was wondering if we can budget a little more shooting time. Or take some time away from the research and pre-production."

"Most of the research is already done," Katz stated, without looking up from his paper. "You just need to do a couple of pre-interviews then get on a plane."

Years of shooting on location had taught Burns that this was simply not enough time to cover a story in the middle of the jungle, let alone enough time to shoot it well. Logistics were logistics. They didn't budge. But the story appealed to him. It was different, noble even.

"It's not breaking news," Katz said. "You know that. It's an evergreen. I need something in the bin when the show runs short."

As long as he'd known Katz, the executive producer always felt a need to diminish his producers. It was his way of reminding people who was in charge. Burns usually ignored it.

"So there's no air date," Burns said, a circumstance he knew could condemn the documentary to the archive vault forever.

"That could change. Depends on what you come up with. Like the professor and the call girl story."

Katz never seemed to stop admiring a documentary Burns would rather forget. It was one in a long line of what Burns considered murder and mayhem documentaries—the bread and butter of prime time television. Katz's favorite was about an Ivy League professor and family man who had become obsessed with a prostitute and eventually killed her. While Burns was proud of the filming and editing, it was a tawdry story better suited to tabloid TV. But Katz had gushed about it from the start, especially the big ratings it attracted.

"This is up your alley, Burns," he said. "You'll make something out of it. Maybe get another one of those gold paperweights."

The canoes continued to putter upstream through the dense, sizzling haze. They were in the middle of the river, far from the shade of the trees, feeling the brute intensity of the tropical sun. Burns splashed a handful of the warm river water on his face, but it did nothing to cool the hot, prickling sensation he felt on his cheeks and the back of his neck. He wondered vaguely how many miles they had come and how much they had yet to travel. Ahead, lining both banks, were more of the endless trees. The haze made their lushness blend together into one unbroken green wall.

Burns wondered what Julie would think of this. He'd been seeing her for almost a year, the longest relationship he'd ever had. He closed his eyes to the heat, picturing his girlfriend in his place, a textured white sheet of paper in her lap instead of his production bible. She would be holding that pencil-thin paint brush in her girlish hands and her delicate, caramel eyes lost in dreamy concentration. She occupied whatever landscape she painted with a presence he envied. He loved her talent for seeing details of color and form that were often invisible to him. It was the side of her he treasured without complication or hesitation.

"I'll miss you," she had said just before he'd left for the airport. Her thin, delicate arms were wrapped tightly around his waist. He liked her close to him, but he was anxious to go and it felt as though she were holding him back.

"I'll miss you, too," he'd said, pecking her full lips, ready to bolt out the door.

"No you won't," she'd said with a wry, coquettish smile. "You'll be where you're happiest. Filmmaking."

"I've never taken on anything like this," Burns said. "I'm going to be tested."

"It's your chance to shine, Michael. It's going to be great. I love you."

Burns hugged her with gratitude. He needed the support. But it wasn't until he was in the yellow taxi, speeding across the Triboro Bridge, that he realized he had not answered her in kind. The East River, pigeon-gray in the flat morning light below him, stretched to the foot of the jagged city skyline, as still as a moat. He would call her when he got to Belize, he told himself. He would say something.

When Burns opened his eyes again, he was facing a hazy blue wall of trees. At the same time, Mr. Green brought the canoe suddenly about, heading toward shore. Burns wondered where they were going. At first, he thought it was some kind of optical illusion, a distortion caused by the heat, the confinement and the growing awareness of his own exhaustion. The impenetrable wall of trees began to separate, each sinewy trunk becoming separate and distinct. The long branches spread like venetian blinds, opening up a view of the sparse forest beyond. There were wood steps the color of the tree trunks, connecting to two stories of stairs that zigzagged up a steep bank, through more tall, skinny trees and scattered scrub. The clearing was sparse and as well maintained as any park.

The transformation of the riverbank reminded him of a painting he'd seen at one of the art gallery openings that Julie insisted on attending. On first glance, the black, textured canvas had seemed to be nothing but a swath of impenetrable color. Burns had wanted to dismiss it as simply another piece of modern, conceptual art that one required a manual to understand. But something—boredom, exasperation—had kept him from walking away, and he'd kept staring at the Halloween black, wondering what the point was.

It was then that the painting had begun to transform before his eyes. There was an image of a man and woman in the left corner. There was a street lamp. There was a park. The images seemed to bleed through the black at the same time they were part of it. The effect was remarkable. He felt the art was coming to life, summoned by his own curiosity and confusion. At first, he'd seen only the black color of the canvas the way he'd seen only the green wall of trees along the shore. He had recognized the painting. But he hadn't really been looking, seeing what was there. The painting, like this forest, had surprised him into seeing.

Mr. Green turned off the engine and glided the last few yards until they bumped gently against the silt bank. Before Burns could move, the wiry old man was out of the canoe and knee-deep in the water. He sloshed through the water with the supple agility of a thirty-year-old and plucked the line from the floor of the canoe.

The grandson puttered in just below, then slid the canoe broadside, pointing the bow upstream. The smooth turn swung the equipment barge across the surface of the water until it bumped the shore. He kept the outboard engine running as Big and Elf jumped out into the ankle-deep water. They followed Burns up the wet bank, slogging through mud the color of coffee grounds.

"We got to go up that?" Big asked, peering at the warped, flimsy planks. The stairway looked as though it had been hammered together in an afternoon.

Burns walked toward the steps, planning to check if they were stable enough to climb. But even before he reached them, Vic's angry voice exploded behind him.

"What do you mean it was there, bonehead?" Vic demanded "I don't see it now, do you?"

Elf had his hands on his hips and was shaking his head in disbelief. "I don't understand it," Elf pleaded. "It was here."

"You is. It ain't," Vic said.

"Well it's not my fault," Elf insisted. "So don't blame me."

"You were in charge of packing up, Elf. Am I right?"

"What happened?" Burns called over to the men.

Vic and Elf hesitated, facing off silently at one another, daring the other to speak. Burns hurried toward them.

"We don't have any stock. Our tape is gone," Vic announced as soon as Burns reached them.

"What do you mean, gone?"

"I knew something like this was going to happen. As soon as I saw that stupid little raft," Vic said.

"It was there, Burnsie, I don't know what happened," Elf said. He peered at the floating raft, waiting as though it might offer the missing clue.

"How can it just be gone?" Burns asked. The ramifications were staggering. It was like the time he was boating on the lake and a dark rainstorm swept slowly but inexorably across the water toward where he waited, frightened and awed by what was about to strike. He couldn't move.

Now, fighting panic, Burns waded into the warm water alongside the cargo raft and began searching through the remaining cases.

"I've got one cassette I brought along in the canoe," Vic said. "And about ten minutes worth of tape in the camera."

Burns swatted away a cloud of gnats that swirled in front of him.

"Thirty minutes of stock. Are you kidding? The show is an hour. Sixty god-damn minutes."

The shooting ratio was generally seventeen minutes to every one minute of a finished program. Seventeen to one was even conservative, Burns reminded himself. He was planning to record at least twenty cassettes. He took a long, deep breath that his girlfriend swore always calmed the mind. It didn't work.

"Are you sure we didn't leave the case of tapes somewhere. Like back in San Ignacio?" Burns asked. "Now think closely, Elf. Do you remember taking it out of the van?"

Elf nodded without hesitation.

"Are you sure?" Burns insisted.

"I'll go back," Elf said. "I'll find it. It's my fault we don't have it."

"No one is going anywhere—yet," Burns said. He calculated that he would lose at least one day of his shoot if he waited for a new case of raw stock to be delivered from Belize City even if he could find someone who sold them.

"If we don't go back now," Vic said, "there might not be enough daylight for the return trip."

"He's right, Burns," Elf said. "Let me go."

Sunset was a few hours away. They might have time. Before deciding, Burns wanted to make contact with their character, Kelly Montgomery, the blanc woman Gilbert said was under the spell of the curandero. The research camp might have their own boat or even a truck that could drive one of his crew back to the city.

"Let's get this equipment unpacked first," Burns said. "I'll go and see if our native doctor can help us."

Burns marched back toward the flimsy stairway that towered a few stories above him. From the first step, the planks did not feel solid. They were also coated with a thin, slippery film of moisture. But Burns ran up the stairs nonetheless, anxious to save time. If he stepped on a rotted plank or lost his grip on a slippery step, there wasn't much he could do about it anyway.

The dank, humid air made him lose his breath by the time he reached the second landing. Burns kept moving, pushing himself as he did even when he was playing tennis in Central Park, always testing his endurance, pushing himself to the limit just for the fun of it. He climbed higher, breathing through his open mouth. Sweat dripped from his chin and made his button-down shirt stick to him like a second skin. As he made the turn onto the final set of stairs, however, his feet went out from under him and he went sliding into the handrail.

Burns immediately pulled himself up. He wouldn't allow himself to be stopped. He ran up the final flight, stopping only when he reached the landing and felt the sunlight on his reddened face. Feeling victorious, Burns raised his arms, then bent over to gain control over his heaving chest and stomach. He heard a rustle in the trees to the side of him. A spider monkey squatted on a branch, his chestnut eyes darting over him with anxious curiosity. Burns stared back. It was the first monkey he'd ever seen in the wild.

After he caught his breath, Burns called down to his crew. They were studying him like they weren't sure what he might try next.

"I'll walk next time," Burns said.

"What about the old man?" Vic yelled up.

"Tell him to wait," Burns said.

"Tell him how, Burns. What language?"

The old man, Burns remembered, only spoke the local patois of Spanish, English, French and even some Creole.

"Use Spanish, I guess," Burns said.

"I speak a little college German. But that's it," Vic called back.

"How about Elf giving it a try?" Elf lived in a Hispanic neighborhood in Jersey City. "He must speak some Spanish," Burns said.

"Elf says nada."

Burns did not want to climb down and run up the stairs again. He was also anxious to get to the research camp before something else went wrong.

"Use English then. Some sign language. He'll get the idea."

"The old man's almost blind, Burns."

"Just do something to make sure he stays. I'll be back," Burns said and turned to follow the sunlight that blazed above him.

Yax-nik: Powdered bark of this tree is used to treat infections

As soon as he stepped out from under the shade of the stairwell landing, Burns found himself at the edge of a sprawling suburban lawn. The scent of freshly mowed grass hung in the humid air. He stood utterly still, momentarily stunned by the screech of unseen birds, the insistent racket of cicadas hidden in the trees. A single morpho butterfly darted over the carpet of grass, its electric blue wings flashing like neon in the hot sunlight.

Burns warily approached a half-acre tilled lot, which was as well ordered as an English garden. It was all so out of place, a botanical Disneyland in the middle of the jungle. The plants, many flowering in yellow, rose and violet, were organized in perfect, cultivated rows. Insects buzzed around the buds as well as the weathered index cards that were planted at the base of each row. Each card identified a row of herbs by its scientific name: *Lantana camara*, *Chenopodium ambrosioides*, *Momordica charantia*. It was a medicinal garden designed and labeled for visitors. Burns wouldn't have been surprised to find a box filled with self-guided tour pamphlets.

He was relieved to find something that appeared more authentic just beyond the garden, where the grass thinned and showed patches of cocoa-colored mud. There was a small gazebo-like shack in the middle of this uncultivated spot that reeked of cooked grains. A faint steam, in fact, drifted out of the open door. As Burns walked toward it, he heard the faint Creole chatter of a radio DJ, followed by the punta rock music that blared in the streets of Belize City. Someone worked inside the shack, speaking softly, almost murmuring like a priest intoning a benediction. Burns slowed his pace, wary of startling whomever was inside, even though he guessed it might be Kelly Montgomery.

Burns recalled the scientists at Pfizer's corporate lab in Connecticut speaking of Kelly with great respect for her skills in gathering information about plants native to the Belizean highlands. Remarkable. Astounding. Like no one else out in the field, they claimed. But one associate had admitted to Burns—after the camera had been turned off—that Kelly Montgomery's long apprenticeship with a local healer had been eroding her high scientific standards. She had recently been sending back new plants with written instructions describing their spiritual properties as well as their chemical compositions. She thinks she's a curandero, he said.

Burns stopped at the doorway of the gazebo, peering into the cool shade of the hut. A middle-aged woman with honey brown, shoulder-length hair was poised in front of a discarded oil drum, which she was using as a pot. She was dressed in blue jeans, rubber boots and a rectangular cotton shirt that reminded him of the embroidered blouses flower children had worn in the Sixties. She had strong, narrow shoulders and held her head with what Burns thought of as a proud, aristocratic bearing, like a queen slumming in a servant's kitchen. Some colleagues had warned that Kelly thought too much of herself, but what Burns read in her posture was an attractive self-confidence.

A faint steam rose past her damp hair, toward the low roof of hanging pots and colanders. Hundreds of clear cookie jars filled with dried leaves and sticks were lined up neatly on the waist-level workbenches that fit snugly against the walls.

"What's brewing?" Burns asked.

"A miracle, I hope," she answered without a hint of surprise, as if American TV producers were always dropping by.

Burns was surprised and disappointed to see a woman much older than her press photo. The portrait had air-brushed away the weathered neck, the deep lines of a face etched in the merciless tropical sun. Her teeth, too, were graying with age, untouched by any caps or professional whitener. Yet her lips were smooth and full, and there was something about her manner that recalled the pretty, headstrong achiever fresh out of graduate school.

"What happened?" Burns asked, focusing his attention on the savage red bumps that coated one arm like the measles.

She told him about the mosquito attack, blaming herself for not coating herself with DEET, especially during the rainy season. As she spoke, Burns made a mental note to shoot a close-up of the arm when filming started.

"So you're mixing up an antiinflammatory?" Burns asked.

"A healing lotion, yes," Kelly said. Her moss-green eyes were beautifully intelligent, with flecks of grey that floated in them like ashes, a fact he found both alluring and disturbing. "How was your trip?"

"Something of an adventure." Burns took her outstretched hand. He was startled by its masculine size and strength. It was an outdoorsman's hand, rough and callused from chopping wood or handling tools. Yet, when he pressed his own smooth city hands against hers, he felt a spark of silken warmth and ease, a healer's touch.

"I'm glad you made it in one piece," she said, returning to her cooking.

Burns leaned close to the pot, examining the amber liquid. With the help of the scientists in Connecticut, he had learned about some of the herbs and native plants. "Ix-canan. And maybe skunk root. Is there also some red mangrove or fiddlewood?"

"Fiddlewood bark. The Mayans call it Yax-nik," Kelly told him, a trace of amusement crossing her parted lips. He smiled back, charmed by her manner.

"That was an informed guess," she continued. "I'm impressed. Where did you learn it?"

"Your associates," Burns said. "I made a visit to the Pfizer campus."

Burns made it sound as if it had been a pleasant, amiable scout. But the Connecticut headquarters facility had been shrouded in a paranoid secrecy, as though the campus were guarding top military secrets like the nearby nuclear submarine base in Groton.

"I'm surprised they let a journalist visit," Kelly said. "Good for you."

"I had a corporate chaperone most of time," Burns said.

"Did they show off their prized toy?"

Using infrared light, a unique, specially designed computer scanner examined any given plant stem or leaf and determined all known chemical compounds and enzymes, and flagged any new ones. It was considered a technological breakthrough and one that saved researchers from countless, tedious hours of examining each plant or herb by hand.

"They're misguided," Kelly said. "They believe they can objectify a plant's medicinal property. But one thing you learn in Belize is that you can't divorce the physical use of a plant from its spiritual one. They're inter-linked. One works with the other. You can learn about every single chemical or enzyme in a plant, how they mix together even, but it will never tell you how it heals."

Burns nodded as though he understood. In fact, he was reminded of her colleague who feared she had gone native.

"How was the river today? I've heard it's calmer than it has ever been."

"The rapids took some getting used to," he said.

"Oh, you never get used to those," she said. "For every three trips up here, one inevitably gets wet."

"So they can capsize? I'm glad I didn't know."

"Hardly matters. It's a quick swim to the shore, and the sun will dry you like a heat lamp. Now how many are you?"

"Four. My DP, a sound man, a grip and me."

"DP?"

"Director of Photography," Burns said.

"Of course. You are making a movie of sorts."

A man's terrified scream blasted over the quiet yard. In the next instant, responding instinctively to the human cry of fear, they rushed out of the hut and into the yard.

Big hoisted a blue anvil case above his head and threw it at the ground like it was a spear. The heavy case slammed to the ground and Big fell back toward the landing, barely missing a collision with Elf, who had just emerged into the sunlight cradling an armful of light stands as if they were a batch of firewood.

"Look out, you big oaf," Elf screamed. The metal stands fell clattering to the ground. Big was oblivious. His attention was glued to the blue anvil case. He was breathing hard, his reddened cheeks glazed with sweat.

"What's going on?" Burns asked.

"A snake," Big said, "and it freaked me out."

Burns grabbed one end of the case, planning to have a look at whatever Big John had almost certainly crushed.

"Be careful," Kelly warned. "It might have been a fer-de-lance. They're very poisonous. And one of the most aggressive snakes in the world."

"Aggressive?" Burns asked. He hesitated raising the heavy case.

"They like to attack. Fer-de-lance means 'tip of the sword.' They don't bite their prey. They slash repeatedly, injecting venom each time. They're feared more than even jaguars."

Burns stared at the anvil box, his curiosity overcoming his vague fear. As soon as he lifted up the heavy case, everyone backed away instinctively. The dead animal puzzled Burns.

"Well?" Big asked.

The long, brown reptile was crushed, flattened the way Burns had seen them on country roads. A dark, brown stripe ran from its head to its long tail.

"I'm not sure, Big," Burns said, "but I think you saved yourself from being eaten alive by a newt."

Kelly stepped forward for a quick look and smiled.

"It's called a shiny skink. It's a type of lizard."

"Well it looked like a snake," Big said, trying to shrug off his embarrassment. "They're all over the jungle, right?"

A shiny skink, Kelly told them, could be mistaken for a snake. Its long, sleek body was similar and, when in a hurry, the lizard abandons its four webbed feet and slithers along the ground, mimicking a small snake.

"Well it tricked me," Big said, "and most everyone else."

"That's because you were looking for a snake," Elf said. "So that's what you saw."

"I'm not looking for snakes, Elf," Big said. "I'm looking to get out of their way."

Burns studied the skink a moment more, intrigued by its use of illusion for survival. Even animals toyed with seeing, instinctively knowing that sight can easily be fooled.

"Let me show you where you'll be staying," Kelly said.

She led them across the open grass and up the slight hill toward the prefab rancher. As he stepped back into the blaze of sunlight, Burns began to worry again about the missing videotape. If he sent one of his crew back and the tape was not found, what would he do next?

"Are you OK, Mr. Burns?"

Kelly was walking alongside him, suddenly.

"Yeah, sure," Burns lied. "I was just thinking about something we left back at the hotel in San Ignacio."

"It's that valuable?"

"No, no," Burns said. He couldn't get himself to tell the simple truth. Part of the reason was that caution was ingrained in him. The other reason was that he found himself wanting to impress Kelly.

"Call the hotel," Kelly said. "We do have phones here, as you know."

"I'll go back, Burns," Elf blurted. "I told you."

"You don't want to tell me what it is?" Kelly asked.

"Can he make it back to San Ignacio before dark?" Burns asked.

"If he leaves soon," Kelly answered, "but getting back may be a problem. Mr. Green lives in San Ignacio. He'd have to overnight here at the camp when they return. I don't know if he'd agree to it."

"I'll talk to him," Burns said, more quickly than he intended because he immediately felt Kelly eyeing him suspiciously.

"No to worry," Burns said.

"You've met Gilbert," Kelly said, grinning. "Of course, there probably aren't many who haven't."

Burns and Elf hurried back across the lawn, through the white-hot sunlight, toward the top landing of the stairwell. Elf kept an eye out for wayward snakes as Burns gave instructions. Elf was to check the bank of the river where they had embarked, then go back to the Hotel San Ignacio, on foot if Mr. Green couldn't help him find a car.

They descended the stairwell in silence, concentrating on their steps. But as soon as they had reached the riverbank, Burns flew into a rage. Their video equipment sat on the bank where they had left it. But Green and his canoes were nowhere to be seen.

"You were supposed to tell him not to leave," Burns yelled.

"You told Vic to do it. Not me," Elf said. "I don't talk Spanish."

"Well did you see them leave?"

"Not sure. I was carrying stuff. But I heard Vic say something."

Burns searched beyond the trees, expecting the canoes to reappear on the darkening river.

"We've lost a day, damn it."

"Well it's not my fault."

Burns's sunburned cheeks made him look even angrier than he was. He glared at the fast-moving river as if he held it personally responsible for his predicament.

THE FIVE LOST DAYS

5

Xcoch: Seeds and leaves used as a purgative

After the sun had finally cooled to a pale blood orange, they hiked to an old wooden cross that marked the summit of the research camp. Kelly Montgomery led the way, climbing the steep grade with an ease that impressed Burns. The humidity made each step even more of an effort, but Kelly stormed ahead, tackling the hill like a deft mountaineer. Her muscular, powerful legs belonged to someone much younger. Burns admired them, curious about her life as a wife living with her husband in the jungle. If one had to live in the middle of nowhere, he thought, this was the kind of partner you would need.

By the time they reached the summit, Burns and his crew were straining to breathe the thick, moist air. Burns swallowed, trying to coat his dry, scratchy throat with saliva. Sweat trickled down the side of his flushed cheeks and fell from his square chin like drops of rain. His long, thin face was gaunt with the strain of the climb.

"You're at the highest elevation in Cayo," Kelly announced.

"I believe you," Burns said. He bent over, hands on his hips, catching his breath.

"I try to climb up here every day just for the view and the peace-fulness," Kelly said, looking out over the jungle.

There was protectiveness about her gaze that reminded Burns of a private landowner admiring her property. It was easy to see why. A jade sea of rolling hills, carpeted in a dense weave of mahogany trees, stretched to the fading horizon. She pointed to the flat, granite crown of the distant Mayan pyramid, which gazed sternly over the treetops like a soldier on guard. But there was no kingdom anywhere, no em-pire to protect. There were no roads, no houses, no radio tower. A vulture circled lazily above another distant summit, a black pencil mark in the vastness that it patrolled.

"We're close to the Guatemalan border, aren't we?" Burns asked.

"You're looking at it," Kelly said, motioning to the hills rolling to the horizon. "Maybe twenty miles, but it's a world away."

"Thousands of Mayans have been killed in their civil war," Burns said.

"Likely more than that."

"Why do they hate the Maya so much?" Burns asked.

"Everyone knows the government wants the land for ladinos. The Maya are out there planting maize and carrying on their culture, so they're in the way."

"You've been over there?" Burns said.

"As far as Peten," Kelly said. "But it's always risky even for a white woman. I spend most of my time right here."

Burns absently touched the old missionary cross. Years of rain and wind had worn it as smooth as bone. It was stark and pale in the midst of the lush, emerald jungle.

"My husband hates that cross," Kelly said. "He sees it as a sym-bol of the ongoing repression against the Mayans." She explained that it started with the Franciscans who controlled the area in the late 1800s and were relentless and cruel in their drive to convert. Like the Ladinos, they wanted to recast the Mayan lands in their cultural image.

"I've heard that story before," Burns said. "But I still like the cross."

"You're Christian?"

"That's not the reason."

"You like it because it might be useful, something you can shoot with your camera."

Burns nodded, liking this woman's bracing honesty.

"I like the cross, too. It's a symbol for me but not one of suppression. I see this cross as a little reality check of where I come from and the attitudes I bring with me. So it helps to question my assumptions."

Burns abruptly asked her to stop. He wanted to get this explanation on tape. She would look appealing if posed next to the cross with the jungle rolling into the deep background. Burns liked people photographed in the midst of their environment with ample depth of field. The landscape acted like a photo caption, telling viewers more about the subject. Without it, all he had was another talking head.

His crew hurriedly set up their equipment with the smooth, natural coordination of a well-practiced team. Big John opened the spider legs of the tripod and spiked them into the soft ground. Elf unleashed his coiled, black roll of audio wire that he had been carrying on his shoulder. Vic grabbed a lens filter from the pouch that was clipped to his belt. Burns, meanwhile, positioned his character next to the cross. He explained what he wanted with the precision and authority of a director.

"Are you making me a star?" Kelly joked.

"You bet," Burns said, not joking at all. Documentary producers were paid to shape their leading characters. It wasn't unlike film directors who shape the performance of their actors.

"Now when we're rolling, I'd like to ask you about what you were just going to say."

"OK. Do I talk to you or the camera?"

"Me. Look right at me. In fact, it's better if you don't glance at the camera at all. We're just having a conversation."

As Vic adjusted the lens and iris alongside him, Burns focused all of his attention on Kelly. He knew it was awkward to suddenly turn a real conversation into a taped interview, so he wanted to relax her so that she would seem and sound natural when recorded. But the problem was that he was nervous in a way he rarely ever was. As he met her unguarded eyes, he suddenly became aware of what he looked and sounded like. Why? She wasn't beautiful or even particularly sexy. If anything, she had plain looks. So why was she making him self-conscious?

"The light's going fast," Vic said. "I don't want to lose her. Can we just shoot with the boom mike?"

"No. I want a lav and a boom," Burns said. Elf hurried to Kelly's side carrying the bug-like lavaliere microphone and asked her if she wouldn't mind running it under her blouse so the wire didn't show. Kelly was agreeable. Burns watched as she slipped the tiny black bug along her bare skin, casually pulling it past her breasts and clipping it to the collar of her embroidered blouse.

"OK," Vic said. "We've got maybe five minutes of light."

"This is a Mayan shirt," Kelly said, glancing demurely at Burns. "It's called a huipile. Women wear it as both a practical and a religious garment."

"Can you say that again for the camera?" Burns asked after Elf had backed out of the shot.

"About the huipile?"

He nodded and Kelly repeated her description like a well-trained actor. Burns was pleased. She would make his job easy. He asked her about the cross, finally, and what assumptions it served to remind her about.

"I bring science and medicine the way missionaries might have brought religion. The Mayans don't need it or even benefit from it. But years of training, of scientific method, have blinded me to the fact that these people probably know more than I do."

Burns encouraged her to continue. But he was reminded of those scientists in Connecticut who worried about her drift away from substantive research into the hazy world of primitive Mayan spells and magic stones.

"It's easy to make light of their beliefs and superstitions," Kelly went on as if reading his thoughts. "But it begs the question, don't you think? If we're so damn smart and sophisticated, if the scientists and the medical researchers know so much, why are we down here looking for miracle cures?"

"Money," Burns said. "There's big profit in medicine. One new drug can mean billions of dollars in profit."

"Nothing wrong with money. But isn't it curious that we are looking to so-called primitive people for these new, miracle cures? What do they know that we don't?"

"I was hoping you could tell us," Burns said.

"I can't say I trust most TV people," Kelly said, glancing directly at the camera lens before turning back to face Burns. "Your colleagues have a habit of simplifying and sensationalizing most issues. God only knows what your camera might make of the curandero."

"What do you make of him?"

Kelly gazed down at the ground as if the words might appear there.

"What do you say about a person who changes the way you look at the world, who leads you to a life's calling? He's the most remarkable man I've ever known."

Burns absently wondered if she and the old man had slept together.

"I know you're skeptical. And you should be. But you'll see when you meet him. The best I can say is that he sees what we don't. In his world, like most native Mayan, the unseen world is as alive as this one. Perhaps more so."

"He's an animist."

"More than that. He's not superstitious in the way we think of it."

Burns thought of the long drive across the savanna with Gilbert, their Belizean driver. He had suddenly slammed on the brakes to save a lumbering turtle that had decided to cross the road. In the States, that turtle would have been road kill, not a kindred spirit.

"Why isn't it enough to see what's really in front of us?" Burns asked. "Why invoke spirits?"

"Maybe because what we see doesn't explain enough."

Burns hesitated and the silence between them, the lapse that most television interviewers feared, only seemed to grow as he struggled to find a retort or at least a response. He became acutely aware of the birds and cicadas, but what he heard most clearly was the faint scrape of the plastic tape casing inside the metallic camera as the machine continued rolling with a faint wobble.

"The light's just about gone," he finally said. "So if we could just pick this up tomorrow. We'll do a formal sit-down interview some-where."

"So this a wrap?" Elf asked. He slid the headphones onto his neck, waiting for confirmation.

"It's a wrap," Burns said. "Thanks, Kelly."

"Anything wrong?" she asked. "Did you not get what you wanted?"

Burns thought he spotted a sliver of the Macal river as it twisted through a dark gap in the hills. But it disappeared like a flash of dis-tant lightning. As night crept over the jungle, he worried if he shouldn't have turned around immediately when the tape was found to be miss-ing. They could have regrouped and been ready for anything.

6

**Pixoy: Handful of chopped bark of
this shrub is boiled then drunk before
each meal to treat diarrhea and dysentery**

Dinner was served by a petite villager with a black braided ponytail that reached to the small of her back. She kept her gaze lowered as she handed out one plastic dinner plate after another piled high with dirty rice and black beans. Burns studied her as he might a portrait, admiring the flat, wide forehead and flared nose common among the Maya. He was impressed with how closely she resembled the cave paintings of her ancestors from centuries past.

"That's our Aida," Kelly said, affectionately. "She's been with us so long, she feels like a daughter."

Aida glanced up with the mention of her name; long enough for Burns to appreciate her wide, dark eyes, gleaming like black onyx. Her high, full cheekbones shined from faint perspiration. When Burns introduced himself, she nodded and backed away, before vanishing into the kitchen.

"The Maya are such a beautiful people. Maybe that's the real reason they meet so much hostility. They're jealous," Kelly said.

"You're talking about Guatemala."

"Here, too. But it's not political in Cayo. Just prejudice."

Aida returned almost immediately, carrying a basket of warm corn tortillas and a steaming bowl of fried plantains. She left both in the middle of the old picnic table. Burns watched her through the steam swirling above the thick, caramelized slices. Her skin was nearly the same color but smooth and unblemished, as flawless as her full lips.

"Is she from the same village as the curandero?" Burns asked.

"Yes. But she lost both her parents to the flu of all things," Kelly said. "She was just three. Somehow she avoided it. "

"People here were dying from the flu?"

"They die from it in America, too. The flu pandemic in 1916 killed millions of people. Flu is a virus. A killer."

"What about medicines?"

"There weren't any then. This was many years ago, before we even began building this camp. The curandero looked after her in the beginning. Sometimes she helps him. She has some knowledge of the healing arts as well."

"How many assistants does this curandero have?" Burns asked. He remembered Gilbert's distrust and disdain for the native healer.

"You're looking at the other one," Kelly said.

"Gilbert, our driver that everyone seems to know, said the curandero was a brujo, a witch who kept a blanc woman and seduced his patients."

"You know the way some Latin men treat women," Kelly said. "Machismo. The curandero is no different. But he is not a womanizer. He's a healer. But too many people misunderstand his work. They mistake his clowning for his medicine."

"He's been married a few times, hasn't he?" Burns asked.

"The curandero is eighty-three years old," Kelly said. "His second wife died nine years ago, and he still mourns her almost every day. He was deeply devoted."

Burns spiked a few slices of the hot plantains with his fork and peeled a fresh, thick tortilla from the warm stack piled high in the basket. The soft, round tortilla smelled of sweet white corn. He watched his crew eating hurriedly, shoveling one forkful of steaming rice after another and scooping up beans with their rolled tortillas. The long, hot journey up the river had left everyone famished, and the last morsel of food anyone had eaten were the stale rolls with butter served at the Hotel San Ignacio. Already, the morning seemed long ago.

"How soon before we get to meet the healer?" Burns asked. He sniffed the plantains, which reeked of old vegetable oil. It was a scent Burns associated with cheap Mexican restaurants and poverty.

"That's entirely up to you. I've told him you and your television crew were arriving. I should warn you that he doesn't understand how you're going to record his knowledge with just a camera."

"We've got microphones, too."

"He's actually never seen television."

"Never?"

"Believe it or not."

"Maybe he's better off."

"He's afraid you won't understand his medicine," Kelly explained. "So much about his medicinal knowledge is wedded to Mayan spiritual beliefs. Our everyday world, in his cosmology, is merely a shadow of the real world of the spirit."

Burns thought they might have common ground. Like this curandero, he saw the real world as source material. Whatever he filmed would be edited into something else entirely.

"So is that why no one has ever come to film this bush doctor?" Burns asked.

"Who knows? None of his medicinal knowledge has ever been written down or recorded, either," Kelly said. "It will be a tragedy if it dies with him. We'll lose thousands of years of Mayan botanical knowledge and healing techniques. It's invaluable. But none of his people have the calling to be a curandero. He'll have no heirs. The closest thing has been the work I've been doing with him."

Kelly described her daily work with the curandero, from their long excursions into the jungle to collect medicinal plants to her acting as nurse to his patients. By helping him, she was able to see which plants actually seemed to cure and then send samples to a lab in the States where the plants could be studied in depth.

Kelly's description of her daily life disappointed Burns because it was the same thing she had said on the telephone, almost word for word. It was a prepared speech created for probing journalists. Although many subjects he interviewed also were ready with made-for-TV sound bites, Burns had hoped she would be different, less calculating.

"That's the big challenge in our research," Kelly continued. "Many of these plants and barks heal, but it's difficult to isolate why or under what conditions. You have to isolate the active and inactive compounds to create a treatment. The more we know about it, the more applications, the less debilitating the side effects."

"That's the kind of investigation that your company does up in Connecticut with their scanner. But you don't really believe in what they're doing, right?"

"Their science is good, just incomplete."

Burns waited for her to continue. He was playing a game with himself now, listening to discover how closely Kelly repeated what she had already told him.

"Their prejudice is to have everything measurable, quantifiable, or it doesn't exist. But it's precisely what can't be proven that fascinates me the most."

"You've seen the curandero's methods work then?"

"I told you all this on the telephone," Kelly said, suddenly impatient. "Are you prepping me for the camera?"

"Yes," Burns acknowledged.

"At least you're honest," Kelly said. Her easy, confident smile reminded Burns of the well-bred women that were everywhere on the Yale campus. During those undergrad years, at least, they had seemed always out of reach, members of a class so far above his own that they were unobtainable.

"How did you end up in the middle of the jungle?" Burns asked, recalling what he knew about her privileged background. She had been born and raised in an exclusive suburb of Main Line Philadelphia, the only daughter of the Montgomery family, who had made their fortune in railroads. She had attended college nearby at Bryn Mawr and eventually went to Harvard, where she earned her Ph.D. in Ethnobotany.

"I didn't end up here," Kelly said. "I chose it. I would like to tell you it was for a cause, a purpose. But then I wouldn't be very honest."

She was restless and unhappy living in Cambridge. She wanted a more adventurous life, like that of one of her mentors, Dr. Shultes, a legendary ethnobotanist at Harvard who traveled throughout South America for months on end. He would stay in remote Indian villages, learning the local language and culture and gathering their knowledge of the indigenous plants. He traveled by foot and canoe, oblivious to personal dangers, driven by a passion for learning.

"Professor Shultes was everybody's hero," Kelly continued. "We all wanted to be like him, to be him. So when the pharmaceutical companies started to get interested in medicinal plants in the jungle, it didn't take much for me to get interested."

"You're one of the only women who do this kind of work," Burns said.

"I hope there'll be more."

"I knew a woman from the Main Line," Vic Colt said, taking a break from his food. Burns was jealous of his cameraman jumping into their conversation and stealing Kelly's attention. "Wildly rich family. For her sixteenth birthday, they trotted her out at a cotillion ball. Didn't even know people still had debutantes."

"You're looking at one. You see, the Main Line likes to think of itself as genteel society," Kelly said, adding a wry, knowing smile. "But it's really just another wealthy suburb."

She was something of an aging tomboy, Burns thought. He had less trouble picturing her as a debutante than imagining her in a tailored city dress.

"It was a great party. We had a rock band and danced until two or three in the morning."

Burns was impressed. It would have taken considerable conviction and self-confidence for anyone to walk away from a privileged life for the hardships of a remote rain forest and then remain there for over a decade. It would, he thought, require unshakable belief in one's purpose.

They heard a pickup truck come to a shuddering stop outside the house, followed by the creak of the rusted driver's door. The bearded visitor appeared a moment later, shuffling across the wooden floorboards, looking for a place to sit. He was tall with a lanky build. His rugged face was a reddish-brown from exposure and his scruffy beard was nearly blonde.

"This is my husband, Frank," Kelly said. She leaned away from Burns with a suddenness that startled him. He felt a sinking disappointment when she became rigid, sitting on the bench as if at attention. The liveliness that had lit her eyes vanished.

Frank acknowledged the television crew with a polite nod. His long, bearded face was drawn, worn out from a long day. Kelly introduced the crew in turn, ending with Burns, who extended his hand. He felt an instant competitiveness with Frank.

"You live in New York?" Frank asked in a way that made it clear he found the notion incredulous.

"Manhattan is home sweet home," Burns said. "Born and raised on the Upper West Side."

"Never thought of anyone growing up in Manhattan," Frank said, shaking his head.

"My father was a teacher at Columbia, a professor of nineteenth century British literature," Burns said, trying to be agreeable. "He's retired now."

"And he can still afford to live there?" Frank asked.

Aida appeared with a plate of rice and beans. She set it down in front of Frank and backed away as if from a dangerous animal.

"Mind if I light up?" Vic asked. He took a plastic pouch of tobacco and rolling papers out of his pocket. The sweet but acrid scent clung to the humid night air.

"Not at all," Kelly said. "Make yourself at home."

Aida returned with a bottle of Belikan beer. Burns recognized it as coming from the case of the local beer he had transported upriver at Kelly's request. But Frank showed no sign of being pleasantly surprised. He merely nodded his approval and Aida scurried back into the kitchen. Frank picked up his fork, examined it for cleanliness and then lowered his head closer to the plate. He ate as ravenously as the crew. Burns watched him attack the food, one forkful after the other. He didn't pause until he was halfway through his plate.

"They've offered to give us a video copy of everything they shoot, Frank," Kelly said, struggling to please her husband as if atoning for a past slight or argument. "So there'll be a record of all the work we've done in addition to whatever they put in their report."

Frank nodded and then turned his attention to Vic, the cameraman, who sat smoking silently. He blew plumes of smoke at the screen, scattering the mosquitoes that climbed the wire mesh, looking for a route inside.

"You spare one of those?" Frank asked. Vic opened the pouch of tobacco, preparing to roll a cigarette. The sharp scent wafted over the table.

"Let me," Frank said. "I can roll pretty well."

Vic closed his tobacco pouch and handed it to Frank along with a loose paper. Frank sprinkled a few pinches of the tawny sprigs along the seam of the paper and made a fast, tight roll. He licked the end of one side to seal it expertly. Vic handed him a lighter as an apprentice might hand a tool to a master.

"So what's your angle for this?" Frank asked after lighting his cigarette. Smoke leaked from the corners of his thin, severe lips.

"No angle," Burns answered, feeling attacked. "We're doing a doc about the work you, your wife and the curandero do here."

"And you're going to get everything you need in a couple of days?" Frank shook his head. "You guys kill me."

"Personally, I think we need months to do this story right. But there's no budget," Burns said.

"You must know about the history of the Spanish conquistadors," Frank said.

"Of course," Burns said.

"So you must know they came through here centuries ago the same way they trampled through the rest of Central and South America. All in the name of Spain and the Catholic Church's greater glory. But—of course—what they really wanted was gold. They didn't come to learn shit. They came to take, to steal. That was the holy quest. They tortured and murdered, and when they finally rode away on their horses and returned home, the bastards left behind their calling card—disease. My wife will tell you that, to this day, it's those diseases that afflict the Maya. Almost none of their ailments are indigenous. So when the people down here see blancs coming, they suspect they're being used somehow, no matter what anybody says."

Frank took his last breath of smoke and squashed the butt of his rolled cigarette in the middle of his bean-stained plate.

"We're hardly conquistadors," Burns said.

"No," Frank said. "But reporters and filmmakers and media people always have an idea of what they want their story or interview to come to. You're not down here to just see where things will lead. You have your own idea of what you want out of Cayo and the curandero and us."

"That's a little unfair," Burns said, although he knew better.

"That's what the conquistadors claimed," Frank answered.

"You got a thing against the media?" Burns said, not liking this man at all.

"In the end, it's up to you, isn't it? You make the story. Not us. Not the Maya. Not anyone from Cayo."

"The camera records whatever we point it at," Burns said, feeling as though he were being treated like a child. "It's not like we make it up."

Frank's thin lips spread with a sardonic smile.

"If you're on the government's side and pointing the camera, you see pictures of protestors or insurgents. But what if it's pointed from the other side? What do you see? It's all in the point of view, whoever is behind the camera. Seeing is all in here," Frank said, putting his finger to his head like it was a gun.

"We're not on anybody's side, " Burns said.

"We know you'll get the story right," Kelly interrupted. She thought the men were snarling at each other like dogs. "You have to remember we've had other journalists come down here and miss the whole point. Frank and I were made to look like a couple of eccentrics running around looking for the cure to cancer. So we're more careful now. Would anyone care for some coffee?"

The hostile silence that followed her question was broken by the sound of coffee being poured into mugs. A spoon dug into the sugar bowl like a shovel thrust into sand. The tin spoon clanked against the ceramic mug. Burns sipped his coffee.

"I have another story for you to point your camera at if you're interested," Frank said.

Burns stared back at him.

"A Guatemalan woman is coming to our village in a few days to lend her support to the Mopan. That's just one of the many different tribes of Maya. Many of them settled here from Guatemala a century ago when they had to flee for their lives."

Frank explained that the government had tried to kill this woman many times, but, so far, she had managed to stay ahead of the thugs. Her family had not been as fortunate. They were tortured and killed by Ladino government goons. Her sole crime was to support her people who wanted equal rights and opportunity in Guatemala and throughout Central America.

"Mayans are treated like they're gypsies," Frank said. "They're seen as dirty and shiftless with strange ideas and rituals. Some otherwise brainy people still think they have human sacrifices like they did thousands of years ago."

"Your hero have a name?"

"I doubt you would recognize it."

"Try me."

"Frank," Kelly said. "Don't you think the crew has enough on its hands? They're only here for a few days. As you made so clear just a few moments ago, that's hardly enough time to get the details of our story."

Frank stroked the thin blonde hair under his chin. Burns recognized it as a nervous tic. On some level, he seemed to be afraid of his wife. Or he was simply devoted to pleasing her. Either way, Burns waited to see how husband and wife would square off.

"Maybe they can come back," Frank said, finally.

Kelly smiled strangely—like a hostess at a restaurant, Burns thought. A mask more than a smile.

"Can I show you and your crew where you'll be staying?" she asked.

7

**Hatz: Leaves boiled, cooled and placed
on the head to relieve aches and pains**

The flat, stark light of the moon illuminated the camp. The cabins, trees and open ground gleamed with a faint, silvery sheen like a fine black-and-white photograph. Burns felt as if he were walking through a carefully lit movie set. The moon distributed the diffuse light with the efficiency of a bank of filtered HMIs, turning night into a ghostly day.

"You consult an astronomer for this shoot?" Vic asked as they strolled toward the nearby cabins. Everyone was full from the starch-heavy dinner and eagerly anticipating a long, deep sleep.

"I did check into the local calendars," Burns said. The Maya had long ago created three separate calendars—civic, religious and lunar. It was part of their cultural obsession with keeping time. They tracked it with mathematical precision, but the numbers and days themselves carried more weight than counting.

"If we were following the Mayan civic calendar, or Haab', this is the month of Uayeb, a time when tradition calls for contemplation, not action. It's considered bad luck to work during this month. Some people don't even leave their homes."

"Maybe that's why my wife didn't want me coming on this shoot."

"You're kidding."

"No. Said she had a dream."

"Which was?"

"Never heard. I had to get up and take a leak."

Burns laughed. His girlfriend Julie often was eager to share her dreams with him, but the so-called dream world held little interest for him. He rarely remembered his own and when he did they were nonsensical and not worth the time to decipher.

"What's the plan if Elf doesn't find the tapes back in town?" Vic asked.

"We'll get them, Vic. Don't worry about it."

"Well, Burns, it's gonna be a challenge to shoot a story when there's nothing to record it on."

"That's occurred to me."

There were always two realities on a shoot. The world that unfolded in front of their eyes and senses and sensibilities, and the world captured by the camera. Sometimes they were similar, sometimes not. Cameras were dumb. They saw only what they were pointed at and recorded only what was within the parameters of the lens. So Burns could shoot a colorful sunset over a river, an image of pristine beauty, and leave out the sewage treatment plant in the foreground and its rancid odor that nearly choked him on the actual location. He had produced too many shoots with this willful deception. But he had never been in this situation. He had his camera but little or no tape to record his story. He had only himself, and it made him uneasy.

Their footsteps crunched along the narrow gravel path that led to the cabins. The aluminum facades of the prefab A-frames looked like cutouts in the lunar light, more a studio set than genuine living quarters. Virtually a projection on a screen, Burns thought, not real. But beyond the peaked, cinematic roofs he could hear the cacophony of birdcalls and insects and the rustling of leaves as monkeys and other animals scampered among the branches, hunting for food.

"I wouldn't want to get caught out there at night," Elf said.

"It's all in your head, Elf," Vic chided him. "There's no goblins or ghosts out there. Just animals, like you and me."

"Yeah, well, some of those animals get hungry," Elf said.

"Or they're just mean, like snakes," Big added.

"You've seen too many movies," Vic said. "I've been out in a jungle at night and it's not a nightmare. Just dark. Serious dark. You can't even see your hand."

Vic Colt had been a grunt in Vietnam. He liked sharing war stories, often ending his tales with an expression of amazement that he'd stumbled through his six-month tour of duty without being wounded or even suffering mild injuries. He made it sound like war was an exciting adventure, not death and misery. Either way, Burns longed to see and experience a war. It was the ultimate story in news. He still had vague hopes of covering a war somewhere even if he was too old to fight in one.

"I'd be freaked being out there," Elf said. "But I know I'd be less freaked if I was wandering around in the dark with a fully loaded M16."

"The gun doesn't help you see," Vic said.

"Maybe not," Elf said. "But it does better the odds if it's just you and the beasts."

"Most animals are not that aggressive, Elf. They're not out to get you," Vic said.

"You know, Vic, it would be just my luck to prove you wrong."

"One thing is for sure," Burns said, peering at the black wall of trees at the edge of the clearing. "Whether you have a gun or not, it would test your survival skills."

"One night wouldn't test anything," Vic said. "Except maybe your patience. I told you. I've been there."

Burns didn't contest his cameraman's experience. But he didn't believe anyone would survive a night in the jungle unarmed. It was feeding time and every animal became a predator. Man, without benefit of sight, would be easy prey. The possibility of being in complete and utter darkness unsettled Burns. He couldn't imagine a more terrifying scenario.

"So how did you make it out there in the jungle?" Big asked.

"Beats me," Vic said. "One thing was that you listened like you never listened before. Every bird call, every leaf that shook, you listened. It got so you could recognize one of your own by the sound of their breath. And then there were the booby-traps."

"Did anyone ever trip a mine?" Big asked.

"One poor guy," Vic said. "He stepped on it and lit up the forest like fireworks. Medics saved him but it blew off one of his legs. After that, no one moved until it was dawn."

"Well that's a nice bedtime story," Elf said. "So what's our call time tomorrow?"

"Dawn," Burns said. "I want to try that one again from the hilltop. An establishing shot of the research camp just at the magic hour."

Burns preferred to shoot in the rich, photogenic light after dawn. The day's first hour cast a glowing grandeur to almost everything it fell upon, from buildings to landscapes to people, a kind of magic wand of photography.

Elf and Big said good night and disappeared inside their cabins. But Vic loitered outside. He lit up a cigarette and leaned against the railing near Burns, who stood gazing up at the moon, which seemed close enough to touch.

"Nice out here," Vic said. The moist air felt as soft and supple as freshly washed hair. "That scientist is pretty well preserved for an older woman. Must be those herbs she was yapping about."

"She's a strong woman, " Burns said. "You see her make him back off from the fugitive nonsense?"

"I didn't see any contest," Vic said.

"There was something going on," Burns said. He felt a hostile tension between them, an unspoken, unacknowledged resentment.

Vic shrugged. "Who knows. I don't figure it's easy on a marriage living down here. I know if it was Cheryl and me living in the middle of nowhere, we'd get pretty odd ourselves. It's too much time together. Spending time apart is good for a marriage. Keeps it fresh. That's one reason I love what we do for a living. It keeps me on the move."

Burns leaned against the wood railing on the porch. He pictured Julie back in New York, her yoga-limbered body curled on her favorite couch, wrapped inside one of the antique quilts she collected, even though she probably had the heat in her apartment turned up to eighty. She often complained of being cold and loved to snuggle close to Burns when they slept together. The chill of her small, girlish hands surprised him, but he liked the close heat of her naked body against his. She smelled of soap and the bath oils that she liked to soak in nearly every night. Too often, however, it felt as if she clung to him with the fierceness of a drowning swimmer, and he instinctively pulled away.

"What are you so afraid of?" Julie had asked.

"I'm not afraid," Burns had said.

"You have this thing about people being close to you, Michael. It has to happen on your time and under your conditions. But intimacy doesn't work like that."

Burns stared at her dry lips, which made them seem thin and harsh, disliking her impulse to render judgment. She couldn't or wouldn't simply accept what he said. She had to find some other explanation, like the Freudians who insisted that a slip of the tongue always had to be more than a slip of the tongue. Julie simply could not accept things as they were. She needed to uncover hidden motives, unspoken desires, whether they existed or not.

"Sometimes I just don't like to sleep glued to a person like a barnacle," Burns said, finally. "Is that so hard to understand?"

"I don't think that's the issue, Mike."

Burns shrugged. He didn't want to get into it. He was content to let whatever problems they had work themselves out. For him, talking about a relationship diminished it.

"Why is it you want to date me?" Julie asked.

Burns groaned inwardly.

"It's just a simple question."

"Can't we talk about something else?"

"We don't have to talk about anything, Michael. But just tell me. What do you like about being with me?"

"Julie. Don't do this. I feel like I'm being interrogated."

"One question is hardly an interrogation," Julie said.

"I don't want to get into a fight."

"This is a discussion, Michael, not a fight. Just tell me what you feel."

"You know how I feel," Burns said.

"Sometimes I do, sometimes I don't. Right now is one of those times when I'm really not sure what you feel."

"What do you want me to say?" Burns asked.

"Something. Anything. Why are you making this so hard?"

Burns shook his head, annoyed. She was so beautiful that he could sometimes be happy just admiring her without a word spoken.

"You won't say what you really feel."

"Sex. I see you for sex. OK?" Burns said, trying to make a joke, a bad joke, admittedly. But his face and voice were humorless. He was angry—at what or whom he didn't know.

Julie fell silent. He knew he had hurt her and he was sorry he had. But instead of explaining, telling Julie he was making a bad joke, Burns remained equally silent.

"I feel sorry for you," Julie said. "You don't really care about anything or anybody, do you? Except maybe your work. God help you if you ever lose that."

"It's no different than your painting, your art-making," Burns said.

"Oh yes it is," Julie said. "It's what I do, not who I am."

"Well, tough," Burns said. "It's just who I am then."

Making documentaries was not an occupation. It was a calling, a lifestyle in the true sense of the word; a way of life; a way of seeing the world. Burns felt he was always working, and he was in love with it.

Vic took a long drag on his cigarette. He blew an extra large smoke ring and watched it spin like a flying saucer. Burns could tell his cameraman was still musing on marriage and his own wife, Cheryl.

"Sometimes I think it would have been better if I'd stayed single longer, like you," Vic said.

"I'm not trying to stay single, Vic. I just am. Haven't found what I want."

"What is it you want?"

Burns didn't have a ready answer. He wasn't sure when it came to a partner. He was content with his own company.

"Maybe I just haven't found 'the one,'" Burns answered, finally.

"Is there a one?" Vic said, clearly believing otherwise. "You can spend a lot of time chasing that one."

Burns heard those words as the gripes of an older man. He liked the pursuit just as he always liked staying on the move, travelling on location. He was never more content than when he was moving, going somewhere. Being in a new place, like sitting here in the Mayan night, was more comforting to him than anything or anyone familiar. Here there were only possibilities.

"This is going to be a breakthrough film," Burns said.

"You're the producer," Vic said.

"No one has ever captured the kind of footage we have a chance to. I didn't think there was still such a thing as never-before-seen images—of a curandero or anything else."

"Yeah, well. Let's hope we get some videotape."

"We'll get it," Burns said. "We'll get it."

THE FIVE LOST DAYS

8

**Xmutz: Dry leaves smoked as tobacco to
relieve backache and nervous irritability**

Frank flicked his Bic lighter and cupped his hand around the high
flame, even though the air was utterly still. A plume of Xmutz
smoke rose from his wood pipe, a hand-carved block of ceiba in the
shape of a canoe that he'd bought off the street in Belize City. Over a
decade had passed since he and Kelly had christened the pipe as their
good luck charm. He had filled it with a gooey piece of hashish, lit it
in full view of anyone who cared to look, and took his first drag. When
he handed the pipe to Kelly, she had hesitated, fearful of getting in
trouble with the local police.

"You're not afraid to set up shop in the middle of the jungle for a
year, but you're scared about smoking some dope in public?" Frank
remembered asking her.

"I don't want people thinking we're just some more ex-pats out
for a good time and cheap ganja."

"Who cares what they think?"

"We do. I mean, we should. We're representing a major pharmaceutical company, not to mention our country, whether we know it or not."

"What's next, honey? Are you going to vote for Nixon?"

Kelly gave a look of mock-horror and finally took a hit from the pipe. But it was to be one of her last. Within a year, she had ceased being the quirky, experimental grad student he'd fallen in love with in Cambridge. She became obsessed with her research and he'd watched, listlessly, as her one-year contract with Pfizer Pharmaceuticals drifted into a dozen with no end in sight.

Frank took another hit, held it in as long as he could to help his bloodstream absorb more of the hash vapor, then exhaled loudly like a swimmer bursting to the surface. He was mildly addicted to this Xmutz tobacco in a way that he never had been with pot or hash. He liked the way the local herb relaxed him and eased his muscles better than any Jacuzzi.

"Why on earth did you tell them about Manuela coming here from Guatemala?" she asked, watching the ashen cloud drift out through the fine mesh screen.

Frank took another long, deep drag from the dory-shaped pipe and held it. He waited with a single-mindedness that annoyed her.

"You know it won't do her cause or ours any good."

Frank exhaled loudly, but only a wisp of smoke leaked from his mouth. He nodded.

"I know that, Kel. But you saw how he reacted. He could really care less about your research. He wants a story to make a name for himself."

"So now you're going to give him one?"

Kelly met her husband's bloodshot eyes. The pupils were dilated from the effect of the Xmutz. *Mimosa pudica*, the binomial identification. She'd sent it to the Connecticut lab with a description of its local use as a pain reliever and to treat insomnia. But only Frank had developed any serious interest in the herb. He used it the way he once used marijuana.

"He's got no access to Manuela unless I give it to him. At least now we know where he's coming from."

Kelly shook her head even though she knew what her husband said had some merit. But when it came to protecting her research camp, nothing else mattered, and she needed these journalists to give her camp a boost.

"It's a sucker's game, Kelly. He holds all the cards."

"I have a good sense about him. He's basically honest."

"Where do you get that?"

"He's different than most journalists that come down here."

Frank tapped the ash from the pipe into a tin can by the side of the bed and lit a spice candle. Kelly watched him look through his audiotape collection, wondering about his sudden departure for San Antonio earlier in the day.

"What is Manuela going to do anyway?" she asked.

Frank flipped though the cassettes with one hand before plucking out his choice. He popped it into the portable radio-cassette player that sat on the night table.

"Morale," Frank said as he pushed the play lever. "She will raise morale, maybe for months."

"But do they even know who she is? She's from Guatemala and from an entirely different Mayan region. She doesn't even speak the same dialect."

"Doesn't matter. She's one of them. A poor, working woman from a poor village that is under the thumbs of the government and the military. She's putting a thumb in the eyes of the corrupt establishment."

Kelly was surprised to hear "Workingman's Dead." It was their favorite LP when they first met, and she hadn't heard Frank play the tape in a long time. The folk-rock ballad skipped along like a happy, unexpected breeze.

"What is she like, Manuela?"

"I haven't met her yet. This is all happening through UNRC contacts."

Kelly leaned her cheek against his shoulder and held his arm with both hands. She could remember clinging to him like this in Cambridge, a young student clinging to the apparent safety of an older graduate. He seemed so strong and confident, a rebel fighting a cause. He wasn't going to get sucked up by The Establishment. He was going to do his own thing, his own way. He had inspired her with his passionate talk, his wild if unfocused ambition. She, too, would continue to follow her own path, wherever it led.

"I love this song," Kelly said, humming along with Jerry Garcia's guitar. "It makes me feel like a kid again."

Frank remained still and silent.

"You were such a rebel," Kelly said, squeezing his arm. "I wanted to sleep with you the way my roommate wanted to sleep with Mick Jagger. You were just so sexy."

Frank was snoring lightly. It was common when he fell asleep on his back. Kelly let her hands slide from his arm. She sat up, watching his peaceful face, deciding whether or not to wake him up. She wanted to talk, to share some of the memories conjured by the music of the Grateful Dead. But she could see her husband was already in a deep sleep. He would be furious if she woke him.

Kelly slipped out of bed and walked to the small window that looked over the forest. She felt restlessness. The moon lit up the trees like the spotlights on the campus at Harvard. She remembered all the late nights, strolling out of the lab, tired but happy, and meeting up with Frank at a coffee shop on Harvard Square. He would be waiting for her at one of the wood tables, sitting in his faded jeans and white T-shirt, a cigarette dangling insolently from the side of his mouth. He didn't have a job, and she assumed it was because he had other resources or because, true to his philosophy, he was searching for a different lifestyle. Either way, it didn't matter. He was there, waiting for her. Why, she wondered, was she so afraid of being alone back then? Now she could wander for days, untroubled by solitude.

Whooa-oh, the song played, *where does the time go?*

A rare breeze ruffled her cotton nightshirt. The feeling of the soft air against her skin reminded her of one of the first days in Cayo as if it had been only weeks ago. She was sitting at a plastic cafe table, her hands wrapped around a cold bottle of Belikan, relieved to be under the shade of a tree. A breeze like the one that touched her now rose up from the fast-moving river, cooling the sweat that trickled down her back.

On the bank of the river, a young Indian woman stood ankle deep in the lush stream. She leaned over the avocado water, knees locked, dipping a man's shirt into the current. Downstream, her two naked children scurried along a narrow, sandy shore. The boy clutched the neck of an empty wine bottle filled with the pristine river water and the silver flashes of minnows. His delicate sister skipped after him, excited and crying gleefully. They stooped at the edge of the river, solemnly gazing into the water as if into a deep well. Kelly was enchanted, studying them with the concern and wonder of the mother that she might have been.

A sacrifice. They were too young to be parents. The creation of the camp took all their time and energy. But a dozen years had made her look at that decision in a different way. She hadn't thought of it as a sacrifice at that time. There was a moral and emotional choice. But it seemed outweighed by their youth, the many childbearing years that stretched ahead of them. Instead, the camp had been born and raised. Now, she thought bitterly, it faces being ripped away from her by the corporate parents who demand profit, not research.

Kelly stepped away from the window and strolled back to her sleeping husband. The moonlight turned his motionless face into a chiseled, alabaster relief. It reminded her of one of the Greek reproductions at the Philadelphia Museum of Art that her doting father took her to see many times when she was a young girl. The statue radiated truth and integrity and strength. But when she told Frank they were pregnant, his face was guarded. He could have been more forceful, more authoritative, she was sure. But he acquiesced. It was her decision, he said. Whatever she wanted to do, he would go along.

THE FIVE LOST DAYS

9

**Sayab: Water from the bark of this tree is
used to wash tired, burning or irritated eyes**

Burns lay utterly motionless, his body pleasantly spent from the travel and the heat, listening to the buzz of cicadas and chattering birds, the screeching and howls of monkeys as they rustled along the limbs of nearby trees. The jungle. He was surprised to hear the clamor. He'd imagined that the deep jungle would be still and quiet at night, even peaceful. But nighttime was feeding time, and most of the animals seemed to be foraging restlessly. The din disturbed Burns more than he felt it should. But there was something about being in this environment, and especially about meeting Kelly, that was unsettling him. She triggered emotions he could not identify or understand. But it felt like fear.

He studied the fine netting that was spun around him like a cocoon. He ignored the whine of the mosquitoes, indifferent to whether they bit him or not. He just needed to get some rest. Soon, gratefully, the din of the forest became so much white noise, and he fell gratefully into a deep, welcome sleep.

Moments before dawn, Burns was startled awake. He was surprised that he had fallen asleep at all. But what unnerved him was a sudden, undiluted silence. It was as if someone had hit a switch and turned off the forest. The roar of the cicadas had vanished into the night. Burns sat up and rolled the canopy of mosquito netting away from him. He stepped onto the cool, bare wood floor, absently checking for any bugs and snakes that might have wandered in, and walked to the window.

The moon had faded and the stars over the forest were weakening at the approach of dawn. Burns checked the empty porch. No one else had been disturbed by the queer silence.

As suddenly as it had vanished, the sharp, foreign cries of the jungle exploded through the trees, annihilating the silence. Burns stepped away from the window as if the noise might come flying through the screen like shrapnel. He waited, deciding whether to go outside. The dense forest screeched and chattered, now at fever pitch. Burns willed himself to be calm. He told himself he feared only what he did not know. There was an explanation for what he had just experienced.

He opened the screen door and stepped onto the empty porch. The sky above him was brightening, the horizon tinged with an intense red-orange dawn. The dark wall of trees cracked open, providing glimpses of the loud forest. He could see that it would be a priceless Magic Hour for his camera. At least he had enough raw tape stock to record that. Burns ran across the wet grass to the hut where Vic was sleeping.

Halfway there, a sudden, visceral fright stopped him in mid-step. Without knowing why, Burns searched the edge of the forest, his heart racing, his breath tense and short. He could not understand what had come over him. He felt as vulnerable as prey. He searched the deep shadows underneath the distant trees, hungry for a clue. Every sense, especially what he could see and hear, was unusually alert. There was a slight, almost imperceptible movement at the base of one of the dark trees, and Burns felt a rush of adrenaline. In the next instant, the movement took form. The tail of a large, stocky cat. Burns was sure his mind was playing tricks with him. But then he recognized the feline eyes, electric green as if seen through a night scope lens. They were locked on him.

Burns ignored the fear that trickled through him. He wanted to capture this image. He needed to wake up his cameraman and film this rare moment, but he didn't want his movement to spook the cat. At the same time, he couldn't just stand there. Finally, he took a small, awkward step toward Vic's hut. As soon as his foot touched the ground, he stopped and checked for the distant eyes. He was relieved to find them motionless. Satisfied with his pace, Burns took another step, then another, all the while keeping track of the animal in the shadows. After what felt like a slow trapeze walk, Burns arrived close enough to the cabin to attempt to call out his cameraman's name. He checked the shadows one last time before breaking the silence.

"Vic. Get out here," Burns whispered. When there was no response, Burns called again. The third time he spoke louder, angry and frustrated that his cameraman was not responding. Still, the green eyes did not move. They were so still, in fact, that Burns again doubted his own sight.

"Is that you, Burns?" Vic called. Burns winced at the loud voice.

"Get out here and keep your voice down," Burns whispered.

The wood floor creaked as Vic finally stepped out of the bed. He shuffled to the door, pushed it open and stumbled onto the porch. The commotion made Burns fear the worst. Sure enough, when he checked the edge of the forest, the green eyes were gone.

"What's going on?" Vic asked.

"I just saw something over there, in front of the woods."

Vic searched the trees. The low light level and the distance made it difficult to discern more than the dark, featureless tree trunks.

"You scared it away," Burns said.

Vic studied the forest again, his close-set, ferretlike eyes drawn with skepticism.

"Burns. Those trees over there are like a football field away. I hate to break it to you, but you'd be lucky to get a look with a zoom lens."

Burns followed his cameraman's gaze to the edge of the forest. The shadows remained dense and nearly impenetrable, even as the red clouds above the trees were beginning to meld into the faint yellow and blue of early morning. Burns knew he could easily have been seeing things. The dance of light and shadow could create all kinds of possibilities. It wasn't unlike his experiences hiking in New York's Catskill Mountains. There were many times when he mistook a stick on the ground for a black snake. Sometimes your mind just played tricks.

"It's going to be a hell of a Magic Hour," Vic said. "Amazing light."

"Let's get everybody up," Burns said.

As Burns hurried back to his cabin, he realized his entire body from neck to bare ankles was drenched in sweat.

The crew set up the shot with a quiet precision that impressed Burns, even though he'd watched them work together before. Elf spread the black spider legs of the tripod a few feet from the weathered cross, while Vic clipped the camera on the fluid head, his eye glued to the viewfinder as he screwed it into place. Big quickly uncoiled the wire to the boom microphone, found a spot far behind them and clipped on his earphones. The sun would be climbing above the distant hills in a matter of minutes.

Burns marked his log sheet: Dawn. He couldn't remember the Mayan name but made a note to ask Kelly. In the distance, a morning mist rose from dark gaps in the brilliant green trees like steam from city grates. Burns felt utterly in his element. These were the types of cinematic images he had hoped to capture in Belize. He sensed a similar expectation in his crew as they worked through their fatigue without complaint, knowing they had a chance to capture a rare glimpse of the jungle's beauty.

"This could be the opener," Burns said.

"It's your movie, Cecil B.," Vic said.

Burns checked the sun. Shafts of orange light flickered above the trees like flames. The beauty soothed Burns. The sun appeared blood red and lit the rolling hills of Cayo in a shimmering electric green. Burns felt the same wonder he'd experienced on the Western highway when they were speeding across the flat grasslands of the savanna and the rain forest had risen suddenly into view. For an instant, it made the world new again, and there was nothing to be worried about. No Julie. No missing tapes. No problems.

"Anything else you want?" Vic asked after another thirty seconds had passed. The sun was rising quickly, already beginning its swift transformation into the lemon-white disc that had hounded them on their trip upriver.

"Yeah," Burns told him. "A shot of the Mayan pyramid over there on the hill. You know, that's where they used to have human sacrifices. The high priests tied the victim down and ripped out the heart."

"That's nice," Vic said. "Almost as nice as nailing a guy to the cross when he's still alive."

Of course, Burns thought. No wonder the Mayans were said to have assimilated Christianity so seamlessly. The stories echoed their own. They would probably have even recognized the Bible as a version of their own Popul Vul, the Mayan religious book that recorded moral stories that some followers took literally and others accepted only as metaphors.

"You want nat sound on this, right?" Vic asked.

"Just what we're hearing," Burns confirmed and ordered everyone to remain silent. Elf held his boom pole high in the air like a flag. Burns studied the fat windscreen that clung to the end of the boom, his attention on the anxious chorus of the jungle far below them. The raucous noise ignited a sudden elation within him. It was like a developer unexpectedly glimpsing the potential of a vast tract of otherwise useless land. Burns understood that he was in a new, photogenic world that promised more than he had at first imagined. He could make a story out of this setting alone. But he had a great character in Kelly, too. The camera loved her. He just had to make her love the camera. Katz was right. Burns was unquestionably the right producer for this job. He had the skill and the knowledge and the experience to bring TV viewers inside this world that howled wildly below him. It was still, untouched, under-photographed and, most importantly, gorgeous to look at. Cayo was taking him to a new place, a new way of approaching his life's work .

10

Zubin: Bark of this small tree is chewed to treat snake bites

Pedro Meza crouched in the damp shade of his cement hut, studying the morning light as it flickered through needle-sized holes in the tin roof. He had intended to plug those leaks for months but never seemed to find the time or the energy. There were almost always patients waiting to see him, always healing work to be done. But today, he had to admit to himself, today was different. No one waited outside his open door. Only the sun greeted him this morning, dancing on the floor of his home like Dreams and Spirits of the Ancestors.

Many of his fellow Mayans had begun to distrust his ideas about healing, preferring the synthetic medicines imported from Belize City or Miami, like the powerful, cocoon-shaped pills that cooled the lethal fever of malaria. The young, especially, thought his ideas about healing spirits were quaint. He was a relic of an older, less-educated time when the village had no contact with the outside world. Some, like the two boys who carried their boom box everywhere they went

in the village, openly ridiculed him about his sastun and his chanting, calling him a witch doctor or, worse, just a crazy old man.

Although Pedro Meza often surprised himself with his youthful
energy, he admitted he was an old man. Every morning, his arthritis
seemed more severe, his breathing more difficult. At eighty-three, he
was one of the last surviving curanderos in the Maya Mountains of
Belize. Despite the ridicule of the younger residents of the town, many
patients—some not even Mayan—traveled miles to be treated by him.
Payment was food or articles of clothing. Pedro Meza was content to
live simply, focused on his work, and there were days when he did
not eat at all.

On those nights when he went hungry, Pedro Meza would remember the warm, caring smiles of his second wife, Rosita. She cooked
fresh, steaming tortillas and hot bowls of beans, always concerned
for his health and well-being. He remembered cool mornings, like
this one, when they would lie together in the soothing, happy light
and make love, massaged by the sounds of the awakening forest. She
had died nine years ago, but a day never went by when Pedro Meza
didn't think of her or remember the joy inspired by her broad, loving
smile.

A lone, painful shriek shot through the morning, echoing through
the village. Pedro Meza heard the slap of feet on the wet ground. The
strides were light, young and frightened, and they grew louder, approaching his hut. The curandero pushed himself off the coarse mat,
an effort that seemed to require more strength than ever, and stepped
out into the angry sun. He squinted at the skinny boy running down
the path toward him. For once, Pedro Meza ruefully noted, the boy
was not carrying his annoying music box.

Tumil was terrified. His bare chest heaved, ribs pressing through
his taut skin. He told his story quickly, his eyes darting in every direction. His cousin Mazdara was hurt and rolling on the ground. Not a
snake. Something else. Something inside him.

The curandero remembered the ridicule the boys had given him.
They had been merciless, laughing as he trudged by their home on

his way to fetch water from the rain collection tubs. But curanderos took a vow of healing, and Pedro Meza knew that he could not allow his own pride to get in the way of a sacred vow.

Tumil pointed into the forest, angry now and impatient. He expected immediate action. Pedro Meza motioned for the boy to wait with a slow, calming wave of his hand. The healing could begin only with the cessation of panic. The curandero found panic to be especially tiring and unnecessary. Tumil's dark, obsidian eyes bulged from his gaunt face, and he nodded, struggling to catch his breath.

The curandero stepped back inside his hut and walked to the far corner, where loose plants and herbs were set in clean, even piles. He carefully selected three and wrapped them inside a large plantain leaf, tying the bundle with his sacred string. It came from the same ball of string that tethered his kite, both treasured gifts from Kelly. He had accepted them reluctantly, out of politeness, until he had seen the wind dance of the paper diamond, rattling high above the trees like an anxious spirit, struggling to be set free. The image had been as striking and immediate as any of his dreams, and he accepted it as an omen of progress, of the living force of his medicine given new life by this pale blanc. What was life worth, he wondered, without a woman to share it with?

The curandero stooped out of the entrance to his hut, wincing at the sharp pain in his lower back, and motioned for the boy to lead him to his friend. As they hurried into the forest, the curandero became annoyed at the boy's brisk pace. He hated that the boy was so consumed with fear and his own needs that he did not have consideration for the limitations of an older man. The young were oblivious of the old. But the curandero let go of his petty irritation, knowing that he would need every ounce of his strength.

They arrived next to the body sooner than the curandero expected. Mazdara, chubby from the candy lavished on him by his grandmother, was curled up, fetus-like, foam gurgling from his mouth. The rancid smell made the curandero flinch reflexively. He searched the boy's body for snake or spider bites, but there were only a few minor scratches on his ankles and calves. Yet the boy's symptoms were uncannily similar to the havoc wreaked by the venom of the fer-de-lance snake.

"Tommy-gutt?" the curandero asked, using the Mayan nickname for the deadly snake.

His friend Tumil shook his head slowly. The curandero grunted with dissatisfaction. He placed both hands on the boy's heaving chest. There was no doubt the boy was reacting to a powerful poison. The curandero unwrapped the makeshift pack of herbs he had brought with him. He took a long stem of brown Zubin—Kelly called it Cockspur—and measured it against the boy's forearm. He murmured a brief prayer, calling on the medicine's spirit for help and guidance before cutting the bark to match the exact length of the boy's forearm.

"Mazdara," he said, holding the bark in front of the boy's frightened eyes. "Chew this. Like candy."

The boy stared up at him, past the long, skinny stem, as if it didn't exist, and moaned.

"Chew," the curandero repeated. "Now."

The boy's round, dark eyes welled with tears. The curandero laid his frail, weathered hand on the boy's forehead and was alarmed that it was already burning with fever. He had absorbed a great deal of poison. But chewing the root delayed the action of most poisons and would buy the boy time. Without it, whatever was inside him would spread quickly, and he could die in a matter of minutes.

"Tumil," the curandero ordered. "Mazdara must chew the bark."

Tumil jumped alongside his friend and took the bark from the curandero. He chewed on the end, trying not to make a face from the bitterness, and passed it to Mazdara. The boy grabbed the bark and bit down on the end as his friend had done.

"Good," the curandero said. "Swallow the juice."

The curandero quickly scraped the leftover bark with his knife until there was a small pile of fiber shavings at his knees. He added the other herbs to the mound, mixed them together and lightly pressed the makeshift poultice onto the boy's damp forehead. He worked slowly and methodically, chanting a prayer to the healing spirits each time he pressed the poultice. After covering the herb paste with the plantain leaves, the curandero wiped the bubbling foam from his patient's chin and rubbed it between his palms until the moisture evaporated. He blew across his open hands in a gesture meant to whisk away the deadly spirit.

"Swallow the juice from the root," the curandero said sternly. "Pretend it is candy."

Mazdara's body began to tremble. Tumil cried out but fell silent when Pedro Meza raised his hand as he had outside his hut. The curandero took the sastun from his pants pocket and clenched the clouded blue marble as though it were a nut he was trying to break. The sastun was his link with the healing spirits, a special diviner given to him by his Mayan ancestors by way of a dream. He then sat in the mud, closed his eyes and prepared himself. He would join the forces of his sastun with Mazdara's will to live. He hoped the boy's youth would prove decisive. The curandero feared his own spirit, like his aging body, was losing strength. Contrary to the hopes of many who came to see him, the curandero believed everyone and everything entered this physical world for a predetermined time and that this life could not be prolonged beyond its limit. Healing was a matter of the spirit, not medicine alone.

THE FIVE LOST DAYS

11

Xa-ax-como-che: Leaves are used in bathing to treat insomnia

Kelly perched on the edge of her bedroom chest and slipped on one of the rubber boots. The sides were pockmarked from sharp sticks and rocks and snakebites. She checked the next boot for scorpions, then pulled it on, stuffed her jeans inside and stood up to regard herself in the mirror. After she had slipped on her favorite cotton huipile—hand-sewn by a Maya woman in the village using soft greens that reflected the color of her eyes—Kelly found herself doing something she hadn't done in quite a long time. She couldn't even remember the last time she worried how a man might see her. Frank didn't seem to care or notice and, in time, neither had she. There were a few strands of unmistakable gray in her tawny hair, but they were barely noticeable. Crow's feet and faint laugh lines marked her face, but it didn't look as old as she feared. Not half-bad, Kelly decided. Still attractive. Not gorgeous. But attractive. Age had thickened her hips, but her legs were still lean and the hard work demanded by the forest had otherwise kept her fit.

The voices of the television crew percolated from the distant porch. They were eating breakfast and drinking coffee. Burns's voice excited her. It had a slightly higher tone than the rest and projected easily so that she could even make out the words. His vocabulary was more complex and schooled than that of his crew, one of many things she liked about him.

"It's a complete protein, Elf. Legumes and small-grained rice. The nutritional equivalent of steak and eggs."

"I'll take the steak and eggs, Burnsie."

"And the fresh corn tortillas," Burns continued. "You know the Mayan believe that corn is the only real food. We're lucky to be eating this well."

"Aren't these the same beans we ate last night?" Elf asked.

Kelly slowly buttoned her soft denim shirt, liking the snugness because it made her feel fit and sexy. She smiled inwardly at herself, conscious of why she was feeling like a schoolgirl, ready to flirt, to tease. Finally, she tied a clean bandanna on her head, knowing it would be wet and soiled within ten minutes of hiking through the jungle. But it looks good, Kelly said to herself. A few moments later she was strolling through the bedroom to the kitchen where Aida was beating eggs in a white ceramic bowl. A cast iron pan smoked faintly with oil on the stove. Kelly said good morning in Spanish and continued past her and out onto the cool, shaded porch.

"Scrambled eggs are on the way, " she announced as she entered the room. "If anyone is interested."

Burns sat stiffly at the wood table, his hands cupped around a coffee mug. She was thrilled to feel him check out her jeans and open blouse.

"I know some crew people might be interested," Burns said.

"Did you get good pictures this morning?" Kelly asked, sliding onto the bench next to him with an ease that surprised even herself. She didn't usually do this sort of thing.

"We caught the sunrise up on the hill, " Burns said.

"Did you?" Kelly said, remembering his face the day before, how handsome it looked in the bronze light at dusk. "It must have been beautiful."

Burns took a sip of his coffee, regarding her. Kelly felt as though he knew exactly what was going on in her mind. So she was disappointed when he immediately turned to business and reminded her of the TV equipment that had been left in San Ignacio.

"Frank already left with our only truck," Kelly said. "So I'm afraid he won't be able to give you a ride to San Ignacio."

"He gets started early," Burns said, clearly irritated.

"These days. Yes."

Kelly pictured her husband's face, taut with unmistakable excitement, telling her he was leaving to meet Manuela, the peasant woman who had become nearly as well-known as the icon of the movement, Rigoberta Menchu. Kelly thought of Menchu as Guatemala's Martin Luther King.

"Are you going to tell her about the TV crew?" she asked, careful to make the question sound casual, off-the-cuff.

"I haven't decided," he repeated. "I don't want to do anything that could endanger her."

Kelly was jealous of her husband's protectiveness but not because of the Guatemalan woman herself. For Kelly, it was an unwelcome reminder of all that was missing. Over the years and the hardships, there had been a slow but inexorable loss of intimacy. It had worn away the unspoken bond between them, leaving them with separate, duller lives. How long had it been, she sometimes wondered to herself, since they had felt the mutual passion, that impatient, glorious need to share everything they felt and dreamed? Was it just youth that had gone?

"What time will he get back?" Burns asked.

"I don't know. I'd suggest calling your hotel first. They might have your equipment. It's a small country and everyone knows everyone else. Something like high-tech TV equipment wouldn't easily be overlooked."

"I'd like to send one of my crew back to the hotel anyway," Burns said.

She felt his eyes on her bare neck and raised her chin as if basking in the warm sun. "I can call Mr. Green, the canoe guide who got you here. He'll be happy for the work."

"Good, good, good," Burns said. "I don't want to lose this morning light. You can't buy lighting like this."

"What do you want to film?"

"You, among other things."

"Again?"

"You're the star of this show."

Burns opened his bible and removed two sheets of paper listing every character, scene and shot he planned on capturing in Cayo. The list extended to cutaways of specific animals, birds and even insects. Kelly could see that the producer had considered many of the scenes he was likely to confront. She was impressed with the meticulous care he had brought to his preparation. It was worthy of a scientist, except that Burns seemed to have worked out the results before the experiment was undertaken.

"Nothing we shoot needs to occur in this sequence," Burns explained, handing the paper to Kelly. "We can do it in any order and then cut the piece to sequence after we get back to New York."

Kelly scanned the shot list. They were here to get what they wanted and take it back to New York, not unlike the drug companies, who paid scant attention to helping the people who could lead them to new, lifesaving medicines.

"It's more of a wish list than a schedule set in stone," Burns continued. "There are some things that might not apply to you or the curandero, but I put them in anyway. When you start laying out the acts, every little image comes in handy."

"The acts?"

A documentary was structured into acts, just like a play. Act One introduces the issue and the main characters, other acts examine the conflict, and then the final act provides a resolution and, sometimes a denouement. Classic Aristotelian dramatic structure, Burns said.

"Aren't we talking about facts?" Kelly asked.

"Yes, but you need structure," Burns said. "You have to start with some kind of framework or you won't walk away with a story."

Kelly remembered a researcher similar to Burns who also needed to control all of the variables. He was extremely knowledgeable and observant but was unable to identify any plant or herb that wasn't already catalogued. He simply passed over anything he didn't recognize because he was so focused on confirming only what he already knew. He couldn't discover any new species because he didn't know how to see.

"You look worried," Burns said. "But you shouldn't be."

Kelly suddenly felt like a fool for flirting. He was treating her as if she was naive and didn't understand what story he was after.

"So you make up your 'documentary' in New York and fill that story in with the pictures and interviews that you film here," Kelly said.

Burns shook his head emphatically, a gesture that only confirmed what she had said.

"No. But you have to have a plan. You do try to be objective. We're not making things up."

"No? Even scientists are hard-pressed to be purely objective. Any experiment has a point of view. The scientist herself distorts by the act of observing it. Physics calls it the Heisenberg Principle."

Kelly was appalled at herself. What was she trying to prove?

"The Heisenberg Principle," Burns repeated, shrugging. "OK."

"I'm lecturing. I apologize."

"Why is it academics despise television so much? It's like pictures don't count even though that's how most of the world communicates, including your Mayan friends."

"I don't despise TV, and I'm not an academic," Kelly answered sharply. "But it does seem like you're making up your mind about Cayo before you've really seen or experienced it. And it wouldn't even matter except that what you do influences many, many people in the States."

Burns remained silent in frustration. Here was the same issue that came up time and again. Filmmakers took shortcuts, weren't willing to take the time to plumb an issue to its depth. But no one appreciated the pressures that went into creating a program. Time was a luxury. The equipment, the technicians, the travel were all eating up money, lots of it. He had only five days for this story. He had to make some decisions before any shooting began or he would end up with nothing. He would love to mull over the topic for months. But that just wasn't the way it worked. However, that didn't mean informative, even important work, couldn't be created.

"We need to start shooting," Burns said, finally. "This will all make sense the further along we get."

"You want me to trust you."

Burns nodded. That's what it was all about, wasn't it? People had to trust the people providing the information and the pictures. Otherwise, it was all just so much gossip.

12

**Salvia divinorum: Herb with hallucinogenic
properties taken during religious ceremonies**

Frank took the new logging road that bypassed the village and climbed deeper into the dark hills. He drove fast, wired on the strong Guatemalan coffee that helped to clear his head of the morning-after grogginess. The pickup rattled over the hard, packed dirt, spewing a cloud of dust and broken twigs in its wake. Frank had been driving this stretch of the road every morning for over two months and knew every dip and curve as if he'd built it himself. In fact, he often thought of it as his road because it represented a shining, new path, the yellow brick road that had always eluded him. He couldn't lose this time. No one could accuse him of another half-baked business scheme.

People still joked about his grand plan to sell the native chicle to chewing gum makers. He had tried to convince companies to create a "natural" line of chewing gum using the tree resin. Chicle, after all, was what everyone had used to make chewing gum before Goodyear stumbled upon a cheaper, synthetic substitute. Chicle had even been the country's chief export crop back when Belize was still a colony of England. But the companies had balked at the idea of reintroducing chicle, not only because it was expensive to harvest but also because it would draw unsavory attention to the synthetic rubber compound that had replaced it.

"Rubber is better than chicle anyway. It lasts longer and has no aftertaste," the most sympathetic executive told him.

Frank interpreted the rejection of his business proposal as timidity on the part of the business community. He'd never developed any great affection for corporate America to begin with. He believed most large corporations were slow and cautious and basically stupid when it came to the development of innovative products. Personal computers like the Macintosh, for example, were the direct result of inspired entrepreneurs working out of their garage. Despite vast economic resources, no corporation would have ever had the nerve or vision to create the Macintosh. They were always more concerned about screwing up than succeeding. Frank had learned this years ago while working for a huge commercial bakery in Boston. No one wanted to try anything new, especially a new flavor of bread, without years of tedious research and test marketing. Fear of failure had been their collective concern. How else to explain the layers upon layers of "managers" and "supervisors," a virtual army of blue suits looking over one another's shoulders? Many of his bosses knew next to nothing about baking as a craft. Most were MBAs who were more comfortable with marketing strategies.

Frank would have no bureaucratic burden in this new venture. He was the sole proprietor. He'd have to hire some cutters and transporters and give a cut to the exporter in B.C., but that was it. There would be a pot of cash to go around, for the Mayan rights movement and a little to himself. It was almost too good to be true, and he only regretted not stumbling on the idea sooner. Looking back, he could see the concept had been there all the time just waiting to be discovered. The old adage was true: do what you love and the rest will follow.

Frank was beginning to feel a little too jittery from the coffee, so he lit up a thin joint of Xmutz to smooth things out. A hit or two in the morning always helped his attitude anyway. But this morning he felt he deserved whatever he wanted. He was proud of himself and what he was about to accomplish. Kelly, too, would come to respect him more. She would look up to him as she had at Cambridge when he had turned her on to the whole scene. He'd been the one who had introduced the Philadelphia debutante to pot and mushrooms and LSD. He'd encouraged her to explore the boundaries of botany, to take a chance on this odd new discipline called ethnobotany. But last night, like too many times in the last few years, the tables seemed to have slowly turned, leaving Frank feeling as though he had failed to live up to her expectations.

The dirt road was suddenly transformed into a pale orange lane by the morning sun. The light nearly blinded Frank as it shot over the dark treetops. He slowed down the truck, checking absently in the rearview mirror. He rarely encountered anyone this early, especially since the regular loggers had suspended their tree hauling for the rainy season. Still, he could never be too sure.

Frank checked the road again after he had pulled off to the side and parked his truck at the edge of the forest. He followed a path as it led underneath the trees and then back up the side of the hill in the direction from which he'd come. Finally, he came to a clearing. A dense half-acre of what almost anyone—except perhaps for Kelly or Pedro—would think was mint. And it was mint, only a type with special properties that had become very popular in natural food stores from Berkeley to Austin. In one Malibu shop, the herb was retailing for $120 an ounce. He estimated his crop would weigh in at one hundred and twenty pounds.

Frank took a deep, grateful breath and looked out over his private garden and the sparkling river that meandered at the bottom of the hill like a sapphire necklace. He'd begun with just a handful of seedlings. Over time, armed with botanical advice from his wife, his little open-air greenhouse had grown and prospered, and he felt a deep satisfaction with his accomplishment.

The crop represented at least half a million dollars wholesale—money that could be used to fund the UNRG and its nascent efforts to gain power and respect. Repressive governments like those in Guatemala and, to a lesser extent, the regime in Belize, would soon be facing the best-financed indigenous movement in the Americas.

Still, Frank could not predict how Kelly would react when she discovered what he had done. *Salvia divinorum*, as the herb was known in the scientific world, was chewed by healers to invoke visions, healing visions. Hallucinations worthy of LSD. But American spiritual seekers used the sage as well. It wasn't classified as a drug, and it wasn't illegal. A natural food store could sell it as readily as echinacea. Kelly knew this. Would she be pleased, impressed with his cleverness? Would he hear her girlish, infectious laugh that he'd fallen in love with the moment he'd heard it? Or would she be dismayed by his willingness to market a sacred herb? He couldn't be sure. But there was no stopping now. The plants were mature, close to harvest, and everything was in place. He was buckled in, his plan already launched.

13

**Callawalla: Root of this plant is boiled
and ingested to treat high blood pressure**

Burns crouched at one end of the garden, deciding how best to shoot Kelly. He wanted her main interview conducted while she was busy doing something else, a visual counterpoint that made a talking head more interesting to watch. He also understood that a good interview was really a focused conversation. It was not a producer reading a list of questions from a pad or paper. The interview was an engagement with the subject, an attempt to draw out unexpected comments, especially short, pithy stories that took even the teller by surprise. Burns had long since learned that an interview began with the sole intent of relaxing the person being filmed and making her trust him. The best producers got their characters to lose their awareness of being on camera and to speak without any fear. Burns often thought of it as a seduction.

Kelly, he decided, was going to make or break his documentary. He had long since assumed that a key ingredient for creating an entertaining story about medicine hunting was the hunter herself. Characters, after all, made better viewing than issues. So Burns hoped to create a portrait that persuaded viewers not only to like Kelly but also to want to fall in love with the quirky ethnobotanist.

"Where the hell did she go?" Vic asked. He stood alongside Burns, holding his Ikegami like a weapon. The soft, bluish light of morning had toughened into a harsh, white, midday sun. It dangled directly above the medicinal garden like a bare light bulb, and its overhead position would create deep, ugly shadows under Kelly's eyes that reflectors could do little to soften.

"She had to take a telephone call," Burns explained. He felt responsible for her tardiness even though it was out of his control. Kelly was his "character," his charge.

"I know that. But it's been over an hour."

"So what do you want me to do?" Burns asked.

"I don't know. Go get her. You're the producer."

"Give her a couple more minutes," Burns said. He was as annoyed with his character as Vic, but he did not want to give the impression of doing Vic's bidding. He was the producer, and he would make the final decisions. He was in control.

"What are we going to do if Elf doesn't find the tapes back at the hotel?" Vic asked.

"You hate to wait, don't you?"

"I just want to know what the plan is."

"We'll fly some in from Miami or New York. Don't worry about it."

"We'd lose another day," Vic said.

"I know that. That's my problem. OK? If I need your help, I'll let you know."

"Get them flown down now. As a backup. You can do that. Call Katz."

"That's the last person I'm calling," Burns said. He believed it would raise far too many questions about his competency as a producer.

"I'll call him," Vic offered.

"You the producer now?" Burns asked. He worried suddenly that Katz, his executive producer, might have a closer relationship to Vic Colt than Burns knew. After all, the EP had to approve the hiring of the shooter and the rest of the production personnel. Maybe he had tapped Vic as a way to keep tabs on Burns, to make sure the shoot stayed in line. Execs had been known to do that, Katz in particular.

"Whatever," Vic said. "But I think you're making a mistake."

"OK," Burns said. "I'll go and get her. Will that make you happy?"

"It's not going to change the light," Vic said, flicking his index finger at the white-hot sun overhead.

Burns found his character in her small office, poring through a book of plant classifications. Kelly had put on a pair of knee-high rubber boots, and an old, worn machete was lying on the ground next to her, its long blade as blunt as a garden tool. At least she was ready to go, Burns thought. But it annoyed him that his character was being so casual about an important interview.

"I haven't forgotten you," she said, "but I have to square something away with Pfizer this morning. It's about a specimen I sent to them."

"A new drug on the way?"

"No. Just some arcane botanical details."

Burns studied the multicolored yarns of her Mayan blouse. The border of the neck had been stitched into a repeating pattern of diamonds. Diamonds, according to his research, represented the Mayan boundaries of Space and Time. Each point followed the movement of the sun from east to west.

"They believe when a woman puts her head through the neck-hole, she emerges in the axis of the world," Kelly said, meeting his eyes for a moment. "She stands between heaven and the underworld and between the supernatural and the ordinary."

"Well, you look pretty in it," Burns said.

"Are you flirting with me?"

"My cameraman is worried that we've already lost the good light with this delay," Burns said, looking away.

"He likes to run the show, doesn't he?" Kelly said.

"We really have to go," Burns said.

"I'm nearly finished," she said, breezily. "I promise."

Burns studied her, admiring the clean simplicity of her dress. It fit her personality.

"Why the boots?" Burns asked.

"Snake bites," Kelly said. "They can be woefully easy to step on by accident. I'd suggest you and your crew wear them as well. There are extra pairs down by the gazebo. We keep them for tourists."

"You really get that many tourists up here?" Burns asked, concerned that he was not in a remote enough area of the jungle.

"Here it is," she said, repeating a plant's genus in Latin. "I knew I'd seen this before. Well, problem solved."

"How many visitors do you get?" Burns persisted.

"A few hundred a year," Kelly said. "More lately. They get bored out on the cayes with the beaches and rum punches and want a little adventure."

Burns sighed inwardly. Was there anywhere, any end of the earth, that hadn't been visited by either cameras or eco-tourists? Was there really any location untouched by the footprints of someone's media?

Kelly closed the book and stood up slowly. She was close enough for Burns to touch. He hesitated, aware of her smooth, bare neck and the sweet, floral smell that enveloped her.

"What are we doing now?" Kelly asked, her eyes teasing him.

"Now? What are we doing now?"

Kelly waited, waited like a lover waits.

"We have to do your main interview now," Burns said, the words acting like ballast, slowing the feelings racing through him. It was not unusual for him to feel affection for his characters; in fact, it was necessary if he was to mold her into the main character of his film. But this feeling, this experience, was different.

"I want to have you in the middle of the garden where you gather your medicinal plants. The background needs to tell us something about you. It works like a caption."

"You really think in pictures."

"Can you do it?"

"I told you this morning. I don't gather plants from the garden. They're for show. I hike a special trail through the forest."

"How far do you hike?"

"I don't decide beforehand," Kelly said. "The plants decide."

"The plants?"

"They lead us. Not the other way around."

"You're kidding, right?'

"Yes, a little," Kelly said, followed by a teasing laugh, the practiced, coquettish laugh of a debutante. "Michael, you've become so serious."

Burns felt as foolish and helpless as a young boy. He couldn't think of what to answer or how to act. He hadn't become serious. He'd become frozen with self-consciousness. She got to him.

"OK. I hike until I find the plants I need," Kelly continued. "So, in a sense, the plants do determine where I hike."

Burns wondered how often Kelly might talk to her colleagues in this flippant way, daring them to take her literally. Maybe this was the real source of their distrust of her research. She was always goading their presumptions.

"So most of your medicine hunting happens on the trail, not here."

"All of it, really. But we can do your interview in the garden if that's what you want."

"We'll follow you," Burns said, "on your medicine hike."

THE FIVE LOST DAYS

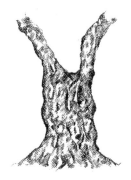

14

**Willow Bark: Chewed to treat aches
and pains; basis of modern aspirin**

Each crew member wore a battery belt, including Burns. The black vinyl straps buckled in front with the battery cells strung side-by-side like square bullets on a gun holster. Each five-pound cartridge packed enough electricity to power a portable quartz light for a little over fifteen minutes. Collectively, the crew slung two hours of artificial sunlight on their hips, far more than would be needed to illuminate the forest for a few minutes of shooting. But Burns didn't want anymore screw-ups.

His crew also outfitted themselves with a few pieces of production equipment. Black rubber audio wire dangled from Big's thick neck like strands of odd jewelry, and a set of headphones was clamped to his head, just behind the ears. He also wore a small pack filled with extra portable lights. Vic, as always, trusted no one but himself to carry the camera.

"Do you really need to take all that tribal gear?" Kelly asked. "We won't be going all that far."

"We usually have more," Burns said.

Kelly led Burns and his crew to a wide, grassy road that fed into the forest. They hiked for only a few yards before Kelly stopped alongside a thick green curtain of vines. A dry, rotted tree was barely visible inside.

"Shortcut," Kelly said. "Through these strangler vines."

"What is it they strangle?" Big John asked from behind them.

"Trees—not television grips," Kelly said. She explained that strangler vines germinated in treetops, their roots dangling in the open air until they reached the ground. Eventually, they steal the nutrients from the tree's roots. The vines multiply, getting thicker and healthier with nutrients until they grow big enough to block the sun and water from the tree, slowly strangling it to death.

"So they're parasites," Burns said. "Using another living thing to live."

"They're a type of epiphytes," Kelly continued. "There are all kinds of epiphytes on that tree if you look close enough. There are orchids, bromides—all crowding the branches."

Burns recognized the spiky bud of an orchid about to bloom. He saw other plants sitting on the tree branches, their roots dangling in the air. Suddenly, the tree itself seemed to come alive as he noticed scores of these plants and flowers on every square inch of branch. It was extraordinary. Burns felt as though he were seeing the tree for the first time.

Kelly led them onto the path through the forest. Thick, hairy roots crisscrossed the ground or curled up by the tree trunks like garden hoses. More of the vines dangled everywhere like string ornaments. The skinny trees, some thin enough to enclose with two hands, soared above them, seeming to stretch desperately for a glimpse of the sunlight. The forest canopy blocked the direct light and splintered the sun's rays, like a stained-glass skylight, creating a dappled jade roof.

"Be careful of the roots. They're slippery and tear up your joints," Kelly warned. "Also, try not to step in any of the red ant piles that you come across."

"Killer ants?" Big joked.

"They won't kill you, but they can peel your skin off."

The crew followed Kelly and Burns up the trail, single file, under the thick canopy of steamy trees. The sponge-like moss absorbed the sound of their steps. They were careful to step over and around the undulating roots that slithered along the ground or twisted around the hulking bases of trees. The sound of percolating water was everywhere. Shallow creeks burst in patches of forest off the path. Water dripped from the leaves above them. Every leaf, every root, gleamed with moisture. The smell reminded Burns of the charged air just after a rainstorm.

Unfortunately, Burns could also smell the DEET he and his crew had used to coat their arms, legs, shoulders, faces and ears to protect against the mosquitoes. But other tiny, nearly invisible bugs danced around them in swirling defiant circles, landing on lips, eyebrows or crawling through their damp hair.

A burst of tropical rain rattled the leaves, a few drops leaking down, only to be stopped and greedily absorbed by a lower tier of leaves. Little rain ever reached the forest floor, nothing to cool the sweat that fell in a steady trickle down their necks and under their damp cotton T-shirts.

As they continued along in silence, Burns became aware of a pleasing floral scent. At first he thought it was a tropical plant or flower. Then he remembered smelling it back in Kelly's small office when he had come upon her studying her book.

As Kelly hiked ahead, Burns found himself again admiring the poised, regal way she carried herself. She was not a young, raving beauty, nor was she anything like the petite, delicate women he liked. Kelly was something of a tomboy. She was tall, fearless and exuded a natural, unaffected directness.

"So you always walk this trail alone?" Burns asked.

"I never think of it that way. There's so much to see and study."

"You don't think about your safety?"

"The jungle isn't dangerous if you know it. People I worry about more anyway. They can do the real damage."

"You just told the camera about four things that kill or maim us."

"I still feel safer here than in a city," Kelly said.

The full sun was obscured by the treetops. The tall, inscrutable trees reminded Burns of walking through the canyons of Wall Street. Instead of a narrow strip of blacktop hemmed in by the skyscrapers, there was a footpath crowded by trees soaring out of sight. Instead of taxi horns and car alarms, there were the squawks, cries and the whistling of unseen birds.

Occasionally, a branch would snap in the distance followed by a long, hollow whistle until the rotted wood exploded on the forest floor, rumbling like artillery rounds. Kelly explained that dying trees were a common problem in Cayo.

"Stay alert for the dead wood," Kelly said. "They've been known to hit people."

Burns peered at tree branch after tree branch, hoping to discover a macaw or other parrot or any piece of wildlife. But the path wound through an endless maze of dense woods. Kelly suddenly stopped in front of one of the trees, its bark lighter, the color of cinnamon.

"Genus, *Cinchona*," Kelly said, gently touching the tree with her outstretched hand. "First known to medicine as fever bark or Jesuit's powder. It probably changed our collective history more than any other species in the jungle, except maybe the coffee plant."

Burns studied her hand, again disturbed by its size and apparent strength. They were the hands of a tough lumberjack, and their ugliness jarred with the feeling conjured by her graceful neck.

"Centuries ago, Indians in Peru used to peel the bark of a similar tree to this one and then dry it in the sun. Later, it would be ground into a powder and ingested to treat malaria."

Vic suddenly bolted from behind Burns and Kelly and hurried past, holding his Ikegami camera against his side, lens pointed to the ground the way hunters often moved from one location to another.

Kelly paused, searching Burns for an explanation, but he smiled as if nothing unusual was happening. In fact, it wasn't. He knew Vic was getting into position for a B-roll shot of Kelly hiking toward camera.

Vic stopped far ahead of them, crouched just above a protruding root and aimed his camera at their approach. Burns was pleased that Vic was returning to form by taking the initiative, hunting for the best shot.

"A Jesuit priest traveling in the jungle carried a sample of the bark back to Rome in the mid-seventeenth century," Kelly continued. The New World wood cured several priests of malaria and was hailed as a miracle cure. But few in the establishment trusted the bark because it was a folk remedy, like chicken soup. So neither doctors nor the apothecaries took it seriously, even though it worked. Only the traditional healers used the bark.

Kelly suddenly jumped away from the tree and brushed off her boots. On the ground next to the tree, a swarm of ants was charging over an exposed root, headed toward Burns and his crew.

"We better move, " Kelly said, leading them further up the trail.

"So how did this bark catch on?" Burns asked.

"King Charles II was cured in 1678," Kelly said. "And the rest is history. The bark caught on, and all those doctors and apothecaries who wouldn't have anything to do with the Jesuit powder were falling all over themselves praising the amazing curative properties of the 'fever bark.' It eventually saved the lives of millions of people all over the world."

"Is it still used for malaria?" Burns asked, absently checking the ground for other insects.

"It was, up through World War II, and then synthetic substitutes were created. Malaria itself permutated into different strains that required new and different alkaloids to fight it."

"So it's not used," Burns said.

"The bark still has been shown effective. The one identified alkaloid in the bark is quinine, but there are many others in the tree that we don't understand but potentially contribute to healing."

"Someone must have done an analysis of this bark after all this time," Burns said.

"It took over two hundred years before the scientific community bothered to make a proper study of cinchona bark, and even then the only thing they came up with was quinine. But not once did anyone think to return to the source and investigate the other properties of the plant."

"What other properties?" Burns asked, even though he suspected the answer.

"The spiritual properties, of course," Kelly said. "There are reasons beyond chemical analysis that explain why some plants work against a disease and others don't."

"Is there evidence of these spiritual properties?" Burns asked.

"Everywhere," Kelly said. "Like you said yesterday, many of the Mayan are animists. They believe anything from a twig to a passing cloud is imbued with spirituality. In practical terms, it means all living things are in some way sacred. Everything has meaning."

Burns checked to see if Vic was still rolling. Kelly was full of good, pithy sound bites. They could easily be pared down to the ten- to fifteen-second hit that Burns had learned worked best. His bosses, like Katz, were always pushing him to make sound bites shorter.

The path soon grew to the width of an old carriage trail and began to level off. The thick roots at their feet vanished, soon replaced by scattered granite rocks. The humidity that had dogged them for the entire hike was carried away by a sharp, fresh breeze that swept off the surface of the river. Burns, like the rest of the crew, was reenergized by the sudden change and hurried further up the trail toward a clearing that shimmered with a white, milky light.

The path emerged alongside the river. A series of small waterfalls tumbled down through a wide corridor of smooth boulders and gentle rocks. Natural swimming holes gleamed with a cool, aqua tint that reminded Burns of the Caribbean. He directed his crew to the base of the waterfall to set up for a scenic shot. But he was disappointed when Kelly told him they were at a swimming hole that was popular with tourists and Mayans alike. He had hoped they had stumbled upon untouched, virgin nature.

A pair of blue-green Morphos fluttered at the edge of a tree branch that stretched over the water. In the next instant, the Morphos spun away from the tree and vanished into the blue sky.

"They'll be back for your camera," Kelly said, following Burns gaze. "Morphos are plant-specific. They eat only one kind of plant, and that tree is it. And they only fly in the sunlight, so you should be able to get a good picture."

Burns strolled over next to the boulder where Kelly rested, gazing up at the waterfall as it spilled from the ledge.

"Can we get a shot of you here, next to the water?"

"Is there something you want me to be doing?"

"What would you usually do?"

"On a day as hot as today? Go swimming, I'm sure."

Kelly grinned before Burns could ask the next question.

"No chance, Michael. We don't need to see a middle-aged woman splashing around like a teenager."

"How about just wading in the water? I just want an image of you at rest in the middle of pristine nature. But without the boots."

THE FIVE LOST DAYS

15

Ix-ti-pu: Boiled leaves are used to reduce fever

Kelly leaned against a rotted tree trunk, slipped off the rubber snake boots and peeled off her damp socks. She closed her eyes as the cool air rushed over her bare feet and swept away the heat-induced ache that had pounded in her head. She waited until Burns gave his cue before she strolled over to the water's edge. As soon as she felt the cool water, she wanted to dive in and lose herself in the blue womb of the river. She had begun to wonder if she was doing the right thing in being so cooperative with Burns and his crew. After all, there was no guarantee that he would produce a documentary that was flattering to her research camp or, even if he did, that it would influence the bean counters at corporate headquarters in Connecticut.

"Can you turn a little to your left, so we can see your profile?" Burns yelled from his post alongside the camera. He was like his camera, she mused for a moment. Burns watched everything closely, sometimes perceptively, but she could no more tell what he was feeling than if she were peering into the deep, opaque video lens itself.

"OK, thank you," Burns called as if he were dismissing her from a set.

"Got what you needed?" Kelly asked.

"You made the water look inviting," Burns said. He and his crew immediately plopped down on the nearest rock and started taking off their boots, preparing to wade into the pools themselves. Burns was the last one to enter the water. Unlike his crew, he tested the water first with his hand and then his bare foot, wary of jumping in too fast.

Kelly slipped out of her damp huipile and draped the embroidered blouse over a log. The clamminess that had enveloped her vanished and she felt clean and limber. She unbuttoned her jeans and stepped out of them, relieved to feel the breeze on her thighs. It made her feel more youthful, like the avid dancer she had been as a teenager in high school. Her mother had urged her to make a career of it, but Kelly had neither the desire nor talent. Her mother became dismayed when her only daughter developed an avid interest in science. Even decades later, on Kelly's last visit to her childhood home in Philadelphia, her mother had looked admiringly at her daughter's figure, strong and lean despite her age. Still, her mother could not resist judgment. "You could have been a dancer."

Kelly walked to the water's edge, ready to dive in. But, at the last moment, she recognized, belatedly, that the men had stopped undressing. They stared, appraising her. Although she still wore a sport bra and panties, their eyes made her feel stark naked.

Slowly, mechanically, Kelly turned back to face the water. She would not be shamed into putting her clothes back on and acting in a way she did not feel. So she dove into the deep pool. She drifted underwater, relieved to be in this aqua womb of silence. But her air was used up quickly, and she rushed to the surface, gasping for breath. When she opened her eyes, she found that Burns was back on shore, his face raised to the drying sun. Vic was checking something on his camera under the shade of a tree. Only Big remained in the river, not far from where she was treading water. They no longer paid any attention to her and, for a moment, she was angry that she had been so easily dismissed as an object of their interest.

She swam back to shore slowly, her chin dipping into the water as she made a sidestroke. The soft water caressed her skin, and her shoulders and legs became light and limber. She felt young and energetic, a girl playing innocently in a pool. As she neared the bank, her muscles tightened. She anticipated stepping onto land, again in full view of the men. But now she had become acutely aware not of her nakedness but of her physical flaws. Breasts beginning to droop with age. Thickening hips. Pockmarks on her upper thighs. It was absurd to be so critical of her own body, she knew. But she couldn't help it.

After Kelly crawled onto shore, she stood up slowly, preparing herself for the men's belligerent gaze. But no one so much as glanced. They seemed intent on their own activities. Kelly looked down at her body. The cotton bra clung to her hard nipples. Beads of water rolled over her smooth belly and onto the white panties that clung to the dark wedge of pubic hair. There was mud and flicks of grass from the riverbank on her bare toes.

She tried to stroll casually toward the clothes hanging on the tree trunk, but her body felt awkward, stiff—moving parts that were somehow not working together. She was afraid of falling, tripping on an unseen stone or stray piece of wood. When she finally reached her clothes, she glanced back and caught Burns admiring her. But he quickly looked away, pretending he was concentrating on some picture angle.

As Kelly dressed, she had to keep herself from laughing. Sitting with his face raised blindly to the hot sun, Burns reminded her of the lifeguards on the beach at Bethany where her family summered. The young, solitary men sat high on their white plywood thrones, staring out to sea. Kelly and her sister made a game of distracting their attention, playfully disturbing their somber vigil by stopping to ask questions or, when they felt confident wearing their bikinis, sauntering into the lifeguard's field of vision.

Burns had that same cool aloofness that taunted Kelly, made her want to shake him up, disturb his self-assurance. Surely the man had doubts. He wore that masculine mask like a second skin. Still, she liked his intelligence and, especially, his enthusiasm for his work. She'd been charmed by his fascination with her sacred hill overlooking the research camp. His eyes, too, had betrayed a boyish, troubled longing as he watched the sun slip behind the darkening trees of Cayo.

Burns was lulled by the rhythmic splash of the waterfalls. He lounged on the bank with an unusual sense of contentment. He felt younger, more limber. The brief swim had left his skin feeling clean and smooth, his body relaxed and supple. The tropical sun no longer seemed harsh. Absently, he picked up a handful of the dry dirt at his feet and rubbed it between his fingers and sniffed the reddish, dank soil. He couldn't remember the last time he'd felt this relaxed, this alive. Every limb, every pore, was alert, stimulated, yet there was none of his usual anxiousness. The drive that pushed him to be active, to always be doing something useful or productive, utterly vanished.

He glimpsed Kelly as she stepped out of the pool, water dripping down the slight folds of her stomach and sliding down her strong but imperfect thighs. He liked that imperfection of age. It made her somehow more authentic in his eyes, more real. A tuft of wet, reddish-brown hair pressed through her white underpants and curled just outside the seams, touching her damp skin. Instinctively, Burns searched for her lips and found those moss green eyes, bright with girlish amusement.

Kelly strolled past the camera and tripod and sat down alongside Burns. Swimsuit shot for the promos, he thought ruefully. She reached behind her back and gathered her wet hair in both hands and wrung it gently, letting the cool water slip down her back. Burns was both excited and utterly at ease, a feeling he rarely experienced in the company of women. He often felt safer and more readily understood with men.

"You just jump right in," Burns said.

"Sometimes," Kelly said.

Burns nodded, feeling both excited to be alongside her and guilty that he had been less than honest. Well, he told himself, he could always just not use the scene if it were too revealing. Erase it if necessary. Kelly leaned back on her hands. She closed her eyes and turned her face toward the hot sun. The steady rush of the waterfalls echoed from the granite walls around them.

"So is this the end of your medicine trail?" Burns asked.

"Most of the time, I climb a little further into the hills and then follow the path to San Antonio where Tato lives."

"Who?"

"Pedro Meza, the curandero. Tato is what we call him. It's an affectionate name for elders, a sign of respect and a sign of love. Genuine love."

"Tae-to," Burns said, pronouncing the title slowly, feeling vaguely jealous, as if this old man were a rival.

"He's the real star of your show," Kelly said.

"There can be more than one. Is the village far?" Burns asked. He suddenly felt a need to get back to work.

"A few miles yet," Kelly said, her voice soft and languid.

"Miles? How long would it take us?" Burns said. He stood up, peering into the forest beyond the clearing.

"You don't want to go today?" Kelly said, sitting up, shielding her eyes with her hands. Burns glanced at her rough hands, callused and etched with old scratches and cuts. Again, the masculine toughness made him uneasy, like seeing women who opted against shaving their underarms.

The cassette clicked to a stop a moment later, signaling the end of the tape. Burns had one, single tape remaining. It was a fraction of the 30 to 1 shooting ratio that was needed to make a documentary. The prospect of not recording anything he witnessed seemed more than absurd. It was a mockery of his best intentions.

"Were you recording me?" Kelly asked, peering at the camera.

"Were we?" Burns asked his cameraman.

"At least you're a bad liar, Michael," Kelly said, standing up. "I like that about you."

16

Ix-im: Cultivated corn; boiled and drunk for treatment of measles

Pedro Meza squatted on his soiled hemp mat, facing the cross that stood against the east wall of his bungalow. He had placed an offering of fresh flowers to the Ancestors at the base of the cross and now waited for the water to boil on his hotplate. His clothes still smelled of copal, the incense used for the funeral. The sweet scent was reassuring and, he believed, helped to ward off the dark Mayan spirits that moved freely through the village in the aftermath of Mazdara's death.

The village itself was empty. Everyone had remained on the riverbank, where they had prayed over the boy's body then tied rocks to it before letting it sink into the depths of the turgid river. His soul, his essence, they believed, had long since returned to the spirit world. The body was a gift to the spirits of the great river upon which they depended for food and transportation.

The loss of the young boy would be a tragedy anywhere, but in the dying village of San Antonio, it was devastating. Most of the young, childbearing couples had long since been lured away by the promise of the city. The few remaining represented the last chance for the town's survival.

Pedro Meza studied the steam escaping from the tin spout of his tea kettle as it rose in a faint, metallic-smelling cloud, only to dissipate before it reached the low ceiling of his hut. He was drained by the long hours fighting to save Mazdara. The healing Maya spirits had not come to his aid. The people of the village didn't blame him, but they also did not credit him with administering to the boy with the competence of a regular doctor. Pedro Meza was used to this doubt among the villagers, but he now wondered if he had done everything possible to invoke the healing spirits. He had used the correct herbs, uttered the sacred chants, but Mazdara had died.

Pedro Meza closed his eyes and imagined Rosita was pouring the water over the leaves of the Hatz plant to make a calming, aromatic tea. He could feel her warm hand on his neck, softly reassuring him, her fingers scented with the Ix-im she had been mashing to make tortillas. Corn, as many Mayans believed, was more than sustenance. It was a gift of the Gods, given to man as a benediction. In Rosita's hands, Pedro Meza had always felt blessed.

The curandero opened his eyes to an empty room. The solitude was as oppressive as the stale air. He did not want to live like a lonely old man. He needed a woman to share his home, his meals, his moods. He did not want to just wither away. Despite his age, he believed there were years ahead of him still. Above all, he did not want to die alone. There were the spirits, of course, but he also needed a living person, someone to help him make the journey when the time came.

The lid of the teapot began to rattle. Pedro Meza grabbed a small towel and plucked the tin kettle off of the hotplate and poured the steaming water over the chopped branches and leaves of the Hatz plant. The tea would calm his nerves and help him to sleep later. He again smelled the copal on his clothes and breathed a sigh of relief. The herbs, he reminded himself, always helped. They carried the spirits with them, and the spirits were always present, their power waiting to be tapped.

The curandero's melancholy lifted. He was reassured by the message from Kelly. She was planning to visit today and was also bringing the movie people who would record his work. He did not appreciate how the cameras could record his medicine. All that could be viewed were the plants, which were merely the beginning of his work. But Kelly had been so excited about the power of the cameras that he had not objected. He adored her enthusiasm and, besides, there was the possibility that the cameras were as powerful as she believed. Perhaps they could record some of his healing knowledge collected over a lifetime. Pedro Meza yearned to leave a legacy and, if not through Kelly, perhaps these cameras.

The curandero strolled out of his dark hut and into the hot, midday light. The scattered, concrete bungalows slung on either side of the dirt path seemed tired and drained from the heat. A neighbor's horse, tied under a nearby tree, snapped its tail, vainly trying to stir the humid air. Pedro Meza rebelled instinctively against the oppressive weight of the day. He needed to act, to atone for his action, to prove to himself and his neighbors that his healing art remained powerful. Pedro Meza began walking down the path, away from the village toward the jungle. He did not know where he was going, but he could not ignore the instinct that was calling him forward. It was the same sense that he relied upon when searching the dense forest for rare medicinal plants. The destination would reveal itself when the time came.

In the meantime, he was only too happy to move. The act of walking itself quickly began to ease his anxiousness. The familiar smell of the wet leaves, the chatter of birds and insects, the deep, soothing green of the canopy, all worked to clear his mind and focus his attention on the moment. Pedro Meza found himself taking joy and satisfaction in each step, as though being alive and healthy were something new and curious.

THE FIVE LOST DAYS

17

**Bukut: Juice from the pod is drunk
to treat tiredness and general malaise**

Burns trudged far behind Kelly, feeling nauseous from the unrelenting heat. He wanted to ask how much longer they would be stuck out in the open, hiking without the protective shade of the trees, but he said nothing. Instead, he readjusted his leather battery belt to try and relieve the weight of the lead battery clips that hung from his hips.

The crew was further behind, moving single file, each struggling in his own way. Vic shuffled forward, scowling at nothing, absently hugging his camera as though it were a sleeping infant. Big's wide, flushed face and dazed eyes made him seem lost or disoriented. Still, neither he nor Vic made an attempt to stop. Burns was struck by their resemblance to an Army platoon trudging through the woods. Their battery belts looked like ammunition, their light poles and camera could easily have been mistaken for firearms.

"How's everyone holding up?" Burns asked.

"Haven't had this much fun since I was a grunt," Vic said.

"I thought I was in shape," Big added, his nose wheezing with the thick air. "But that woman can go."

Kelly was far ahead, strolling toward the trees. Burns wondered if his decision to hike to the Mayan village had been rash. But he had wanted to experience the jungle firsthand. He had been consumed with the need for each image to be authentic. He had duped himself into the fiction that the camera captured life. Burns knew it was more complicated. The Heisenberg Principle, Kelly had defined it. The act of seeing influenced what was being seen. Pictures lied more than they told the truth. They were not neutral recording devices. Images were made.

"Burns," Vic pleaded. "This is insane, even for you. Why the hell don't we have our forced march tomorrow, when we actually have something to record it on?"

"We have tape," Burns said.

"Exactly one tape. About enough for the credit roll."

"We're scouting, Vic. We're seeing what we need to get later."

"When's later?"

"You know, you're really getting on my nerves, Colt," Burns said, knowing his cameraman was being sensible. But the last thing Burns could do was sit around and wait until they had their raw stock.

Kelly leaned under the trees, watching. Her eyes sparkled in the dappled light of the green leaves, and it gave Burns a start. Bizarre as it seemed, it was a similar feeling to the sighting, the dream or the vision of the animal or whatever it was he had witnessed earlier in the day.

"You look like you just saw a ghost," Kelly said.

"It's the heat," Burns said.

"Most people take time adjusting to the climate," Kelly said.

"We're fine," Burns said.

"Make sure you keep drinking the water. Whatever you do."

Big had already poured out a handful and was slapping it on his burning cheeks like after-shave. Burns stared dumbly at Kelly as she brought the plastic water bottle to her lips, the corners wet with perspiration. She tilted her head back, spilling her tawny hair over those regal shoulders. As she drank deeply, her exposed neck strained higher, like one of the elegant herons that fished on the shore.

"The good news," Kelly said, gently wiping her moist lips, "is that we're near the Rio Frio caves. The closest we have to air-conditioning in Cayo."

The mouth of a slate gray cave appeared just inside the trees, arching above a slow-moving stream. Burns and his crew stopped at the foot of the cave and dropped the tripod, microphone poll, wire cables and other video equipment to the ground. There was a collective sigh after the last coil of black cable slapped into the loose, sandy soil.

Burns leaned against a tree, grateful to be in the relative cool of the shade. He chugged more water, then splashed some on the back of his neck. It cooled him instantly, sending welcome chills down his spine. The headache that had dogged him during the hike vanished, and he looked at the dense trees and rocks around him as if for the first time. The river had slowed to a glassy, silent current, rippling only when a bug scampered across it like a skipping stone.

Burns felt an unexpected peace. There was nowhere else he wanted to be, no lost video stock to be worried about for the moment. In the middle of nowhere, surrounded only by trees and the chattering of cicadas, he was home. It was a world away from the drab apartment facades that lined West End Avenue in Manhattan. In winter, the soaring, prewar buildings blocked all but a miserly sliver of sunlight, entombing his neighborhood. Compared to this lush, sun-drenched world where every sense was engaged —the pungent smell of moist leaves, the warm spray of humidity that tasted like the soft tips of asparagus, the melodious chirps and calls of unseen birds—the city was lifeless. The concrete and the glass, the steel and the brick, all walled off the immediate experience of the natural world. Here, in the jungle, Burns felt his senses opened like pores on the skin, quickening the sense of being alive. In the city, except for meals and sex, he felt his life was guided by sight and mind. Like TV, his chosen profession. The city was busy and full of fast-moving visuals—the people, the traffic, the garbage, the homeless—all manmade, some seductive. His daily life, Burns thought, was guided by disembodied voices on radio, in music; electronic representations on a glass screen; plastic computer keys; a metal subway. All removed as far as possible from contact with the natural world.

"This is a good spot," Big John said. Kelly and Vic both nodded. Burns wondered if he looked as tired and spent as his crew did. They weren't used to the heat and, even more, nature itself. He thought of Elf on the river, floating on the dugout canoe back to San Ignacio. Burns trusted Old Man Green to get him safely back.

"There are good spirits here," Kelly said. "As they should be."

A sudden, light breeze brushed Burns's face. The air was as soft and silken as a woman's hair. He let Kelly's reference to spirits wash over him as well. There were no unseen, disembodied spirits here. It was much better than that.

"How do you think Elf is doing?" Big asked.

"As long as he got through the whitewater, he's golden," Vic said.

"You know he can't swim, don't you?"

Burns didn't, and he was disappointed in himself for not thinking to ask. A producer was supposed to think ahead, to be ready for anything. He felt as if he were stumbling from one mistake to another.

"He doesn't have to swim," Burns said, reassuring himself as well as the crew. The brief peace he had known was already gone as quickly as someone hitting a light switch. "He'll be fine. We need to get going."

The cave was cool and damp. Sunlight filtered from the opposite end, highlighting the rough-hewn walls and the dark river that swept silently below. A path was cut into the limestone along the ridge that wound its way to the other end. Burns peered over the steep cliff. A thin crescent of beach was dimly visible. The black, slow-moving stream slithered alongside. The atmosphere invited superstition like the musty Catholic monasteries in the remote mountain villages of Italy. Burns remembered sitting on the hardwood pews in a medieval chapel in the Apennines, where priests intoned their prayers in ancient Latin and clouds of pungent incense billowed through the dim candlelight toward the rugged stone ceilings.

"The Mayans and their descendants still believe caves like this are sacred places," Kelly announced from the darkness just ahead of him. "Fathers take their sons to a cave to teach them about the spirits and the Maya underworld." The Maya underworld was called Xibalba, which translated roughly to "Place of Fright." It was a dark hell equal to the one imagined by Dante and equally rich with allegorical monsters and evil rulers.

"If you turn on one of your TV lights, you'll see what I mean," Kelly said. "This cave has one of the few walls with glyphs not looted either by thieves or archaeologists."

Big lumbered past Burns and plugged a connector into his battery belt. A few moments later, the wall was blasted with electric daylight from the portable light. The wall gleamed with a massive rectangle crammed with glyphs painted the color of terra cotta and surrounded by various Mayan figures. The glyphs resembled Chinese characters, only they were rounded and more compact. The figures were either seated or standing, and all were festooned with elaborate headdresses.

"Where are the monsters?" Burns asked.

All the human figures had flared noses on smooth oval faces and the protruding lips Burns had admired on Aida, the striking Mayan woman who had served dinner last night at the research camp.

"These are the gods," Kelly said. "One I do know something about is Ix Chel, or Lady Rainbow, the Goddess of Medicine. The curandero pointed her out to me. And Lizard House, the patron of writing and science."

Lizard House was an old man with the prominent, flared nose. Burns was reminded of his father. An accomplished academic, Burns's father spent most of his time either buried in early nineteenth century British novels or perched over his beloved IBM Selectric typewriter, tapping out another article on Jane Austen or George Eliot. He was not impressed by computers and contemporary culture and certainly not by television. Books and learning were his father's religion. He revered what he called their "timeless stories." Burns didn't share his father's passion. The plots were interesting enough, but he did not have his father's tolerance for the mounds of prose description, taking pages and pages to communicate what a photograph could accomplish in a single frame.

But there was another reason Burns disliked the novels. His father was a natural loner who preferred solitude to the company of even his family except for short periods of time. He seemed most comfortable only in the company of books, and Burns had always been jealous of the sway those musty pages held over his father.

"This is Ix Chel with the snake," Kelly continued.

Ix Chel was hunched over what looked like a tree stump with a serpent coiled on her head, replacing the long, dark Mayan hair. Burns was reminded of the staff with a coiled serpent that was the symbol used by the American Medical Association. But most of the doctors he knew would have rolled their eyes at any comparison to the superstitious curanderos who practiced medicine in the jungle.

"Placebo effect at best," one doctor sniffed when he told him about his upcoming story on medicine hunting in Belize. "The power of suggestion is a powerful medicine."

"You don't think the plants work?" Burns had asked.

"If they did, don't you think the pharmaceutical companies would have rounded them up by now?"

The sun gun began to sputter, the white light quickly fading before it went out all together. Big cursed at the dead battery. The light had drained all the power from his battery belt.

"Burns," Big called. "I'm going to need someone else's belt if you want to keep shooting."

"Take mine," Vic said.

The sunlight at the far end of the cave traced Big's monster-sized profile in the darkness. Kelly and Vic were rendered into elongated, cartoon-like shadows that climbed the walls. Burns carefully backed away from the narrow trail to get a wider perspective, wondering if this was a shot worth getting. He tested each step to make sure he was putting his weight on solid ground.

"Stay close to the path," Kelly warned. "There are sharp drop-offs you won't be able to see."

Burns was confident he would be able to sense an approaching drop-off, so he kept moving, anxious to find the ideal angle for filming the group. Moments later, he found what he was looking for.

"Vic," he called. "Over here. This is perfect."

"Perfectly dark."

"Indulge me, " Burns said. "You can see just enough."

Vic gave a sigh of disapproval but nevertheless hiked over to where Burns waited.

"Like something from a Scooby-Doo cartoon," Vic said.

"Or a horror movie," Burns said.

As Vic filmed the silhouettes, Burns heard new sounds rising in the silence. Water dripped from a distant boulder like a leaking faucet. The river below hummed with the force of its current.

"OK. Got your shot," Vic said.

"You like it?" Burns asked.

"Shadows on the wall, mostly. It's OK."

"Perfect. We're in the shadow world, right?"

"We're in a cave the last time I checked."

"Metaphorically. I meant the Maya world."

"Right."

"We're on our way to you," Burns called to Kelly and Big as he and Vic picked their way through the darkness, struggling to get back to the narrow dirt path.

"Please keep talking so we can find you," Burns said, feeling his shoe sink into what felt like wet sand. A moment later, he couldn't tell if Vic was behind or ahead of him.

"I'm back here taking a rest, Burns. I don't want to bang this camera into anything."

Burns turned to look for him in the darkness. This time, his other foot felt open air. He calmly jumped sideways to catch his balance on another stone or crevice. Only there wasn't any. Instead, he was falling, too startled to even scream. He hit the warm stream a few moments later, felt a sharp, jarring tear across his thigh, and he was under, gulping water as he sank.

The battery belt clung to his side like dive weights. His rubber snake boots, too, were heavy anchors, dragging him deeper into the river. He kicked wildly, afraid the equipment would drown him. But he was reluctant to give anything up. So he continued to descend. Air. His head was pounding as he clawed at the water. He opened his eyes, but there was only darkness. Water shot up his nostrils, and he gulped a mouthful of water. He was drowning. It was impossible. He kicked furiously, arms flailing. This time he reached down to his waist and unhooked the battery belt. He felt it fall off and release him. He could not tell if he was swimming toward the surface or simply moving sideways—or if he were even still sinking. The confusion only made him swim harder. Suddenly, inexplicably, he burst through the surface, hoarsely coughing up the water, wheezing as he sucked in the air.

Burns tried to orient himself, but he was afraid of sinking and continued to kick. Then his head banged into a rock. The sharp, unexpected pain shocked him into awareness. He wasn't going to sink. He was OK. He glimpsed a gray swath of sand a few strokes away.

The sand soon was scratching his chest, and he pushed up to a standing position, relieved to feel the firmness underneath. He dropped onto the dry sand, angry with his boots for being so heavy and clumsy. Burns leaned over, willing himself to control his breath and in doing so control the panic. So he forced himself to take long, deep breaths, fighting the urge to hurry. Soon the fast, anxious rasping subsided, and he was beginning to feel safe. Water dripped from his nose and fell across his lips. It tasted vaguely metallic.

Slowly, Burns examined his environment. The beach extended far upstream, narrowing until it vanished altogether.

He searched above him, gauging how far he had fallen. Three or four stories at most. But it had felt endless. He scanned for any sign of the group. But there were no racing footsteps or calls for his whereabouts. There was only darkness and the faint gurgle of the river. Burns searched for toe- and handholds on the rock face, thinking he might try climbing back to the top. His aching leg persuaded him otherwise.

He squinted at the blood, which looked like the chocolate syrup used to fake it in movies. It leaked from mid-thigh in a slow but steady stream, and some had congealed on the gray sand. He was surprised at the depth of the gash on his leg but could feel nothing arterial had been cut. He remembered the moment of impact and the sharp pain that had shot up his leg, probably from landing on a submerged rock.

Burns called for help, expecting his voice to resound through the cave, but there was not even a hint of an echo. Had he fallen into a crevice within the cave? The stream was less than ten yards across, the current flowing swiftly away from him. When they first entered the cave, the stream was also flowing away from him, back toward the rain forest. He could try wading into the tea-colored water and allow the current to carry him back to the entrance. It appeared simple enough. Except for two things. One was the presence of small eddies that marked every stream and river he'd seen in Cayo. Most were harmless, but some were powerful whirlpools that could easily suck him under. The second factor was his leg. He was confident he could swim with the injury but worried about the blood. It could act as bait, attracting whatever lurked in these waters.

Burns heard his name. The calls were soon followed by the piercing white beam of a sun gun bouncing off the river. He leapt up with a strength he didn't know he had. He yelled in the direction of the voices, waving until the light blinded him.

"There he is. Are you OK?"

Kelly. Her voice had never sounded so welcome. She seemed to be speaking to his crew, but Burns couldn't hear what was being said. He waited. The talking continued as if he weren't there.

"What's going on?" Burns yelled, finally.

There was silence. For a moment, Burns feared they had left.

"Can you swim?" Kelly asked.

"Yes. Why?"

"Because that's the only way out."

"Are you sure?"

Kelly didn't answer, but Burns heard the rise and fall of her words.

"We'll shine the lights on the water, Burns," Vic yelled. "Just follow the light."

"I could climb up one of these walls," Burns yelled back, even though he knew he couldn't.

"The river is the only way," Vic said.

Burns thought he heard impatience in Vic's voice. His cameraman had, after all, supposedly been in more threatening situations. Hadn't he trudged through rice patties and streams, praying there were no booby traps or Viet Cong waiting to shoot him? Burns took a deep breath to calm himself. The snake boots, at least, had to go before he was going back into that river. He plopped down on the cool sand and prepared to remove them. He paused when he saw the leg wound. It was midway down his left thigh, about four jagged inches long and a little wider than his fingernail. He'd need stitches.

"Are you in the water yet?" Vic called.

"No. Give me a minute."

Burns couldn't afford to lose the boots. They would be essential for a safe hike back through the jungle to the research camp. He could still kick with them on, he decided. It was worth the risk.

He stood and inched his way to the water's edge. The long beam from the sun gun patrolled the middle of the river. He moved toward it and into the water. It was surprisingly warm, even soothing. He waded further out until the rocks poked the bottoms of his feet, then slipped in chest-first. The current took him with surprising swiftness. Before he knew it, Burns was in the middle, drifting downstream.

The spotlight bounced off the surface ahead of him.

He turned over and floated on his back, his feet ahead of him as he'd learned from whitewater rafting. He raised the injured leg out of the water and held it just above the surface. It was spotlighted a moment later by the sun gun. The thigh was candy red, but the bleeding had stopped. Burns watched it float just above the water like the red bow light of a boat, leading him to safety. A minute later, his raised leg was gliding around a dark bend and into the halo of hazy sunlight at the mouth of the cave.

He relaxed and let his head float. He gazed up at the roof of the cave. Stalactites dangled like stone chandeliers. He tried to slow himself, wanting to study what he'd only seen in storybooks and movies, but the current was picking up speed, and he was gliding out into the white, hazy light of the afternoon.

Burns rolled onto his stomach and tried to swim toward the muddy bank. He was surprised at his own weakness. Each stroke was an effort. His chest was heavy with congestion, and he wheezed as he fought for more air. Still, he pushed himself as he always did, fighting the desire to give in to his tiredness. When he bumped into the bank, he dug his fingers into the soft mud and crawled. He clawed his way up the bank until his knees hit solid ground.

Burns was on all fours. Like a baby, he thought. As he prepared to stand, however, he heard footsteps on the nearby ground. No voice followed. He tensed with fear. The steps were soft, nimble, animal-like. He was about to cry out to his crew but sensed the loud noise could provoke the animal. He lowered himself to the ground and slowly began to back toward the river. If the animal attempted to stalk him, he would jump back in and let the current carry him to safety.

Burns stopped when he felt the water lapping against his boots. He remembered the blood flowing down his leg. The animal could smell it. Instinctively, the animal would know it was stalking injured prey. Burns was helpless. With the fresh blood, he feared he was luring the predator forward. He had no weapon to defend himself. Even if he managed to slip into the river in time, there was the likelihood that the jaguar—if that's what it was—could still come after him. He needed to go now, to anticipate the attack before it was too late. But he wasn't sure if he had enough strength to swim.

Burns slid into the warm water as quietly as he could. The current nudged him off and away from the bank. He rolled onto his side, keeping his eyes locked on the forest where he had heard the approaching steps. He stroked with his right arm, using it like a paddle. The current steered him slowly downstream. As he drifted away, however, he was startled to see what likely had been stalking him from the forest. A short old man wearing a baseball cap had stepped out from behind the trees, evidently from a forest path. Burns tried to call to him but swallowed a mouthful of river water instead. He gagged, rolling back onto his stomach and swam furiously back toward the bank. He reached it quickly and crawled back through the mud, coughing hoarsely. Finally, he caught his breath and stopped. When he looked up, the diminutive old man was stooped in front of him.

18

**Zutz Pakal: Young, green fruit of this
tree is carried to ward off witchcraft**

Frank drove up and over the deforested hill, the rotting stumps scattered everywhere like bones in a killing field, speeding toward the tiny village of San Antonio. The destruction wrought by the American logging company hardly registered with him anymore, although his anger at their casual devastation still smoldered in him, mixing with his general disdain for all those corporations getting rich on the backs of the Mayans and their land.

But Frank was riding high. Music played in his mind, and he broke into the lyrics of the Dead song from the night before. He sang with a crazed exuberance, anxious to hear himself over the straining engine and the rough road. He felt some of the same cockiness he'd known as a student, the kind that had spurred him to join the Independents, an alternative to the fraternities that dominated the social life of the campus. He had quickly become one of their chief spokesmen, publicly railing against what he called the "repressive regime" of the fraternities on the college radio and in the school newspaper. He attacked their hazing practices and drinking binges with the fervor of a fundamentalist, galvanized by the power of a just cause. It had given him the only direction he had known in higher education.

Frank parked at the edge of the village and jumped out of the cab into the early morning sun. The heat stung the back of his neck like a wasp, and he took an involuntary breath. He never got used to it. Never. The hot, hazy sun was a constant, debilitating presence. He yearned for one of the rare, cloudy days that made the heat bearable. But he put the discomfort out of his mind and focused on his meeting with Manuela. She would have arrived at Carlos's house sometime in the early dawn, traveling at night across the border. Finally, he smiled to himself, here was the chance to make a connection with a world-class activist, a woman rumored to be a rival to Maya icon Rigoberta Menchu. If her presence did nothing for the village, he knew it would inspire him to even greater efforts. He would make a better life for these people, whether they wanted it or not.

But as Frank strolled up the dirt alleyway, he was met not by the familiar kid, such as little Tumil, or the crows of Santi, the withered old rooster, or even the chatter of Belize City DJs, but by silence. The village was deserted. He continued in the direction of Carlos's bungalow with apprehension, worried one of the marauding bands of Guatemalan "soldiers"—fifteen-year-old boys carrying AK-47s—had slipped across the border on a traitorous tip. As Frank turned the corner, however, he was relieved to see his friend in the usual spot, slouched in a faded plastic chair, smoking a Marlboro Light. He pinched the end of the cigarette the way one usually held a fat cigar.

"If it isn't our own Che Guevara," Carlos greeted him, waving his cigarette like a small flag.

"Hey, bud," Frank said, grabbing his friend's warm, bony hand in a tight, brotherly grip. "Is she here?"

Carlos fell silent, staring at the dirt floor. He was gentle and self-effacing, qualities that also made him hard to read.

"There was a message here this morning, before the funeral, from those who were to bring Manuela. There was trouble."

Frank closed his eyes and held them shut. He was beyond disappointed. He felt as jilted as a lover. He had worked hard to get her here, using money he didn't really have to grease the in-betweens.

"What happened?"

"Someone tipped off the army. They set up roadblocks everywhere between here and the roads leading to Guatemala. She had to turn around at the border."

Frank felt all the energy go out of him. He knew he had been thrilled to meet Manuela, but now he recognized that he had been living for it. Months of planning had given new energy to the organizing efforts that had slowed in the village. Most just wanted to be left alone.

"Where the hell is everyone?" Frank asked.

"Down by the river," Carlos said. "Burying Mazdara."

"Esposita's boy?" Frank asked, surprised. He hadn't known the boy well but remembered how happy and healthy he had been.

"What happened?"

"No one knows. Pedro Meza says he had symptoms of a snake bite."

"Was it a snake?"

"Many say the boy was under a spell."

"Spells don't kill people," Frank said, throwing up his hands. Virtually the entire village was illiterate, with schooling hours away in San Ignacio. They had no defense against superstitions. They had only their cultural knowledge to inform what they witnessed.

Carlos took a slow, worried drag on his cigarette.

"It is a sad day in any case," Carlos said.

Frank grabbed a footstool but hesitated to sit.

"So Guatemalan soldiers crossed over the border to track down Manuela?"

"They move at will. You know that."

"What about the BDF?" Frank asked. The army, such as it was, had been created precisely to protect against incursions by the Guatemalan military. They were a purely defensive force.

"You know as well as me, my friend. Only the spirits know when our government will operate a patrol. It's been months since a plane has even flown over Cayo."

"Who told you about the roadblocks?"

"Our people," Carlos said. "I am sorry, my friend. I know how much you were looking forward to meeting her. Myself as well."

Frank thought he had been prepared for this turn of events. He knew Manuela's arrival was risky and provisional. It was something of a long shot to begin with. Yet he had held such hopes, and that faith had kept him going and bolstered his own confidence and belief in his purpose, not to mention his scheme for funding the movement. Now, he told himself, he could not—would not—lose momentum. It was up to him. He alone would have to generate the enthusiasm. Of course, this wasn't the first time he'd been out on a limb by himself. He'd survive. This was only a temporary setback.

19

**U-tu-it: Large leaf is warmed and placed
on muscles to treat spasms and pain**

The old man made a clucking sound with his tongue as he crouched to examine Burns's bloodied leg. He scooped a handful of water from the river and poured it over the wound to gently wash off the mud, then pressed his finger against the red, congealed gash. Burns remained still throughout the examination, curious about the man he knew to be the curandero.

"No esta mal," the curandero said after he took a taste of the blood from his finger.

Tasting someone else's blood seemed a crude and dangerous way to test for infection, Burns thought. What if he had a disease?

"Vamonos," the curandero said, standing upright.

"No go," Burns said. "My crew is coming."

"Vamonos a mi casa," the curandero insisted. "Por medicina."

"You speak English? Habla Ingles?"

The curandero shook his head.

"Kelly," Burns said. "Kelly."

The curandero grinned with something more than recognition.

"You know?" Burns asked.

"Si, si." The curandero nodded eagerly.

"She comes soon," Burns said. He struggled to remember the few Spanish phrases he'd picked up from living in New York City. But his fatigue made it too difficult to concentrate.

"Vamonos," the curandero repeated and tapped his own shoulder, gesturing that he would help Burns up. Before Burns could protest, the curandero grabbed one of his arms and slung it over the shoulder. With surprising strength and agility, the curandero quickly brought him to his feet. Burns winced from the pain that shot up his back as soon as he stood on the injured leg. He shifted his weight to the healthy left leg and leaned on the old man's bony shoulders. The curandero smelled strongly of incense—copal, a sandalwood-like scent common in Mexico. In New York, the Mexicans burned it all day and night to celebrate their most revered holiday, El Dia De Los Muertos, The Day of the Dead. The devout welcomed back the souls of their beloved who, they believed, returned to comfort the living.

The curandero stepped forward, forcing Burns to move with him. He repeated the action until Burns and he were off the riverbank and headed toward the path from which the curandero had first appeared.

"We have to wait," Burns insisted. He felt almost as if he were on the river again, fighting the current that prevented him from reaching shore. The curandero ignored his pleas, forcing them forward with small, quick steps. Finally, Burns yanked his arm off the curandero and hopped away on his one strong leg. He extended both of his hands as a gesture for the old man to stay away.

"Kelly," Burns said. He pointed toward where he remembered the cave entrance to be. The curandero turned, following Burns's outstretched arm.

"Donde?"

"The cave, the cave."

The curandero studied him calmly. Where was the crew? Burns

asked himself. They should have been here by now, unless the stream had taken him farther than he assumed.

"You know, the cave. How do you say in Spanish? Cave, cave," Burns repeated, pointing again.

"Ah! Cueva," the curandero said. "Cueva. Comprendo."

"How far to Cueva?" Burns asked. He could feel the throbbing return to his thigh even though there was no weight on it now.

"No comprendo," the curandero said.

"Cuanto. Damn it. Cuanto. How far?" Burns said, gritting his teeth from the surging pain.

"Ah," the curandero said. "Esta lejos de aqui? No muy lejos."

Burns could not concentrate fully enough to try to infer what the old man's Spanish meant. Instead, he let himself sink to one knee, hoping for some relief from the aching wound. It was then his chest constricted and his mouth grew dry and irritated, followed by the inevitable urge to cough. He sensed the curandero's clinical, inquisitive gaze as he lurched into a coughing fit and fell to his hands. It seemed to Burns as if he were falling apart right in front of the old man's eyes, and that infuriated him. He shook his head, feeling betrayed by his ailing body. He was rarely sick and had never once visited a hospital as a patient.

The curandero remained still, pensive. Finally, he crept forward. His movements were tensely cautious, feline. Burns felt his approach but was too preoccupied to challenge the native healer. This time he did not protest as the old man helped him to his feet and led him back toward the path.

The sound of barking dogs echoed in the distance. As they came closer, Burns heard the anxious chatter of radios and the intermittent squawking of the roosters. Soon they were out of the forest and into a grassy clearing. A weathered, wooden sign announced "Welcome to San Antonio. Population 680." in black, hand-drawn letters. A score of weathered bungalows and a few traditional thatched huts were scattered like cans on the hills just beyond the sign. The bungalows were painted in bright candy colors—lime green, sugar white, Jell-O blue—topped with either a thatched or corrugated tin roof. Small vegetable gardens were crammed in between the houses. As they walked closer, Burns felt an unexpected sympathy for one of the town's roosters. The scrawny cock strutted back and forth at the edge of a narrow garden, asserting its presence, refusing to be humbled by the string tied around its clawed foot, tethered to a wooden stick otherwise used to train a thriving tomato plant. But the moment Burns was alongside the houses, he was surprised to find them empty. The sound of the dogs and the radios and the roosters echoed from one empty doorway to the next. Everyone seemed to have left in a hurry.

"Donde los otros gente?" Burns asked.

"El funeral," the curandero said, his eyes cast somberly to the ground.

"Who died?"

"El chico," the curandero answered. "Mazdara."

Pedro Meza made Burns stoop low to enter the cool shade of his bungalow, then helped him to sit on the dirt floor. His one-room home reeked of copal. The incense made Burns think of Catholic funerals. As a boy, he'd been captivated by the ritual of the priest, cloaked in flowing robes, who strolled down the aisle near the end of mass, dangling a brass incense burner by its thick chain. Burns would follow the sweet, oily smoke as it wafted over the low wooden pews crowded with stern-faced adults dressed in suits and formal dresses. The smell and the reverberations of the pipe organ conjured a sense of mystery, not grief. No one spoke except the priest, who called out Latin phrases as though invoking the spirits in a low, hypnotic cadence, punctuated by the clang of the incense holder when it bumped the brass chain.

"Donde el funeral?" Burns asked. The curandero shuffled behind him, turning on a hotplate. He poured a cup of water from a plastic barrel against the wall.

"El Rio Frio," the curandero said. It was the same river that also coursed through the cave where Burns had fallen.

Burns wondered why the healer seemed to be the only person in the village who was not at the ceremony. Maybe the old man was like his old man, who avoided wakes and funerals. Burns's father claimed they were useless. "What's my going to the funeral going to do for the poor fool?" his father would ask.

The curandero picked two small bundles of herbs from a dark corner, where scores of similar bundles, some wrapped in tent canvas or plastic, were piled almost to the tin roof. The curandero plucked dark green leaves from the wiry stem of one of the herbs and dropped them into the cup of water. He whispered a prayer over the rising steam, like a priest chanting a somber creed. Burns was about to ask about the prayer when the curandero reached over to the small table behind him and retrieved a small, handmade, ceramic jar that looked like it was made to hold sugar or salt. The old man closed his eyes and shook the jar, rattling a coin or stone inside it. The intense concentration on the curandero's face made Burns think of a gambler rolling the die in one last pitch to win his bet.

The curandero turned the cup upside-down onto his opposite palm and slowly lifted it away. A smooth, gray and blue marble rested in his dirty, weathered palm like a pearl in the midst of a mottled oyster shell. The old man peered at the marble ball, studying the imperfections with the scrutiny of a jeweler. The marble remained still as the curandero moved his head from one side to the other for a different perspective. Finally, he grunted with what Burns assumed was either surprise or recognition and closed his short, thick fingers around the marble and returned it to the ceramic cup.

"Is that your sastun?" Burns asked.

He had learned about the sastun from the research that had been done back in New York before they left for the shoot. The sastun was the divining tool of the curandero, a sacred object that aided the healer in determining the source of a patient's illness. Somehow Burns had expected something else—a stone, a relic evocative of Mayan culture—not a kid's marble.

"Como conocerlo?" the curandero asked, finally. He studied Burns

141

with a new, guarded focus.

Burns struggled to answer the old man in Spanish, but no words suggested themselves. The fatigue and throbbing in his leg were making it even more difficult to think clearly. Finally, he thought to repeat the one word that would at least satisfy the curandero.

"Kelly," Burns said. "Kelly told me about the sastun."

"Ah," the curandero said, his elfish, weathered face visibly relaxing. His deep-set, chestnut eyes flashed with understanding.

"Televisione?" the curandero asked. He spoke further in Spanish, and Burns understood that he was asking if he was one of the men from the television crew.

"Si, si," Burns said. He smiled at the old man, who suddenly broke into a toothless grin. The joy of simple communication. Burns wanted to ask what the curandero had discovered from his sastun, but his Spanish was not up to the task.

The native healer plucked the boiled leaves out of the water with a large wooden spoon. He laid the wet, steaming greens on a large plantain leaf that he had spread open on the table. It would be the poultice he would wrap around Burns's leg wound. Next, he took the pot off the hotplate and poured the tea into a blue coffee mug that was chipped around the lip.

"Beve," the curandero instructed and handed him the mug. The water smelled faintly metallic, but there was no trace of the plant's scent. Burns sniffed a second time, hoping his sense of smell would give him at least a hint of what he was about to drink. He was generally careful about what he ate and drank, especially in third-world countries, where he feared food poisoning or worse.

"Beve," the curandero repeated, this time even more emphatically.

"Si, si," Burns answered, hesitating. Whatever he was about to drink, it was hot enough to have killed any major germs. So Burns brought the beverage to his lips and tested the water. It was hot, but not scalding, so he sipped it, immediately disliking the bitterness that filled his mouth. He considered spitting it out, but the curandero's intense gaze somehow made him swallow it. Burns was surprised to find himself trusting this little old man. Back in New York, Burns rarely took any medicine. Even when he had contracted a mild bronchitis in the summer he avoided going to a doctor until Julie made an appointment for him and walked with him to the Upper West Side office. After the diagnosis, the doctor had prescribed an antibiotic that Burns never ended up buying. He thought it was too expensive. Besides, the doctor had told him the bronchitis would eventually clear up on its own if he took care of himself. A month later, his lungs did clear up, but not before Julie discovered he'd never purchased the medicine.

"What on earth are you trying to prove?" Julie had demanded.

"Pharmaceuticals are a racket most of the time," Burns had said. "If I'd really needed the medicine, I would have taken it. "

"We're not talking about Alka-Seltzer, Mike," Julie said. "Bronchitis is a serious illness. It's not stomach upset."

"Well I feel better."

"And if you didn't it would probably be too late. Did that ever occur to you?"

"Hey, there's no reason for you to get upset. I'm the one that was sick. It's my choice."

"It drives you crazy when anyone tries to help you, doesn't it? You get afraid. Like they're going to find out something you don't want them to find out."

Burns fell silent. He could feel Julie's temper rising and the discussion escalating into an argument. He didn't want to argue. As far as he was concerned, the whole thing was no big deal.

"Bueno, bueno," the curandero said approvingly after Burns gulped down the rest of the tea. Then he motioned for Burns to remain on the floor with his injured leg stretched out in front of him.

Burns winced. His injured thigh had grown stiff and awkward. The blood had congealed into a black, muddy paste. He felt a slight tingling sensation as soon as the curandero pressed the poultice onto the wound and covered it with the huge plantain leaf. The old man chanted another prayer and closed his eyes. He looked heavenward the way priests did at Sunday Mass as they offered the body of Christ to the congregation. Then, as now, it was a ritual Burns watched with vague curiosity.

The curandero stopped his prayer abruptly and put his hand on his chest. He pointed to the interior of his bungalow and invited Burns to move to a blanket in the corner.

20

Pasmo: A tonic herb said to be helpful to all conditions

There was no sign of Burns. They retraced their path from the mouth of the cave, following the winding stream, but there was no body, no piece of clothing, no boot print in the mud. He had simply vanished. Kelly searched the river for eddies or any small whirlpools that might have recently formed. But the surface was as smooth as glass, the fast-moving current posing little danger.

Kelly would not let herself think of the worst. Wounded by the fall, of course he could have simply lost the strength to swim or stay above water. More likely, she thought, was that he had slipped out of the river, become disoriented and hiked in the wrong direction. He seemed too impatient to simply sit wherever he washed up and wait for them.

"It's easy to get lost here," Kelly said. "He's probably wandering in the woods, trying to find his way back to the cave."

"What if he didn't make it out?" Vic asked. "He could have cramped up."

Kelly stared at the river, listening to the indifferent hum of the current. A leaf riding the surface floated past, then drifted toward the bank.

"No," Kelly said. "No, he's here."

"He could be ten feet under and a mile downstream," Vic said. He knelt alongside his camera, squinting through the acrid, briny sweat that dripped from his thick eyebrows. They had hiked to and from the cave twice, searching.

"The current isn't swift enough. He could have swam to the bank anytime he wanted," Kelly said.

"And if he passed out?"

"What about animals, snakes?" Big asked. "Aren't there snakes in the water? And he was bleeding."

Kelly recognized that the men had been pushed to their physical limits and that the exhaustion was fueling their worst fears.

"Anything is possible," Kelly said.

"So what are we going to do?" Big insisted.

"Think," Vic said. "Catch our breath and think."

"And observe," Kelly added. "Take the time to observe."

Kelly's long apprenticeship in the rain forest had given her the conviction that patience was always rewarded. Whether she was medicine hunting or trying to decipher enzymes, she had learned that waiting to see what presented itself was often the most effective way of finding whatever it was you were looking for.

"What are we watching for?" Big asked.

"Clues."

"Well we can't do that sitting here, for Christ's sake," Big said.

"Watch the forest," Kelly told him.

"She's going to tell you to hug a tree next," Vic said, shaking his head.

Kelly was used to people reacting with disapproval to her ideas. The scientists back in Connecticut would have exchanged just the same sort of look with one another as these men did. Kelly has lapses in judgment, those eyes said. She takes all this native lore too seriously.

Women are just too emotional. They think with their hearts instead of their heads.

"You have a better idea, maybe?" Kelly asked.

"Yeah. Let's stop staring at our navel and get back on our own two feet," Vic said.

Kelly ignored him. She listened to the chatter of birds, the scampering of unseen monkeys on the tree limbs, the gurgle of the adjoining stream. The afternoon sunlight leaked through the canopy, falling on trunks and branches, smelling of heat. She recognized a medicinal plant growing in the protective shade of two mahogany trees like an infant being watched over by her towering parents. In fact, she knew the roots of those trees would eventually starve the plant, but Kelly was charmed by how much they appeared like a botanical nuclear family. Pedro Meza spoke of plants in family terms, one being cousin to another, all as moody and idiosyncratic as people. "Sometimes they like to help. Sometimes they can't be bothered with healing," Pedro Meza had said, throwing up his hands as a father might gesture about his ungrateful, quibbling family.

"I knew I should have never set foot in that canoe," Vic said. He still had not moved from his resting place. "Burns is always pushing it."

"But you still work for him," Kelly said.

"I didn't say I was smart," Vic said.

Kelly heard a faint, unusual rattle of leaves. Any other time, she would have paid the sound little attention. Birds of all sorts commonly rambled through the dense forest, tumbling through leaves and branches. Only this sound came from the forest floor. She leaned forward, motioning for the men to remain silent. They turned in time to see a brown, quail-like bird scuttling through the underbrush. Kelly followed it as it turned a corner and disappeared silently from view. She continued staring long after the bird disappeared.

"Just a little quail," Vic said. "We used to shoot 'em and eat 'em in Vietnam."

"That was a tinamou, not a quail."

The birds were common in Cayo, moving about on foot rather than flying, although they could ascend to a tree limb if necessary. The tinamous were prized for their meat by the people throughout the country, Maya and mestizos alike. But they weren't easy to catch since tinamous had a remarkable ability to remain largely hidden from view on the forest floor. They were also loners, preferring to travel without companions, which only increased their elusiveness.

"I think we should get moving," Vic said.

The tiny bird had appeared suddenly, then vanished into the green silence of the trees as quickly as it had come. Kelly saw the tinamou appearance as a puzzle, a kind of Zen koan whose answer she felt might help them locate the lost producer. She retraced the appearance of the tinamou in her mind. There was no way to tell where it was traveling from since it had appeared so suddenly from the underbrush. The bird had also left without a trace. Even without a sound.

Kelly jumped up. She hurried to the spot where the tinamou had disappeared, feeling almost giddy with anticipation. The bird had vanished without a sound because it had scampered to a place where there were no branches for it to disturb.

A path. It was probably right in front of them. Paths wound all through this part of the forest, some used often, others used so sparingly that sometimes the forest reclaimed them with new undergrowth. Sure enough, when Kelly reached the spot where she had seen the tinamou, she also found a narrow, almost hidden path. There were footprints in the moist earth. One was from a snake boot. The other was a flat, small indentation, much like one would expect from a young child. Kelly recognized the imprint as that of Pedro Meza himself. His prints were especially close to the boots, suggesting that one was helping the other to walk.

Kelly called out to the crew, who had lingered behind, watching her as they might one of the exotic toucans that sometimes flashed through the high canopy.

"No wonder they think she's lost it and gone native," Vic muttered.

21

Cho-Otz: Tree leaves used to treat high blood pressure

Elf lounged at a cafe table on the cement veranda of the Hotel San Ignacio. The late morning air was becoming more humid by the minute, smelling of wet leaves and the burnt oil from the town generator, which now chugged and clanked at regular intervals. The sound of the machinery was oddly comforting, like background music. Elf had been the only customer at the hotel's cafe when he first arrived and had amused himself by watching a green lizard dart from one section of the low brick wall to the other. Its skin shimmered like a sequined costume in the bright sunlight. A thin, red tongue shot from its round puckered mouth at regular intervals before the lizard slurped it back inside. Elf tried to feed the animal, but the only food he had to offer was the half-finished bottle of tepid Belikan that rested on his table.

"Sorry, buddy," Elf said and took a long swig. He didn't care for the bitter taste of the local beer, but he was grateful for the slight buzz that allowed him to relax. The trip back down the river had unnerved him. The canoe had come close to capsizing, even though Old Man Green hadn't flinched when the dugout had pitched dangerously as they slid down a rogue wave in the rapids. Elf had never learned to swim, and deep water terrified him. He stayed in the shallow end of swimming pools, never ventured into the ocean higher than his knees and always found the two-foot waves on the Jersey shore to be vaguely threatening. He still remembered dreams from childhood as vividly as if he'd had the nightmares the night before. In one, he'd fallen off a dock on a lake and caught his ankle in a rope used for moorings. He'd panicked when it managed to wrap itself around one of his bare legs like an octopus. No matter how hard Elf kicked, it only served to strengthen the grip of the rope. He gulped for air. When Elf opened his eyes in the darkness, for a moment he still felt as if he were underwater, about to drown.

Green had steered them through the worst, however, and Elf had arrived safely. He'd walked the two miles to the hotel, grateful to have his legs on solid ground. No cars had passed him on his solitary stroll even though it was a workday. The town, too, was empty except for a few men he noticed loitering outside a bodega. They had stared at him with a hostile indolence, like the stray dogs that seemed to be everywhere.

At the hotel, the young boy who greeted Burns and the crew the night before was standing behind the front desk as if he had never moved. Color brochures from the 1960s were stapled to the wall beside him, offering trips to Tikal, the great Mayan ruins just across the border in Guatemala. But there was no sign of other guests. When Elf asked about the missing videotapes, the boy had smiled, reached under the counter and presented him with a cardboard box with the Sony label.

Elf stared at the boy, dumbfounded. He hadn't expected to find the missing tape stock at all. He was sure the case had fallen in the river or had simply been stolen. But he'd volunteered to return to the town because he'd felt responsible. Without the tapes, the shoot was a bust and they would all look like fools back home.

Elf's first instinct was to hurry back to the research camp as quickly as possible. He knew he had just saved the shoot, and he looked forward to being something of a hero, at least in Burns's eyes. But he hesitated, picturing the river's swift, threatening current. Maybe this time he would not be so lucky. The young boy watched him with a calm, disinterested expression. His eyes were as dark as coffee grounds and gleamed like his coarse black hair, parted neatly at the side. Elf liked that he and the boy were the same height. He was usually the shortest person in any group.

"Is there a place to get a beer?" Elf asked. He decided he would need some time to get himself prepared for the trip back upriver.

"Cafe," the boy answered cheerfully and pointed to the back of the hotel.

"Not that porch out back where we had breakfast?" Elf asked. It had all the charm and comfort of a cement loading dock.

"Cafe," the boy repeated.

"Tell me, are there any other guests in this joint?" Elf asked.

Elf slid back in his canvas chair, letting the sun and alcohol massage him. The lizard was as still as a porcelain statue. An empty swimming pool gaped from the overgrown lawn beyond it. Hairline cracks were scattered across its alabaster walls like dark veins, sprouting bits of pale, anemic grass. A steel fence, by far the most recent update on the grounds, separated the deserted pool from the ragged green hill that rose beyond it.

The truth was that Elf was used to being stuck in cheap hotels. On location, crew were almost always given budget accommodations. There had been a few exceptions that Elf remembered fondly. Once he'd done a shoot on Oahu, Hawaii, and the producer had put them up in what was known as the Pink Palace, an oceanfront hotel on Waikiki Beach with a circular driveway and a marble lobby bursting with oversized vases of tropical flowers. He remembered hearing the surf from his room, realizing it was the only time in his life that he had ever stayed anywhere so grand.

Ernesto "Elf" Paladino lived only a few blocks from the soapstone house in Bayonne, where he'd grown up. It was an old industrial town across from New York's harbor, too far away to be attractive to Manhattan commuters and too poor to attract anyone interested in traditional suburban homes. So the town relied on itself and became tight-knit and suspicious of outsiders. One of Elf's aunts, in fact, took perverse pride in never having ventured across the river into Manhattan in the entire seventy-six years of her life. "Why bother?" she liked to say. "I got everything I need right here."

Elf looked at his watch, a waterproof Casio. It was close to noon. He'd arranged to meet Old Man Green at the river at one o'clock, which meant he was going to have to begin his hike back unless he could order a cab through the hotel. The sun had burned away the last remaining mists above the distant hills and was beginning to bore down on the jungle. Elf took one last swig of his warm Belikan. It was time to face the river. He picked up the case of videotape and strolled back inside the hotel. He was surprised to see a vanload of older American tourists at the front desk. They seemed stunned, a few of them gawking at the austere lobby as if they had arrived at the wrong address.

Elf waited for the group to sign in before he approached the boy at the desk about a taxi. He learned they were part of a Mayan Ruins tour and had just been driven from the airport at Belize City, following the same route Elf and the crew had endured the day before. The tourists, however, had detoured to the Belize Zoo, and it remained vivid in their imaginations. A tall, thin man with silver hair and thick glasses pointed to a poster of a jaguar on the wall.

"There she is," he announced as if it were the photograph of the very jaguar he'd admired in captivity.

Elf was surprised to find a familiar face. The driver had just stepped inside the double glass door and was grinning. Elf hurried over to meet him.

"Gilbert," Elf said. "This is great timing, man."

Still smiling, Gilbert nodded.

"You drove us yesterday, remember? The television crew."

Gilbert's smile faded, and he seemed to see Elf for the first time.

"You not go to the camp?" Gilbert asked, mildly puzzled.

Elf explained his situation and added that Mr. Green was due to meet him in less than an hour.

"Could you give me a lift to the dock?" Elf asked. "I was going to call a cab, but since you're here...."

"A taxi? In San Ignacio?" Gilbert grinned.

A few minutes later, Elf was back inside the familiar air-conditioned van, speeding to the outskirts of town.

"So you bring in groups every day?" Elf asked, fumbling for the seatbelt. Gilbert swerved to miss a pothole and sent Elf flying against the door.

"No, no. This week very busy. I'm happy."

"Are we in a hurry?" Elf asked.

The calm Elf had gained from the beer and the warm sun had vanished. Worse, in less than an hour, he was going to be alone in another dugout canoe, charging up the rapids under the steerage of the blind old man. Elf's growing fear inspired a new idea.

"You ever drive this van to the research camp?" Elf asked.

Gilbert nodded. "Very fast."

Elf could hardly believe his luck. He could hire Gilbert to drive him to the camp and avoid the river, at least until the entire television crew returned in a few days when all the shooting was over.

"How much would you charge?" Elf asked.

"Today?" Gilbert asked. "No today. Today is rain. Roads fill like the river."

"There's not a cloud in the sky," Elf said.

Gilbert grinned. "It comes very fast."

"I'll give you forty bucks, cash," Elf said. He took two twenty-dollar bills out of his wallet and laid them down on the dashboard. Gilbert studied them for a moment as if checking for counterfeit.

"Alright. Fifty," Elf said, adding his last ten-dollar bill to the dash.

Gilbert glanced up at the clear blue sky and grinned.

"We go," he said. In one effortless motion, Gilbert scooped up the bills, folded them in half, and slipped them behind one of his dark, worn socks as if it were a holster.

22

Xix-el-ba: A vining fern that is boiled to treat skin fungus

Frank nodded and hurried out into the sunlit path that coursed through the village like a dry riverbed. The heat bore into his face and eyes, a momentary pain that Frank had never really adjusted to, even after over a decade in the jungle. He followed the path to the road where his truck was parked, which was in the opposite direction of where he knew his wife had gone.

Frank resented the time Kelly gave to the little old man. She spent at least a few days a week with Pedro Meza, playing adoring pupil to the Mayan sage. Kelly had followed the same pattern at Harvard, fawning over Professor Shultes, the Pope of Ethnobotanists. These men could do no wrong, and Kelly acted more concerned for their welfare than her own. But her enthusiasm had been part of her charm. She exhibited a passion for living and knowledge that had attracted Frank immediately. But here in Cayo, her devotion made him feel overshadowed, first by the jungle research, then by the little old man.

Frank relaxed when he reached his pickup and climbed back in behind the wheel. Sometimes it was the only place that felt like home anymore. As he steered down the dirt road back toward the research camp, the deep disappointment he'd felt at the absence of Manuela drifted away. The excitement that he'd known that morning began to seep back into him like a smooth, smoky draw of Xmutz. *Salvia divinorum.* The name of the mint plant in Latin meant "divine leaf." It was a divine plan, to be sure. He was helping men and women in need, both here in Belize and the many Americans searching for self-discovery. It was a win-win scheme, the best he'd yet designed. The future had never looked so noble or so profitable.

A few miles out of town, however, Frank was reminded of another future. A tasteful, prefab wooden prairie house—not unlike those that had been built outside of his hometown of Chicago—was poised just beyond the dirt logging road. The expansive front windows of the living room mirrored the open fields and the cattle pens. Hundreds of acres of mahogany and spruce trees had been cleared to make way for the beef barons. After only a year in operation, the land was already semi-barren, the grasses consumed by the hordes of cattle and the unchecked runoff from the heavy rains common to Cayo. A company from El Paso had bought the land from the government for next to nothing and was siphoning its considerable profits out of the country. The only people who benefited from the operation, as far as Frank could see, were the hamburger lovers of America. Otherwise, the operation was destroying the native habitat faster than the logging companies. Frank would not miss the virgin jungle if it were to disappear, but he did mind the wholesale, mindless destruction of pristine land by corporate America. They were the world's strangler vines, living off healthy trees and people until they were sucked dry and rotted to an early death.

The Texans had hired experienced ranchers from Guatemala to actually run their operation. The family had visited the research camp soon after their Midwest prefab was nailed together. Their three children were as scrubbed and overly groomed as their middle-aged parents, a couple from one of Mexico's elite families. They reminded Frank of stories he read about plantation owners at the turn of the century: polite, restrained and thoroughly obsessed with clothes and manners.

He remembered Kelly had played the gracious hostess, even though the ranch was destroying the rain forest plants only a mile from the research camp. He wondered if she was trying to kill them with kindness, serving them wine and making Mexican chocolate milk for the kids. Frank thought she doted on the children, especially the youngest, a precocious five-year-old girl with long, black hair and wide, round eyes the color of tubroos bark. Kelly had been quick to take the little girl's hand and lead her just outside the porch to point out the macaws that often loitered on the roof of the house. Frank was surprised at the ease with which Kelly assumed a maternal role. It was out of character for the driven scientist who doted on plants, not kids.

A decade earlier, Kelly had not wanted anything to do with children. Plants and their medicinal properties were her offspring. She'd had no honest desire for motherhood, as he remembered. Of course, for his part, he'd never even entertained the idea of a family. He was content to have just the two of them. But that day, watching his wife stoop alongside the Mexican girl, engaging her with ease, Frank had been rudely reminded of his own rewriting of history.

He pictured—in full, living color—what he had allowed to dim with memory. Kelly stood by their bedroom window, the moon a ghostly white in the starless Mayan night behind her, telling him she was pregnant. The cicadas and jungle insects seemed to roar in the shocked silence that followed. Quickly, in what he would later understand was panic, she had announced it was a poor time to take on this enormous responsibility, neither fair to the child nor to the life's work to which they had committed themselves. Didn't he agree? Frank hadn't objected, had said nothing, in fact. He was overwhelmed. He was thrilled at the prospect of being a father, terrified of the responsibility, alarmed at the change a child would bring to his lifestyle. But he communicated none of this and resolved nothing for himself. He simply followed what seemed to be her conviction. It wasn't until long after the abortion in a Belize City hospital, in yet another recollection of that night, he heard the desperate cry of help in her voice and decisive manner. He heard the plea to take charge and demand to have the baby. But he was more frightened and confused than she was.

"I don't know how a couple survives this kind of thing," a friend back in the States had told him long after the abortion.

"You just don't think about it," Frank said. "That's how you do it."

The ranch faded from his rearview mirror, and Frank was soon headed downhill toward the research camp. With his plantings now soon ready for harvest, he needed to focus his attention on transportation. An importer-exporter in Pensacola was arranging for a pickup at a grass airstrip near San Ignacio, but it was up to Frank to transport all the crops to the airstrip. He'd thought to barge it down the river, a route that was fast and would avoid any wandering bandits or stray Guatemalan conscript soldiers. The problem Frank had yet to work out, however, was how he would get the harvested plants to the river and then on from San Ignacio to Belize City without arousing unwanted attention.

23

**Ku-che: Handful of grated tree bark is
soaked for six hours in water, then sipped
to treat bruises, falls and internal injuries**

B urns rested pensively on an old, soiled serape, watching the curandero searching a medicine bag for more healing leaves or bits of magic bark. The old man moved slowly and deliberately, handling the native medicine plants with the care of a jeweler. Pedro Meza was not what he imagined a bush doctor would look and act like. Physically, he was broken. The old man resembled a hunchback, his shoulders slumped, his skin wrinkled and sagging. His brilliant onyx eyes were intelligent and alert, but they peered out from an oval, mocha face, scarred with deep wrinkles that looked like cracks in a weathered clay pot. The flared nose, so common on all the Maya Burns had met, seemed battered more than proud. On camera, Burns was certain he would photograph as either a withered old man or a wise, primitive elder.

What the camera would not record was the feeling emanating from the man. Julie might call it his "aura." But Burns didn't believe in such things. What he felt was a natural healer, warmth that was at once deeply intimate and wholly impersonal. There was an unseen power that Burns would have scoffed at only a few hours earlier, before he was injured. He had trusted this old man at once, instinctively, and he was sure this healer's quality he felt was behind it.

He understood how Kelly might go native, or appear to, in the presence of this old man. He was a natural doctor, a presence that probably brought as much medicine to the ailment as his herbs. He seemed as worthy of study as his botanic knowledge.

Immediately, Burns began thinking about how he might capture this remarkable old man on film. Extreme close-ups to be sure. But more than anything, he would have to be filmed with patients, the camera recording their reactions to the bush doctor. The reactions would communicate what a participant felt but what remained unseen.

Burns attempted to stand up. It felt as if a knife had been stuck into his right thigh and he cried out, embarrassed by what he was afraid sounded like a weak and womanly yelp.

The curandero waited until Burns was looking at him. The old man held up one finger and waved it from side to side like an admonishing mother.

"No," he said. "Early."

Burns nodded, understanding that the poultice on his leg had merely numbed the gash, not miraculously healed it. He wasn't going anywhere yet.

The old man hobbled over to the hotplate and poured his brewed herbs from the pot into a chipped coffee mug with a Dallas Cowboy emblem on the side. He carried it over to Burns and offered it to him, urging him to drink it.

Burns blew over the top of the steaming water that now smelled even more off-putting than boiled cabbage. Again he was touched by the old man's instinctive kindness. The only person in his life that had ever shown such concern was his mother. Growing up, she had always been quick to comfort even his most benign injuries, such as a stinging paper cut from his school books or a stubbed toe. He took that maternal care for granted, as most children did.

She also mothered his quiet and remote father, bringing him coffee and pillows like a home nurse. As a young child, Burns barely noticed his mother's doting treatment of his father. But, after college, when Burns moved to the city, the women he knew were anything but deferential. Those he chose were independent-minded and self-conscious about taking care of men, frequently going out of their way to insist they weren't about to coddle anyone.

"Beve," the curandero urged, motioning to the cup.

Burns obediently took a sip, hoping this smelly brew might make it possible for him to stand.

The curandero knelt beside him and studied the mixture on his leg. He deftly brushed off a small clump and peered at the wound underneath. He nodded at the gash that stretched from just below the knee to the top of his ankle, the jagged strip dyed brown by the poultice.

"Bueno?" Burns asked.

The curandero grinned with his gums. "Bueno. Si. Bueno"

Outside, the lone bark of a wandering mutt was followed by the sound of familiar voices. He recognized Kelly's instantly. It had a softness and teasing lilt. Oddly, he found that it didn't make him picture her or yearn to do so. The sound was attractive in and of itself.

"Kelly!" the curandero said, excitedly.

A few moments later, two men blocked the sunlight at the door.

"It smells worse than a shit bucket in here," Vic said.

"What took you guys?" Burns asked.

"You're lucky, Burns. Your star is an animal tracker among her other talents. She tracked you."

"You do that on your fall, Burns?" Big asked, staring at the long mound of wet leaves and herbs covering his right leg.

"It's already feeling better," Burns lied.

"Lucky you didn't bust your head with that stunt," Vic said.

"Thanks, Colt. You're a sweetheart."

"Scared the hell out of me," Vic muttered.

The curandero met Kelly as she strolled into the bungalow. Burns was dismayed to see them hug warmly. The old man spoke quickly, gesturing to Burns. Kelly listened attentively, nodding as she absorbed the information. She looked at him with clear affection and rested on one knee beside him.

"I'm so glad Tato found you. Anything could have happened."

Before Burns could answer, Kelly was distracted by the mix of leaves and barks displayed on his leg.

"Fascinating," she said, leaning closer. "These plants have either antiinflammatory or antibiotic properties. This Ix-Canan, for example, is very commonly used for antiinflammatory applications. This Ku-che bark treats bruises. Pain?"

"None if I don't move."

"Really. No plant here, either alone or in combination, would carry anesthetizing applications."

"Maybe it was the tea," Burns said.

Kelly told him he'd been drinking Pasmo, an herbal tea the curandero brewed every day to relieve the rheumatism that plagued his old body.

"Then again, it might have been his marble," Burns joked.

"His marble?" Vic asked.

"A sastun. A divining instrument," Kelly explained. "It can be any object. Tato found the marble."

"The marble," Vic repeated.

Burns explained it was part of a fascinating treatment process they would have to attempt to capture on video. He described what the curandero had done with his leg, the prayers, the plants, the herbs, the sastun.

"We should film him with the people here, his patients. Follow the process across a range of ailments. Focus as much on the patients as the curandero. Go for the reaction shots to tell us what's going on that we can't see."

"You mean film this as soon as we have some tape," Vic said.

"The challenge is to show something that can't readily be visualized," Burns said, straightening with a burst of enthusiasm.

"That sounds more like a disaster than a challenge," Vic said.

"It's a wonderful idea," Kelly said. "Tato treats the whole person, not just bodily symptoms. Everything is brought into play—emotions, psychology, spirituality. There's no dividing line, no separation between illness and the person being treated."

Burns took a deep breath and attempted to push himself off the rug. He stood for a moment, testing the weight on his bad leg, then tried to walk. Big caught him before he fell.

"It's getting there," Burns insisted.

"His Nagual is very strong," the curandero said, speaking to Kelly in Spanish, as he poured himself some tea from the sauce pot.

"What are you talking about?" Burns asked.

"The spirit that protects you," Kelly told him. "Some Mayans believe everyone has a Nagual, an animal spirit that reflects who you are."

"I was lucky," Burns said.

"It was more than luck that he found you," Kelly said.

"You're going to tell me that the spirits are responsible," Burns said.

"Why couldn't it be?"

Burns recognized the look in Kelly's eyes. It was a complete, unwavering acceptance that he had seen reflected in the eyes of two Moonies he had interviewed in San Francisco a decade earlier. He had interviewed them for a story about the spread of cults in America. The two young Californians were smart, well-educated and articulate. But, like Kelly, they accepted Sun Young Moon's assertions uncritically. Seeing this quality in Kelly, however, was alarming. She was too well-grounded, too rational a scientist to believe this kind of comic book cosmology.

"So you believe in the Naguals?" Burns asked.

"What's so odd about that, Michael? Christians believe in protective angels and no one blinks an eye. Yes, I think someone or something looks after us in some way."

Burns shrugged. He wanted to get back to his planning for the shoot. When the videotape did arrive, he wanted to be organized so that not a moment was lost or wasted.

"When do patients usually visit?" Burns asked. As soon as Kelly translated the question, Pedro Meza pursed his lips, clearly disturbed. He spoke rapidly in the local patois this time instead of Spanish and gestured repeatedly to somewhere outside the bungalow. When he finished, Kelly looked stricken. She stood quietly, thinking.

"What?" Burns asked, impatient.

"A village boy died," Kelly said.

"I'm sorry about that," Burns said. "But how does that affect his practice?"

Kelly explained that the curandero had heard a boy's cry for help and rushed into the forest just beyond the village. He showed symptoms of a snake attack even though there were no bite marks on his body. The curandero had tried to get the boy to chew on a bark known for its ability to counter the potency of the venom. It didn't work, and the boy's parents found him dead with the root still jammed in his mouth.

"So they blamed him?" Burns asked.

"They don't blame him," Kelly answered. "They blame evil spirits."

Burns tried putting more weight on his injured leg. It was still too weak to walk.

"OK. I still don't get how that affects his practice."

"They believe the evil spirits have come here for a reason. So they do not want to tempt them by approaching a healer."

"So it's like a curse," Big said.

"Uayeb," the curandero blurted. "Uayeb."

Burns forced himself to take a step. He felt the pain all the way to his head, but he took another step anyway.

"Look," Burns said. "It's OK. People are superstitious the world over. But we can recruit some patients. We'll find the characters we need."

"Where?" Vic asked. "We're not exactly in the middle of a Manhattan."

Burns took another step, his leg throbbing now.

"First things first," he said.

THE FIVE LOST DAYS

24

Flor-de-Pato: Vine is chopped and served as a tea to treat hangovers, stomachache

Gilbert pushed the accelerator to the floor. The van barely surged ahead, but it somehow continued to climb the steep dirt road. Both he and Elf accepted the slow progress without complaint. Gilbert had shared a joint with Elf, and the strong pot had left them both dazed and dreamy. So it took longer than it might have to recognize the roadblock when the van came whining over the crest of the hill and dropped into the next gear.

Initially, Elf thought it was a gang of bored teenagers loitering around a broken-down truck. Except everyone was watching them approach, and each kid held some kind of rifle or automatic weapon. Too weird. These kids reminded him of a news story he'd worked on in East New York where gangs were a way of life and even ambulances refused to enter the neighborhood without a police escort.

"No good. No good," Gilbert said, his face drawn.

"No shit," Elf said.

"Soldiers from Guatemala," Gilbert said.

"Those kids are soldiers?" Elf asked. "When do they start down here? When they're ten?"

"They want money."

"So we'll give them a couple of bucks," Elf said, suddenly sober and hoping to appear unconcerned.

The soldiers waited for the van to come to a complete stop. No one pointed a rifle at them, but the boys cradled their secondhand weapons with a casual insolence. Elf wished Burns was with them. He would know how to deal with this situation. He'd intimidate these punks. Guns or no guns. Elf was sure of it.

"Buena," Gilbert said, greeting them with his wide smile. A schoolboy with smooth, round cheeks and a bowl of thick, black hair came to the window. Elf was encouraged. This soldier seemed about as threatening as an altar boy. But when his dark eyes regarded both of them with a cold, reptilian indifference, Elf was put on guard. There was also a nervous, racing buzz about him like someone who had drunk far too much coffee or, Elf thought, was high on uppers. The boy searched the interior of the van with quick, darting glances as though he expected something to appear at any moment.

"Donde vamonos?" he asked, bristling.

Gilbert clenched the steering wheel like it was a life raft.

"We go to the American research camp," Gilbert answered him in Spanish. "You know it?"

Elf watched the other teenagers. They had fanned out around the van, sniffing around its perimeter like a pack of dogs testing desirable new territory.

"Americanos?" the boy asked with a strained voice.

"He is American," Gilbert said, smiling at Elf. "He is with an American television crew."

The reminder that he was part of the American media gave Elf a curious sense of power. He was someone to be reckoned with.

"Televisione?" the teenager said. He looked at Elf but couldn't focus for longer than a moment. He was definitely high, Elf thought.

Like some of the pill-poppers he'd gone to school with.

"Where are your cameras?" the soldier asked as if he had caught them in a lie.

"With the other Americans," Gilbert explained. He nearly jumped when one of the soldiers suddenly opened the back double doors. They kept their guns drawn as if they expected something or someone to emerge.

"Where are the others?" the boy demanded.

"An American camp near San Antonio. Not far."

The boy's eyes lit with interest.

"San Antonio," the boy said back to him.

Gilbert nodded agreeably, happy to have struck upon some information the soldier might want.

"Tell him we got to get going," Elf said.

The boy soldier either understood English or simply felt the general tone of Elf's demand, because he turned instantly more hostile as if he'd been personally insulted.

"Get out," he ordered, stepping away from Gilbert's door. He raised the iron black nozzle of his rifle and, again, Elf wondered if the safety was engaged. He didn't want to get shot by accident.

"Give him twenty bucks," Elf said.

Gilbert didn't move. His hands remained glued to the steering wheel. A bribe would only increase their suspicion that he and the American were hiding something. Gilbert guessed it was a fugitive they were looking for, maybe someone important fleeing the brutal civil war. For years, Gilbert had heard stories about the brutality of the Guatemalan army. Innocent men, women and even children had been shot or burned alive for opposing the army.

"I'd give him the money," Elf explained, "but I gave you all my cash. Just give him twenty and I'll pay you back when we see Burns."

"Get out," the boy soldier repeated and raised his rifle higher, pointing it level with Gilbert's head. One of the other teenagers suddenly hopped inside the back of the van and began ripping up the carpeted floor.

169

Gilbert opened his door while keeping one hand on the steering wheel. He needed to show they had nothing to hide.

"Don't get out, you idiot," Elf snapped. "Just give him some cash."

The side of Gilbert's licorice black face shone now with patches of glimmering perspiration. He let go of the steering wheel, his long, bony fingers trembling.

"For Christ's sake, Gilbert! Give him the god damn twenty bucks!"

Gilbert finally turned to look at Elf as if he'd heard him for the first time. His eyes were wide and blank with fear. Maybe the American was right. A faint sheen of yellow shimmered at the edges like a blemished egg white.

"Get a grip, man," Elf snapped, "and give it to him."

Gilbert stepped out of the van, wincing when he found himself less than an arm's length from the end of the soldier's gun. But he remembered Elf's order, so he crouched down to recover the money from inside his socks, his usual hiding place for cash. But the boy soldier, afraid the Belizean was reaching for a concealed weapon, stepped forward and slammed the butt of his rifle against the side of Gilbert's head. It sounded to Elf like the crack of a baseball bat. Elf stared in disbelief as Gilbert pitched forward and collapsed onto the dry, dirt road.

"Who the hell do you think you are?" Elf demanded. But the soldier merely stared back at him with his lizard eyes and motioned for him to get out of the van. Elf was staying right where he was. He'd defy this punk with his rifle. At the same time, he recognized that he could well get himself killed. Reluctantly, Elf threw open his door in a calculated show of defiance and jumped out of the van.

Almost immediately, the ragtag group of soldiers started piling inside, hustling past Elf as if he weren't even there. Meanwhile, their leader had moved around the front of the van. He pointed his rifle at Elf's chest and motioned for him to move away.

"Donde Manuela?" the soldier ordered.

"I don't speak Spanish."

"Manuela," the soldier repeated.

"No comprendo, asshole." He was tired of these punks; kids no different, he thought, than the teenagers who loitered outside the corner convenience store in Bayonne, and his fear was overcome by a sharp, indignant anger.

The boy's dark eyes darted to the commotion in the van. One of the gang members had climbed in behind the driver's wheel and started the engine. He yelled for their leader to go. Vamonos. Vamonos. Elf peered into the tinted windshield, amazed at the brazen car-jacking. They were stealing the van in broad daylight, and no one was going to stop them.

The schoolboy leader swaggered past Elf to the passenger's seat. He jumped inside, slamming the door behind him, and the driver threw the van into reverse. Elf shook with an impotent fury. Somehow, he vowed to himself, those punks were going to pay. He'd hunt them down himself if he had to. They were not going to get away with this.

The van made a short, circular turn and sped back down the hill. Elf ran to Gilbert, who lay motionless in the dirt. A trickle of blood had pooled on top of the dirt alongside the Belizean's open mouth. The side of his jaw was swollen and discolored. But he was still breathing and when Elf grabbed his left shoulder to turn him over, Gilbert moaned and his glassy, unfocused eyes were blank with pain.

"Can you hear me?" Elf asked. Gilbert blinked slowly and moaned louder.

"You need help," Elf said. The empty logging road stretched for miles in the distance. "How far are we from the research camp?"

Gilbert opened his mouth to answer but only groaned. Elf waited for Gilbert to speak again, but even the slightest movement caused him too much pain. Elf knew he had little choice but to hike to the research camp no matter how far away it was. Gilbert had told him that the logging trucks did not operate until a month after the rainy season ended, so the likelihood of anyone's driving down the road to rescue them was remote.

"Do you think you can walk?" Elf asked. Gilbert's eyes remained glassy and unfocused, and Elf worried that the blow to the Belizean's head was even more serious than he feared. But Elf knew little about medicine or injuries—he'd always relied on the family doctor for any of his own problems—so he was at a loss to know what could be done for Gilbert immediately. He only knew that Gilbert needed help.

Crouching behind him, Elf slipped his arms under Gilbert's shoulder blades and lifted him to his feet. Elf steadied Gilbert from behind, his face and nose buried against the Belizean's back. His dark skin smelled dank, like wet clothes left for weeks in a hamper. Elf let go of him and stepped back. Gilbert immediately lost his balance and would have fallen flat on his face for a second time if Elf had not caught him.

"Great," Elf said, feeling Gilbert's dead weight. "This is just great."

Gilbert was far too heavy to carry. Where was Big when you needed him? Elf thought. The oaf could have slung this Belizean over his shoulder like a rucksack. Elf was too small and slight and he'd never worked out a day in his life. Where was the big weightlifter? Where was Burns? Where was anyone that could help him?

Elf had a sudden realization that made him fear for his own life. He was late returning to the research camp, but no one would know to search for him on the road. Burns would be expecting him to return by way of the river and, if they looked anywhere, it would be on the Macal. Outside of some great stroke of luck, no one would be venturing along the logging roads to rescue him or Gilbert. Elf felt a tinge of panic. What would Burns do in this situation? He wouldn't panic, Elf reminded himself. He'd stay cool, figure his way out. I can do that, Elf assured himself. I can do that.

Gilbert, he decided, should be left behind. Elf would return with help as soon as he reached the research camp. The only problem was that Elf wasn't certain whether the camp was a mile or ten miles away. In any case, it was a good idea to get Gilbert off the road and out of the sun. The trees were no more than twenty yards from where they stood. So Elf took a deep breath and hoisted Gilbert off his feet and tried to carry him to the shade. After only a few yards, however, Elf couldn't hold the body up any longer and found himself dragging

Gilbert to the tree line, like he was carting an oversized equipment case.

He tried to prop Gilbert against the tree trunk, but the smooth bark was too slick. Elf decided to leave him flat on the moist ground. When he stepped away, he was reminded of the first corpse he'd ever seen. He was working local news and had raced to Riverside Park with a crew who'd been dispatched to get what they could at a murder scene. When they arrived at a remote wooded section of the park, police tape had already been wrapped around the trees to mark the site, and the NYPD detectives were standing around in their navy blue windbreakers, chatting about the unusually warm spring weather. The body was sprawled under brush, black and white high-top basketball shoes poking from its hiding place. Its dark, olive-skinned face was smeared with dirt, its eyes closed, not wide open in the way Elf had come to expect from the movies. The boy's rigid calmness fascinated him. But the terror of what he witnessed did not sink in until later when Elf woke up in the early morning, the death mask in his mind's eye, staring back at him like a mirror.

Gilbert, however, was still breathing. His skinny chest rose and fell with regularity, and Elf could even hear a slight wheeze as the air passed through the Belizean's open, bloodied mouth. He told Gilbert he was leaving and would be back with help. But Gilbert showed no sign of having heard. Elf remembered hearing that someone with a concussion or head injury should not be allowed to sleep for fear of slipping into a coma. So he tried to rouse Gilbert, shouting and shaking him gently.

"Gilbert. I'm leaving, man. I'm leaving. You got that? You hear me?"

Despite his bending down to within inches of Gilbert's ears, there was no response. Elf sprang up suddenly, knowing instinctively that Gilbert's condition was getting worse. Yet he was now fearful of leaving him alone, virtually unconscious. But there was no choice. At least, Elf told himself, if he went for help, Gilbert had a chance. Out here, with nothing but the forest and the sky and a frightened guy from

Bayonne, there was little hope.

"I'll be back, Gilbert," Elf said, finally. "I'll be back, buddy."

He hurried to the road and headed in the direction of the research camp. After a few minutes, he allowed himself to glance back to the spot where Gilbert lay under the trees. He could make out the tips of his black rubber sandals, but little else. God protect him, Elf said to himself. Instinctively, he tapped his wet forehead and trembling chest with the fingers of his right hand, a gesture he used whenever he entered Saint Clement's Church in Bayonne. But it had been years since Elf had been to mass or even stepped foot inside St. Clement's, or any church for that matter. He looked up at the sky as he might glance at a holy cross. The sun had just begun its afternoon descent. He had a few hours of daylight left and prayed that it would be enough.

25

Frijolillo: Midwives do a pregnancy test by having women urinate on the leaves of this bush; if the leaves look scorched, a baby is due

Frank was expertly rolling a Xmutz cigarette, carefully pinching the thin paper between the thumb and forefinger of both hands, savoring the damp tobacco-like aroma, when he heard the footsteps. He exchanged looks with Carlos, who looked equally surprised. Reluctantly, Frank set aside the makings of his cigarette and crept out of the door and crouched in the shade of the tin awning to keep himself concealed. He spotted Burns immediately as the tall New Yorker hobbled up the road, the curandero at his side. Frank waited for them to pass, expecting the producer's crew, and especially his wife, to soon follow. But long after Burns had gone inside the curandero's bungalow, the road remained empty, the village retreating back into silence except for the low chatter of a Belize City radio station that came from the empty home of a nearby neighbor.

Frank stood slowly and went back inside. Carlos waited for an explanation, but Frank merely motioned to remain quiet. Clearly there had been an accident of some kind, and he feared it was somehow connected with the thwarted arrival of Manuela. He worried that Kelly and these filmmakers had also fallen victim to the same military threat. It wasn't uncommon for the Guatemalan militia to ignore the Belize border and do as they pleased. Only they had never dared come this far.

"Who was it?" Carlos whispered.

"A documentary producer," Frank answered. "Down here to do a story about Kel and her work. Looks like he had an accident."

"Si?" Carlos asked, impressed. "American?"

"New York City," Frank answered. "Dumb as doornails."

"Why do they come now?"

Frank stared at his friend with sudden alarm. He didn't know why the producer and his crew had chosen these days. It was an odd coincidence they had arrived only a day or so before the expected appearance of Manuela. Maybe they weren't as clueless as he supposed. Maybe, in fact, they were not really filmmakers or TV people at all.

"What is it?" Carlos asked. "What is troubling you?"

Frank remembered they had arranged to send one member of their crew to San Ignacio just that morning—the short guy they called Elf—but had been very evasive about why it was necessary. Kelly had helped make the arrangements with Mr. Green to get him downriver, but had never thought to ask why. Kelly had not been concerned, but Frank now felt he should have been more suspicious.

"I'm not sure, Carlos. But I got a bad feeling about these guys all of a sudden."

"You think they are with the government?"

"Yeah. My government. Not the Guatemalan."

Frank was disturbed by yet another recollection. Burns and his crew had actually done very little filming since they arrived. Other video crews he'd witnessed over the years shot like crazy, hour after hour after hour for a ten-minute story. Not these guys. They were uncertain, ill-at-ease, the way amateurs might be.

"I told them everything last night. Except her name," Frank said, now angry at his own naivete. He'd blurted out the story because of that arrogant producer who probably wasn't even a producer.

"Are you saying CIA? In little San Antonio?" Carlos laughed. "My friend, my friend—we are a tiny village of no importance."

Frank didn't think it farfetched or funny. It was common knowledge that the United States was aiding the Guatemalan government in their fight against the Marxist guerillas because those freedom-fighters were seen as communists. For the U.S., it was yet another front in the Cold War, and American operatives had been eager to lend a hand. Why wouldn't the CIA or some other clandestine arm of the U.S. government help to capture Manuela, who had been nothing but a thorn in the side of the Guatemalan strongmen? In the eyes of American cold warriors, this peasant woman, encouraging Mayans to stand up for themselves and their rights, was a communist, too.

Frank felt he knew. He had been branded a communist decades ago, back in Cambridge. Then, as now, if you protested the policies of the U.S. government, if you exercised your right of free speech to criticize a war, you were a communist. Patriots kept their mouths shut. They didn't raise their hands to question; they saluted.

Kelly's laugh suddenly sounded from the road. Frank bolted to the door instinctively. He found her strolling up the road with the video crew, unharmed and unconcerned. He was relieved she had not been confronted by militia wandering across the border. Still, he did not rush out to greet her. He remained concealed. He would watch and listen to what this crew did next. He had his own reasons for fearing they were government stooges, too. They could just as easily be DEA agents, searching for narco traffickers. Anything was possible these days.

"Frank," Carlos whispered. "Why are you hiding from your wife?"

THE FIVE LOST DAYS

26

**Ki-bix: The stem of this vine is boiled and
used to wash wounds to reduce bleeding**

Elf had no idea how long he had been walking. Maybe a mile.
Maybe more. Except for the occasional ascent up a hill and the
welcome descent that followed, the logging road meandered with a
numbing sameness. He distracted himself for a time by watching the
butterflies that swirled at the edge of the forest. Sapphire blues, apple
greens, blazing oranges and velvet blacks. But it wasn't long before
even their photogenic neon wings left him bored and listless. Sometimes he would simply close his eyes and march forward like a sleep-
walker, listening to the birds and the occasional howler monkey. The
monkeys sounded like barking dogs, and there were moments that
he imagined himself back in Bayonne, strolling along a side street in
mid-afternoon, real dogs barking from unseen alleyways. He could
even smell the city rising from the blacktop and the gutters. It was the
familiar smell of home.

The jungle that towered on either side of him smelled like a working greenhouse, a pungent mixture of wet plants and soil and decay.

The thick humidity challenged his breathing the further he walked. Elf felt at times as if he were trying to breathe through a wet cloth. But it was the bald, white sun that was most unforgiving. There was no escape from its fierce heat and unrelenting glare. It tortured his every step and thought and hope. He knew his entire face had long since been burned. His cheeks, especially, felt as though they had been pricked by thousands of tiny pins.

His tube of sun block, like his bottled water, had been left in the van. He could picture the ribbed plastic bottle wedged against the box of videotapes under the front seat, protected from the sun. He imagined the punk soldiers guzzling the fresh, clean water as they took their joy ride to the border. Why hadn't anyone warned him about the soldiers? Or was that the reason Burns had chosen the canoes for travel in the first place?

Burns was not going to be happy with him. No tapes. No documentary. Elf again rehearsed how he would explain the incident to Burns. The producer would want an explanation for why he had taken it upon himself to hire Gilbert instead of traveling upriver. The dory ride was considerably faster than the logging road. Burns would be livid about losing more time. Elf knew he would have to lie. He was embarrassed that he had never learned to swim and was as wary of deep water as any child. He would have to turn the story around and claim he happened to run into Gilbert at the hotel and that Gilbert—not him—had insisted on driving him to the camp.

Elf felt it was a necessary lie, one of those everyday white lies people use to get along in an imperfect world. The only person that might be offended by the lie was Gilbert. Unlucky Gilbert. Why had he waited so long to hand over the cash? Elf still didn't understand. They'd both be walking this route if the man had just handed over the money.

Elf started up a new hill. It was an easier climb than the other hills had been. Only when he glanced into the blue sky without squinting did he recognize why there was less struggle. The sun was softening into a cool amber. It was loosening its grip, slowly fading into harmlessness. The sudden change gave Elf new hope. Maybe there would finally be some sign of the research camp once he reached the crest of the hill.

A few minutes later and the world he'd known all day vanished. At first, he worried his exhaustion was playing tricks on his mind. But the flat, treeless field ahead was too expansive to be some kind of tropical hallucination. In the far distance, he recognized cattle and what he was sure was at least a mile-long fence. Elf had never seen such a vast ranch. The jungle had been completely razed on either side of the road. In the midst of this sprawling land was a modern ranch home like he'd seen off Route 4 in New Jersey.

Elf stopped at the entrance to the house, taking a moment to catch his breath. He faced a strangely familiar wooden door. It was like the well-to-do Jersey suburbs. He pushed the doorbell button near the molding, and a chime echoed pleasantly inside. He waited impatiently and, when no one appeared, he pushed the button again. Still no one. Elf banged on the door with a clenched fist. What is it with rich people? he thought. They have these magnificent houses that are the envy of the world, but they're never home. Elf had been on countless shoots in wealthy neighborhoods where dwelling after dwelling inspired awe, but not a single person blemished their parklike grounds. They reminded him of the marble mausoleums in the Bayonne cemetery. If wealth entombed you in this cold and lifeless existence, he wanted none of it.

Elf backed away from the door and shuffled around to the side of the house. He peered in through one of the expansive wall-to-wall windows. A bright, rainbow-colored Mexican rug covered part of the polished floor. The country-style furniture and oversized pillows were showroom quality. Tall, floor-to-ceiling plants were parched, many of the green leaves withered to the color of tobacco. Whoever lived here, Elf concluded, hadn't been around for awhile.

As he stepped away, Elf glimpsed a strange reflection in the window. An angry red mask with cracked lips and bulging, bloodshot eyes glared back at him. He barely recognized his own image. Fearfully, he reached up with his thin, bony index finger and gently tapped his right cheek. He winced as though he'd pricked himself with a needle. His stiff, cardboard skin was hot to the touch.

Water. The wretched thirst that he'd put out of his mind for so long came rushing back, more violently than ever. He searched frantically for a source of water outside the house, but there was no hose or faucet. He ran to the locked door and banged with his fists and his shoes. But no one came and there was no getting inside. He considered smashing the window but didn't have the strength. He lingered by the entrance, deciding what to do.

The road led somewhere, and he hoped it was the camp. If not, he felt sure there would be a village or at least another house, one that was inhabited and had water. Absently, he licked his lips with his leather tongue and started from the sting of the cracked skin. But he was grateful to taste a delicate drop of wet blood. It was almost like water. He turned, finally, and walked back onto the empty dirt road, wondering how long he had before the darkness descended. He pictured Gilbert at the edge of the jungle, gaining consciousness, calling out for him. Immediately, Elf picked up his pace, determined to find help somewhere.

27

Cruxi: Leaves of this vine are boiled to prepare a bath to treat nervousness and sleeplessness

Burns had a new dilemma. The curandero was willing to be filmed as he treated patients of the village. The problem was there were no patients.

"He believes patients come to him because they are called to him," Kelly said. "He has never gone in search of patients. That makes no sense to him."

"But we don't have time to sit around and wait for ill people to show up," Burns said. "If we don't find some patients in this village willing or needing to be treated, and if he won't treat them, we don't have a film."

Burns was being dramatic, hoping it would inspire Kelly to help him at all costs. She wanted and needed this documentary as much as he did. A good program, he knew, could save both her research camp and some of the curandero's vast knowledge of healing plants.

"You still have a few days," Kelly reminded him. "And today, with the funeral, is not the best time to approach the people of San Antonio village."

"There's no perfect time for this," Burns said. "I've had to deal with reluctant characters before."

"I don't think you understand, Michael."

"Sure I do. They're feeling sensitive and vulnerable after a young boy dies. They're struggling with their own fear and grief. But I've had to go up to mothers after their kids have been shot or stabbed and get an interview. It's not easy and it's not what I would choose. But sometimes you don't have time to wait."

He felt Kelly's clinical gaze evaluating him. He remembered one assignment when the story required him to visit the home of a teenager who had been murdered the night before. Burns had been ordered to get an exclusive interview with the bereaved family before his TV competitors did. He had stood outside the family's home for a long time, deciding whether or not to go through with it. When he did, and marched up to the door with his cameraman and soundman, he'd been startled to find the parents agreeable. He hadn't been proud of that moment, but it had taught him that it was impossible to predict how people would react to cameras and being on television.

"This is different," Kelly said, finally. "First, many of the villagers will be distrustful of the curandero because the boy died in his hands. Think about it. How would you feel about seeing a doctor when his most recent patient just died on the operating table?"

Burns frowned and shifted his weight onto his makeshift crutch. The curandero had given him the branch of a tubroos tree that had been cleaned and carved by one of the men in the village after everyone had returned from the funeral.

"He treats patients from all over Cayo, correct?" Burns asked.

"Of course," Kelly said. "Even accident-prone New Yorkers."

Her coquettishness thrilled him, but he pretended not to be affected.

"Too bad we weren't filming when he was doing his magic on my leg," Burns said.

"There's another thing," Kelly said. "Anima."

"Spirit?" Burns said.

"Yes. There are some Maya who still believe the camera steals the soul. So they're not going to let you film, especially at a time like this."

"The curandero is Mayan. He had no problem with the camera."

"We don't have tape to go with it anyway," Vic reminded him.

"Elf is sure taking his time," Big agreed.

Burns gazed up at the afternoon sky, the light already shifting to a warmer hue, signaling the approach of the photographic luminance of magic hour. He not only had little to film, but darkness would not be far off.

"What are you saying?" Kelly asked, suddenly. "You don't have tape?"

Burns avoided her eyes.

"We have some, of course," Burns answered, pretending to look over the squat bungalows of the village. "Just not as much as we might be."

"Cut the crap," Vic snapped. "Tell her the truth. We screwed up. We don't have tape and that's why we sent Elf back. Why pretend?"

Burns shook his head, exasperated at Vic and himself. In the past, he would have had the time to research the story properly, to set up all the elements to be filmed, to anticipate most of the challenges inherent in a shoot like this. In the past, they might even have sent him to do a brief scout to actually see what they were getting into. But not anymore. Now news and documentaries were funded and assigned with nanoseconds in mind. Get the story fast, get done fast, get it on air fast. Time was money, and that was what mattered.

"Why didn't you say something, Michael? Why keep it a secret?"

Burns looked up and, for a moment, Kelly's questioning became an echo of Julie's. Why couldn't he just say what he was thinking? There was a disconnect in him, an inability to speak without premeditation as though he feared being found out.

"I thought it would be easier to just take care of it quietly," Burns heard himself say. "I was afraid for the shoot, the film."

Kelly listened calmly, without judgment.

"And I didn't want to look like an idiot."

Where on earth did that come from? Burns asked himself. Since when did he start making lame excuses?

"Maybe Elf is already back at the camp," Big said.

Kelly quickly offered to drive them back to the camp in her husband's pickup, which she had spotted behind Carlos's bungalow when they had first arrived in the village and gone to the curandero.

"Look, we can't just throw away the light or the time," Burns said, annoyed. "I want to do at least a short interview with the curandero while we're here. We have enough tape for that, Vic."

"Fine with me," Vic agreed. "I want to get something out of that long trek you just put us through."

Burns hobbled back inside the curandero's bungalow to look for a good area to stage the interview. The angry light of the afternoon sun punched through fist-sized holes in the wall, creating rough circles of light on the dirt floor. Dust particles swirled in small but fierce rays that provided just enough illumination to film the curandero's deep-set eyes and weathered face.

Kelly spoke to Pedro Meza in simple Spanish, explaining where he was being asked to sit and assuring him that she would be present the entire time, translating. The curandero sat as requested, but his old, weary eyes darted from one blanc to the next, hostile and suspicious. It was obvious the old healer was cooperating only because of his relationship with Kelly, who had persuaded him that some of his medicinal knowledge could be preserved by the camera.

Vic positioned himself a few yards in front of the old healer, then knelt on both knees to make the curandero's eyes level with the camera lens, a point of view that brought intimacy and an air of candidness to the shot. Once, Burns had made the mistake of setting the camera angle below the subject which made him appear more demonic than heroic. It had fit the CEO being interviewed, but neither the network nor his boss was pleased with the choice.

Burns used his crutch to ease himself to the ground and to sit as close as possible alongside the camera, another subtle placement that would encourage a sense of viewer intimacy. As the curandero spoke to Burns, his eyes would be filmed just shy of looking directly at the viewer, maximizing the voyeuristic pull of listening to a talking head on television.

"Kelly, sit where you're comfortable translating," Burns instructed after he had found his own spot. "We're recording this so we'll hear you but not me. The only person on camera will be the curandero. "

"Fine with me," Kelly said, sounding genuinely relieved.

"You're not off the hook," Burns said. "You're back in the starring role as soon as we get the new stock."

"Don't hurry on my account," she said, smiling playfully.

"*If* we get the stock," Vic said.

"Later we'll figure out a way to convince these Maya to be on camera," Burns said.

Kelly smiled at him, certain he didn't know what he was dealing with.

THE FIVE LOST DAYS

28

Cordonsillo: Leaves of this shrub are mashed and mixed with water and drunk to treat headaches

Pedro Meza was running through the forest. He moved with a youthfulness he'd not known for decades. Despite the utter darkness, he ran without fear as if he knew every step by heart. Yet the curandero had no sense of his destination. He simply ran, following his bare feet as they sprung from each step into and out of the soft earth. Suddenly, he leapt out of the forest and onto what he recognized as the logging road, the wide lane that his own people had carved out of the forest without the least attention to the invaluable trees and plants they killed along the way. They did not accept that these trees and plants were an extension of their own flesh and blood. These leaves and roots and the living bark were healing spirits, waiting to be called upon for help. Few among his own people believed this anymore. Most assumed that they were separate and distinct individuals bounded by the physical body. They believed themselves to be apart from the natural world, making contact with it only through their eyes and ears and other senses.

Pedro Meza turned without knowing why and ran up the road, in the opposite direction of the village. He was moving toward San Ignacio and the beginning of Western Highway, which led to the coast, and Belize City. But he was stopped, suddenly, by the unmistakable cry of a wounded animal. The moan pierced the busy hum of the forest night. With the instincts of a healer, the curandero turned and ran toward the cry. But no sooner had he reacted than the moan vanished. He stopped, waiting for it to resume. But there was only the hungry chatter of unseen monkeys rattling the tree limbs. Had he simply mistaken the sometimes anguished screech of a monkey for a human cry? Soon, however, he managed to catch a glimpse of a pair of black, outstretched wings, floating in a moonlit circle. The lone vulture was joined by another and another until the trinity glided in unison, waiting for their chance to descend.

Pedro Meza opened his eyes, finally, and looked about his dark room. He'd fallen asleep just after sunset. The dream had awakened him, and he knew there was a reason. Throughout his lifetime, even before he became a healer and used dreams to help him discover the source of his patients' illnesses, the curandero knew that dreams were significant. They were a dialogue between the visible world and the real world of the unseen. The spirit world made itself known through dreams.

The curandero rolled over onto his knees and pushed off his padded bed mat. His knee joints snapped like dry twigs when he stood up straight. The rest of his aging body ached as it always did when he first woke. He still felt tired, as if he hadn't slept at all. He trudged to the door of his bungalow and stretched, searching the moonless sky. The smell of approaching rain invigorated him. He welcomed a long, cleansing storm.

The ground under his bare feet was cool in a way the curandero hadn't felt in the dream. His slow, heavy steps were also a contrast to the feline nimbleness of his run. Clearly his spirit self was engaged. But to what end? He gazed up at the night sky again, but no clues appeared. The answer to his question was as hidden and inscrutable as the stars masked by the storm clouds.

Pedro Meza went back inside his bungalow and plugged in his hotplate to make his Pasmo tea. The radios had all been turned off in the village, and most of his neighbors were asleep. The jungle chattered in place of the DJs from Belize City, a welcome relief. The curandero collected leaves for his tea and dropped them into his tin mug. The action made him remember the television crew when they asked him to perform this same movement over and over again for their camera. Kelly had explained that it would remember all that he said and did, but Pedro Meza had known infants who learned faster. If the television was to preserve his healing knowledge for future generations, as Kelly promised, Pedro Meza remained skeptical at best. Yet the blancs had gathered around their camera as though it were more intelligent, important and powerful than any one of them. The tall blanc named Burns, especially, had watched everything with intense concern, as if he doubted that his camera and recorder would remember all the words.

The dream, he decided, must in some way be connected to the tall blanc and his machines of illusion. Why else would he have found himself on the logging road, a path he rarely ever took? Blancs used that road for their trucks piled high with the bare, limbless corpses of the trees. The curandero had no use for the logging road. Forest paths took him anywhere he needed or wanted to go. Clearly the dream was aimed at those who would use the road.

For Pedro Meza, there was no coincidence, only connections. When he had stumbled upon the tall blanc on the bank of the river, he assumed there was a reason for the unlikely meeting. At first, he guessed that it was merely a timely call of the Healing Spirits. But as the tall blanc crawled onto the muddy bank, Pedro Meza was distracted by a sudden disturbance in the brush. He caught only a glimpse of the animal's lean, powerful shoulders before it darted silently into the shadow of the forest. A Nagual. The protective spirit surrounded and supported the injured blanc as solidly as the deep roots supported the trees that towered above him. Yet, later, while Pedro Meza treated him at his home, the tall blanc seemed as blissfully unaware of his own animal spirit companion as a child who takes his parent's support for granted.

There were, of course, many of his own people who neither recognized nor believed in the presence of Naguals, just as they refused to accept the work of spirits behind their own actions. They thought him drunk, mad or simply senile when he pointed out their own Naguals. They laughed or snickered behind his back, sometimes even to his face. The curandero sees angels of the dead everywhere, they jeered. He was made to feel like a relic of a distant, uninformed past.

Recognizing the Naguals, however, was essential to Pedro Meza's healing work, and he ignored the ridicule. Plants and medicines alone could not cure most patients. Illness was as intimately linked to a person's spirit as it was to his body. The tall blanc, for example, carried an injury within him that was far more debilitating than the puncture wound on his leg. The Nagual had prevented his drowning in the river and helped him to reach the village. But Pedro Meza had discovered another, more worrisome injury in the man's body. He'd felt an unusual constriction in the jawbone and skull of the blanc, a stiffening that resisted every probe of his fingertips, and he found it extended to the man's wide shoulders and chest. When Pedro Meza had consulted his sastun, it had gleamed alternately dark and light in the full sun, its natural translucence dimmed—much like whatever shadow of fear or pain the blanc clung to within himself. Over time, Pedro Meza was certain even the tall blanc's powerful Nagual would be unlikely to protect him against this unseen danger. The curandero had treated other patients with a similar inner constriction that expressed itself through illness or sleeplessness or, in a few rare cases, persistent headaches. Through the course of treatment, he discovered some of these patients harbored deep resentments or jealousies against loved ones, clinging to their disappointment until it hardened into a knot in the body. As a result, an essential part of their cure was the recognition and removal of these debilitating feelings. If they did not cause the illness, the curandero was sure they at least impeded any plant-based cure.

But Pedro Meza did not know the tall foreigner, nor could he communicate well enough with him to draw out the source of that unseen wound or fear. So the curandero had treated the tall blanc for it as best he could, having him drink tea of the Ix-canan, the most sacred plant of the Maya.

Pedro Meza shrugged. Even now, he still did not know why he had been called to treat the tall blanc. Outside his dark bungalow, the forest was pensive, anticipating the rain. He peered out into the warm, still air, wondering if the vision of the black-winged vultures drifting over the logging road was, in fact, an omen. An omen meant for him, not others. He was an old man, after all. He knew his own death was not far off.

But why had he felt so youthful as he ran through the forest? Surely, this was not an image of weakness or death. The vision teased him with interpretations. If only he had a few more clues to help him solve the puzzle the spirits had sent him, he thought. So Pedro Meza decided to do what he had always done when a dream or a vision had roused him in the middle of the night. He would add one precious herb to his tea, a minty leaf that generations of healers had used, however sparingly. *Salvia divinorum.* The leaf of visions. Then he would go back to bed and wait until visited by another dream from the spirits, who would fill in what he did not know. He trusted in them, and they would lead him to where he was needed.

Pedro Meza gathered three of the sacred mint leaves and held them between his forefinger and thumb and raised them up over his head, much as the Spanish priests lifted their unleavened bread during a mass. Pedro offered his leaves to each direction of the sun—east, west, north and south—turning each time to face the life-giving movement of that sacred incandescent orb. Finally, he let the leaves drop into the hot, steaming water and whispered a prayer. He called for assistance to the spirits of his father and his father before him, lifelong curanderos who had taught Pedro many years before. He called to the Maya spirits of healing. He called to Mother Earth. The steam wafted through the dark and drifted out the door with a sud-

193

den, stiff breeze. The curandero stopped, startled by the wind. Ik was the name given by the Mayan language. The evil wind. The rain fell in the next instant, pouring out of the sky, banging like angry fists against his tin roof.

29

**X-anal: Leaves and flowers mashed
and applied to infected sores**

Kelly didn't ask Frank about his meeting with Manuela right away. She was too high on the interview they had filmed with the curandero, gushing about the performance of her beloved Tato.

"Frank, you've got to get us back," she said, as she hurried to meet him outside of Carlos's bungalow. "Wait until you see this. I can't wait to watch the replay."

Burns and his two men trailed just behind her. He glanced at the producer's makeshift crutch and the plantain leaves wrapped around his thigh and tied with long strings of weed. He recognized it as the curandero's handiwork.

"What did you do to your leg?" Frank asked.

"Slipped on a rock," Burns said, shrugging.

"All that from a rock?"

"That's right," Burns answered with a quizzical expression.

As they sped along the dirt road, bouncing back toward the camp, Kelly began recounting each moment of the interview, quoting her mentor's wisdom about medicine and healing. Frank was happy for her, but over the years he had heard much of it before. Burns, he noticed, didn't seem to be paying attention either, focusing intently on the blazing red sky with the foreboding of a mariner reading rough weather in the color of the sunset. His distracted manner only made Frank more suspicious about what this producer was really doing here in Cayo.

"This may be only another interview for you, Michael," Kelly said, "but this is history. This is knowledge that would otherwise vanish without your cameras."

"There! There!" Burns cried out. "It's Elf!"

Elf had seen them first and was waving his arms high in the air. Frank brought the truck to a shuddering halt a few yards before they reached him, smothering Elf in a cloud of dust.

"Burnsie," Elf called out. "Am I happy to see you!"

Burns was puzzled by the sight of Elf's scorched face.

"Do we have any water?" Kelly demanded. "Frank. Is there any in the truck?"

Frank hurried back to retrieve the emergency bottle he always kept behind the seat. There was never enough drinking water for this tropical heat.

Burns peered at Elf's swollen red face. A whitened blister on one side of his cheek had popped, and yellow pus dripped down like candle wax. Another blister was rising, threatening to split open as well. But what sickened Burns was the news of the brazen mugging by the soldiers in broad daylight. It was more menacing, more vile than anything he'd heard about in the city. Burns felt personally violated, and it nearly choked him with a rage he'd never felt before.

"They can't get away with this," Burns managed to say. "They can't."

The water from the bottle was dribbling over Elf's chin as he gulped as much liquid as he could.

"They do. And they can," Frank said. He stood alongside Elf now.

"They sound like they were militia from Guatemala and they, like their government, don't pay any attention to the Belize border. They go and do as they please."

"What about the Belize army? The Belize government?" Burns demanded.

"You see any?" Frank asked.

Burns felt a hand on his shoulder suddenly. He recognized it was Vic, delivering a gesture to calm him down.

"The last thing we need is to get caught up in a war," Vic said.

Elf shook his head.

"Burns," he said. "I have to tell you. The videotapes were in the van. A whole fresh case."

Burns released an odd, muffled chuckle. Everything that had happened so far could be traced to that one small oversight—not making sure that raw stock was on board before they headed upriver. With that seemingly minor oversight, all hell had broken loose. But Burns was laughing to himself because he realized he didn't give a damn about the video right now. What he worried about was Gilbert, the amiable fixer who had generously set them off on this journey.

"How far back did you leave him?" Burns asked.

"Miles. I don't know. But Gilbert's out there. He was hit real bad."

No one had to speak the obvious. The sunlight was waning rapidly now. Even if they went on a search for Gilbert this minute, it would be in the dark.

"Well we have to go," Kelly said. "We cannot leave an injured man alone in the jungle like bait for the animals."

"How do we see out there?" Frank asked. "That's a lot of real estate we're talking about."

"We got lights," Vic said. "They're not called sun guns for nothing."

"But Elf here won't be able to recognize where we are in the darkness."

"Yeah he will," Burns objected.

"I know I can find it," Elf insisted. "I know I can."

"Frank?" Kelly asked. Burns was jealous of the intimacy he heard in that single, endearing syllable.

"OK," Frank said. "Let's go. Elf up in the cab with me. Everyone else in the back of the pickup."

"We'll need to run by the camp," Vic reminded them. "Unless you want to use matches."

Burns searched the black, starless sky for a glimmer of the rising moon. But the sky, like the passing trees and the dirt road beneath them, was hidden behind the darkest night he had ever witnessed. He could not see his own hand, let alone Kelly, Vic or Big, who shared the back of the pickup.

"Frank!" Kelly yelled, straining to be heard above the wind and the truck's engine. "Do we need to be going this fast?"

When there was no answer, she yelled again, only this time she was answered by the truck plunging into a deep pothole, tossing her against Burns. He caught her and held on to keep them both from being bounced out.

"Hey, moron," Vic screamed. "You almost threw us out with the lights!"

"What?" Frank yelled back.

Burns held onto Kelly, telling himself it was for their own safety. But the closeness and warmth of her body thrilled him. Her strong shoulder fit snugly against his side, and her hair smelled of the damp, charged night. He noticed, with pleasure, that Kelly made no motion to move away from him.

"This is gonna be a bitch of a ride," Vic said, less than a foot away from them.

But they might as well have been in another world. Burns hoped this ride would go on into the night even though he knew that was impossible. Without a word spoken, Kelly nestled her head against him, snug under his chin with a natural intimacy and familiarity . He kissed her hair silently, intoxicated by her. He could see nothing in this absolute darkness, yet she felt more beautiful than any woman he'd ever held. She was so strong, so resolute, so impassioned by her calling, it was a wonder to behold. It didn't matter to him what she looked like as a woman, an admission that utterly astounded him. He didn't think to give it a name. But he knew he was heading into dangerous territory.

Frank had driven along this stretch of road too often not to recognize it as much by feel as by sight. The trailhead that led to the clearing where his *Salvia divinorum* flourished was difficult to detect from the road, even in daylight. But Frank had worked too long not to feel as if he could step out of his truck at any moment and march straight to his concealed trailhead. It was exactly the reason he had an overwhelming urge to get away from here as quickly as possible.

"My face is on fire," Elf said.

"It looks it," Frank said.

The rains erupted out of nowhere. One moment they were driving along a dirt logging road, the next moment everyone and everything was being pounded by a downpour. It was another thing Frank couldn't stand about living in this place.

"Oh, God. Not rain," Elf blurted.

"Do you see anything out there?" Frank said, wishing he hadn't volunteered to try to find this Belizean driver. He'd have been better off to stay uninvolved and letting Burns and his covert buddies deal with it.

"Yeah, rain," Elf said.

"Don't be cute," Frank told him. "We find something soon or I'm turning around."

"Tire tracks!" Elf said. The headlights illuminated deep, semicircular tracks in the road ahead, filling up with the black sheet of rain. Elf explained that the tracks had to have been made by the van since the soldiers had spun in a circle before speeding off down the hill. Gilbert lay just inside the forest nearby.

"Anyone could have made those tracks," Frank grumbled.

"Who?" Elf asked. "Not one god damn truck passed me all afternoon."

Frank stopped the truck and threw the transmission into reverse. "What are you doing?"

"Turning around," Frank said. "While we can still make it back."

"We can't turn around," Elf said.

Frank didn't respond. He was concentrating on the tires, hoping they still had traction on the fast-softening road. With luck, he was confident they would make it to the research camp. But it occurred to him that the search for the Belizean driver would almost certainly resume tomorrow if he wasn't found tonight. Kelly would insist on enlisting help from the villagers in San Antonio, and he didn't want dozens of the villagers stumbling upon his sacred mint, even if it was unlikely they would recognize what it was.

"OK," Frank agreed, throwing the gear into park. "We can look more. But there isn't much time."

Frank waited, staring at the rain falling across the headlight beams.

"I ain't going out there alone," Elf said.

"Somebody has to stay with the truck," Frank said.

"But I don't have a light," Elf said, turning and staring out his open window. "Burns has the sun gun."

Frank screamed for everyone to get out. This was where they could search for the missing Belizean driver on foot using the HMI sun gun.

"I ain't stepping out of this truck without a light," Elf insisted.

Frank took the truck out of park and turned it so that the headlights faced the forest. But the heavy rain doused even the high beams long before they reached the black trees.

"That's the best we're gonna do," Frank said. "It's up to you."

"No way," Elf said. "I don't know what's out there."

"Your friend is out there."

"Friend?" Elf snorted. "I caught a ride with the guy. I've only known him for twenty-four hours."

"Well, my wife is out there now," Frank said. "Let's go."

Frank turned off the engine and yanked out the keys without uttering another word. He stepped out of the truck, sinking in mud up to his ankles, and slammed the old, rusted door behind him. He marched toward the forest, following the high beams that he had left on. Soon, however, he left their pale white glow and trudged further into the darkness. He preferred walking without the aid of light, liking the exercise of his other senses to help guide his movements. He'd spent many early evenings around his crop, moving without a flashlight or any other illumination that might call attention to himself. He'd almost liked the jungle at times like these.

"Wait," Elf yelled behind him. The sound of his door slamming was quickly followed by a genuine wail of pain. No doubt the rain slapping his sunburn. But there was nothing to be done about it, and Frank continued walking through the mud.

He was disappointed when he spotted the TV light, blazing like a surreal white torch along the edge of the forest. He'd hoped to find this Belizean driver long before Burns.

THE FIVE LOST DAYS

30

Cucu: fruit is crushed and applied to boils and skin sores

The sun gun bathed Gilbert's body in a bright, white theatrical glow. Kelly stepped out of the darkness and knelt down alongside him. Bugs snapped and sizzled through the vapor slowly forming as the TV light's heat mixed with the cooler rain. Kelly leaned close enough to kiss him, eyeing him clinically as she knew she must: the thick, glistening blood flowing out of his ear, spilling over dark, dried patches from earlier in the evening; the gash near his forehead, which had deformed his round, smooth head; the subtle tremor of his eyelids. She knew enough about internal medicine to recognize that the Belizean had likely suffered severe hemorrhages.

Kelly searched for other signs of injury. But she stopped when she felt his ankles and bare feet. They were cold, much cooler than the rest of his body. His hands, too, were losing their warmth. Kelly let go of them gently as if his hands were as fragile as a sun-dried leaf.

"He needs a hospital," Burns said.

"Might be too late for that," Vic said, standing alongside him.

"Gilbert. Hey. It's me. Elf. We got help. We got help."

Kelly began chanting, a low, almost imperceptible prayer she had learned from the curandero. It was a plea for assistance from the Mayan spirits. There was no herb, no root, no medicine that could stem the flow of life from Gilbert's body. But there was hope and faith and the promise of a miracle. She'd seen others fall into a coma only to step out of it under their own power. What else could explain it but the intervention of the healing spirits?

"Let's get him to the truck," Burns urged.

There was a splash of footsteps behind them, and in the silence that followed, Kelly knew that her husband recognized what Burns did not. She resumed chanting, louder, more insistent, as if she were competing with the rain and the cacophony of the interior forest beyond. Suddenly, she felt a change, even though there was no physical manifestation. Gilbert's presence was sinking, draining away. She felt his leg just below the knee and was not surprised to find it ice cold.

Kelly witnessed the next moment with a sobering clarity. Although she had never met Gilbert, she could sense the energy that animated his face and body, the uniqueness that was as apparent as the laugh lines at the corners of his wide eyes. In an instant, that animation—spirit, soul, whatever one called it—evaporated into the stormy night. Gilbert left behind not himself but a corpse, a body whose time was spent.

Kelly clapped her hands in short, sharp bursts, then spread her arms wide as if she were releasing ashes into the wilderness. It was a custom among some of the villagers, a gesture that communicated a release of the man's spirit back to the world from which it originated. Kelly repeated the clapping and release two more times before rising slowly. She felt the mute silence of the men behind her as though it were a physical wall.

As if obeying custom, the men broke rank, circling the corpse at her feet. Burns handed the portable light to Elf before helping Frank lift the body and carry it to the truck. Kelly followed the small procession as it ambled its way through the cool, tropical downpour. She began chanting once again, only this time the prayer was not for Gilbert but for their own protection. The rain she tasted on her lips was fast turning the road into an impassable mud bank.

She helped the men hoist the corpse into the back of the truck and then climbed in alongside it. The dark face was as rigid as a mask, impervious to the pelting of the heavy rain. Kelly was reminded of the Mayan reliefs, the stone faces staring back over the centuries. Only those sculptures were infused with a hint of the life that had come before. Gilbert's face was impenetrable, showing only that life visited upon the physical world, but it otherwise existed in its own realm. The curandero taught her that our present time world was merely a shadow of the real, timeless world in the eyes of the spirits. The individual self had a life of its own, according to the curandero, but it was no more substantial than a costume, hiding the real, unseen life that existed within and without. Kelly could not completely accept this mystical view, but she remained sympathetic. Her education and continuing research only served to remind her how little she really knew and understood about the mysterious workings of the physical world.

The back wheels struggled for traction. The truck rocked back and forth as Frank switched between forward and reverse in an effort to pull the vehicle out of its rut. Finally, the truck stopped and she heard Frank's door slam.

"We're not going anywhere," Frank said, his voice barely audible even as he stood at the tailgate less than a foot from the flatbed, where everyone was huddled, including Gilbert's corpse. The rain continued to roar.

"Let's get something under the back tire, something the wheels can grip," Burns demanded. He turned the sun gun into Frank's eyes.

"Get that toy out of my face, you moron," Frank said.

Kelly could hear her husband's contempt for Burns, and it frightened her.

"We'll get some wood," Vic volunteered. "C'mon Elf, Big."

All three jumped out of the back of the truck and landed squarely in the black mud, sinking immediately beyond their ankles. The road was becoming almost fluid. One step forward only landed them deeper as each tried in succession.

"There is one thing that might work," Frank said. He looked toward the back of the truck.

"Are you crazy? That's a person," Burns reminded him.

"OK," Frank said. "What's your solution?"

Burns thought of the television light. It was as solid as wood and probably heavy enough. But the wheels would crush it, rendering it unusable for the duration of the shoot.

"I don't know. How about our clothes?" Burns said.

"Not enough," Frank said. The road was already close to impassable. If they even had time to negotiate the sinking road, the corpse was the only object that would lay under the tire and provide traction for the wheels. Enough, at least, to get them some forward momentum.

"If we don't take off now, we are here for the night," Frank persisted. "You know that, Kel."

Kelly didn't answer. The sound of the pouring rain filled the dark silence that had descended over them. It was immediately clear that they had no real option beyond what Frank suggested. They were stuck, and no one relished the prospect of spending the night in the rain in the middle of the jungle.

"The rain will stop sooner or later," Burns said.

"This time of year, that could mean days," Frank warned. "Look. I don't want to do this. But we've got to make a choice, and it's not a time to be sentimental."

Again, the group remained silent. It was as though they were all debating what to do through Frank and Burns.

"I can't be part of this," Burns said.

"I can," Vic said. "We have to get out of here and there is nothing else. Nothing."

"Let's go," Frank screamed. He grabbed Gilbert's stiff, cold feet and yanked the corpse toward the waterlogged road. Kelly slipped her arms under the dead Belizean's shoulders and helped her husband hoist the body to the road. Burns stood witness, hobbled from participating by his weak and injured leg. He held up the rain-shrouded sun gun, barely illuminating the back tire where Gilbert could best serve them.

"We're not going to be able to stop and get him if this works, are we?" Burns asked. Once they were underway, stopping risked getting stuck yet again.

"We'll come back," Kelly promised.

There was no cover from the rain that pounded them in the darkness. Burns, like the others, clung to the inside of the flatbed. His head was bowed and eyes closed almost in prayer as the downpour battered his skull and ripped into the still open wound on his leg. He couldn't tell if his leg was bleeding again, but he felt the rain roll under him before gushing out the back of the pickup like a waterfall.

The pickup stayed to the shoulder of the road where there were grasses and fallen branches and scattered rocks to keep them form sinking again into the mud of the lane. Still, the truck shimmied from one side to the next, then bounced when it slammed into and over the very rocks that allowed it to continue.

Burns could not see or hear anyone else in the flatbed. He squinted through the pouring water in search of Kelly, but there was only darkness. He shivered from the cool water and cursed out loud. But he knew no one could hear him in the din of the shower.

Finally, in a moment that felt miraculous, the rain seemed to slow. They were rolling down a solid road, and he sensed a light ahead. There was an umbrella of branches not far above him, shielding some of the rain, and Burns knew they were on the tree-covered lane that curved down the hill to the research camp. His guess was confirmed when they reemerged into the punishing downpour and the truck stopped in the open land that surrounded the prefab ranch—Kelly and Frank's camp.

A spotlight over the front door flickered through the sheets of rain, which shimmered like drops of mercury. Immediately, Burns recovered himself as he watched his crew bound off the truck into the mud. His leg felt stiff and immobilized. Gingerly, he stood up, and the pain ripped through him as he stumbled to the muddy ground.

"We need to report this," Burns said, checking to see if his leg wound had reopened. The flesh was raw, but there was no blood.

"I'll talk to the police in the morning," Frank yelled, raising his voice to be heard against the rain.

"Why not now?" Burns answered.

Frank didn't respond. He hurried away from the truck, up the hill and through the bright security light that illuminated the door.

"Kelly," Burns pleaded.

"San Ignacio is a small town," she said, turning to him. Her hair was flattened, her face pale and wet with the chilled rain. She shivered and, for a moment, Burns felt he glimpsed the young schoolgirl back in Main Line, Philadelphia, and it touched him as if he had seen something meant to remain private and hidden, like an unsightly birthmark.

"It's closed up this time of night."

"Closed up?" Burns asked.

"The police usually have little to do here," Kelly said. She smiled sadly, her lips wet and parted slightly. "Tomorrow."

Burns stared at those lips before they were lost in the darkness, watching until she, too, ran back inside the house as her husband had done. He felt foolish for allowing himself to be attracted to a married woman. It had to be some kind of Pygmalion effect which, of course, was counterproductive. It was selfish and destructive and only made his mission here even more difficult.

"Burns. We're goin'," Vic called behind him.

She was older, Burns thought to himself. Not even his type. She wasn't a beauty. Her hands were ugly, scarred from wielding machetes and tree limbs. Yet none of this mattered for long, he had to admit. It was what couldn't be readily described that charmed him, coaxing him forward.

31

Chink-in: leaves are used in bath
to treat sadness and grief

The rain ended suddenly, just before dawn. Burns woke moments later, the quiet gently punctuated with the sound of water draining from leaves and dripping to the wet ground. He imagined Gilbert's corpse, squashed into the mud like a cigarette butt. The heavy rain might have saved the carcass from scavengers, but now Burns feared the man would be pounced upon for a second time. He'd seen road kill before, ripped apart by dogs and birds and the inevitable army of flies. The stench of rot as much as the eviscerated animal was repulsive. Gilbert was a human being, however, and he couldn't allow himself to picture the young Belizian suffering the indignity of being mauled on the open road.

Of course, he understood and accepted his part in exposing Gilbert to the elements. He had gone along with the decision to use Gilbert. In the end, however, there really had been no choice. They could not risk their own safety out of deference to a corpse. There was survival, not to mention the life of the documentary. So much had been sacrificed already to produce his show that he could not imagine just abandoning what they had come here to accomplish for sentimental reasons.

Besides, after the roads were dry enough for passage, he would amend last night and retrieve Gilbert with the help of his crew. There would be dignity. But that was only the beginning, of course. Who would tell his family and friends? Who would explain why he was on that road and what happened? A man with such a respect and reverence for life that he worried about running over a turtle in the road was, himself, casually cracked open.

When Kelly had knelt alongside Gilbert in the bright television light, Burns had felt a sudden, queer change, and he knew instinctively that the man had just died. Before Kelly raised her head and startled him with her sudden clapping, Burns felt something—energy, temperature—he was at a loss to explain or describe exactly what. Gilbert's body looked no different to the eye. A photograph would not have revealed any dramatic change.

Science taught that matter never died. It merely changed forms. The Druids believed that spirits occupied the space where they died. The Good manifested itself in locations with a special feeling and attraction: the summit of a beautiful mountain next to a gently percolating creek along a welcoming stretch of pristine beach. If that were true, however, Burns wondered why hospitals and hospices weren't teeming with energetic, spiritual forces embodied by the dead, past and present.

The religion of his schooldays explained even less. Burns did not believe that souls rose to a hallowed place alongside God, far from man and the known world. Why such disdain and contempt for the world of our senses? Why could not the souls be among the living, guiding us. The Maya, at least the Maya of the curandero's generation, believed in just such a living spirit world. If Burns had understood it correctly, Pedro Meza literally believed that the physical world was a mere reflection of the spirit world. They were inexorably joined. Authentic life existed in both what could be seen and what could not.

How did he live? Burns asked himself. He watched the world from car windows, computer consoles, movie screens and, of course, television monitors. He listened to voices, music, the racket of the city. He smelled, tasted and touched and yet he was separated, kept at a remove by the very technology he used to view it. The idea reminded him of a long, steep hike he'd taken with Julie in the Catskill Mountains. They were sitting at a small summit, enjoying the expansive view, when a photo buff arrived using the same trail. He had a camera around one shoulder and was holding another with both hands. He'd stopped, put the telephoto lens to his eye and took some snapshots. Then he turned and left. Julie had laughed—that lovely, girlish laugh—at the hiker's single-minded pursuit of the perfect picture, but now Burns remembered that he hadn't laughed at all. The hiker did what he would have done if Burns had been armed with a camera.

The sound of footsteps surprised him. Instantly alert, he followed their movement as they slapped gently along the ground toward the forest just beyond the cabin. Burns rolled off his bed, parted the mosquito netting and limped along the bare, wooden floor to the window. At the last moment, he glimpsed Kelly at the edge of the clearing before she disappeared into the trees.

Burns rushed back to his bunk and retrieved his shorts, still soaked and heavy with rain, and pulled them on, ignoring the throbbing of his leg. He paused to check if it had woken Vic, who was lying in the bed on the other side of the room. When his cameraman didn't stir, Burns hopped out onto the porch, taking pains to close the door as quietly as possible, anxious not to disturb anyone who might ask him where he was going.

He stepped off the creaking porch and into the warm, velvet light of dawn. Above him, the summit of the research camp reached into a blue, beckoning sky. As he limped toward the spot where Kelly had disappeared, he noticed the wisps of vapor that danced above the sunlit clearing and the spinach green trees. He felt a sudden, inexplicable burst of excitement.

Kelly had taken the same path where they had filmed the day before, the so-called medicine trail. He looked around him for another stick he could use as a crutch, but there was nothing. So he limped on, anxious to catch her.

A few minutes later, the forest came to life as if someone had hit a switch. The cicadas roared and the birds called and screeched and a howler monkey deep in the trees barked for his morning meal. Burns was startled by the onslaught. He stopped and searched the jade canopy. He had no real hope of catching her. He could hike a little further before resting his leg and wait for her return. But he suddenly felt as vulnerable as a newcomer who had wandered into the wrong neighborhood.

A rattling of leaves unnerved him. He waited, watching the brush. A branch moved, and Burns held his breath. It was an animal, he was sure. But he had no weapon, nothing with which to defend himself.

A bright green bird suddenly scampered out of the brush, spotted Burns and soared into the canopy. Burns exhaled, only then realizing he'd been holding his breath.

He turned around on the path and hobbled his way back toward the camp. He didn't need to be out here, wandering alone. He needed to regroup and get back to work. This was their third day. It felt as though it had been weeks. But he could feel the pressure of the clock. It occurred to him that the arrival of the police and ensuing investigation of Gilbert's death would likely take hours, if not days. He'd been around this kind of thing many times before, filming detectives day after day. It was time he didn't have. They still had no raw video stock, no documentary. They had a few minutes of footage for a trailer, but it wasn't even enough for a promo, let alone a program. He had to have tape, one way or the other.

32

Romero: Herb used to ward off evil spirits

Pedro Meza had planned to take a long walk to relieve the stiffness in his joints. The night's rain had intensified his arthritis, and the best remedy he knew was to drink an infusion of Pasmo with a pinch of Damiana and walk in the warmth of the morning sun to stimulate his circulation. But as soon as he stepped out of his bungalow, his bare feet sank into warm, ankle-high mud. The heavy downpour had also scattered shallow puddles throughout the village, bubbling with toads. Pedro Meza wanted to walk in the direction of the river, but each slippery step threatened his balance. He feared a sudden, unexpected fall because his bones were brittle with age and could break as easily as dry tree limbs, even in the soft mud. Even a simple bruise marked his body for months instead of days.

Growing old didn't have to be this way, he told himself. If only there was a woman in his life, a loving partner to help soothe the inevitable aches of the aging mind as well as the body. He was certain making love would cure his melancholy. Didn't the entire visible world, from the spore of a plant to the ambitions of a man, gain its impetus and momentum from the drive to copulate? What was more inspiring?

As if to taunt the old man, Marietta, the young and pretty wife of one of his neighbors, stepped out of her bungalow. She was dressed in a loose cotton dress that reached to her bare, elegant ankles. Marietta turned and smiled in silent greeting before splashing down the path toward the river, carrying a straw basket piled with soiled clothes against the curve of her hips. Although it had lasted only a moment, her appearance lingered in Pedro Meza's mind and body, making him feel suddenly younger and grateful to be alive. Did the spirits, he wondered, know anything of this pleasure?

Pedro Meza squinted into the hazy morning sky and shrugged. There was nothing to be done about old age other than to endure it. But he was grateful that it did not prevent him from performing his duty as a curandero. His calling remained as vital and necessary as it had in his youth. From the moment his father had introduced him to the healing ways, Pedro Meza understood he had been given the great gift of purpose and conviction, escaping the aimlessness of many who left the jungle and wandered off to the towns and cities by the sea.

Pedro Meza pulled his feet from the mud and turned back in the direction of his home. He needed to get to work. The spirits had not revisited him in the night after the dream of the logging road and the circling vultures. But he understood that the dream was a sign and that it would be necessary for him to hike to the logging road and allow himself to be guided where the Spirits chose. As he passed a neighbor's garden, their lone rooster blasted the morning silence with his call and darted forward until he was restrained by the string that tethered him to the house. Pedro Meza stopped and became aware of the singular, pungent scent of the herb Ca-cal-tun. A sprawling patch had newly sprouted at the edge of the garden. The curandero crouched alongside the tall, leafy plant as if it had called out to him. He knew from experience that sometimes healing plants found the healer.

Ca-cal-tun was a common cooking herb that Kelly called basil, but it was also occasionally useful as a defense against certain evil spirits. The curandero selected two of the taller plants, whispered an enselmo giving thanks to the beneficent spirit of the sweet herb, then snapped the thin, green stems barely an inch from the wet ground. The rooster crowed again, then trotted back to the shadow alongside the cement bungalow.

At home, Pedro Meza decided to follow the lead suggested by the appearance of the Ca-cal-tun and broke off a chunk of copal to take with him to the logging road. The dark, dried resin was burned to ward off dark spirits. He also added sprigs of Romero, or rosemary, to his cache of herbs. When mixed and burned with copal, Romero was a powerful agent of protection. Finally, the curandero made sure to bring a fistful of Ix-canan, what he considered an all-purpose medicinal plant. The leaves, which resembled human ears, were effective in the treatment of everything from infections to stubborn sores.

Satisfied with his preparations, the curandero hurriedly ate two tortillas, which he warmed on his hotplate and washed down with the last cup of Tan Chi for his arthritis. Feeling nourished and finally awake, Pedro Meza retrieved his sacred sastun and slipped it into the front pocket of his baggy, soiled jeans. Whatever other herb or plant he might need, the jungle would provide what was necessary.

The path inside the forest was damp but firm. The dense canopy had blocked the night downpour as effectively as a roof. The sun, however, was heating the heavy, wet leaves, releasing a warm, smoky mist that drifted gently through the jungle and the filtered light. The mist obscured much of the path ahead of him, but Pedro Meza knew the route by heart. He hiked without concern, listening to the birds and foraging animals that rustled unseen around him. Within a short time, however, he became aware of an unusual lightness in his step, his bare feet springing off the ground with a youthfulness he'd not known for years. It was not unlike the feeling he'd experienced in the logging road dream. He'd been running in that vision, but the curandero was not now even tempted to break into a sprint. He knew his knees and skinny thighs would ache for weeks if he were foolish enough to run like a young man.

215

So Pedro Meza hiked without sense of hurry or concern. He would arrive when he arrived. Besides, walking in the forest, he felt utterly at peace, in his element. The thick smell of vegetation, the green womb of the sparkling jade trees, the pulse of active, unseen life, all inspired him. So he was vaguely disappointed when, sometime later, he reached the edge of the forest. But as he approached the last line of trees that separated the jungle from where he knew the logging road to be, the curandero also felt something far more ominous than disappointment. He could feel it under his skin, like the itch from a poisonous plant.

The curandero hesitated before leaving the protection of the forest, sensing that he would soon be putting himself in danger. Finally, he stepped out into the blaze of the midday sun, his eyes stinging from the brightness of the bleached sky. The logging road was riddled with a maze of misshapen puddles, but he soon spotted a dark cluster of objects in the distance. Only when one of the birds spread its dark wings and hopped to a new position did the curandero recognize the vultures. They were feasting on a carcass, tearing off scraps.

Pedro Meza pressed his canvas bag of herbs closer to his body as if it might shield him and filed alongside the road, avoiding stepping into what was certainly deep mud, toward the vultures. The Evil Spirit of the place was powerful, its presence as palpable as the heavy, humid air. As he came closer, the curandero saw that the carcass was, in fact, the body of a man. All but a few of the mocha-colored toes had been torn off and consumed by the vultures. There was little blood, only the mottled gray of flesh.

Pedro Meza continued walking until he was only a couple feet from the corpse. The vultures paid no attention. They continued to poke and pluck as greedily as before. The curandero realized he was standing in a rut made by truck tires and that the tracks led up into the road and over the dead man. The skull was crushed, the face unrecognizable. The curandero was almost grateful the man seemed to be no one he knew, nor, given the color of his skin, did he seem to be from this part of Cayo. One thing was certain, however. He was the object of the vision.

Man had only one known predator, Pedro Meza reminded himself. While the harsh jungle could deliver a swift death, as it had to the boy Mazdara, it was more an exception than a rule. Men were most in danger of themselves. Fortunately, there had never been a murder in San Antonio in the half-century the curandero had lived there. Across the border in Guatemala, where he was born, killings were commonplace as a result of the civil war. But not here.

The curandero took the two sprigs of Ca-cal-tun herb and broke them into pieces and made a wide, slow wreath around the body. Two of the birds squawked as he circled them but otherwise continued to pick through the dirt and unearth more of the man's flesh. Pedro Meza prayed, wiping the sweat from his forehead, certain of the presence of an Evil Spirit. Next, he removed the copal and the Romero and made a small mound on either side of the body. He lit both with his Bic lighter. The mixture caught quickly, but there was no wind to carry the smoke and spread it over the road. So Pedro Meza removed his canvas bag and used it like a fan, directing the dank, sweet smoke toward the vultures and their corpse.

The curandero raised his voice, calling for protection from the Evil Spirit of the place. The birds angrily flapped their dark wings, trying to deflect the thick smoke. They hopped from one spot to the next, screeching, shaking the mud that clung to their claw feet. Pedro Meza swung his bag, fanning more energetically, continuing to cry out. The vultures slapped one another with their wings, caught in the acrid circle. Finally, one bird leapt above the corpse and flew off. Moments later, the other scavengers followed, screeching as they rose into the sky, then circling on a thermal.

Pedro Meza watched the vultures rise, three of them floating above him as they had in the dream. A light breeze cooled his damp neck and fanned the copal and Romero and lifted the smoke higher into the sky. Pedro Meza was relieved to feel the Good Wind and the departure of the Evil Spirit. He wiped the sweat from his forehead and moved closer to the corpse. He sank to his ankles in the warm mud. The copal and Romero masked some of the stench but not all of it.

Pedro Meza held his nose as he bent over and dropped the last few leaves of the Ca-cal-tun on the body. Satisfied, he raised his hands together and clapped, releasing the life spirit into the open sky.

Uayeb. The lost time, he thought. His father had sworn by those dark days of the calendar, shrugging off smirks, declaring that the spirits chose the time, not men. There were days when men should not tempt their fate. Uayeb was that time.

The curandero backed out of the mud and regained his footing on the side of the road. As he walked back to the forest, he felt the ugly weight of death, of a murder. It was the second death in less than three days. But he was convinced that the cause could be blamed on the lost days of Uayeb. It was only a calendar, after all. Evidence pointed toward the blancs. They had come for Kelly, one of their own, and disturbed the balance.

Of course, he reminded himself as he reached the precious coolness of the trees, much could be traced to his homeland, where the soldiers of Guatemala hunted down Mayans like himself. They wanted to rid the mountains of them, the way the cattle barons wanted to rid the forest so they could raise their own interests in the place of those who had lived and grown quietly here for generations. The dead man in the road was certainly an omen, a warning, he feared, of what was yet to come.

33

**Xiv-yak-tun-ich: Center vein of leaf is
applied to relieve muscle spasm of backache**

Burns telephoned two television stations in Belize City, a small
production company in San Pedro on Ambergris Caye and even
a one-man band wedding shooter on Caye Caulker that was only ac-
cessible by motorboat. One of the Belize City stations was still using
three-quarter-inch tape, which had gone the way of eight-track re-
corders in the United States. The other station could not spare any
tape for at least a week. The production company, however, did have
some stock. The catch was they would not transport it. Someone would
have to drive to Belize City to pick it up. They also demanded C.O.D.

Burns held onto the receiver, weighing his options. The logging
road was hours away from being passable and that was only if it didn't
rain again. He could track down Mr. Green and his dugout canoes,
but that would likely take up half a day just getting him and his grandson upriver. He considered hiring another fixer in the city, but again
that would not happen quickly enough. Burns could not afford another lost day.

The telephone receiver began to make rapid, irritating honks. Burns slammed the phone down, and it echoed like a sharp clap in the silent, empty house. He would have to call Katz, his executive producer in New York, and plead for more time and, while he was at it, a case of raw stock. But Burns knew he was likely to be rebuffed. Katz would not approve more days on location. It would send the project soaring over budget.

One solution could be to pitch additional stories to justify additional money. There was the spillover of the Guatemalan civil war, which revealed the targeting of Mayans who alone lived in this border area in the kind of poverty common to so much of Latin America. There were the stories of the cattle barons and their destruction of the habitat. There was the logging company that planted seedlings in the place of felled trees but whose roads carved up miles of pristine jungle.

"Foreign stories are deadly," Katz said after listening without interruption to his pitch. "They don't get ratings, and no one cares about them except other journalists and the ex-Peace Corps volunteers."

"But we're here. We could shoot the pieces in a few days and come back with three or four stories for next to nothing."

"Medical stories are a sure thing," Katz answered. "They always get viewers. Come back with one. It was what you were sent down there to get."

Burns hung up before he said something he would regret. Katz got under his skin and one day, if he survived this shoot, he was going to tell off that ratings-obsessed junkie and remind him that they were filmmakers first.

Burns hobbled out of the house and into the muggy shade outside the screened porch. The jungle buzzed and squeaked with unseen life. He checked for any sign of Kelly.

"How's your leg?" Vic asked. He was sitting on the landing with Elf and Big.

"We have to get to Belize City," Burns said. "There's a production company there that has stock."

"Oh God," Elf muttered. "That's hours away."

Elf's face was blood red and puffed out like a blowfish.

"Kelly has got to get something for you, Elf. Anybody seen her?"

The crew was silent. Vic stood up, sighing.

"Burns, we all want to make a good film. Hell, just getting something in the can would be enough. But we've reached our limit."

"We still have a few days," Burns said. "Enough to get what we came down here to get."

"It's only a film," Vic said.

"Only a film?" Burns said. He was furious and indignant. He also felt betrayed by his cameraman, who knew better than to belittle what they devoted their lives to creating.

The wooden door creaked open behind him. Frank emerged, tired and disheveled. He'd heard the discussion. Burns could see it in his sardonic glance, as if to say, "I knew you wouldn't last."

"Frank," Burns said, turning on his practiced charm, "we need a little favor."

THE FIVE LOST DAYS

34

**Xucul: Leaves and stems are rich
in minerals, proteins and vitamins;
juice used to nourish the system**

Kelly hiked along the medicine trail in the cool, vaporous light of deep forest. The high canopy above her was heavy with the night rains. Fat droplets fell occasionally, rattling the web of leaves that surrounded her. The ground, too, was soft with filtered moisture, cushioning each of her steps. A melancholy fatigue, brought on by the sad death of the Belizean driver, had convinced her to hike back to San Antonio so that she could have tea with Tato. He would help calm her.

The village was alive with the chatter of radios, the occasional clink of a breakfast plate, the deep murmur of unseen voices. A rooster strutted back and forth in a mud patch, crowing at will. Kelly found the curandero in his bungalow, boiling water on his hotplate and mixing in a fresh herb he had evidently picked that morning.

"Ah, Kelly," he said, genuinely pleased to see her. Immediately, she felt both happy and relieved that she had decided to come and visit him.

"Fresh Tan Chi?" she asked.

The curandero made a sour face and pretended to grumble.

"It is for old age. I have to drink it all day long to keep the aches quiet."

"You're not old in spirit, Tato."

"Maybe not. But my bones are tired always."

Kelly smiled. Like a good-natured crank, the curandero frequently complained about his age.

"All your bones?" Kelly teased.

Pedro Meza's eyes lit with the mischievousness of a young boy.

"Never that one. No," he said and winked. Kelly hugged him, then sat down on the dirt floor in front of the hotplate. She watched in silence as he slipped in first the leaves, then the roots of the herb to make the tea for his arthritis. While he stirred the leaves in the steaming water, he met her eyes, nodding, then returned his attention to the pot.

"What's troubling you?" he asked, suddenly.

Kelly wasn't surprised by the swiftness with which he caught her mood and state of mind. It was a skill that made him a great healer, after all.

"I'm not sure," Kelly lied. Her unexpected feelings for Burns both excited her and made her feel she was betraying her marriage, even if the passion had long been dormant.

The curandero waved away a cloud of metallic steam that drifted into his face. Kelly wondered if he was in some way trying to hide the concern reflected in his tired eyes.

"This morning I found a man's body in the road. He was not from Cayo or the mountains."

"Gilbert?"

"You know?" the curandero asked.

Kelly recounted their troubles of the night before. The curandero received this information in silence, his face a mask of impenetrable folds and wrinkles. He turned off his hotplate and sat down next to her.

"You know this to be the time of Uayeb," the curandero said.

Uayeb was the Mayan term for the "nameless month." According to the Mayan civic calendar, known as the Haab, the year was eighteen months long with twenty days each, adding up to three hundred and sixty days. The five missing days were given their own name, Uayeb. For some Mayans, it was considered an unlucky time, when the world experienced great upheaval and evil was rampant. The most ardent believers would schedule nothing of importance for the month of Uayeb, fearing the worst. They called it the lost time.

"In a dream, I found the dead man," the curandero continued. "When I went to him on the road, it was the fourth day of Uayeb. Before, I discovered your blanc at the river, it was the third. Mazdara died from the fer-de-lance attack the same day."

The curandero slowly smoothed the dirt floor with his hand as though he were preparing to write this information on the ground.

Although Kelly had developed the deepest respect for the spiritual component of the curandero's healing method, she didn't share his acceptance of all things Mayan. There were many aspects of the culture, like the concept of an evil wind or the Uayeb days, that she regarded as little more than superstition. Yet it was uncanny to know that the filmmaker's arrival coincided with these dark days of the ancient Mayan calendar.

"So what does one do when it is Uayeb? Stay home?" Kelly said.

"Many do. In my father's time, it was important. Now, maybe it is like your number thirteen. Yes? One hopes."

The curandero shrugged, then stood and returned to his hotplate. He grabbed a chipped white mug from a wood shelf and set it next to the burner. Before picking up the sieve used to strain the leaves, however, he asked Kelly if she would care to join him for a cup.

"It is helpful for nervousness, too," he said, his eyes smiling.

"I watched the video of you," Kelly said. "It is very powerful."

Pedro Meza poured the second cup of herbal tea and let the hot water pot clang on the hotplate.

"La alma," Pedro Meza said. "In my father's time, it was believed that the camera took not a picture but the soul of the person it was pointed at. La alma. But that is foolishness."

She watched the old man—now a dear friend—shuffle toward her, each hand clasping a mug. She was reminded that Tato was co-operating with the camera because of her.

"The video will preserve some of your knowledge, Tato. That's what the camera can do."

Pedro set the mug in front of her. Kelly felt the steam brush her chin.

"No, my Kelly."

The curandero set his own mug on the dirt floor, then lowered himself behind it. He groaned from the stiffness in his knees.

"The camera cannot see what cannot be seen, and that is medicine."

"Yes," Kelly said. "Yes, of course. But the plants, the herbs. They are important, too."

"For your work, yes," Tato said in a kind tone.

Kelly had allowed herself to forget that her own camp, her own livelihood, was threatened by the corporate owner who wanted more tangible results than she had yet provided. Kelly needed favorable press. It was why she made an effort to have Burns as a friend, some-one who would look on her operation with affection, not criticism.

"You are fond of the blanc, yes?" the curandero said. Kelly was caught off-guard. His eyes met hers without judgment, only curios-ity.

"It is easier to help those we like," the curandero went on, not waiting for a reply. "But it is also more dangerous."

Kelly waited for an explanation.

"We want also to be liked," the curandero said. He bent over and tried to sip the tea. But the hot water nearly scalded his lips.

"Careful," Kelly said as a mother might to a beloved child.

"I have no patience when my bones are hurting," he said.

"We help each other," Kelly said. "The producer and I."

"You must be careful," Tato said.

"Don't worry," Kelly said, impulsively hugging him, feeling her affection for this old, wise man nearly overcome her.

The late morning sun had risen into a pale, lemon sky and burned away the morning mist. As Kelly approached the edge of the clearing and stepped out of the dense shade, she immediately felt the familiar, growing haze silently boring into her as it would for the rest of the day. Over the years, she had come to enjoy the heat and humidity of the jungle, the way it enveloped her body and made her aging skin feel loose and supple as she hiked and collected plants. In the beginning, when she and Frank had first climbed out of Mr. Green's dory and stumbled onto the muddy banks of what would soon be the research camp, she had felt weak and dizzy from the hundred-degree heat. Sitting under the trees, she never imagined she would come to love the climate, never dreamed she would spend over a decade in the midst of it. But the assignment had proven to be more than another project. Once she had met and begun to work with Tato, she knew she had found her life's calling.

Kelly stopped under a tubroos tree to admire the smooth white facade of the research compound that surrounded her. She felt a wave of rich satisfaction, knowing that somehow she and Frank had built this camp. In spite of the disappointments, there was something to show for their efforts.

The men were sitting inside the house, waiting. She had heard their rough voices as she approached, and she listened particularly to hear Burns. She liked his youth and his boyish infatuation with her. It made her feel younger, more desired, both of which had been ground down by both her work and a long marriage.

"Any new medicines out there?" Burns asked. He was sitting at the dinner table, gazing up at her with a thrilling admiration.

"Yes. I just haven't found them yet."

Frank appeared from the kitchen, holding a coffee mug.

"While you were gone our guests came up with an urgent request," Frank said. He explained the plan to drive to Belize City to buy videotapes from a vendor.

"The roads are still mud," she said.

The men fell silent, reminded of the ugly night.

"Tato found him, found the body," Kelly said.

"How the hell did he do that?" Frank asked. "The sun's only been up for a few hours."

"He had a healer's dream," Kelly said, "and it led him there."

Everyone watched her, waiting.

"He blessed the body. Nothing else. He left it to the Spirits."

Again, Kelly felt the pregnant silence, the thoughts and feelings all the men, not just her husband, kept to themselves. A woman would have spoken, would have been compelled to communicate. But most men, she thought, kept a distance, protecting their options. Or, she thought, their silence itself was a response to her talk of Spirits—a world they could not accept.

"Your man needs treatment," Kelly said, going to Elf, who was slumped in a chair next to the table. His skin, she found, was the texture of parchment paper and still almost hot to the touch. She was immediately concerned that he could have a first- or second-degree burn, which she wasn't equipped to treat.

"The sun will dry up that road quicker than it burned him," Frank said. "We can be back by late afternoon."

Kelly was surprised at her husband's eagerness to help the filmmakers. She knew he didn't like or respect them. But maybe he felt differently now or, even more hopefully, he was thinking about their documentary and the good it could do for the research camp and their lives.

"You should go," Kelly said, smiling at her husband with gratitude. In the end, he was a great and loyal partner.

"We'll manage the police," she added. "When and if they come from San Ignacio."

"Why wouldn't they come?" Burns asked, visibly concerned. "A man was murdered."

"They take their time," Frank answered for her. "It's not like the man is going to rise from the dead and walk away."

THE FIVE LOST DAYS

35

Sink-in: Shrubby herb used against spiritual diseases such as envy, fright and grief

Frank was relieved to be out of Cayo and speeding across the open savanna under the blazing sun of high noon—even if he did feel like an errand boy for this hapless film crew. But what got under his skin most was his suspicion that there was some connection between Manuela's aborted visit and Burns. The murder of the driver, who had been employed by Burns, struck him as anything but random. It could just as easily have been premeditated, a planned attack. There was just something off about Burns. How could he lose videotape? It was unheard of. Moreover, he didn't act like many journalists or film-makers. Burns had another agenda unrelated to filmmaking.

"Hey, you mind turning up the air-conditioning?" Big John asked from the passenger seat. Frank had virtually forgotten his existence. But it was hard to miss his oversized passenger now. The top of his head pressed into the carpeted roof.

"It's on super cool," Frank said. The afternoon sun blasted through the glass, unimpeded by any trees.

"Man, I just can't get used to this climate down here," Big groaned. "It just never stops cooking."

Frank didn't like to be reminded of the stifling heat. It was a given in this part of the world, and the best way to cope was to forget about it.

"I don't know how you guys do it," Big said.

"That's what I think about people who live in New York City. You couldn't pay me to live in that sewer."

"I'm from Jersey," Big said. "I don't like the city much either."

Frank could sense his own growing anxiety, so he took a pre-rolled joint out of his madras shirt pocket. He held the joint with his lips and pushed in the cigarette lighter. The engine was the only sound in the cab until the pop of the heated cylinder announced that the coil was ready to use.

"You want some?" he asked after taking a hit.

"No. Don't do drugs," Big told him.

"How did I know that?" Frank said, turning his attention to the passing grasslands. They were as parched as straw.

"I'm pretty boring that way," Big said. "I don't like what pot and stuff does to my body. I feel lousy from it, not better."

Frank took another hit of the marijuana and held it until there was no smoke left to exhale. He caught his breath, finally, like a swimmer resurfacing after a long time under water.

"Tell me something," Frank said. "Has this kind of thing happened before?"

"Sure," Big said.

"You just run out of tape," Frank said, disbelieving.

"Crazy, huh?" Big said. Burns had been adamant that no one should let on that tapes had been lost.

"Yeah. It is. And I don't buy it," Frank said. "I think your producer has something else going on. I just don't know what it is. Not yet."

Big John turned away and hid his face by looking out the window. Frank suddenly remembered the look on his wife's face when she asked him if he was jealous. It bothered him because, hearing it now in his mind, he recognized it as a deflection, a way of turning the issue to him. She was more than interested in Burns. Much more. And both she and Burns were taking him for a chump.

"But I'll do anything to get you and your crew out of my hair," Frank said, adding a short laugh. He had decided to use this trip to Belize City to show Federique a sample of his crop. A bag full of his special mint leaves was stuffed under the seat. Frank was depending on Federique to handle the export of his plants to California.

"I hear ya," Big said, smiling. "People either love us or hate us on these shoots. There ain't much in between."

Frank had little respect for the American media. They had a herd mentality, rushing en masse to the story of the moment, then eventually crushing it underfoot with their sheer relentless attention. There seemed little room in news operations for thoughtful, probing reports. But most Americans did like and trust their daily network news. They seemed to believe what they were told. If Burns and his crew presented the research camp in its best light, then that was how America, too, would see it.

"You like what you do," Frank said.

"Yeah. And it's a great way to see the world. Better than the service. I mean, just the last couple of years, I've been to Italy, London and Mexico. And all over the States."

"You were thinking of enlisting?" Frank asked. He couldn't imagine a more objectionable career. He disliked and distrusted the American military. They took perfectly decent young men and turned them into killing machines. "Highly trained" was the euphemism the recruiters and PR people liked to use.

"ROTC," Big answered. "They were going to pick up the whole tab for college."

Frank could hear the jeers in his mind. It was 1970 and a group of ROTC kids were marching across campus. Ramrod straight, towing the government line. The soldiers-to-be elicited the same kind of response as cops at a concert. Every kid walking through the campus, most changing classes, started to make catcalls. Frank joined in, firing a whistle at the moving herd of uniforms.

"Well you came to your senses," Frank said.

"Sallie Mae came to the rescue," Big said, smiling. "Got a good student loan. 'Course, I'm still paying it back."

Frank's parents had footed the tuition bill at Harvard. From as early as he could remember, his parents had made it clear that he was to have the best schooling, and cost would be no object. Education was sacred, more important than their suburban ranch home, the two new cars, even Sunday mass. They wanted their son to acquire sophistication and status. Frank often wondered if his parents didn't see college as a kind of finishing school. They were appalled, in the end, when he joined the radical movement and made it part of his life's mission to help the poor and powerless of the world, exactly the class his parents had struggled to leave behind.

So far, Frank had to admit, he had little to show for his decision. He'd been involved with the Mayans and the indigenous rights movement for almost a decade. True, he had helped it gain some notice from the international community. But, as yet, there had been little real change in their living conditions. Most still lived in corrugated tin shacks, farmed and fished what they could for sustenance, and depended on the blancs for medicine or the crazy old curandero if they were desperate enough. It was a life doomed to be lived on the edge.

"Mind if I catch a few?" Big asked, sliding down in his seat, preparing to take a nap.

"Whatever you want," Frank said. "We've got plenty of time."

"You're not going to fall asleep at the wheel or anything?"

"If I do, it won't make a hell of a lot of difference."

Big laughed, glancing at the flatlands that stretched in every direction. Frank, too, observed the virtual sea of sargasso that surrounded them. But he was startled to see dark tombstones rising haphazardly in the distance. Turkey vultures floated on a thermal just above them. Frank peered closer, wondering if his mind or the pot was playing tricks on him. Or was it simply the memory of the dead Belizean, ground into the mud?

"What are those things?" Big asked, following his gaze. "They look like tree stumps."

Frank nodded, feeling immediate relief. He was grateful the TV worker had supplied a new caption to the image before him. It helped him to understand what he saw. "They're dying palmettos."

"They're like palm trees?"

"Short versions. Those are shorter than most. And the crowns have collapsed from the heat and lack of rain."

Frank was always surprising himself with his botanical knowledge. Kelly had opened this world to him with her relentless passion to identify every plant that he was just as happy to ignore. Her enthusiasm was contagious. In the end, it had brought him to those mint leaves, and through them, a step closer to making a difference in the strength and reach of the Mayan movement. At least that was the plan. But was Burns who he pretended to be? Or was he a government goon sent here to flush him out? After all, official Washington believed the Maya to be a Communist threat.

THE FIVE LOST DAYS

36

**Dracaena: Leaves crushed and steeped
for tea that alleviates asthma**

Frank had dropped them off at the base of the narrow road that climbed up into the village of San Antonio. Burns insisted they stop at the outskirts so that he and Kelly could go bungalow to bungalow, searching for patients that would agree to be filmed.

"We don't have a lot of time," Burns said, squinting up into the punishing midday sun. He studied the Mayan village sprawled haphazardly among the hills and banana trees. The low-slung homes with their tin roofs looked to be cowering from the searing sunlight. A boy on a pale, skinny horse clomped in the distance, disappearing behind one of the cinderblock bungalows. The anxious cry of a rooster pierced the hot, sullen quiet. The village, Burns thought, had the look of a distrustful old man squinting suspiciously at all outsiders.

"There's bound to be someone who will go on camera," Burns said. He winced from his sore leg as he trudged up the road, shaking off the heat that already had burned his neck, determined to find his characters. He believed in his ability to make things happen no matter what the common wisdom proscribed. In fact, the more he was discouraged by others, the more resolute he became about proving them wrong.

Further up the narrow road, Kelly directed them to a clapboard bungalow alongside the hill with a small clearing hacked away from the jungle by machete. A loose brotherhood of scrawny chickens scampered out of their way as they approached the entrance. Kelly made a clicking sound that Burns understood as a greeting in the local Mayan dialect. Almost immediately, a welcome resounded from within, its friendliness obvious in any language. Burns bounded inside ahead of Kelly, anxious to recruit.

The shade was hot but mercifully dark. A child sat pensively in the hard-packed dirt, lit by the sun leaking in under the doorway. Her head was wrapped in cloth or towel, the ends veiling much of her face. After his eyes adjusted to the low illumination, Burns recognized that she was missing a small part of her nose. Her skin was mottled and flaking like a burned-down candle. There were two chalk-white eyes staring at him from underneath the makeshift veil. At first he thought it was a terrible birth defect, but then he realized the little girl was blind, her eyes literally blanched by the fierce sun.

In the midst of his discovery, Burns had heard women exchanging words. The voices stopped now, and Burns acknowledged the mother who stood near a tin hotplate, dressed in baggy jeans and a T-shirt, not the traditional wraparound skirt. She greeted him politely with a small bow of her head.

"Her daughter's name is Natividad," Kelly said behind him. "And that's her little sister Paula in the corner."

Tiny Paula, who Burns guessed was no more than three, was holding an unclothed Barbie doll.

"What happened to Natividad?" Burns asked.

"Xeroderma pigmentosum—XP. At least that's what they believe. We still haven't got a proper blood sample to Belize City yet."

Burns was upset by the clinical description. It sounded as if she were reading off a chart. He looked at the girl's ravaged face, hating the flies that danced around her wounds. Natividad seemed not even to notice.

"XP is a kind of disease that makes you defenseless against the ultraviolet radiation of the sun."

"And there's nowhere to go," Burns said. He glanced about the tiny one-room hut. They couldn't keep her penned up in here all day, every day.

Natividad giggled and hurried over to her little sister in the corner of the room.

"Did the curandero treat her?" Burns asked.

Kelly explained that the curandero believed her ailment arose from problems that began in her mother's womb. She was born prematurely and emerged from the womb sickly and blue. The mother came from a family that had been chased out of Peten in Guatemala by Ladinos, but not before Natividad's future mother was violently raped—although she did not become pregnant.

"That's not a medical history," Burns said.

But he knew it was equally important, and it reminded him that the old curandero had been a healer for a generation of his fellow villagers. He knew them as far more than patients. It was no wonder that the medicinal plants were only a small part of what he considered when he treated them. The curandero spoke of evil spirits and good, but what Burns understood was that the unique intimacy between healer and patient demanded medical attention that was personal.

"What did the curandero do, exactly? The girl is blind."

"Pain management," Kelly said. "Not unlike what our doctors would do in a case like Natividad's."

"Are you saying there's no cure for her?" Burns asked.

"Yes," Kelly said.

"She's going to die from this?"

"Yes."

Burns was stunned. He'd never even considered the prospect that simple sunlight could kill. At worst, he thought it benign and, at its best, sunlight brought the world to life. Natividad had barely begun her own life, yet she could not, would not, ever see her sister or her mother. The only thing she would know before she died was darkness. Burns felt terrified for her. In his own life, it would be a living death, a world without any hope or possibility.

Kelly slid past him and squatted down in front of the girls. She slipped a pair of hard candies out of her pockets like a magician, and the girls squealed with excitement. Their mother nodded approval, and Kelly handed over the goods.

She spoke softly to them in the dialect that made all the women join in a conspiratorial giggle.

"Will you help me ask her, Kelly?" Burns said. As awful and tragic as Natividad's condition was, he knew it was also great television. He could not have dreamed up a better subject to stir the hearts and minds of viewers about the hunt for new medicines.

"I love these girls," Kelly said, standing up and watching them both compete to see who got the wrapper off first. She spoke to the mother, pointing to Burns and pantomiming a camera. Without pause, the mother answered in an even-toned burst of the dialect.

"She wants to know what you will do with those pictures?"

Burns hesitated. He hadn't expected such a media-savvy question. He'd assumed she might say something about Mayan superstitions, such as the fear that taking a photo stole the soul.

"We want the pictures to show how important your working with the curandero really is," Burns began but stopped when he saw the mother's face change with the mention of the village's traditional healer.

"What happened?" he asked Kelly, who listened to the short, clipped response of the mother.

"She paid Tato for his work in good meals, and so she feels he has cheated her by not curing her young daughter."

Burns didn't press the issue any further. When he returned with Vic and the camera, he would try win this woman over. It was simply too powerful an image and story to let go.

He winced as he stepped out of the shade of the bungalow and was pounced on by the afternoon sun. It was vicious and relentless, he thought. No one had a defense against it.

"Isn't there something we can do to help her?" Burns asked. He felt guilty and angry just walking away. There was another reason to film her, he told himself. Maybe her story could make a difference.

"Find a cure," Kelly said. "Soon."

They walked further up the road into the village. Burns utterly ignored his own superficial leg wound. If a young girl could withstand what that girl did, he certainly could move about uncomplaining. He felt inspired, buzzing with a new energy like a born-again enthused with the holy spirit. He was anxious to make a difference with his film.

"Are you OK?" Kelly asked, noticing the abrupt change.

"Never felt better," Burns said.

Ahead, there was a traditional Mayan thatched hut. On either side of the wood-slatted walls were maize plots, the apple green stalks no more than a foot high. The sacred crop of the Maya. It was grown everywhere, and everyone depended on it to survive.

"Who are we seeing?" Burns asked.

Kelly explained that all but one member of the large Mayan family who lived there suffered from asthma, the most common ailment in the village. The forest surrounding them provided two of the best medicines for treating it.

"Dracaena and damiana," Kelly said. "Undershrub with leaves that pack a powerful one-two punch. Alone they work as well. But when you mix the leaves together and make a tea with it, the person relaxes and breathes normally."

"And these leaves they can just stroll down the path and pick?"

"Of course. You've seen them. The dracaena looks a little like bamboo, and the damiana blooms with small buttercup flowers and smells like chamomile."

"You'll show me later?"

"The ancient Maya used damiana as an aphrodisiac," Kelly said, pausing before calling to the people inside the hut. Her sudden co-quettishness disarmed him, coming at so unexpected a moment, that he was too confused to react.

"Ready?" Kelly asked, pointing to the plank door.

Inside, a family of seven were gathered in small groups along the dirt floor. Cloths spread with brown, rough-ground beans smelled vaguely of coffee. Kelly explained they were cacao seeds that had been dried and hand-crushed to be sold to a factory in Belize City to make chocolate.

"That can't be good for their asthma," Burns said, noting the dust from both the ground and the seeds.

"They have to make a living," Kelly said.

She introduced Burns to the family, who listened to her attentively but avoided any eye contact with the filmmaker. Burns, however, was able to study them as if they were displayed on a television monitor. All had licorice-black hair and skin so smooth and unblemished they could have been in a commercial. They were a dramatic contrast to the festering skin wounds of the blind girl.

"They say, yes, you may film them with Tato," Kelly said after only a few moments.

"Good news," Burns said without enthusiasm. The family appeared perfectly healthy. If anything, TV viewers might envy how they looked. He couldn't immediately understand how their story would illustrate Kelly and the curandero's work.

"Asthma is not curable, of course," Kelly said, standing among the family like a favorite Aunt. "But they drink this tea nearly every morning to help them cope. Some days it works better than others."

"So they would allow us to come in the early morning?" Burns asked.

"Yes. And you would get your before and after. You'll see the forest at work."

When they had left the warm shade and reemerged into the blazing sunlight, Burns was at odds with himself. He remained disturbed by the discovery of the blind girl, doomed to an early death, and he was excited to be with Kelly, who made him feel utterly alive.

"The heat," Burns said, squinting into the cloudless blue sky. "It feels like it's scratching my skin."

"Maybe we should take a break," Kelly said.

"No, no," Burns said with immediate alarm. "There's no time."

"But you don't even have your camera today," Kelly said.

"I just need to see this all for myself," Burns said. He surprised himself with the plain truth. He wanted to witness the people's lives here as much as he wanted to scout for his film.

"The spirits are awakening in you," Kelly said, smiling.

"No spirits," Burns said. "Just reality."

"They're the same thing," Kelly said.

THE FIVE LOST DAYS

37

Box Haaz: Young, green leaves are
used to treat blisters and burns

Elf's swollen, sunburned face had become as stiff as dried leather.
Kelly had wiped off the last of the waxy yellow pus before she
left with Burns. Elf opened his chapped lips to ask for more of the
lemon-flavored electrolytes but was surprised to find his cheekbones
immobile. He tapped the layer of plantain leaves that covered his
cheeks with the tips of his fingers as if testing a taut conga drum.

"Hey Vic," he blurted, breaking through the resistance of his own
face.

There was a long, uncomfortable silence, and Elf feared the cameraman might have left the house, leaving him alone to fend for himself.

"I'm here," Vic called out, finally.

"I need some more of that bug juice," Elf said.

Vic was perched on the edge of his chair in the adjoining room,
rolling another cigarette. Elf called again until he heard Vic finally get
up and trudge to the kitchen and bring him a quart-sized plastic jug.

Elf chugged from the bottle. The drink was slightly salty but otherwise tasted like watered-down Kool-Aid. Kelly kept cases of it in the storage shed of the research camp, where it was used to help patients who were suffering from the dehydration caused by food sickness and diarrhea.

"My face feels like a block of cement," Elf said.

Vic studied his ravaged face with the unblinking intensity of his camera.

"Is it gonna scar, you think?" Elf asked.

"I'm not a doctor," Vic said. "And I'm sure not a nurse."

"Can you get me a mirror?"

"I have to cover your mug with these plantain leaves," Vic said. Kelly had left instructions to place new leaves on Elf's burned face every half hour to minimize the chances of infection. If he avoided infecting his damaged skin, Kelly said, a specialist should be able to perform minor skin grafting to save Elf from ending up with facial scars. He'd suffered a deep, second-degree burn that had damaged some of the underlying nerves.

"I want to see what I look like," Elf said.

"You already know what you look like," Vic said. "Nothing is going to scar, Elf. You'll be back to your ugly self soon enough. You want anything else?"

"A fan or something. The air don't even move in this place."

"If I find one, I'll bring it."

Vic turned to leave. Elf immediately forced himself to sit up, fearful of being left alone.

"Vic. What do you think about Burns? You think he's gone over the deep end?"

"Over Doctor Kelly, yeah. But he'll be fine. She'll make sure he doesn't do anything stupid."

"Are we gonna finish this doc?"

Vic shrugged and turned to walk away to get the plantain leaves, which were wrapped in wet cloth in the kitchen.

"I want to finish this thing," Elf said.

"I'll be back," Vic said.

"You want to finish this thing, right?" Elf asked.

"That's what we came here to do," Vic said.

"That's not what I mean. Do you think it's worth it?"

Vic tried to wipe away a new layer of sweat from his forehead on the shoulder of his T-shirt, but it was already soaked.

"Look, Elf. Things happen you have no control over. It isn't what happens to you that matters. It's how you deal with what happens to you."

Elf waited to see if Vic planned to add anything else.

"It wasn't my fault this all happened, you know," Elf said. "Gilbert dug in his sock to give the Guatemalan punk some cash. If he had just said what he was doing, nothing would have happened. They would have just drove away. I mean, the guy was just so scared, man. Scared for his life, you know? You do all kinds of stupid things when you're scared. And how was I going to carry him? I never would have made it anywhere."

Elf reminded himself how difficult it had been to drag the dead weight of the Belizean off the road. Yet he couldn't shake the memory of looking back at Gilbert lying alone and helpless at the edge of the forest. Elf had hesitated, unsure whether it wasn't best to just stay with the injured man and wait until Burns and the crew came looking for them. They would have been protected from the fierce sun by the thick, cool shade of the trees, and Elf could have gone in search of the water they both would need. Had he heard a stream nearby or was that wishful thinking? There was also the lucky possibility that someone from the town might wander by on foot, car or even horseback and come to their rescue. There were other options than the one he chose. Yet he had turned his back on Gilbert and uttered a prayer to a God he hadn't addressed since grade school. Why had he been so anxious to strike off on his own? Elf could not stop himself from returning to that moment on the open road, picturing what might have happened if he had not been so anxious to leave.

"I could have just come upriver," Elf said.

"Why didn't you?" Vic asked, merely curious.

"I couldn't swim," Elf said. "I mean, I can't swim."

Vic glanced out the screened window a few feet behind Elf and smiled.

"Well I'm a good swimmer," Vic said, "but the old man and his canoes made me think twice. I was afraid of losing the camera."

"I was going to do it anyway," Elf continued as if he hadn't heard. "Then I ran into Gilbert at the hotel, you know? I figured, hey, why not make it easy on myself."

Vic continued staring out the screen window.

"I figured what's the big deal, right?"

"I'm going to go get your leaves," Vic said.

"The truth is he warned me," Elf said. "He said there were these Guatemalan soldiers and they were bad news."

"Look, Elf," Vic said. "Don't torture yourself. It wasn't your fault. Let it go. Forget it."

"It was such a freak thing, wasn't it?"

Vic walked out of the room, and Elf slid back against the damp pillow. He was relieved that his sunburn no longer ached as badly as it had during the night when he had developed a fever and felt the terrible nausea rise up from his stomach, threatening to throw him onto his knees, bent over a toilet, struggling not to choke on his own vomit. But he had gotten through it with the help of some herb Kelly had made him chew and, after a few bouts of the chills, fell blissfully asleep.

"Hey. You think that old Mayan knows some plants that could heal this burn?" Elf asked after Vic returned with a fistful of the long, waxy plantain leaves.

"Figures he would," Vic said. He carefully peeled the old leaves from Elf's swollen face and added them to the discarded pile stacked in a Mayan basket at the foot of the bed. When Elf made a move to touch his newly uncovered face, Vic shook his head.

"Don't touch it. You'll infect yourself."

"Those leaves don't do shit," Elf said.

"They're to stop infection, not pain. Things would be a lot worse if you got an infection."

Elf closed his eyes and waited for the new leaves to be applied to his skin.

"We found ourselves a war maybe," Elf said, his eyes still closed.

"We don't need one," Vic said. He laid a second leaf next to the first. "Viet Cong used these leaves and were still walking after napalm. They had bad burns. Much worse than yours. Skin peeled off their faces like a banana."

Elf opened his eyes wide, staring at Vic in disbelief.

"You, you're not bad. A couple of days and you'll be fine."

"Vic. You think we're safe here? I mean from those soldiers."

"The guys you met were in Guatemala. We're in Belize. There's a thing called sovereignty."

"But where they jumped us, Vic. That was Belize. Not Guatemala."

"Elf. Can you shut up for awhile?"

"I'm gonna get some herbs from Pedro when we go and shoot him again," Elf said. "Maybe he'll have some miracle plant nobody has ever seen, not even Kelly. I mean, why not, right? People down here must get fried all the time."

"OK," Vic said, placing the last plantain leaf on his face. "You're on your own for awhile."

"Where you going?" Elf demanded.

"To the spa. Where do you think? I'll be right next door. Just don't be calling me too soon."

"Vic?"

"What now, damn it?" Vic said.

"Thanks, dude."

Vic slipped out the door as quietly as possible and walked toward the gazebo. The humid afternoon air wrapped itself around him as soon as he stepped into the clearing. He squinted through the hazy glare of the sun, impressed by the thick waves of heat that shimmered in the distance. Like looking through a plastic lens gel, he thought. He heard

Elf call for him again, but he kept walking. He could tell by the relaxed tone of his voice that Elf was just anxious, fearful of being left alone.

Vic had never been on a shoot that had taken this bad a turn. Maybe that was another reason he was reminded of his tour in Vietnam. They were in a situation that was going from bad to worse. Part of him wanted to finish the job they had traveled down here to accomplish, even if the end result would never be seen. He wanted to follow the same advice he'd given Burns: when you take on a task, do it like you mean it, with all your heart and soul. That was the way he tried to live. Yet, another, more practical and seasoned side of Vic wondered if the best thing wasn't just to get out now while they could before anything else went wrong. He had a bad feeling about all this, and he knew to trust those feelings even if they didn't seem rational.

Vic arrived at the weathered, gazebo-like shack where Kelly stored her herbs. He ducked inside and waited for his eyes to adjust to the dark shade. The light from the single window revealed a wall studded with shelves of glass and pottery, each herb and plant labeled with its Latin name. This was the first thing he'd seen when they had arrived at the research camp, a day that seemed to have been months ago. He remembered Kelly describing her room as a pharmacy, and he had taken note of one plant in particular. *Cannabis sativa*. The bright green buds were on display inside one of the clear glass jars that lined the ethnobotanist's shelf. Vic was sure she wouldn't miss a small amount. He doubted if she even got high. Besides, a few tokes of her stash would ease the ache of Elf's burn as well as relieve the vague but persistent unease that he could not readily dismiss.

38

Sorosi: fresh, raw leaves of this vine are chewed for sore throat

The lime-green shack was in the middle of a slum shaded with lush palm trees. Like a few of the other clapboard homes, it sat uneasily on weathered, makeshift stilts—protection from the flash floods that often churned down the narrow concrete street. Frank beeped the horn to coax a stray dog out of his path, then turned off the rough road and parked the pickup truck in the cool shade of the house awnings.

"What's happening?" Big asked. He looked at the skinny, hand-cut stilts alongside them, wondering how the cheap timber could possibly support the weight of the house.

"Making a quick stop," Frank said, hopping out of the cab.

"For what?"

Frank was already hurrying to the warped stairs that rose uncertainly alongside the house. Big shrugged. There was nothing he could do about it, so he sank further back in the seat, folding his burly arms. The still, muggy air had the sweet-sour smell of a garbage dump.

Frank's rapid knocking on the door startled Big. They sounded like rifle reports echoing down the empty alleyways. The noise settled slowly into the disturbed silence before the door creaked open. It opened toward the truck, which blocked Big's view of who answered it. He moved to get a better angle but still could see nothing.

"Another time is possible?" the man said. He spoke with a faint French accent, which Big heard as an upper class arrogance. It was funny hearing it spoken in a slum.

"You have to see them," Frank said.

"But I can tell nothing from only looking," the Frenchman said.

Dogs began barking around the neighborhood, echoing from one empty street to the next.

"You can see that they are healthy," Frank said. "And we can talk about moving them. There's a shop in Malibu that retails it at a hundred twenty dollars an ounce."

Big didn't understand what he was hearing, but the tone of it sounded like a drug deal going down back in New York. Only there was no sense of menace, of violence lurking in the shadows, waiting to be unleashed.

The men clattered down the wooden steps and approached the truck. The Frenchman was short and intense and wore gold, wire-rimmed glasses. He looked brainy to Big, like a college professor. He even rubbed his light brown beard like a teacher who had taught an Intro to Lit course during Big's freshman year at Adelphi.

Big raised his hand in greeting, and the Frenchman nodded politely.

"Sorry about the short notice," Frank said as he led the way to the truck. "But I don't know when I'll get back this way soon."

"You are sure this is legal in America?" the Frenchman asked.

"It's an herb," Frank said. "Like buying valerian or St. John's Wort."

"What is valerian?"

Frank didn't answer. In stead, he pulled the plastic bag from under his seat. It was filled with the green leaves Big had seen him gather from behind the trees on the road out of the research camp. "The best mint money can buy," Frank had explained. Now he presented a handful of the cuttings. The Frenchman slid one sprig against the bottom of his nose and nodded with keen approval.

"Have you ever tried it?" the Frenchman asked.

"Sure," Frank said. "It's a mellow LSD. You get a mild trip but nothing most people couldn't handle."

"Unless they have too much?"

"You'd puke before you O.D."

"Hmmm," the Frenchman said, scratching his beard with the tips of his fingernails. "I have sold peppers and spices but never a drug."

"It's not a drug," Frank insisted. "It's a legal herb. Like valerian."

"What is this valerian?"

"Oh," Frank said, "it's an herb that helps you sleep. For insomniacs."

The Frenchman nodded again. Big was surprised that this knowledgeable-looking man had never heard of valerian. They sold it in every health food store in America. He'd used it himself, popping a few capsules when he was too wound up. It worked almost as well as sleeping pills but without knocking him out or making him groggy the next day.

"So do you think you can move this herb?"

The dogs started up again. What was with all these mutts? Big wondered.

"Yes. It is possible. But I don't know how much. Perhaps a few ounces."

"What?" Frank was exasperated. He was counting on selling thousands of kilos, not a few plastic bags of the herb.

"At first," the Frenchman reassured him. "We must move slowly so we can set the best price for the future."

"Not too slowly," Frank said.

"I provide for a small distributor who, in turn, provides for small shops," the Frenchman continued. "We move at their pace."

"Well this crop won't survive the entire dry season. At a hundred twenty an ounce, that's hundreds of thousands of dollars that could be cooked by the heat."

"I can store it, Frank. That is no problem."

Frank fell silent, staring down at his worn Birkenstocks.

"OK," Frank spoke, finally. "I suppose we can try and do it your way. But I need to get some portion of the revenue to the URNG immediately."

The Frenchman smiled without showing his teeth. He regarded Frank with what Big guessed was affection, even admiration.

"You Americans, always the optimistic ones."

"How soon can you begin?" Frank asked, excited now.

"Leave this with me," the Frenchman said. "Today I can begin."

Big watched them hug. The Frenchman kissed Frank on one cheek, then the other. Although he'd seen this display of physical greeting before, it always made Big uneasy. He believed in a firm handshake.

They drove back down the alley past more of the ramshackle homes. All were on stilts, some sagging, threatening to collapse, others painted in candy colors like watermelon and mango. Big glimpsed one of the dogs that was likely to have been barking earlier. The skinny, haggard mutt trotted out from under a house just ahead of two small island kids who were brandishing bamboo sticks.

"By the way," Frank said, squinting through the sun that blasted the windshield. "You didn't hear or see any of this."

"Why's it a secret?"

"Because there are people who would like to stop me and put an end to the nuisance."

"You mean this rights movement?"

"Maybe you're not the dumb jock I took you for," Frank said. It was the first time Big had seen the man smile.

"Who wants to stop it?" Big asked.

Frank grinned again and seemed to look at him in an odd way.

"You guys really are a film crew, aren't you?"

"What the hell did you think we were?" Big asked.

"But Burns I don't buy," Frank said, shaking his head. "I just don't."

Big didn't understand at first. But after a moment, he understood what Frank was suggesting.

"You think we're down here undercover?" Big asked, adding a laugh.

"Anything is possible," Frank said with dramatic seriousness.

"This heat is getting to you," Big joked.

"Unlikely."

Big shifted in his seat. He didn't know what to make of this guy. He acted superior, like he was better and smarter than anybody.

"Why do you do this?" Big asked. "I mean, it's not like you get paid for doing this, right?"

"I take it back," Frank said, his face sour again.

"It's just a question, man."

"I get involved because I can make a difference," Frank told him. "It makes me feel good. So I give something and get something back, too."

Big understood the sentiment. What he didn't get was why this eccentric, white, middle class guy from the Midwest had developed a passion for poor people. Why the Mayans? Did everyone just need a cause?

"This herb you got," Big said. "Is it really big money?"

"I'm counting on it," Frank said.

They came to the crest of the hill. Below, the city stretched down the slope to the harbor. The vast barrios looked to Big like mounds of tin cans left to rust and decay in the sun.

"Looks like Tijuana," Big said.

"Never been," Frank said. "But the faster we can get your video-tapes and get out, the better."

THE FIVE LOST DAYS

39

**Chacha: bark is used as a natural
antidote to many skin conditions**

The boy soldier jumped out of the passenger van and trudged over to the corpse half-buried in the road. The herbs placed carefully around the body and the stench of the spent copal reeked of the dirty Mayans and their rituals. These people had a prayer and a plant for everything.

What the boy didn't know was who the body belonged to. The skin was ladino or carib. He looked past the scattered patches of flesh left by the vultures in mid-meal and took special notice of the man's thick leather belt. Maybe a tourist? As the boy bent down to take the belt, however, he recognized the man. The boy was surprised to see him dead. But he felt a twinge of pride at his kill even if the tire tracks around the corpse told him others were involved.

His platoon of young soldiers, some even younger that he, all outfitted in loose jungle fatigues, were watching him respectfully from the van. Punta music pounded from the speakers into the still heat of mid-afternoon.

The boy pushed his Ray-Bans against the bridge of his nose to keep them from slipping. He'd gotten those off a dead Mayan sympathizer. But that body had still been warm and smelled only of the shit that had leaked out of him. This corpse was rancid. The boy slipped the sweat-stained bandana from around his neck and slid it over his fine, aquiline nose to block the stench. Working quickly, he undid the fat American buckle and yanked off the belt in one swift movement, sending dirt exploding in all directions.

His platoon clapped and cheered when he held the belt high in the air above him like a dead Tommy-gutt snake. Two of the boys jumped out of the back of the van and held their rifles up in the air in a show of solidarity.

"Marco," a boy called from behind the wheel of the van. "Who is the dead man?"

"Sir," Marco corrected him.

"Marco, sir," the boy said.

Marco stood up slowly, theatrically. He was boss, and he wanted to remind everyone who was in charge. Finally, he looked past the corpse at the road that climbed the hill in the direction of San Antonio.

"It don't matter. He's a mile marker. The town is ahead."

As Marco marched back to the van, he took off his cheap belt and threw it to the ground. Three of the platoon scrambled for it, and Marco grinned, his teeth movie-star straight and clean. He slipped on his new belt, liking its more substantial weight. As he tested out the holes to fit his weight, he wondered absently if that one, swift smack to the head had killed the man. There were officers who didn't have that kind of strength, except maybe the Commander.

The driver slammed on the gas pedal before the door was even closed, rumbling over the corpse. Marco calmly pulled his door shut without comment, staring ahead. It was important to never show surprise or fear to his platoon. If anything, they should fear him. He hoped that one day his guys would be as terrified of him as they were of the Ajete, even though he was a full grown man.

The voice of Ajete, their commander, still echoed in his mind, if not his ears. They had returned to town and were showing off their stolen vehicle when Ajete grabbed the cardboard box in back and threw it on the ground.

"Do you know what this is?" he asked. The tone of his voice made him and the boys stop. Their celebration evaporated.

"This is for a camera to make movies. The men you stole this from were going to take pictures. Now why would someone want to go to that dirty Mayan town and take pictures?"

Marco nodded, knowing he had overlooked something but still not comprehending exactly what.

"Why?" Ajete asked again, this time sounding angry. "Why do you think?"

The commander had launched into his tirade, screaming at them for being stupid and lazy and worthless. No credit to Mother Guatemala. What kind of soldiers are you? What kind? On and on, it had seemed like forever until he stopped and gave Marco one order.

"We are family, yes?"

"Yes sir," Marco answered. He believed it wholeheartedly. It was the army that gave him food, a place to live and friends. He no longer even thought of his parents back in the village.

"You come back with her, Marco. We are depending on you."

Marco narrowed his eyes, hoping to look tough and determined, as he'd seen in the movies. Rambo always gave that hard look before he went to kill.

Just before the Commander dismissed him, he slipped Marco a treat. It was a treasured pill, a "black beauty," the amphetamine which always took away his fatigue and cleared his mind.

"Marco," the driver said to him now. "I am hungry. We are all hungry."

"There is not time to eat," Marco said, even though he hadn't had a meal since the night before.

"Maybe in the village?" the driver asked.

Marco took a long pause as the commander always did before answering.

"When our mission is completed," Marco said.

THE FIVE LOST DAYS

40

Schama-mo-cal: Entire herb is placed
in bath to treat chronic tiredness

Elf had drifted off to sleep with the help of the sweet cannabis. Vic had lost any sense of time as he watched his patient drift into deep slumber. He studied the deep green of the plantain leaves that clung to his face like a multi-pointed Mardi Gras mask. He pictured his son, Charles, at home, drifting off to sleep after being read his customary three picture books. Many times, Vic had lingered on the bed, watching his toddler sleep, the long face smooth, still, peaceful. It always gave him a sense of pride and of love for what he had helped bring into the world. Oddly, it was something he never thought to photograph. Maybe because it left such a living image in his mind that a picture could never have matched it.

It was rare that his sleeping son didn't also serve as an uncomfortable reminder of both his own youth and promise and his current middle age, of possibilities not realized and dreams dropped forever. He had thought he might be in big budget movies by now, entering a time of mature creative accomplishment. He had wanted to go into features, not documentaries. He liked the aesthetic challenges of a carefully lit movie more than this verite shooting, where you took what lighting and images time and circumstance allowed. He'd been the Director of Photography on one independent feature and a couple of low budget music videos, but no doors had opened into the big time. Documentaries and news had offered him a paycheck, and he'd taken it.

Vic peered through the tiny holes of the screen. A speckled moth clung to the top near the eave, its wing twitching open. The sunlight above the canopy of trees had faded into a warmer, redder hue. In a few hours, the light would be saturated with the photographic richness of Magic Hour. Some tape would undoubtedly arrive by then, and he would have his last chance to create some nice pictures.

The film itself was a bust. They had lost too much time and too many opportunities. Now New York had turned down Burns's request for more shooting time. But Vic wasn't anxious to stay even one extra day anyway. He'd had enough of being on location. He was even tired of lugging around his Ikegami, despite how much pride he took in it. The camera was optimized, outfitted with a few choice components that made it his pride and joy.

Only a few years ago, he would have been quick to act more like Elf or Big John, willing to soldier on no matter what. Making films, even documentaries, were obsessions with most of the people involved—not jobs. But Charles had changed his focus. It had happened almost overnight. After the initial euphoria following his birth—days on end when he had felt more alive and energetic than he had ever thought possible—Vic had taken a new gig overseas. He had hopped a plane to Africa on an assignment to shoot some of the famine then gripping Ethiopia. He felt strong, ready to take on anything. But when he saw the thousands of children, their skin stretched like scrim on thin, skeletal bones and more than a few with intestines swollen like grotesque balloons, Vic was overcome. It was the first time he'd ever cried on a shoot. But it wasn't because he hadn't seen or filmed this level of suffering before. Unfortunately, he had. Many times. He cried because he found himself thinking that these poor kids had parents who wanted everything in the world for them—as he did for Charles. It was the most important job in the world, Vic decided, and he wasn't going to accomplish anything being away on location for days or weeks. He needed to be with his son, spending time and effort. The job could wait. But Vic also understood that he was simply older, a little battle weary. If anything, this shoot had reminded him that he was no longer the gung-ho cameraman he once was. He didn't need to travel around the world anymore.

A howler monkey barked from somewhere in the dense canopy beyond the research compound. It sounded like a wounded dog. Vic checked Elf, but the loud call had not disturbed him in the least. He breathed slowly through his open mouth.

Well, Vic reminded himself, once the story of this failed shoot got around, he probably wouldn't need to worry about traveling anymore. No one would be likely to hire him. Burns, of course, would inevitably bear the brunt of this failure. It was too bad. He liked him and admired his skill at putting docs together. You had to wear many hats and, most of all, you had to be like a general in the field, always aware of the bigger picture.

A shrill, muffled ring underscored the busy chatter of the jungle. It took Vic a moment to realize the familiar tone was a telephone. It reminded him immediately of his co-op apartment in Manhattan. It was empty. His son was away at school and his wife at work. He was alone, killing time, waiting for a call for a new gig. It was a memory he didn't relish. The downtime between jobs ate away at him. He would miss shooting, he knew, as soon as they were back from the jungle.

He stood, finally, and strolled toward the kitchen, following the ring as it grew louder. When he answered the old, black rotary phone that rested on a side table, he guessed it had been ringing for quite some time.

"Hey," John's exasperated voice greeted him. "It's me, Big."

"I know."

"Can I talk to Burns?"

Vic explained that the producer had not yet come back from San Antonio.

"There a problem?" Vic asked.

"We don't have enough money," Big said. "The guy wants eight for the tapes. We got four."

"That's sleazy," Vic said.

"I know. But that's the deal. The guy has us by the balls."

Vic laughed mirthlessly. Every move they made unearthed another problem.

"Can you steal them?" Vic asked, half-serious.

"What?"

"Can you steal the tapes?"

"You're not helping, Vic."

"I don't know what to tell you," Vic said. "I really don't. There must be some way you can bring him around."

41

**Naba-cuc: Leaves of this tall tree are boiled
and added to bath to treat exhaustion**

The Brit listened to his plea with utter indifference. Big John tried
to impress him with the fact that they were making a major network program, one that would be watched across America. He, the
production company owner, would be helping an important enter-
prise, one that ultimately was dedicated to preserving knowledge and
helping to tell the world about new and promising medical discover-
ies.

"It's eight hundred, lad," the Brit said. "I told your man."

"No," Big John said, his voice shaking. "It was four. And that's
still more than anybody would pay in New York."

"Well perhaps you should go to New York."

Big felt his face flush. He knew he was a moment away from grabbing this thin, bony weakling by his throat.

The Brit nervously pursed his thin, mustached lip and adjusted
his squared, gold-rimmed sunglasses. He reminded Big of a sales-
man—and he hated salesmen. Whenever he walked into a store, the

hasty arrival of a smiling sales associate, as they called themselves, would send him immediately for the exit. Big liked transactions to be simple and honest with no nonsense or haggling involved.

"Well you know where to find me," the Brit said, backing away to the door that led back into the concrete garage that served as his office.

Big searched warily for bystanders. But the heat kept everyone indoors. The empty concrete road, veined with cracks, was utterly still and silent. Frank remained glued to the steering wheel of his truck that was parked behind him.

"We drove four hours for those tapes," Big said, stepping forward. He was relieved to see the effect of his imposing bulk.

"Six hundred," the Brit said, feeling for the door behind him.

"We have four." Big hated him more than ever. He would not haggle, he would not negotiate.

"Any harm to my person," the Brit warned, "and there will be no deal whatsoever."

Big stopped but still considered hitting the man for spite.

"Where are we supposed to get two hundred in cash?"

"That isn't my concern."

Big nearly hit him squarely in the mouth. He was even anticipating the pain in his knuckles and the blood that was sure to flow from the man's smug mouth. But what would he tell Burns? There would be no excuses for failing to return with what was needed. The documentary came first, Big reminded himself. Always. Besides, he might yet have a chance to clock this guy after he made the purchase.

"How about we give you some collateral for now," Big said, "then we pick it up and pay you when we drive back to catch our flight to New York?"

"What collateral you have in mind?"

Big John handed him a baggie filled with cuttings.

"What's this?"

"Salvia," Big said proudly. "It's worth a hundred and twenty five dollars an ounce."

"To who?"

"You've got four ounces there," Big continued.

"Four ounces of pot?"

"Salvia. It's a rare and prized hallucinogenic."

The Brit smiled, showing his small, tobacco-stained teeth.

"No drugs," the Brit said, handing the baggie back to Big. "You know where to find me."

The arrogant dismissal provoked him. Or maybe it was the cheerful greed. But Big had the Brit's neck in his hand and stared without mercy, as the man swung his hands in surprise and fury.

"Give me the tapes," Big said, evenly. He was surprised to find he liked this sense of power. He had control and wasn't going to give in.

The Brit's face was blood red now, and he sounded as if he was gargling. After a moment, he stopped trying to fight back with his arms. The change made Big feel giddy, flushed with excitement.

"Give me the tapes," Big repeated. "Now."

The Brit tried to shake his head. Big squeezed tighter, propelled by a force he'd never known. The Brit's eyes were bloodshot and bulging. He was hurting and Big was glad. The man had it coming. It should have been just a simple sale. No gimmicks.

Reluctantly, Big let go and watched with satisfaction as the man fell to the ground, coughing, then gulping for air.

"I'll come with you," Big said, towering over the man on all fours. "Then we'll get a price that works for both us."

THE FIVE LOST DAYS

42

**Crescentia cujete (Calabash Tree):
Seeds used to induce abortion**

Burns admired Kelly's long, feline stride as they escaped the hot, dusty village and walked together into the woods. Her gait reminded him of the first day when they had hiked together to the top of the hill that overlooked the Cayo as well as her research camp. There had been other shoots where he grew close to his main character, gaining an intimacy that felt more real and intense than in his normal world. There was a strange alchemy of affection inspired by his work. After all, in order to get the best footage, it was imperative to get his characters to like and trust him so that they wouldn't shy away from the intrusions of the camera. So, in the role of being a filmmaker, he reached out more urgently—and fearlessly—than he ever did in his personal life. He wanted and needed to get close to a person in a way he seemed to avoid in his own everyday existence. Until now, he'd never been troubled by that kind of wanderer's life, where he moved from one character to the next.

"The children," Kelly said, stopping to wait for him. "The children are just so remarkable, don't you think?"

Burns was rarely around children, so he had little with which to compare them. His life was centered on his job and Manhattan, which were overwhelmingly adult pursuits. Families moved out of the city, leaving play to the work-obsessed grownups.

"They adored you," Burns said.

"I so want them to be healthy," Kelly said. "Happiness they have—in spite of their poverty."

"They don't know anything different. Maybe that makes them better off."

Kelly showed him something between a grimace and a smile. But there was something sad in her lovely eyes that beckoned him. He wanted to comfort and protect her from whatever disappointment she harbored. It occurred to him that he had never thought to ask about her own desire for children. She was past normal childbearing age.

"Not an easy place to raise a family," Burns said.

She turned—nervously, he thought—and they walked together in the direction of the waterfall. Burns remained quiet, warmed by her trust and clear affection for him.

"We thought about raising a family," Kelly said. "But the camp, the camp...."

Burns assumed she meant that her work—like his—demanded too much time and attention.

"If you don't have regrets, you have to wonder if you ever really wanted anything enough," Kelly said.

Burns had few regrets because the only thing he ever really wanted was to work, to make films and to make a name for himself. The rest had long since fallen by the wayside. But that was before this trip. He wanted to know and feel everything about this woman. He encouraged her trust and intimacy in a new way, one not tied to his desire to shape her as a character in a movie.

"I don't know why I'm telling you any of this," she said. Again, her moss green eyes reflected a beautiful sadness.

"I want to know," Burns insisted.

The move to the jungle had begun as the realization of a dream, a fantasy even, when she and Frank were suffering the noise, pollution and high rent of their small, walk-up near Cambridge. They wanted to create a more meaningful life for themselves, one that was connected to the natural rhythms of the earth and not the manmade hustle of glass and concrete. Frank, especially, had been a Sixties radical who inspired her to dare a life outside of the Harvard establishment. So when the Cayo project appeared, they had made the leap together. Only they didn't look hard before they made the jump to an entirely new culture.

When Kelly paused, Burns eagerly nodded encouragement.

"What we didn't spend too much time exploring was what each of us wanted out of this new future," Kelly continued. "It was going to work out on its own."

Burns waited. He could feel how difficult this was for her. She spoke with an eerie calm.

"So then I missed my period," Kelly said. "It was months before I even knew. I didn't have any of the usual signs, like morning sickness, but I did feel different. Until I went to Tato, I assumed it was connected to living in the jungle. You have to remember, until then we had lived in downtown Chicago and Cambridge, Mass. Never the conditions you've witnessed in the village. In the beginning, we had no running water and no electricity."

"Not too family-friendly," Burns said.

"I didn't give Frank or myself an option," Kelly said. "I was terrified. I made a snap decision."

"Who wouldn't be afraid? Caring for a child here wouldn't be anything like the city."

Kelly's delicate nose flared slightly in a gentle exhale that Burns found only enhanced her unusual beauty.

"When I look back," Kelly said, "I sometimes think that decision, that act, forever changed not only our marriage but who we believed we were. It's one of those decisions that never stops having consequences."

Burns reached out and took her hand as if he were offering a life preserver. Only he felt like the one who was drowning. In his eyes, she was utterly connected to her life and her emotions in a way he was not.

"I'm sorry," Burns said. "I'm sorry that happened to you."

They stopped in unison at the edge of the narrow creek. Upstream, a small waterfall plunged from a smooth, rounded cliff. At the base of it, a short, burly Mayan woman with black hair tied in a braid to the small of her back, slapped a wet shirt against a flat boulder. Milk-white detergent dripped down the sides of the rock and into the green water. The woman struck the rock again and again with a sturdy patience that captivated Burns. Even at this distance, he could smell the handmade soap, carried by the sweet, cool breeze that wafted off the waterfalls. Her life was felt and lived directly through the senses. There was no glass, no electronics to objectify the world, no living inside her mind, no lens that kept the body separate from the mind.

"You're lucky to live here," Burns said. "In spite of everything."

"I know," Kelly said.

"In the city, you live in your head most of the time. There is so much coming at you that you have to block it out or risk being overwhelmed. If you really embraced all the noise and people and commotion, you'd go crazy."

Kelly moved so close that Burns felt her bare arm nearly touching his. He impulsively took her hand. It was as rough and callused as a construction worker's. But he was relieved when she made no effort to resist.

"Your hands are beautiful," Kelly said, gently squeezing his palm. Burns glanced at her scarred knuckles, wondering at the transformation of this former debutante into a rugged outdoorswoman.

"They're city hands," Burns said. "You don't get callused from computer keys."

"Follow the river?" Kelly suggested, leading him in the opposite direction of the village woman washing her clothes. He embraced the unspoken urge for privacy, entering an intimate pact that included only them and no prying eyes.

They strolled together in a vibrant silence. Burns felt the soft grass underfoot as they passed under the shade of the tree. The sudden coolness revived him, and he slid his arm around Kelly's waist. The firm, womanly curve both relaxed and excited him. Kelly leaned into his arm, and he pulled her closer.

Burns turned to find Kelly watching him, waiting. A wisp of hair had fallen across her face, creating a veil over her admiring eyes. Her lips, moist and parted, were flush from the heat. For a fleeting moment, Burns saw it as an extreme close-up, a richly textured image of a woman's face. He wanted to film it, to capture the beauty and the feeling it gave him.

When they did kiss, Burns immediately liked the fit and feel of her lips. It always surprised him how few women he actually liked to kiss. She hung onto him, her hands clasped together on the back of his neck. She slowly sank closer into him, her body cleaving to his. Burns found himself resisting. For what reason, he didn't know.

THE FIVE LOST DAYS

43

**Cot-acam: Sacred plant used
to ward off evil influences**

Pedro Meza was among friends. On either side of the sun-beaten
path outside the village were patches of chin-chin-pol-ojo, their
delicate green flowers the shape of a baby's tears; chink-in, with its
bright, butter-yellow petals; chac-te-pec's long, red stems. All common healing herbs that grew naturally as they had since his father's
time. The curandero often strolled out to this grassy lane to relax and
regain his strength in order to be prepared to treat more patients. But
today, again, there were no patients, and ever since he had talked
with Kelly about this camera preserving his legacy of healing, he found
himself thinking about his father. While his father's breath had been
stolen many decades earlier, the loss had faded but never left him. It
was, he often thought, like the amputee he had once treated for infections. The young man had told him that while he knew his arm was
gone, he often continued to experience a faint, ghostly ache from his
blunt shoulder to where his hand had once reached out to the world.

Pedro Meza took a long, deep breath to try to relax. A scent of sage hung in the humid air around him. The short walk had already eased the ache of his arthritis, and he was grateful. He had little tolerance for pain. His father, he remembered, was physically fearless. Pedro Meza would never forget the night his father had crossed the Macal in a canoe, the river swollen and treacherous from the summer rains. He had watched in terror as his father shoved off from the dark shore. At the last moment, Pedro Meza had caught his father's smile in the starlight, reassuring him. In the next instant, he was battling with the raging current to keep from capsizing. All this risk was taken in the name of treating a patient who was too ill to travel to the village.

Pedro Meza shook his head in admiration. But his father also was bold to a fault. There was a time he had experimented with the other side of the healing arts—the curses and hexes fixed on people to bring them harm. His father believed in them as he believed in the unlucky days of the Uayeb. Once, at least, his father had called upon this sorcery out of petty jealousy. A woman he desired had spurned him.

Now that Pedro Meza was old, too, he better appreciated how deeply his father might have felt that rejection when the world itself seemed to treat the old like forest brush—just something to be cleared. But turning away from healing spirits for whatever purpose was a betrayal of the curandero's calling. Worse, he had come to believe that exploring those forces as his father had inevitably brought harm to the user. Sooner or later, you were bit. Hadn't his father fallen ill soon after he had put a hex on a rival for that woman's affection? It was no coincidence. One did no help or good by calling on the evil spirits.

While Pedro Meza himself had never followed his father's path, he had sometimes worried that the son might one day pay for the sins of the father. At his father's funeral, in fact, he had lit an extra offering of copal for just this reason. He hoped to release his father's great and loving spirit and, at the same time, forever extinguish the other forces that tempted him with power.

Instinctively, the curandero ambled over to the bright yellow flowers that graced the roadside. These were the tools of the healer, of good. But when he reached down to touch the plant, he felt an odd tremor in the ground. He looked wildly about him, fearing that he had just had a premonition. In the next instant, however, he recognized the vibration of the road. Vehicles were approaching the village. Soon, he heard the whine of the engines. There was one large vehicle, and he could tell they were in hurry. It was then that the curandero felt a sudden gust of wind. Ik, the evil wind.

Pedro Meza turned back to his village without knowing what this omen meant. But he knew enough to fear the forces that were blowing around him. When he arrived back at the edge of the village, the engines were roaring, gears grinding as they slowly rolled up the middle of the street. He didn't recognize the blue van. It stopped only a few yards from his bungalow. When the boys in fatigues jumped out, clinging to their guns, Pedro Meza started. It was the Uayeb. They might merely be the lost days on the calendar, but they were a reminder that there were times when the best-laid plans went awry, taunted by the dark spirits, and there was nothing anyone in this world could do to change it. The curandero felt older and weaker, and when the Ik blew again, stirring the dry dust into his eyes, he called upon the memory of his father, the fearless healer who smiled at threatening storms.

THE FIVE LOST DAYS

44

Ya-ax-ak: Vine is chopped, boiled and drunk to cure constipation, indigestion or any ailment of the digestive tract

Frank drove without saying a word. The truck rumbled along Western Highway, past the dead grasses and tired palmettos of the savanna. It was his least favorite part of the country, but right now he welcomed its desolation. He felt as though he had betrayed himself twice: first, by helping this crew to get their tape because he was angling for them to produce a valentine report on his wife's work; second, because he was implicitly supporting a thug. Here he was devoting time and effort to help shield the Maya from marauding Guatemalan gooks, and who does he chauffeur to Belize City, the nation's capital? A common thug. This over-pumped monster had almost choked a man to death. Sure, the man was trying to hit them up for more cash. But you don't try to kill him for it.

"How much further?" Big asked, soberly breaking the hostile silence.

"Couple hours."

"Will it be dark?"

"Most likely," Frank said, staring at the drab road.

"That guy was a punk," Big said. "A punk."

Frank noted the square chin, the wide, innocent face. So American, he thought. So cocksure of being in the right, morally superior but using whatever means necessary. Hell, Frank thought, recalling his earlier suspicions. He and Burns and the whole crew could easily be CIA.

"I never did that to anybody. Ever," Big said.

"No?" Frank didn't believe him.

"Last time I even hit a guy was in sixth grade," Big continued. "And it hurt like hell. Had to put my fist on ice for an hour."

Frank concentrated on a flock of birds sweeping over the savanna. Nothing worth stopping for, he wanted to tell them.

"I know you don't approve of what I did," Big resumed. "But I had to do it. We were past being out of time. And I gave that guy plenty of chances to come clean."

"Well. You got your tapes."

"Yep. We got 'em," Big said. "Ain't proud of how. But we did get 'em."

"Well history has a long line of apologists who said that the end justified the means."

"What?"

"It doesn't matter," Frank said.

"You know, something got hold of me back there. Something I ain't ever felt before."

Big paused and turned away. It seemed as though he was talking to himself.

"You give into that and you can do some damage. Must be what gets soldiers to do what they do. No matter the cause."

Frank was startled by the man's introspection.

"I hope I never feel that again," Big said, finally.

Later, as they drove across the concrete bridge that led over the river into San Ignacio, Frank decided he'd been too harsh in his judgment. This film crew believed passionately in what they did, however misguided. They deserved something for it. How different was he himself? Wasn't he tempting fate by dealing with covert funding and shady dealers?

They drove past weathered, clapboard homes that were slung at the road's edge. Mayan condos, his friend Carlos called them. Dirt-poor men and women worked maize fields for a few bucks a day, then trudged miles to these ramshackle homes, exhausted. They did the work no one else would touch and, in the process, made themselves into untouchables. Frank was surprised they could maintain any hope at all. Even more galling, they were ground into a weary subservience by just a few landowners, who profited immensely and disproportionately from their daily toil. The government, democratic in name, perversely aided the landowners, passing laws that kept land ownership rights out of Mayan hands.

But his mint leaves could well revolutionize that one day. Frank would fight money and power with money and its power. The profits from his hallucinogenic plants would bring on nightmares for the current elite. Not a shot would be fired. Affluence would lead a gentle battle.

"You did what you had to do," Frank said, deciding that he had been too harsh and judgmental about his passenger. "That creep will recover."

"What?" Big asked. He'd been dozing.

"Nothing," Frank said.

Impulsively, Frank reached under the seat for the baggie of *Salvia divinorum* leaves. He let them rest on his lap, reminding himself that he had never actually tried ingesting the leaves. He'd been waiting for the right moment. Now seemed ideal. The effects were said to be mild, and they would almost certainly help the last miles go by more easily. Frank had tried any number of hallucinogenics, from mushrooms to LSD, all of which were more powerful than salvia.

"You taking that stuff?" Big John asked.

"Care for a sample?" Frank asked. The leaves were bitter with little flavoring. Like chomping on parsley, Frank thought.

"No," Big John said, staring straight ahead.

"Trust me," Frank said. "Drinking and driving is a lot more dangerous."

"I don't even drink," Big said.

"Well, I can't sell a product I haven't tried now, can I?"

"It's really legal?"

"For now. Who knows what the government will do if the leaves are any good. The government will find a way to screw everything up."

45

**Ok-pich: Leaves of this fern are rubbed
on head to get rid of dandruff**

Carlos was eating lunch in his dirt courtyard when he heard the vehicle come to a hurried stop. At first, he assumed it was Frank returning. Maybe he had forgotten something for the long ride to Belize City. Carlos set his half-eaten plate of dirty rice and beans on the ground, climbed out of his plastic chair and hurried to the side of his bungalow, eager to help.

Frank had become a close friend over the years. He liked the American's wild schemes and causes. The people of the village, especially the Mayans, might be put off by his strange talk of organizing and demanding land and money from a government that never touched their lives. But Carlos thought there was merit in organizing or at least raising people's awareness. Neither the government in Belize nor the one in Guatemala had any interest in San Antonio. The village was too small and poor to be on the radar. As a near border town, deep in the jungle, it was also something of a no man's land. Guatemala didn't even recognize the border, and Belize didn't much care.

Except when the loggers came and then the cattlemen. With all that big money, Carlos began to think Frank's plan wasn't so farfetched.

As he neared the corner, Carlos started. He heard the voices of boys and felt a chill like ice water dripping down his spine. He'd been told about the brazen attack and the car-jacking in daylight by the Guatemalan boy soldiers.

Carlos turned and ran, first for his bungalow, then, afraid he would be found, veered suddenly into a narrow gap between two homes and sprinted toward the waterfalls that were in the woods just outside the village. He could not even remember the last time he had run so hard and so fast. Maybe not since he was a kid, running the jungle paths for fun. But at this moment, he was running for his life.

As he neared the water, he was nearly choking, struggling to breathe. Sweat stung his eyes and soaked his T-shirt. He smelled the copal, still burning along the meandering stream to honor the spirits of Mazdara, the boy who had been killed by the mysterious fever from the virus. The last few days, he thought in passing, have been a dark curse.

Carlos was relieved to hear the familiar splash of the waterfall upstream, where it plunged out of the dark shade of the trees and spilled onto the sunlit boulders he had known since he was a child. The sound had always calmed him. But Carlos recognized another sound as well. Footsteps, lighter and faster than his own.

A cool breeze drifted downstream and brushed his cheeks. It immediately calmed his breathing, and as it came under control, Carlos understood that he had panicked. He felt like an absolute fool. It would have been far wiser to continue walking toward those soldiers. It was possible they knew nothing. They were likely just searching for information. Carlos peered downstream, wondering whether to follow it as it flowed back into the forest and then down into the valley near the Macal. It was, he knew, his best escape. He had run and in that act all but screamed he had something to hide.

Carlos closed his eyes and called silently to his Nagual. The stream went through rugged territory whose boulders and rocks were known to be the preferred home of many a fer-de-lance. Carlos understood that once he entered the forest, his life would be in the hands of his guardian spirit. He reminded himself that he was a good man, committed to his people. Surely this would count for something. The spirits would take mercy on him. If he did not run, and surrender himself to the forest, Carlos knew he would be at the mercy of men, of soldiers. These he feared more. Men were cruel and vicious in a way the spirits never were. Men brought darkness upon each other.

The smell of the copal, however, weakened his resolve. It was the smell of funerals, of life in another realm. Carlos was afraid. He did not know what the other world held for him. So he hesitated—a moment too long. One of the kid soldiers was yelling excitedly behind him. If Carlos ran, he felt sure he would be shot. The soldiers were known to kill for less. Hadn't they murdered that driver just yesterday for no apparent reason? So Carlos remained still, too terrified to even turn around, listening to the footsteps and the angry, excited shouts behind him. When a gun went off, he felt the loud report in his eardrums a moment after the bullets plunked harmlessly into the emerald stream. Carlos closed his eyes, feeling the warm urine trickle down his leg.

THE FIVE LOST DAYS

46

**Pa-al: Crushed, green berries of this shrub
are rubbed on feet to cure athlete's foot**

Kelly rolled out of Burns's arms and sat up. They had been lying together in the warm, dappled shade by the stream when she heard the screaming. She searched frantically for her huipile, anxious not to be discovered, at least not like this.

"What's going on?" Burns whispered.

Before she could even slip on her blouse, she spotted Carlos, her husband's closest friend. The sight of him hit her like a physical blow. She felt sickened, dirty and angry with herself. She had never imagined betraying anyone, let alone her life's partner. Yet it had happened—or *almost* happened—so casually and with such easy desire that she wondered if she hadn't just been fooling herself for years, pretending to be someone she was not.

As Carlos came closer to the stream, the terror on his face shocked her. He seemed to be running for his life. Her first impulse was to cry out, to offer help, but she hesitated. It was then the soldiers emerged, teenagers dressed in olive fatigues, their guns drawn, anxiously chasing down their prey. Carlos stopped at the water's edge, no more than thirty yards away from where Kelly sat. He remained as motionless as she. The gunfire made her jump. But Carlos remained still in the charged air as the soldiers rushed up behind him. They ordered him to turn around and broke into laughter the moment they saw he had peed himself. Carlos, shaking, obediently marched back to the village, one soldier ahead, another behind. They looked to her like boys playing soldier, which made them seem even more threatening.

"Where did they come from?" Burns asked.

"Guatemala," Kelly said. "They must be chasing Manuela."

"The one your husband talked about."

"Manuela," Kelly repeated, startled by the threat fast gathering force before her eyes. Rumors of Guatemalan soldiers crossing the border were common, but in all her years in Cayo, she had never witnessed an incursion herself. The war had never come to her camp or San Antonio.

"We need to get help," Burns said. He grabbed his shorts out of the dirt and slipped them on over his leg wound, which had formed a paper-thin scab. He remained on the ground, dazed by the sudden change of circumstance, and pulled his T-shirt on awkwardly over his head.

"Let's go," she said, standing up and absently brushing the dirt off her shorts.

"Where?" Burns asked, squinting up at her.

"Somewhere," she said, suddenly uncertain what to do.

"Let's think, let's think," Burns said.

"OK," Kelly said.

"Hey. I'm just as scared as you, OK?"

Kelly felt a rare anger burst inside her. He was so utterly self-consumed that he could not see anything or anyone with any clarity. If he felt something, everyone else did, too. Other people were just reflections that offered new glimpses of himself.

"I'm not scared, Burns. I'm worried. There's a difference."

She considered following the stream up to the landing by the research camp. From there, they could contact the Belize military. But it would be a long journey, too long to be of any use to the villagers or Carlos or Tato. Burns balked when she suggested their only option was to go back into the village and try to intervene.

"We can't do that," Burns said.

"Do what you want," Kelly said.

"I want to help," Burns said. "I really do."

"Good," Kelly said. "Let's go."

Burns walked unsteadily alongside Kelly, using her shoulder as a crutch whenever he felt the strength go out of his injured leg. In truth, he simply felt young and foolish. He had been on the verge of screwing his main character, even though she was married and he was committed to Julie—or at least wanted to be. Instead, like some young producer jock, he'd been playing romance instead of maintaining his focus on the film.

"Kelly," Burns began, his voice testing the air.

"Don't say anything Michael," Kelly answered. "Please."

They walked together in a strangely intimate silence. Burns felt very close to her, liking the feel of her strong yet delicate shoulder. He didn't want to let go, even though he was now capable of walking on his own.

They passed under the trees that rose up on either side of the path like sentinels. Burns peered upwards at the jade canopy, dazzled by the perfectly white jeweler's light. Yet, as they continued forward, he found himself feeling apprehensive, even though he knew he wasn't a person who frightened easily when it came to physical danger. But they were taking a foolhardy risk returning to the village in pursuit of these soldiers. He felt he was stepping over some line that shouldn't be crossed. A filmmaker had to resist becoming a part of the story or lose any chance of telling it. But he was drawn forward, against all his instincts.

A hot, dry wind kicked up the dust from the sun-beaten path. Everything changed so quickly in this heat, Burns thought. From mud to dust in a matter of hours. He watched the dust swirl into a faint tube, then sweep toward the forest like rolling surf. Ik was the name the curandero had given it once before. The evil wind.

"What if they just start shooting?" Burns said.

"You were the one who told me no one messes with Americans."

Burns swallowed but his mouth was dry. He licked the salty perspiration off his lips, grateful for any moisture. He'd never felt more vulnerable in his life. He knew that the only thing keeping him moving forward was this woman who did everything with such selfless resolve.

"Don't say or do anything to provoke them," Kelly said.

Burns stared ahead with a feverish clarity, hoping luck was with him—even if it hadn't been so far.

They stepped into the clearing, in full view of the soldiers who were downhill about fifty yards away, grouped in front of a bungalow. The kid soldiers paid no attention to them at first. All were focused on Carlos, who slouched fearfully before them, being questioned at close range by a skinny soldier who was half his age. The boy kept one hand on the assault rifle that was slung over his shoulder. Despite the automatic weapons and olive uniforms, Burns thought they seemed less military and more like the troubled teenagers he'd often spotted next to the bodega that served his neighborhood, pretending to loiter until they scored a drug buy or a sell. Most people instinctively avoided them.

"Donde?" the soldier demanded. "Where is she?"

Chickens in a nearby bungalow chortled nervously in the silence. Carlos stared at the ground.

"Donde?" the soldier screamed in his face like a drill sergeant. "Donde?"

Even at a distance, Burns could tell the interrogator had smooth cheeks and a helmet of thick black hair. He was as neatly groomed as an altar boy. So when he spit in Carlos's face, Burns was startled.

Carlos made no attempt to wipe away the spittle that dripped from one of his cheeks. He continued to stare at the bare ground, waiting for this humiliation to end.

Another, more powerful gust of wind whipped the dust from the street, and the cloud swept past them. Burns shaded his eyes momentarily to keep the dust out. He wondered if the sudden gusts of wind were bringing a rainstorm. But the sky was clear, and the wind itself was hot and dry, drained of even a hint of moisture. Burns had felt winds like this in the desert but never in a rain forest, even one undergoing the deforestation that surrounded this village.

"Tato," Kelly blurted. She spoke with a frightened, maternal alarm as the short old man in a soiled baseball cap, stooped slightly forward, shuffled up the street toward the soldiers with a hemp bag slung over one shoulder and leaning on a walking stick. Despite his tired gait, the curandero moved with an uncanny confidence. Burns was reminded of his first meeting with the bush doctor, moments after washing ashore after his fall in the cave. The curandero had seemed imposing at that moment and as sharply alert as any man he'd ever seen.

The altar boy soldier halted his interrogation, startled to see this old man and, in the next instant, spotted Burns and Kelly. The boy turned back to Carlos, slipping his gun off his shoulder.

"Donde?" the boy demanded, this time pointing the barrel of the gun at Carlos's forehead.

Yet another gust of wind roared up the street. It blew ahead of the curandero as though he were shepherding it forward. He stopped at the crest of the hill. As if on cue, the wind howled again, whipping the dust into their faces. It was a stronger, more violent gust than before, and Burns was forced to turn away before the dirt blinded him. When the wind finally died down, Burns was startled to find the little old man almost alongside the soldiers.

The pop shattered the queer silence. Burns stared, disbelieving. A spurt of blood blew out of Carlos's forehead. He looked merely surprised. But his wide eyes lost focus, and he crumpled to the ground like a worn-out doll.

The altar boy remained utterly still. He looked down at Carlos and back to his gun as if trying to make the connection between the two. He continued pointing the barrel at the now empty space where Carlos's forehead had been.

Kelly's wail knocked Burns out of what felt like a trance.

The soldiers turned in their direction. The boy was dazed, one of his smooth cheeks splattered with a tribal-like streak of blood. He seemed overwhelmed, struggling to register what he knew had just happened and what he had just done. There was an immediate, youthful contrition to his expression, and Burns wouldn't have been surprised if he had walked over and surrendered his weapon.

"Vamonos!" the boy called out instead. "Vamonos!"

The platoon hurried past the curandero, who remained stoic and motionless, back toward the blue van as if they had been granted a school recess. The boy backed away from his kill before turning to join the other kid soldiers. At the last moment, he glanced toward them, but there was not even a flicker of recognition. Before the boy marched off to his waiting soldiers, Burns glimpsed what he thought was a dazed smile.

The curandero leaned on his walking stick, studying the dust cloud left by the departing trucks. Pedro was ashamed of himself. He had acted like his father but not in the way he intended. He had been able to maintain his physical courage, but he had been weak in attempting to marshal the dark spirits. It had been worse than foolhardy. Violence and the threat of it only managed to breed the same.

Kelly was sobbing, tears dripping from her cheeks like rain from a leaf. The curandero felt responsible for what had happened, and he wanted to comfort her. But the tall blanc held her protectively in his arms. The blanc was strong of spirit and his youth impervious to the dead soul at his feet.

The sound of the engines lingered in the distance long after the soldiers disappeared from view. Pedro felt weak, defeated. I am truly an old man, he said to himself. Older than I ever dreamed I would be. He turned sorrowfully to the corpse of Carlos, whose head now rested in its own thick puddle of blood. The curandero clapped his hands rapidly above the body, setting free the spirit. He squinted into the haze of the late afternoon sun, hoping for a sign. The roosters were crowing again, and he could hear the snorting of pigs from one of the pens. Some of the neighbors had emerged from their bungalows and were hurrying downhill with the dread and excitement of wanting to discover what caused such anguish with the blancs. Pedro thought he could feel their suspicion turn to him as soon as they saw the body motionless on the blood-soaked ground. The evil spirits had been unleashed.

THE FIVE LOST DAYS

47

**Eremuil: Dark green leaves
used as a tea to treat hysteria**

Marco was dead silent as they drove along the logging road, away
from the village. He swallowed, wishing they had thought to
get water, and tried to ignore the racing feeling that coursed through
him. The glare of the sun through the dirty window made him cross
and irritated. He didn't care about this Manucla anymore. He just
wanted to be back across the border and out of Belize.

He didn't remember flicking off the safety. There would have been
no reason. He wanted only to frighten and intimidate the man. Maybe
it was the wind. Si, Marco decided, it was the gust of wind. If he had
chosen to kill the man, he would have done so. But the man was Ladino, not a Mayan pig.

Marco remembered the two older blancs staring at him. Where
had they come from? He should have questioned them. But it was
best they left. There would be problems. Marco closed his eyes and
felt a sharp pang of hunger. He imagined a heavy plate of steaming
rice and tangy beans with tiny flicks of onion and pepper. How long

had it been since they had a meal?

They rumbled along the tree line and turned uphill where the road widened. The sour, yellowing sun was ahead of them, dangling in the bone-white sky like a bare light bulb. They would likely be home by sunset, Marco decided. There they would have a meal and tell the Commander they could find no trace of this Manuela and, anyway, there was nothing in the village. He would not mention the blancs. Americans, Marco realized, picturing them again. They were tall and pale, and an air of importance clung to them like a second skin.

As they rumbled over the crest of the hill, Marco spotted the jeep in the middle of the road, both doors swung wide open, about a half mile away.

"Stop," he ordered instantly. "Stop!"

As the van shuddered to a halt, Marco glimpsed the two Polizia. At first, he assumed it was a roadblock. But then he knew it was the corpse, half-buried in the middle of the road. The driver he had hit with the butt of his rifle.

"Reverse," Marco said. He tried in vain to get a sense of what the men were doing, worried they had either heard or seen the van. As they rolled backwards, Marco checked the doors of the jeep and was relieved to see nothing had moved. Of course, that didn't mean he and his soldiers hadn't been spotted.

His platoon was talking excitedly all around him at once. Marco cursed, unsure of what to do. They could not go forward and risk a confrontation with the Polizia. The Commander would be furious. They had never been allowed to take independent action without even seeking his approval. Ajete would punish them severely, that was certain. Perhaps they could pass by the Polizia without incident, brandishing their weapons as a warning. But what if there was resistance?

"Turn around," Marco ordered, finally. The chatter stopped. He remembered another road when they had driven out of the village. It had gone to the east and Marco had wondered absently where it led. Now they would find out.

"Where do we go, Marco?" the driver asked.

"We take another road," he answered. He could sense the puzzle-ment among his men but made no further comment. It was best they simply obeyed him.

THE FIVE LOST DAYS

48

**Pay-che: The 'thinking herb' of the Mayas
used in a great variety of complaints**

The darkening, indigo sky was painted with brilliant strokes of tangerine and salmon and burnished gold. The sunset soothed Frank, and he gazed in appreciation at the rust-colored glow of the dirt road and the wrinkled bark of the trees towering alongside. Even Big's otherwise bland face was transformed—his smooth cheeks, square, all-American chin and wide forehead all bathed in the same other-worldly orange. His hair flickered like flames in the early evening breeze, and the whites of his wide eyes were made super white and piercing. Frank felt an uncommon sense of wonder as if he were seeing the rain forest and Cayo for the first time.

"Frank, are you OK?" Big asked. "You're sweating bullets."

Frank was made aware of the perspiration running down his cheeks and dripping from his chin. It was warm and pleasant, and he didn't feel unusually hot. In fact, he felt cool and calm despite the jungle humidity. His body was so weightless as to be almost without gravity, and that sense made him giddy. He laughed, finally, in answer to Big's question. It began as a giggle, found strength and rolled into a genuine belly laugh. He caught Big's surprised smile and sensed the good humor was contagious, like a contact high.

"I got to stop and take this in," Frank said and brought the pickup to a measured halt. He slipped effortlessly out of the cab and planted his feet in the glowing road. He felt he was on top of the world. The chatter of birds in the forest sounded like a group of schoolgirls at recess, and it made him laugh again.

"You're not going to freak out on those leaves you chewed, are you?" Big asked, crossing around from the other side. His burly arms were folded tightly against his barrel chest.

"Big," Frank said, smiling at the production assistant's nickname, "the answer is no. But I highly recommend the experience. There's more under the seat."

"No way," Big said.

There was a small garden of this remarkable herb not far from where they stood. The knowledge of it filled Frank with satisfaction. He had made the right choice in cultivating the *Salvia divinorum* after all. It acted like a benign drug, but it was legal in most of the world. At least until some communist-baiting conservative Republican got wind of the fun. It would surely be demonized. But for now he had an herb that was fun for people and good for the indigenous movement. It was like selling candy to raise money for the disadvantaged. Everyone wins.

"Look at this country," Frank said with the sudden fervor of an evangelist. "Have you ever seen anything like it?"

"It's a great sunset," Big agreed.

Frank giggled then burst into another fit of hearty laughter.

"Too much," Frank said after the laughing subsided. He felt a surge of simpatico with Big, a sense of shared experience and camaraderie.

"I've been down here in the jungle for a long time. Fourteen years. And most of the time I hate the place. Not the people. The place. The heat, the bugs, the rain, the humidity. If it weren't for my wife, I'd have been gone long ago. And you know what? Right now, I have to say, I appreciate the place. Love it, even. I mean it's just so beautiful."

"You're high," Big said.

Frank turned quiet and philosophical. Salvia magic, as advertised. So much about what we see, he decided, is affected by what we bring to the seeing. He could see this rain forest in a different mood, and it would be a different place. If he looked at it like Kel, it was a research laboratory. If he was a curandero, the jungle was an extension of ancient spirits. If he gazed upon it like Big, like a filmmaker, it was a photo opportunity, a place to be captured and remade. Frank saw it as a dismal place that needed to be fixed, improved. A place that brought both life to the living Maya and oppression from those that hated them for it.

All of us live in a world of our own making, Frank decided. It took the liberation of this remarkable herb to look past our own prejudice, to recognize things as they were, not through the filter of our own minds.

"How about I drive?" Big asked.

"What do you see out there?" Frank asked, deciding to test his sudden insight into the world.

"The jungle," Big said. "Look, everyone is waiting for these videotapes we have."

"Do you like the jungle?"

"It's OK to visit," Big said. "I really think we need to step on it."

The anxiousness in the man's voice touched him. Frank wanted to soothe him. The truth was they would reach the village of San Antonio in less than half an hour—likely just as these magnificent colors that so transformed everything bled away into the soft darkness of twilight.

Frank heard the jet first, its distant approach cutting through the chatter of the forest. Then it shot out of the sunset, headed right to the clearing where they stood. Frank was awed, even though it was by no means the first fly-by he'd ever seen. The BDF ran occasional sorties by the border as a warning to Guatemala. The tiny Belize Defense Force, in fact, had been trained by the British to defend its territory if

Guatemala ever attempted to invade Belize and take what they claimed was their historic land.

The Harrier jet roared overhead. Frank ducked even though the plane was far above the treeline. A few seconds later it was gone, and the chatter of the forest returned.

"What the hell?" Big asked.

"Patrol," Frank said. He knew it was likely to have been prompted by the death of the Belizian driver.

"OK," Frank said. "Let's go. You drive." He tossed Big the keys.

Sometime later, using the truck's headlights, they spotted wood stakes marking the middle of the road. Each had a white rag tied at the top like a flag. Frank recognized it was a crime scene stakeout. The police had come to investigate after all.

"Slow down," Frank said. Watching the flags stir, he was reminded of the corpse below it and the role he played in using it. They might have found a better way, he admitted to himself, even in that punishing downpour.

"Cops do this?" Big asked.

"Yeah. They probably drove on to the village from here."

As they drifted slowly around the flag poles, Frank was relieved to see that the body had been covered with a tarp and pinned to the ground with an assortment of bricks from town. It would keep the vultures and the other animals at bay.

"That fighter jet," Big said. "I can't get it out of my head. It came right at us."

He accelerated up the hill, away from the crime scene and toward the village.

"Yeah," Frank said. "If you get lucky, you might even get some pictures to take back with you."

Frank smiled at his own joke. But he was no longer feeling giddy or euphoric. The plant was wearing off. He'd learned from one of Kelly's pharm books that this was the normal cycle. If you smoked it, the book said, the effect lasted even less time, often no more than five minutes. For the shamans of the world, who used this plant to induce their visions, that was probably time enough. Frank wouldn't have minded a little more time. But he liked that the salvia let him down slowly, returning him to his normal state.

"We're almost back," Frank said.

"Burns will be happy," Big answered.

"You can be filmmakers again," Frank said, still uncertain if that's who they really were, if Burns wasn't just pretending to be a film-maker and was actually some government goon.

"We got two days to wrap this up," Big said.

Frank thought of Carlos back in the village. He was anxious to tell his friend what he had discovered about the salvia. Of course, he'd have to guard his supply from Carlos afterwards. Carlos liked his mood enhancers, whether it was pot or a bottle of Belikan or that country mash one of his cousins in Belize City liked to cook up.

"You're not sweating anymore," Big said.

The road widened as they approached the village.

"I'm stone sober," Frank said.

THE FIVE LOST DAYS

**Chin-chin-pol-ojo: Entire herb is boiled
and used to treat internal infections**

The sight of the immaculate hacienda awed the soldiers, but none more than Marco. The village where he once lived with his parents and sister was an assortment of cinder block homes scattered alongside the region's only road, and not even Senor Jorge's casa was as grand as this, even though Jorge owned the coffee and cardamom plantation where his father and so many others worked for twenty measly quetzals a day. Marco was certain the home with the impossibly tall windows before him, gilded now with the last burst of the sunset's russet light, had to be owned by an Americano. They were all rich beyond belief. Maybe not like he had seen in the cinema, but they had far more than he believed he or his family would ever possess. The Americans were lucky, even if none he had met ever acted like it. They seemed to believe most everyone lived as they did. He had never forgotten the well-fed, privileged American missionary who had come to their house and beamed when he had spotted mama's ceramic crucifix on the wall, as if it marked them as equals.

Marco's soldiers remained motionless in the van. They stared as he did. But they were fearful that the owner of this hacienda and the vast grazing fields that lay before it was very powerful. They should not have risked stopping even when Marco ordered. The road continued past it, plunging further into the forest. So their anxiety heightened when Marco opened his door and jumped onto the gravel driveway.

"Marco, Marco," one of them called out in a loud whisper, fearful of unseen guards. "We must go."

Marco didn't respond. Instead, he walked purposefully to the floor-to-ceiling window. He was surprised to see his own reflection mirrored in the golden glass. He looked shorter and thinner than he imagined himself to be. His thick, dark hair could have been a helmet. But his round face was indistinct, and his eyes seemed like the dark, empty holes of a Mayan mask. He leaned closer, and the image vanished. He was looking inside a vast room with a dark leather couch and polished tables. There were thick rugs on the tiled floors and paintings on the smooth walls. How would it be to live like this? He was sure he would never leave a home like this. Of course, he wouldn't have to.

The recognition that this was someone's home, maybe even the home of a boy his age, weighed on him. He fought the disappointment, telling himself it was just the black beauties wearing off. He was a soldier of Mother Guatemala. She was his home. He had brothers and the Commander. There was purpose and meaning. He was not destined to work at the plantation as his father still did. Marco had a greater destiny. He was sure of it.

Yet, he could feel the tug of his old home. He could see his mama setting the heavy yellow plate in front of him for dinner, steam rising from the rice and beans and roast pork, smelling sweetly of her mama's spices. He could feel the warmth of her standing alongside him, silent, her gentle brown eyes watching him with quiet admiration.

"Marco!" a boy called out loudly.

Marco ignored him and made a quick inventory of the riches displayed behind the glass. There was clearly no one at home or they would have been confronted long ago. Here was an opportunity that would certainly be appreciated by the Commander. If he were with them, the Commander would order them to take what was needed to further the fight against those who hated Mother Guatemala. They had taken things before, but those were from the dirty Maya and other peasants who had less then they did. Marco had never seen anything approaching this opportunity.

He took a quick, emboldening breath and walked up to the richly stained door and tried the handle. It turned effortlessly. He pushed open the door and was greeted with the smell of lavender. He spotted an overflowing basket of it in the entryway. The tile beneath him shined as though it had just been mopped. He looked at his own boots and was surprised to see the dried blood splattered on one. He gained courage from the sight, a badge of his toughness as a soldier.

"Come, come," he ordered to the boys, who had still not dared leave the van. "We will take before we go."

The soldiers stumbled out of the van like they were drunk. Their faces were incredulous, yet they moved forward on Marco's orders. Within moments, they followed their leader through the door and grabbed whatever was in reach. They took vases, clocks, rugs—anything that could be taken without wandering further into the house. The recognition that they were stealing excited them, and they moved more quickly. One ran into a bedroom in search of jewelry. They shouted and laughed like boys at play. And it was a game. They were risking getting caught, and it was fun.

Marco assumed a more mature stance and began barking orders for the loot to be carried quickly to the van. There wasn't much time. He couldn't help but smile when he said this. They had stumbled upon riches and were claiming them. The Commander would be jealous and proud of them when they returned.

The roar of the fighter jet stunned all of them. They stopped, listening for its flight path. As soon as they recognized how close the plane was, they dropped everything and ran, panicked. Even Marco froze, terrified the fighter was about to strafe their position. One of the boys started running for the van, and in a moment it was a stampede. They saw the fatigue green jet in the distance, skimming the trees, racing ahead of its own sound.

"Vamonos, vamonos!" Marco yelled. Once everyone was in the van, they peeled out of the driveway, shooting gravel into the windows, and sped back to the road, anxious to find cover deeper into the forest.

50

**Cho cho: leaves and fruit are boiled in water
and used to treat high cholesterol**

The curandero used the swath of hemp, smelling strongly of the bitter cacao, to cover the body. But the rough-hewn cloth only reached to the knees, exposing the corpse's thin legs and sandaled feet to the hot, rancid sun. The bare toes, caked in dust, reminded Burns of a murder scene he had covered in the Bronx. The victim had been found in a city park in mid-afternoon, stripped of belt, jewelry and his shoes. Burns had touched the cold toes, more curious than anything.

But Burns felt none of that remove here. The sound of the single gun blast still echoed in his mind, playing like a soundtrack to the image of the man's eyes bulging as a hole was torn through his skull. It was the moment of his death, and it kept looping in Burns's mind like a video. He had clung to Kelly for what had seemed a very long time. Shock slowly gave way to a sickening fear that still festered in his empty stomach.

Kelly had left to help the curandero, kneeling with him alongside

309

the body in what struck Burns as the pose of an apprentice. She handed the curandero chunks of copal as he moved gingerly to set it at the shrouded head and then the bare toes of the dead man. Kelly followed with a worn Bic lighter, igniting the dank incense until the caramel smoke lifted into the dusty air.

Like a lens slowly bringing its subject into focus, Burns became aware of the others who had also come to witness. A boy was perched bareback on a skinny mare, the tail sweeping the air like a frayed broom. At the foot of the pale horse, the parents of the blind girl and others he had not yet met lingered, watching in curious, respectful silence. The women stared at him with what Burns took as a kind of accusation, as if he were somehow an accomplice to the tragedy.

The fighter jet screamed overhead, startling everyone. The horse reared backwards, and the villagers ducked even though the plane was above the trees. Burns cringed, obeying the same protective instinct, as the plane shot past the edge of the village and disappeared over the darkening canopy as quickly as it had appeared. Burns gazed at the spot where the sharklike wings had vanished, listening to what sounded like a drain emptying unseen in the sky. Dazed, he looked down at his clenched fists as though they belonged to someone else. He felt lightheaded and dizzy and he struggled to keep his breath from racing.

Kelly and the curandero began chanting in unison. They clapped their hands in short, rapid bursts meant to release the spirit—at least that was what Burns remembered from Kelly using the same technique attending the death of Gilbert. But the chanting sounded childish to him at this moment, annoying spiritual mumblings. He wished they would stop. He wanted to get away from here, away from this village. He yearned to be alone where he could take everything in slowly, piece by piece, not all at once, rushing at him.

Burns turned away and stumbled back toward the path he and Kelly had followed from the waterfalls. He worried that he was going out of control, crazy even. He had witnessed too much, and he had no tool or technique to help him make sense of it. He shivered and closed his eyes. The chanting grew quieter, more distant, and he stepped through the shade of a cluster of banana leaves. Soon he could hear the gentle waterfalls and the occasional chirping and buzzing from the forest. He opened his eyes, and the emerald stream appeared ahead of him, rippling over small stones. Upstream, the portly Mayan woman was collecting wet garments from the sun-beaten rocks that were cooling quickly as the day faded. The clothes were strewn haphazardly, like crumpled items tossed from an open suitcase. The woman sensed his gaze and turned toward him. She waved slowly, her arm extended high above her head, then returned to her chore.

Burns felt his breathing return to normal, and the lightheadedness vanished. He wondered if he had just experienced some kind of anxiety attack or even flirted with having a breakdown. He knew people back in the city who took medication to avoid these kinds of regular attacks—if that's what it was. He didn't know. But he was beginning to feel like himself again. The stream ahead was translucent, and he watched it flow silently past the grassy banks, thinking it was the most beautiful river water he'd ever seen.

When he returned to the village, he spotted Frank's now familiar truck. Behind it was a jeep emblazoned with Polizia across the side doors. Two cops in short-sleeve Khaki shirts and matching pants stood shoulder to shoulder talking to Kelly. Frank sat on the ground, alongside the covered body. He wore a glazed look, staring at the dry dirt between his knees. As Burns came closer, Frank glanced up without the least recognition.

Burns heard his name called. Big was struggling up the road, his face tired and haggard. But he broke into an amiable grin and held a cardboard box aloft with one of his huge, bare hands. SONY was printed in blue on the case of tapes.

"Got a treat for you, Burnsie," Big called.

Burns felt a surge of relief. He grinned back at his loyal production assistant, admiring his tenacity. They finally had the missing tapes. Before he even greeted Big, Burns was anxious to get their film started at last. They would hurry back to the camp, pick up Vic and his camera, and get some shots of this before the daylight was lost. There was so much to be captured, so many images waiting to created. In his mind, he was already composing a new narrative for the documentary, encompassing all that he had witnessed and felt, giving shape to incidents and people that otherwise would mean little to him. Filmmaking, the process of it, helped him make sense of what he experienced.

"Man, am I glad to see you," Big said.

"You really pulled it off," Burns said, grinning and grabbing the back of the big man's neck with his hand in a warm embrace.

After a moment, they both became aware of the morbid scene behind them, and it quickly tempered their enthusiasm.

"They killed him point-blank," Big said.

Burns considered saying something about the smile on the killer's face, but he remained silent and simply nodded.

"Looks like we found that war you were worried about," Big said. "They are sending some troops up from Belmopan, the capital. Is that how you pronounce it?"

"We've got to go and pick up Vic," Burns said.

"But the light's almost gone," Big said.

"We got to get this," Burns said, motioning to Kelly, Frank, the police, the curandero and the villagers, all rooted in their place like characters on a set. "This won't wait until sunrise. And then the army will be here."

"Well, I got the keys," Big said, holding up Frank's key chain. "If you know the way."

Burns was about to tell Kelly where they were going but stopped himself. She would think it coldhearted of him to exploit this tragedy. Her affection for him would vanish. He was certain. In her lovely and loving eyes, he would no longer be the principled filmmaker and compassionate man he pretended to be. But how could he explain that an incident like this was rare and important and cried out for documentation. It was more than a murder; it was what the government would call an international incident. Going after this story wasn't a decision. It was instinct. He wanted to be more like the person she seemed to see. He liked seeing himself that way.

"Let's go," Burns said. He bounded forward, wondering for a fleeting moment if he was making a bad decision.

"What about them?" Big asked.

Burns shrugged as if the question had never occurred to him.

"We'll be back soon," Burns said. "At least we better be if we're going to get this."

As soon as they reached the truck, Burns opened the door and quickly hopped inside. If anyone called out to him, he could say later that he had not noticed or heard because he had been in a hurry. But after the engine rumbled and shook to life, Burns abandoned his pretension and stuck his head out the window, looking for Kelly.

Kelly and the short, stocky Polizia were watching him. Kelly raised both of her lean, bare arms, a friendly gesture asking 'what was going on?' There was nothing hostile or accusatory in it. She trusted him implicitly. Burns felt guilty as he waved back to her in a spirit of camaraderie.

"We'll be right back," Burns said loudly. He was relieved to see Kelly leap back into conversation with the cops. But Frank was alert, his bearded, suspicious face following them as they disappeared down the hill. He seemed to guess exactly what they had in mind. They were filmmakers before they were anything else.

THE FIVE LOST DAYS

51

Cuyche: Leaves of this tree used as a tea to build blood and strength

They lounged on the porch listening as the trees darkened around them and the sunset drained from the once blazing sky. The sound was almost deafening: the buzz of thousands of cicadas—the cries and whoops of unseen birds, the barking of howler monkeys. Vic lit the last nib of his expertly rolled joint. He held it between his index finger and thumb like a specimen. He flicked his lighter at the end and inhaled almost simultaneously and welcomed the hot smoke that shot down his throat. He held his breath, coaxing his tired body to absorb every last molecule of the cannabis, before handing the joint over to Elf.

"I'm good," Elf said, shaking his head. "I'm feelin' no pain."

Vic exhaled, but only a wisp of the sweet smoke came out of his mouth.

"Best medicinal herb down here," Vic said. "Cancer patients use it to get through the day. Helps them deal with the pain better than any synthetic."

"They don't get arrested?" Elf said.

"They're dying, Elf. Who's going to handcuff a corpse?"

Outside, a car rumbled down the dirt road and came to a slow stop outside the house. It should have meant that everyone was back—Big with the tapes from Belize City and Burns and Kelly back from the village. It would have meant they were in business again.

No footsteps or voices followed the arrival of the truck. There was a long, pregnant silence before a door opened. It was immediately followed by the scrape of the side door of a van. Vic sobered instantly, every sense on edge. He knew the feeling that came over him even though it had been decades since he had felt it. Sure enough, he heard the familiar clink of AK-47 hardware, followed by the stalking steps of soldiers.

Vic bounded out of his chair and knelt alongside Elf. He put his hand gently over Elf's mouth and whispered a warning. There were men with guns. They needed to quietly scramble to another part of the house. Elf followed dumbly, not clear on exactly what was happening.

As they hurried through the kitchen, Vic glimpsed the soldiers through the screened window. He counted five, all of them armed. But he had a sense they were more nervous than he was. Belize had a tiny army stationed down in the capital somewhere. So Vic had to assume these were Guatemalan.

"It's them," Elf blurted behind him in a strained whisper.

Vic motioned for him to be quiet, but it was clear the soldiers had heard. They had crouched low, their weapons drawn. It was too dangerous to move because the soldiers were listening. Vic doubted they would shoot, but he saw no reason to take a chance. Together, he and Elf remained perfectly still, waiting.

Vic felt a sense of dread. When he had been a grunt, he had been too young to be very afraid. He never once believed anything would happen to him—like most of the boys in his platoon. Wounds and death came to others. But Vic was under no self-protecting delusion anymore. Everything changed in an instant. One day you were fine, the next day you woke up with a disease or a blood clot or a chronic pain, and your life was never the same. He knew any of a number of things could happen. They could be shot and killed. They could be kidnapped. They could simply be robbed. But whatever happened, Vic knew it wasn't going to be good.

The best thing he and Elf could do was to hide. It would buy them time, maybe even their safety. But their movement would be heard and might even be perceived as hostile by the frightened soldiers. So Vic decided to call out, make their position known, give themselves and the soldiers a new option.

"Who are you?" Vic said loudly and calmly out the window. He ignored Elf's pleading, wild eyes, bloodshot from the marijuana. "Who are you?"

As a unit, the soldiers all looked in the direction of the kitchen. Vic was relieved to see that none aimed their guns. He had made the right guess. They were out of their element, searching for what to do.

"Americano?"

"Yes, American," Vic called out.

"Espanol? Speak Spanish?" the boy asked.

The screen door creaked open a moment later and a handsome, young soldier stepped into the cold luminance of the ceiling light. Vic was startled to see the boy wasn't much older than his son Charles. But it was a black rifle—not the strap of a tennis racket case—that was slung on this boy's shoulder, the barrel pointed to the ground near his muddied boots. Blood had congealed and dried on one foot. There were also matching candy-red spots splattered randomly on his fatigues like house paint. Vic was dumbfounded more than fearful. The blood was undoubtedly human from someone shot at close range. But the smooth faced boy hardly looked like a killer.

"It's him," Elf said. "The one who hit Gilbert."

"We are hungry," the boy said. "And drink."

Vic laughed inwardly at the seeming innocence of the boy. Just like Charles bounding into the apartment after an afternoon playing with a friend pleading for dinner in just the same tone of voice. But there was an air of indifference about this boy that made Vic certain that he would use his gun as casually as he asked for a meal.

"What the hell, Vic?" Elf snapped. "He wants us to cook him dinner or something?"

The boy cocked his head, straining to hear something outside the house. A moment later they all heard the distance approach of a vehicle. It was rumbling over the dirt road, its twin lights projecting high into the forest canopy. A few of the soldiers called for the boy, and he spun around and hurried out the door, barking orders in Spanish. The screen door slammed behind him, echoing like a gun's report.

Through the kitchen window, Vic watched the Guatemalan soldiers scramble out of the ghostly luminance of the security light and take up positions behind the wall of black trees. He knew he needed to act so the soldiers wouldn't fire on the approaching truck out of nervousness or fear. At the same time, any movement or sound could spook them. They were boys not professionals. They weren't capable of the patience that training and age gave to older soldiers. He'd been green once himself, quicker to shoot than to think.

Vic reminded himself that the boy soldiers were grouped in defensive positions. Someone had taught them that much. So they were being careful more than aggressive. They were waiting to see if whomever was approaching them meant harm or nothing. Vic only hoped they weren't going to drive into the wrong place at the wrong time.

The truck emerged from the darkness, the chassis creaking like old box springs. It was impossible to recognize who was driving, and when the cab came closer, the window caught the bright light and lit up in a flash of white. The truck skidded to a stop at the foot of the parked van. But no one emerged; not driver, passenger or anyone from the flatbed.

In their place, the cicadas buzzed and screeched from somewhere in the forest canopy. Flying insects shot through the light like tracers in the night gun battles Vic had known in Vietnam. He braced himself like he was watching a lit fuse.

Finally, the passenger door flew open. Burns emerged from the darkness into the white, vaporous glow of the security light. He used the door as a crutch, still favoring his bad leg. Vic caught that familiar look of annoyance on his producer's face, the pursed lips expressing concern about a surprise delay or a missed shot. Big John climbed out from behind the driver's wheel and pulled a small box out of the seat. He'd been able to get the videotape after all. Vic wondered how he had managed to pull it off after the panicked telephone call.

Without a shot being fired, the teen leader sauntered out of hiding, his AK-47 assault rifle leading the way. Burns froze, a shock of recognition registering in his face. The gun was pointed casually at his chest. A moment later, the other soldiers also stepped out of position and edged closer.

Vic felt an enormous wave of relief. The kid soldiers had shown restraint. No shots were fired out of nervousness or fear.

"Food," the boy said in English. "We eat."

"We're in a hurry," Burns said, absurdly acting as though they couldn't be bothered.

"We eat," the boy repeated, raising his gun until it was level with Burns' forehead.

"Right," Burns said, nodding.

THE FIVE LOST DAYS

52

**Cascabel: a variety of hot pepper,
the powder is used to treat burns**

The downpour exploded on the porch roof, and the open windows flashed with lightning. Burns waited for the peal of thunder, but it was at least a minute before there was a faint, distant rumble. The soldiers paid no attention to the storm. They remained utterly focused on their meal, stuffing themselves with beans and dirty rice and the cold tortillas. Burns and his crew acted as silent spectators, listening to the boys chew and slurp. A husky kid with a round, cherubic face was oblivious to the bean sauce that dribbled down his chin.

"Mas tortillas," the same kid demanded, chomping on the last corn pancake he had pulled from the woven basket.

Burns made no attempt to hide his disgust.

"I'll get it," Vic volunteered, his eyes warning Burns as he ambled by like a servant.

"Gracias," the leader said, his dark, blank eyes directed at Burns, nodding with approval. The teen leader, whom his boys called Marco, had recognized Burns from the village, or seemed to, because he smiled just before they had marched inside the house. It was the same chilling smile Burns had seen cross his unblemished cheeks moments after he had shot a man in the head.

Burns struggled to keep himself in check, but a mix of fear and fury coursed through him. He was afraid of what these boys with their lethal guns were capable of doing. He'd seen how casually they murdered. At the same time, he was angered by their indifference and their cruelty and wanted desperately to fight back. But, for the moment, he was powerless to do anything but watch.

Vic returned under the hostile gaze of one of the eaters, who kept the barrel of his AK-47 balanced on the edge of the table. All the young Guatemalans seemed to gloat at having the adult Americans at a disadvantage.

Burns spotted the small carton of videotapes alongside the door. It was a rude reminder of his unfinished film. He had promised Kelly he would return to San Antonio village as soon as he picked up Vic and the video equipment. He had ignored her look of disappointment at abandoning her at such a painful moment so that he could get his camera. It was the kind of gross opportunism to be expected from a tabloid producer, but not Burns. Now, as he recalled her reaction, he recognized the coolness in her eyes, too, the loss of respect. He had not lived up to his best self. He wanted to be better than he was, to share the remarkable faith and passion Kelly possessed.

"Mas cervezas," the same, hostile boy demanded.

"I'll get it," Vic offered yet again.

Burns was annoyed at his cameraman's appeasement of the soldiers. He felt they had to resist these young thugs. But how? What weapon or power did he have to confront them with?

Soon after the soldiers had eaten, they wore the comically pained look of having consumed more at one sitting than they should have. They looked like teenagers anywhere. Only Marco was different. He took a long swill of the Belikan beer and looked around the room like a collector appraising stock.

"Vamonos!" Marco announced, standing up and pushing his

empty plate away. "We go now."

Burns knew they weren't about to leave without some booty—or worse. Sure enough, Marco dispatched two of his boys to the kitchen, where they began collecting food supplies. Anywhere else, Burns thought, and these kids would be in the playing fields or the basketball courts or racing down the block on their bicycles—certainly not shaking down a scientist's modest home.

The image gave him an idea. He would offer to film them. It would be powerful footage; a look inside the world of child soldiers. He couldn't recall a single documentary that featured what was becoming a worldwide scourge. He could play to their adolescent vanity, holding out the promise of TV exposure, of fame. What kid didn't want to be thought of as the best, the most special? It was a risky proposition, but there was too much to be gained not to try.

"We want to film you," Burns said. "To interview you with the camera."

The soldiers reacted in the worst way possible, and it chilled him to the bone, fearful that he had made a terrible miscalculation. Marco, especially, stared at him as if he were a stray dog, snarling from the insanity of rabies.

"Movie, camera," Burns said, pantomiming the video camera pointing at them. "We make a movie about you. You will be on TV all over the world. All of you."

Burns hurried over to where the camera rested in its blue protective shell next to the videotapes. He picked up the case and turned to find guns once again pointed directly at him. He pretended to ignore them and tore off the case covering and held the camera up to the light, presenting it like a sparkling, coveted trophy.

"Comprende?" Burns asked. "Now I film you."

The leader studied the expensive camera held aloft, calculating. His dull eyes brightened slightly, and he spoke to one of his boys, who ran up to Burns.

"What?" Burns asked crossly. He was taller than the boy soldier and kept the camera high and out of reach. "No. We use this."

The soldier speared him in his stomach with the barrel of his gun. Burns felt the air rush out of him, and he doubled over, stunned by the sharp pain. Somehow, he clung to the camera.

"Journalista," the leader said, his voice laced with suspicion. He continued in a fractured English. "Why you here? Why you come?"

Burns straightened, his face frozen in a grimace, holding his hand to his stomach.

"You help the Maya, yes?" Marco said. His dark eyes locked on Burns. "Ajete tell us."

"So you speak some English," Burns said, relieved that he might be able to persuade the young men to cooperate. "We are doing a documentary about ancient medicines, how the Maya use plants to heal and how we can use that knowledge to find new medicines that will help everyone. We film the curandero and the American scientist. Now we can film you."

Marco tightened his grip around the rifle, its barrel still pointing to the floor. Marco looked menacingly around the room at the video crew, who stood anxiously against the wall.

"I don't think he got the point," Vic said. "He thinks it's about that woman organizer. The leftist Frank wanted us to film."

"Why the hell would he think that?" Burns said.

The rain rumbled along the roof and splashed into puddles already forming outside. Marco raised his rifle barrel at Burns.

"What?" Burns asked. "What did I say? I just want to film you. Take pictures. A movie."

"Donde?" Marco asked coldly. "Donde?"

"Where what?"

"Manuela," Marco said. "The Maya."

"No, no, no," Burns said, smiling in confusion. "We film the curandero, not this Manuela."

One of the soldiers spoke in a rapid-fire burst of angry Spanish. When it was over, Marco stared at him, calculating whatever advice he'd been given.

"Vamonos," Marco said, motioning to the door.

"Me?" Burns said, stunned. "You don't understand. We know nothing about this Manuela. We filmed the curandero and the scientist. You saw them at the village."

"You show us," Marco said.

"What am I going to show you? I don't know where this Manuela is," Burns said.

"You show us," Marco said.

"I'm not going anywhere. I'm not leaving."

"Vamonos," Marco repeated and marched over to him until he was standing inches away. He smelled of beans and rancid sweat. Burns braced himself, expecting to be pushed or even hit. But the boy's coffee black eyes, alert and impersonal, simply studied him as one might an injured animal.

"We give you a lift," Marco said, smiling at his own use of the American slang.

"I'm not going anywhere."

Marco slowly raised his AK-47 until the metal barrel was pointing at his forehead, exactly as the soldier had raised it in the village.

"OK, OK," Burns said, lightheaded from the fear that drained him.

The soldiers followed eagerly behind him as Burns was forced to lead the way outside. The warm rain slammed into his head and shoulders like pebbles. But Burns ignored it, making his way to the parked van. He was afraid—not of dying, but of being hurt. Pain was far more frightening to him than death.

He heard Vic's voice behind him from inside the porch. He was speaking rapidly to the crew. He broke off in what seemed like mid-sentence.

"We'll be right behind you," Vic said.

Burns was stopped outside the van as one kid soldier, then another, opened the back doors in the pouring rain. The uniformed kids tossed wet bags of rice, beans and jars of vegetable oil inside. It was already stuffed with rugs, lamps and a framed mirror, as if they'd stopped by a yard sale. There was no room for him.

Burns waited as soldiers hurried to the side of the van and clamored inside. He was startled by the gunfire and a short series of loud blasts. But only the rain bored into his back. He squinted through the downpour and picked out Frank's truck. The tires had just been blown apart. No one was going to be following him anymore.

There was a sharp, steely jab to the middle of his back. He was pushed forward and would have fallen if he had not been standing so close to the van. No sooner had he recovered than he was jabbed again, ushered this time to the back doors. He was made to climb inside and make room for himself. He stuffed himself on top of the supplies as best he could, his neck and head twisted against the interior as if he were trying to press his ear against the plastic but couldn't quite reach it. The doors slammed shut behind him. He looked out the porthole-like windows in momentary shock. The rain obscured even the refracted light of the security lamp. Burns panicked and clawed at the objects around him. He screamed, desperate to escape. But the van bounced forward over the road, past the disabled truck, and slipped under the deep cover of the trees.

53

**Ox: a Mayan staple, the pulp and seeds of
the fruit are boiled and eaten like potatoes**

There was nothing to see. Burns's neck and back ached from the awkward, crammed position he'd been forced to assume in the middle of the carpet and stolen food supplies. His injured leg had throbbed steadily now. When the van hit a rock, rut or muddy pothole, he was flung against the roof like cargo. But it was the peculiar pitch-black blindness of being within the forest that grated on him. He couldn't even make out his own hand.

The rain stopped, and he could smell the damp air blowing in through the window and hear the chatter from the different layers of the rain forest beyond. As the soldiers drove on without speaking to either him or one another, he was reminded of that first night when they had arrived at the hotel in San Ignacio. He believed he had come to one of the ends of the earth. He had stared out into that darkness beyond the hotel room door and been frightened by what he could not see, by whatever it was that awaited him in the blackness of the jungle. He had never imagined this.

The leader broke the silence, barking an order. The van emerged from the cover of the forest and turned onto the logging road. The road and grasses were visible out the back porthole window, illuminated by the rising moon. He recognized this stretch of the road from the botched attempt to rescue Gilbert. Somewhere beyond that makeshift grave was the Guatemalan border, where they would likely have little use for him. He would be a liability, proof to government authorities that a line had been crossed. They would want him to disappear.

The van slammed into and out of another pothole before Burns could get his hand up, and his head banged into the ceiling. He grabbed his head with both hands as if it were a helmet, bracing for the next hit. Instead, he found Marco studying him, weighing options.

"I'm a journalist, a filmmaker," Burns said. "I don't take sides."

"Journalista, si," Marco said, doubtfully.

"There are people who know more about your Manuela than me," Burns said.

"Si?" Marco said. "Manuela."

The platoon leader was uninterested in the information. It was apparent the teenager had made his judgment that the American was not to be believed. Hostages would say anything to win their freedom.

The van's inside door handle, Burns realized, was within reach. He remembered they had not locked it from the outside. He could, in one motion, open the door wide and jump out. Of course, they were traveling at least thirty miles an hour. He would hit the ground hard enough to fracture bones and burst tendons like they were overripe melons.

If not for Frank, Burns thought, he would not be trapped in this van. He had disliked the bearded ex-hippie from the moment they met. Frank had been openly disdainful of the media, quick to believe the worst as though every producer were cut from the same mold. But it was Frank who was really in it for his own gain, Burns believed. He didn't deserve a woman as passionately ethical and committed as Kelly.

Marco reached into the blue nylon camera bag at his feet and pulled out the Betacam. He held the camera in the moonlight, appraising the worth of all the switches and miniature dials that covered the back. His youthful eyes betrayed a hint of wonder at the technology. It was likely the first time he had ever laid eyes on a broadcast camera, let alone held one. When he flicked the metal power switch, a red light flashed, and the electronics clicked on like a computer.

Marco grinned, and the boys in the car laughed. Their leader pressed one eye against the eyepiece, the lens pointed at their hostage. Burns peered at the dark lens glass aimed at him. He heard the faint scrape of tape rolling over metal. There were evidently a few seconds of tape still remaining, and the camera was recording him now.

He froze, remembering that the precious two recorded tapes were tucked away somewhere in that camera case itself. One cassette was of the curandero, the last surviving traditional healer in all of the Maya Mountains. The other was of Kelly, hiking on the medicine trail when he had begun to see her as more than a character for his film. It wasn't nearly enough for a documentary, but it was invaluable, images never captured before to his knowledge. In an age when cameras had been everywhere—from the bottom of the sea to the highest, most inaccessible mountains to the minute capillaries of the human body—it was extraordinary. He couldn't just let these tapes go with this band of killers.

"Talk," Marco ordered.

"You think I'm some monkey?" Burns shot back.

The van swerved off the road and rumbled over stones and rocks. Burns clenched his teeth and used his arms to keep himself from being bounced against the ceiling and door. A moment later, they swung back onto the muddy lane, sliding over the softening ruts like a boat bobbing over swells. Out the porthole window, Burns glimpsed the cordoned-off crime scene, the unwitting burial site of Gilbert. They raced past it in the very car that Gilbert had lived to drive.

"Talk," Marco ordered again. This time Burns was hit hard in the shoulder by the butt of someone's rifle.

Burns glared at the camera lens. He was cramped, his injured leg shaking. Now his shoulder was bruised. But they could beat him as much as they wanted. He wasn't going to give up. He was going to get himself out of this mess.

"My name is Michael Burns," he said to the camera lens. "I am being held captive by soldiers from the government of Guatemala. I am not a combatant. I am a journalist and filmmaker. This is against all international law."

The tape clicked to an end, then immediately began whirring in reverse. Still, Marco looked through the eyepiece, his white teeth gleaming from behind the camera casing. It occurred to Burns that these twisted kids were capable of filming his own death. Just for kicks.

"Talk," Marco ordered. Burns recognized that the army platoon was watching him as if he were a character or a performer on a TV set, something not quite real. They wanted him to squirm, to show fear, to reflect their own power over him. Burns understood at that moment just how helpless he really was. If he stayed with his camera and the precious tapes, he'd increase his chances of being harmed, if not simply murdered. He had no real choice. He needed to jump.

Burns did it. In one motion, he grabbed the stainless steel handle, unlatched it and pushed the double doors open. He sprung from his perch and was airborne. For an instant, he was weightless, suspended over the road. But then the ground rushed up and slammed his shoulder, and he flipped sideways, smashing his ankles hard until he was caught violently by the mud as if he had rolled into a waiting bear trap. His body hurt everywhere at once.

The red brake lights lit up the dark road. The gear dropped with a thud, and the van started to back up. But the wheels whined as they spun uselessly in the mud. Burns rolled onto his side and forced himself to stand. The tree line of the forest was a long run away. But it was his only hope. He bolted like a terrified animal. He glimpsed the doors of the van as they slid open. The soldiers were shouting, excited like kids anxious to start a game. Burns knew he was an easy target in the moonlight, but there was nothing to be done. Naguals, the curandero preached. If there were such a thing, he needed their help now.

The guns went off, their deafening racket like jackhammers pounding concrete. Red tracers, trailed by wisps of phosphorous, streaked past and behind him like crazed fireflies. They had a fierce, high-pitched sound that terrified him. There were hordes of them, whizzing by or slapping into the ground. Burns knew it was absurd to try to dodge or outrun bullets, but that was exactly what he was trying to do. The individual trees appeared out of the forest as he came closer, their trunks ashen grey in the moonlight.

The shooting stopped. Burns kept running, the hoarse wheezing of his own breath amplified in the sudden quiet. The soldiers must have heard it as well, because there were anxious shouts, and the assault rifles exploded again. He screamed when he felt the sharp sting in his shoulder. It felt like a wasp burrowing into him. The recognition rushed through him. *I'm going to die,* he thought. *I'm really going to die.* Another round came so close to his head that it could have been a mosquito buzzing his ear. He ran faster, shaking from his own fear and wild bursts of adrenaline. The trees were getting closer, but before he even reached them, he panicked and dove for their protection. He fell short and rolled the rest of the way until he banged his forehead against a thick, exposed root. Shards of wood blew off the grey trunks above him. He rolled and crawled deeper into the wooded darkness.

The guns stopped. There were no voices, and Burns struggled to muffle the sound of his rapid, raspy breathing. A moment passed, and the chatter of the forest returned. The adolescent voices jeered, "Journalista...Jounalista...," and mocking laughter followed. But the taunting soon ceased. The familiar whine of the wheels echoed over the road. There were anxious shouts. He heard the side doors of the van open and the engine rev up. He couldn't decipher what was going on.

The ache in his shoulder came alive. It burrowed into him like an animal, tearing and thrashing. He worried that the bullet had ricocheted and lodged in some other part of his body. He put his hand on the wound and felt the warm, sticky syrup that was his own blood.

The van was accelerating as if it were driving toward him. He knew he would have to venture deeper into the forest, where they would be unlikely to pursue him. Night was feeding time in the jungle, he remembered Kelly warning him. But what choice did he have? The jungle was safer than being hunted by kids.

No sooner had he begun to crawl than the sound of the engine faded. He'd been wrong. The van was not driving toward him. It was fleeing toward the Guatemalan border. He turned around and crawled through the brush to the clearing to confirm what he heard. He was soon relieved to spot the driving lights riding into the distance, like one of the nocturnal reptiles that wandered through the black forest.

Burns rolled onto his back, gazing up into bright night sky. He heard a spider monkey foraging in the black web of branches. The cicadas buzzed from unseen perches. He closed his eyes, feeling the warm tears that burst from the corners of his eyes and rolled down the sides of his sunburned face. He began to shake, hugging himself with his arms to get control. But he couldn't, and soon he gave into his overwhelming relief and sobbed, mucus rushing out of his nose as if he were a little boy.

It was a long time before Burns picked himself up and ventured toward the road. He was alone, more alone than he had ever felt in his life. He studied the logging road as though he expected it to speak to him, tell him what to do, what to think. He felt weak and disoriented, and his shoulder burned. He worried vaguely that he might have broken his ankle in the fall from the van.

He took one long look at the vast wilderness that surrounded him. There was no trace of civilization outside of the logging road. It was a true wilderness. The luminance of the sprawling night sky traced mountain ridges in the distance. Burns searched the landscape, hoping to spot flickering lights, the glow of a home, even a distant open fire. But there was only the jungle, neither threatening nor comforting. It radiated a staggering indifference. There were no good spirits or bad spirits or spells—not that he wouldn't welcome them now. There was only an overwhelming sense of insignificance.

Burns started walking in the direction of the research camp. He felt new, fresh blood drip over his triceps, and he wondered if there was a faint smell to it that would alert the instincts of scavenging animals. He pressed one hand against the bullet wound, feeling the hole with his fingers. He pressed it gingerly to stop the flow. His ankle throbbed as one step followed another, and his injured leg only added to the fatigue. With a slow, sickening realization, he knew that he would not be capable of walking miles back to the research camp. At some point, his battered body would give out, no matter what he thought or believed.

There was time, Burns reminded himself. Sooner or later, word would get out, and someone would come looking for him. They wouldn't just wait. He gazed at the road that climbed up the moonlit hill in front of him like a long, foreboding gauntlet. On either side, the forest chattered voraciously. He kept to the middle of the logging road, as best he could in the mud, as though the center offered some special protection.

ABOUT THE AUTHOR

William Petrick's short fiction has appeared in a variety of literary journals, including *Confrontation, Worcester Review, Palo Alto Review* and *The Distillery.* Formerly a senior producer with *Bill Moyers Journal* on PBS, he is an Emmy Award[®] winning documentary producer/director who has created programs for National Geographic, Discovery, MTV, Court TV and many other cable and broadcast networks. He lives with his family in Brooklyn, New York.